CW00859488

MARK A. HEROD

The S.H.A.D.O.W.'s Of Sedona

outskirts
press

Outskirts Press, Inc.
http://www.outskirtspress.com

Paperback ISBN: 978-1-4787-7779-3
Hardback ISBN: 978-1-4787-7780-9

To my lovely wife Sarah of 39 years, a very special thanks for putting up with me and all of our adventures, thank you for following me all over the world all the while raising our son's, you're an incredible woman and I am so lucky for having you in my life. You are truly my soul mate and I will love you till the end of time.

CONTENTS

APPRECIATION

To all my friends in San Diego, thank you all for the support you gave me in writing this book, thank you so much, I couldn't have done it without your positive reinforcement. A special thanks to Rachael Madland for the insight she provided pertaining to the subject matter regarding the ending and its direction, thanks again everyone.

PREFACE

This book was written with the unbelievable appreciation and wonder of the American Indian Tribes of the United States of America and all that they represent, we must never forget the importance of their traditional values regarding life, the planet, mother nature and most of all, the spiritual world that is so ever present in everyone's day to day life. Someday maybe the high tech world that we all live in today will come together with the ancient traditions and values of these wonderful people who have never lost their way. I would recommend to all the readers of this book to learn as much as possible about the history and the importance of the spiritual values of the American Indian tribes, it would be a great benefit to anyone who is looking for a way to achieve peace of mind and eliminate the day to day stress of our society in the modern world we live in today, also I would suggest listing to some of their wonderful relaxing and spiritual music that is so calming to one's soul that it's almost magical. I would like to recommend the music from a man named Carlos Nakai, I do not know this man personally but discovered his unbelievable flute playing while writing this book, it will truly give you goose bumps and touch your soul as it did mine, the writing of this book has changed my life in so many ways it's hard to explain, all I can say is that I'm at peace with myself and the life I have lived so far and now I truly appreciate what we all take for granted every day.

INTRODUCTION

I wrote this book to give people the hope that someday in a time not so distant in the future there might be a way to change the world we live in today for the better, to rid the evil that has infected the human race and only seems to get worse with every day that passes. Until our rapidly advancing technology can help with making our world a safer and less tumultuous place to live in we can all do our part by showing a little more compassion and good will towards each other, at least that's a good start until the miracles of science and the grace of God like the scope of this book can one day maybe just help save humanity.

1

DAY IN & DAY OUT

It was just another gorgeous morning in the canyons of Sedona, as if every sunrise was brush stroked on canvas by the hand of God, not even the fact of having to go to work here every day as a park ranger could spoil the mood and serenity to the start of my day. I was just heading out the front door of my southwestern ranch style home when I turned around just to look at this wonderful place I called home and realized how lucky I was. It had belonged to my father who passed it down to me, he had excluded my sister from the will due to her lack of faith and abandonment of her Indian heritage, I wasn't in agreement with the decision he had made but I was extremely grateful for what I had. I was a Navajo tribal member by my bloodline and a park ranger by necessity, I had bills to pay like everyone else. I was also the best tracker and most knowledgeable geographical expert in the states of Arizona, New Mexico, Colorado and Utah or commonly known as the Four Corners, which made my job that much more interesting and demanding. My lifetime experiences or resume would read as somewhat of a hero or expert when finding missing persons and probably a malcontent when it came to the policies and regulations dictated by the governing agency of the Parks and Recreation agency, sometimes I just didn't see things the same way as our government. I had just finished breakfast at my favorite cafe owned by my sister Miralani, the food was great but the prices were even better, because I never had to pay for a meal.

Miralani and I were very close and all we had were each other in regards to family, even though our father had cut her from the will there were no issues or bad feelings between us, besides she was quite successful in her business adventures, Miralani owned several establishments in Sedona which included a travel agency, 4wd Jeep rental business and of course her cafe "Miralani's". As I was getting ready to leave the cafe Miralani came up to me and said, "Hey Cole are we still on for this weekend?" looking up towards my sister with what was probably a sure look of concern on my face almost as if I had just been told I was going to be audited by the IRS, I then quickly replied, "Of course." I then remembered why I was looking for a way out of this weekend's excursion with her and her friends, not that I didn't love my sister but her friends are nothing but a bunch of snooty yuppies who have never worked an honest day in their lives. I told her we could all meet at the cafe for an early breakfast then get started with our outing. I gave her a kiss and hug goodbye and headed off to work.

This day was starting out like most except it was nearing the end of the week and I had not been out on any rescues or missing persons calls which normally consisted of two or three per week. Although it was a Thursday I knew being past hump day didn't mean things would start to wind down like most jobs. Being a tourist town most people here on vacation normally would try to finish off the week with a flurry of events which usually meant trouble of some kind. When I arrived at the ranger station the parking lot it was almost empty, meaning I was either very early or a few of the other rangers had called in sick. I checked my watch and indeed I was 15 minutes early, during the daylight hours there were usually four rangers on duty. I made my way in and headed to my desk. The desk of Cole Youngblood I thought to myself, how cool was that, not the fact of having my own desk but my name, I mean it was so cool, what if my dad had named me something else like Burt, Harold, Ralph or George, thank god it wasn't George, there are way too many Indians named George, especially on TV and in the movies. I began my day by catching up on the leftover paperwork from my previous shift which was not too bad this time, usually it's around two hours of my day. This part of the job was the only downside of being a ranger, the unbelievable amount of waste in regards to paper files and required documentation. Even with all of the modern advances of computers our agency was still 20 years behind modern civilization. The only good thing about all of that paperwork was the faster I got through it the earlier I could get out of the office and make my rounds of the designated campsites and check for the required permits involved. I rarely gave out citations, I just liked interacting with people and telling them a little about the history of Sedona and the surrounding areas, after all I was born and raised in this beautiful part of the country and considered myself a local expert.

When I finished my paperwork I quickly headed to the key rack which held all of the Parks and Recreation Jeep keys, another reason to get to work early and finish my paper work ahead of the other rangers, it gave me the choice of vehicles to use for the day. The big advantage to that was three out of the four jeeps were six cylinders and the fourth was a V-8, which had all the power I needed to get to a few remote locations that always brought a smile to my face. The off road trails in the Sedona area were some of the most challenging and scenic in the country. Being a tracker and a ranger gave me the confidence I could pretty much go anywhere I wanted to and not get lost or stuck anywhere. I would sometimes lead private weekend excursions in very remote locations for family and friends, like what my sister and her friends had planned for this weekend. I was not allowed the use any of the Parks and Recreation vehicles for my personal use and I had no problems with that, mostly because my own vehicle was fully restored 1973 Ford Bronco with a supercharged 302 V-8 small block that could pull a five-hundred pound "Sumo" wrestler out of a Vegas buffet line, in other words it had some torque or grunt is the word I like to use. I had it custom painted red, white and blue and on the hood an "American Bald" eagle with stars and stripes on its wings, I must say it was my most cherished possession and the only love of my life, currently that is.

As I was leaving the ranger station parking lot in the V-8 powered Jeep I decided to head out towards the northern portion of Sedona to start my checks of the most populated camp sites and trail heads. It would take me about 20 minutes to get there doing the speed limit, which I never did. As I was driving by "Chimney Rock" headed to "Capitol Butte" I received a call on the radio to check out a report of an abandoned vehicle near my present location. The road had transitioned from pavement to dirt just a few miles back so maybe someone had broken down and decided to walk back to the main road, at least that's what I was hoping for. This is the part of the job day in and day out that still makes me a little uneasy and I have been doing this for over 10 years and being in my early thirties I consider myself to be somewhat of a veteran at this point in my career. The report on this vehicle was filed by some local hikers who noticed it early this morning and that they had looked for a required State Parks and Recreation permit that should be placed on the dash or window to provide a verification number and length of the occupants stay in the park.

I arrived on scene around 11:30 am and noticed right away that this was a very expensive looking vehicle, a current model black Escalade that had government V.I.P. written all over it. The plates however did not reflect that of any government agency known to me but I knew better, I had worked with the F.B.I. on several occasions finding missing persons and hired to track some of their most wanted and this vehicle had the looks of that kind of agency. I knew at this point there was not going to be a quick resolve regarding this call. I reported back to the station I had arrived on scene and gave them a brief report on the situation and I was about to investigate on foot. At this point standard procedure was to check back in every fifteen minutes until the situation was identified or resolved.

As I approached the Escalade from the rear passenger side I could tell that the scene was very quiet and peaceful, I mean there was no traces of any footprints or dragging of any equipment or even any signs of staging any gear before trekking out. It was very alarming and disappointing to a person of my skills and knowledge of tracking and being able to read the signs in order to provide any direction of pursuit. I started to circle the vehicle when I did notice something out of place, the dirt on the trail road did not match that of the dirt up under the wheel wells, it was much darker in color, this could only mean one of two things, the Escalade had passed through water recently or this vehicle was towed to this location by a tow truck then abandoned. I knew that there were no water crossings in the Sedona area without having a pretty stout four-wheel drive vehicle to get there and overcome them. With that bit of knowledge understood I came to the conclusion that the Escalade must have been dropped off here by a tow truck or other mode of transport that had brought the vehicle from another location that had a much different dirt compound from its current location. This made absolutely no sense in why someone would want to do that unless it was used in a crime of some sorts and they just wanted to throw off the authorities and any investigations pertaining to the matter.

I made my check in with the station and updated them with my theory of the present situation and let them know that I was heading on to "Capitol Butte" to see if there was anything out the ordinary along the way. The weather was very good and the temperature was around 80 degrees, not bad for the middle of July so at least there would be no weather issues with tracking someone if they were in need of assistance or lost. I was still hoping that would be the case here and I could clear this up by the end of the day but something inside me kept telling me that too many things just didn't add up. It was rapidly approaching midday and still no leads or any new information on the Escalade. I gave Miralani a call to let her know that I was out on a call and that I would not be in for my usual lunch today. She wanted to know what kind of a call it was and if it involved any missing persons so that she might be of some assistance with her large inventory of 4WD Jeeps and employees that could help, she had done so before on many occasions and had helped locate dozens of people over the last few years. My sister was a wonderful person who would do anything to help others in need, I guess she got that from our mother who was of Hawaiian descent and had the biggest heart in the world, she had instilled so much into the both of us during our upbringing which we were so very grateful for during the short time we had her, she had passed away at the early age of forty eight due to complications from her surgery to remove a tumor from her abdomen, to this day my sister still holds the doctors responsible for her death believing they were negligent during the surgery. We both took it hard but I have tried to move on with it knowing there is nothing that we could do to bring her back and besides she wouldn't want us to hold anyone accountable for her death.

Once I arrived at "Capitol Butte" I checked in again with the ranger station to let them know I didn't see anything out of the ordinary along the way. I decided to head back to the Escalade via a north western loop towards Boynton Canyon Vortex, just one of many here in Sedona. The trail would be a little rough but I did have the V-8 Jeep which would make some of the more difficult areas easier to navigate through. The drive would take about two hours in order to make sure I didn't miss any telling signs of human activity or distress. As I was nearing Boynton Canyon I started to notice a lot of bird chatter overhead of my position, they were mostly Red Tail hawks and buzzards flying together in the same direction away from the canyon and they seemed very stressed about something, normally just the fact of being so close together would annoy the hell out them both. This was indeed something you don't see every day out here. I pulled over along the trail and got out the Jeep to see if something had spooked them like a bigger predator or some kind of manmade machine in the area. Nothing, the sky was clear other than the birds flying away at a very good pace, there had to be an explanation, hawks are a very aggressive predator and usually don't back down or flee from anything other than man. I jumped back into the Jeep and continued down the trail deeper into the canyon. I radioed the station to see if there were any reports of military aircraft doing any training or testing in our area. About five minutes later the dispatcher called back to inform me that there was no testing or training going on anywhere today in this part of Arizona. At this point I made a decision to get off the main trail and head west as far as the Jeep would take me.

As I headed towards the "Boynton Canyon Vortex" located near this area I had a thought that maybe there was some kind of energy disturbance that could have caused the bird's erratic behavior. I was not a huge believer in some of the theories that the all of Sedona's vortex's had some kind of magical powers of healing or anything else but I did believe there could be some kind of magnetic anomalies that could affect animal behavioral actions. When I reached the end of the trail as far as the Jeep was concerned I headed out on foot. I decided to take the long way around to the vortex location then return on the shorter route. It was a good two and a half miles the long way which circled around towards the north, then dropping off a few hundred feet back towards the southwest. There was still plenty of daylight left so I was in no rush and I was still looking for any possible signs or leads that may provide some answers about the abandoned Escalade. After a very long and thorough slow hike I reached the vortex site without seeing any traces of human presence along the trail. I checked in again with the station and gave them my location and update on the situation. I took a short break at the site and didn't see anything that alarmed me to warrant staying any longer. As I started back taking the shorter route I thought I could hear something that sounded like a swirling mechanical turbine of sort, I looked up to see if there was a helicopter or light aircraft overhead but there was nothing, the sky was totally clear around me. I told myself it must be something in the nearby canyons echoing to my location, that's the only thing that made any sense. As I got closer to the main trail where I left the Jeep I once again heard the same noise only faintly this time. I turned and looked back towards the vortex location and thought I saw a couple of bright flashes of light for a brief second or two, so I headed back to the vortex as fast as I could to investigate. It took me about fifteen minutes to get back there and when I did there was nothing to see or hear.

I started back towards the Jeep again with even more questions and concerns regarding this whole mysterious call I had been working on now for most of the day with no answers or clues to what the hell was going on with the Escalade, the noises and the flashes of light and still there were no signs of human activity in regards to the whole situation. I was starting to get a little pissed and frustrated that I had nowhere else to turn to in the investigation. The only thing left to do was to get back to the Escalade and have it towed to our impound yard and have the local authorities give it a thorough inspection and just maybe that would lead to who abandoned it and the legally registered owner. I was still leaning towards the F.B.I. or some off shoot of their agency that was not officially acknowledged by our government, if this was the case I'm sure we would be encountering some kind of legal intervention soon. As I arrived at the Escalades location it was already being loaded on the tow truck. It would be tucked away in our impound yard for the night and gone through in the morning to look for any leads that might help answer some of the questions I had. Being the senior Ranger and the guy in charge most of the time I decided to make this case all mine mostly because of my past dealings with the feds, we had sort of a working relationship and have been known to scratch each other's back on several occasions, hell I was even offered a job by the F.B.I a few years ago but didn't think I could wear those monkey suits every day to work.

When I arrived back at the station Miralani was out front waiting for me and she had that look on her face, I knew she was going to grill me on the case and if it was going to affect this weekend's plans. The fact that I had nothing to go on regarding this case would not interfere with our weekend plans unless something big came up tomorrow, so before she could even ask her first question I greeted her with a hug and asked her if she and her friends were all packed and ready for the weekend, she gave me a smirk then smiled, then proceeded to ask about the case and if she could still be of any help, "I wish you could but there was nothing but a string of unanswered questions and that the inspection of the Escalade tomorrow might get us some answers," I reassuringly replied. I then changed the subject very quickly and asked her if she had eaten dinner yet and if she would like to join me and it was on me for once. My sister gave me a big hug then said "Cole you know I love you but please not that taco place down the street or some other fast food joint that you love." I then remarked, "No nothing that fancy, I'm going to cook for you back at the house." She then replied "Wow what's the special occasion?" and I said, "I just feel like spending some time with you because we never get to do that enough anymore with our busy schedules." She gave me another big hug and said "Okay then on one condition, we stop and I get to pick out a nice bottle of wine," I agreed.

I followed Miralani to her café where she kept a pretty good selection of fine wines for special occasions. She was in and out in a few minutes and then we were on our way. My house was only a couple miles away just on the outskirts of Sedona up Highway 89 along Oak Creek canyon. She was keeping up pretty good in her little BMW but then again I was driving the Bronco like a little old lady, as we got to the turn off which lead to my house a black Escalade passed by in the opposite direction, I had almost stopped thinking about the events of my day up until that point. I just kept getting that feeling that this case was going to lead to some kind of federal involvement which would lead to something pretty serious. Oh well, I guess I'll try to concentrate on the big New York fillets that I would be cooking shortly. Miralani loved steaks, I guess that must be the Indian in her or she was just like about eighty percent of the population who loved beef. I on the other hand liked anything cooked on an open fire, I guess that must be the Indian in me. As we pulled up to the front of the house I could still hear that wonderful sound of the Bronco's supercharger echoing through the canyon, it was truly magnificent. Miralani got out of her car and said, "Damn Cole when are you going to get some new mufflers on that thing, your neighbors must really love you early in the morning when you go to work." I then proudly told her, "These are new mufflers and you don't understand the dynamics of exhaust pressure in relationship to engine performance." I had tried to teach her about cars in the past but she just had no interest, as long as they were reliable from point "A" to point "B" and with some comfort and luxury that's what mattered to her.

When we got to the kitchen I pulled the steaks out of the fridge and began preparing them for the barbecue, Miralani helped with the salad and cracked open the wine. We headed out to the back side of the house where there was twenty acres of open land, it was a beautiful view towards Oak Creek and the sound of the running water was so peaceful, this is where I would sit after a hard day's work to unwind and relax. Miralani and I had played here when we were kids and on many occasions and we would explore the canyon for hours upon hours until sunset, those were very special times in our lives where we became so close as brother and sister, we learned about trust and integrity which has become so important in our lives as adults. Our childhood had clearly influenced our outcome as to who we are today. As we drank our wine and the steaks were marinating my sister and I started to talk about where our lives were going and what future plans we had. I knew where she was heading with this topic of conversation and I knew it would end up with her asking why I was not in a relationship with someone, then I would give the same answer I've been giving her for the last few years, which was the job didn't provide me the time to get involved with anyone and the fact it wouldn't be fair to the other person that I was always on call and traveling out of town quite often. I know she means well but I was getting tired of her trying to set me up with some of her friends, besides most of her friends were still a little too immature in my opinion. At this point I decided to put the steaks on the grill.

Once the steaks were done cooking we moved to the patio table and began to eat our dinner, Miralani's salad was fantastic, she definitely knew how to prepare meals by working and owning her own café. The conversation switched back to the case I was working on today and we both seemed to be on the same page about the Escalade and whom it might belong to. Deep down inside

I knew Miralani sort of regretted not following in my career path and becoming a ranger and getting to work outdoors in the place we both grew and loved so much but I also knew that she was a brilliant business woman who had the desire and education to be quite successful. She was a few years younger than me but in many ways acted like a big sister, which I didn't mind at all. We started to wonder why a government vehicle like the Escalade would just be abandoned on a dirt road that led to basically nowhere other than a tourist attraction for those who believed in the spiritual and supernatural theories of Sedona's vortexes. Some people believed they had some kind of healing powers through magnetic anomalies but only on a temporary basis. Myself I pretty much was open to anything except alien bases hidden in the mountains of Sedona, I think I would have found them by now. After dinner, Miralani and I sat by the open fire pit continuing to rack our brains about this case but then after a while we started to gaze upon the stars on this unbelievable clear night. We both were interested in astronomy as kids and always had telescopes to learn about our solar system and the universe overall. It was so fascinating and mysterious we still enjoyed just scanning the heavens in the beautiful night skies of Sedona and we always enjoyed the time together.

As the evening grew Miralani remarked, "Cole I'd better be heading back to town it's getting late and I have an early morning at the café, it's always a madhouse on Friday's when the regulars come in for breakfast." I also knew that tomorrow could be a busy day for me if anything had turned up on the Escalade and I had planned on only working half of the day. Miralani asked if she could help clean up the kitchen and I quickly said, "No thanks it's still not dirty enough, I could go another day or two before I have to do the dishes." She started to chuckle and we both headed towards the front door. I gave her a hug goodnight and told her, "I am really looking forward towards our weekend outing and the time together." She then replied, "Cole I know you're not too crazy about my friends and I really appreciate you being our guide for this weekend and sharing some of Sedona's hidden treasures." I told her that I would do anything for her because we were family and all that we had was each other and besides I never did feel comfortable with her exploring some of those hard to get to spots on her own. I then reassuringly said, "I will see you in the morning for breakfast and we can cement our plans for getting started early Saturday morning." She then gave me a big hug and said, "Cole, I love you big brother, I don't know what I would do without you." I told her that goes for me too and that I would probably starve to death without her, she laughed then we headed towards her car, "Drive careful on the way home and I will see you in the morning," I remarked.

The next morning, I was jolted out of bed by my obnoxious ("Good morning Vietnam," by Robin Williams) but effective alarm clock at five o'clock. I could just see the beginning of what was going to be another beautiful sunrise in the canyon, the colors of the surrounding hills in Sedona were breathtaking, especially in the early morning and late evening. The red and orange colors of the hills just exploded upwards into the skies during those times of the day, it was truly magnificent. As I was getting dressed I couldn't help but wonder if there were going to be any leads that might turn up today on the Escalade. I just wish I could close this thing out today and not have to think about it over the weekend on our outing. I know that my sister and her friends were really looking forward to this camping trip and I didn't want to be distant or preoccupied with this case.

2

READY FOR THE WEEKEND

As I headed out the front door looking forward to my breakfast at Miralani's and eager to get the day and my Bronco started mostly because of that wonderful exhaust system that Miralani had eluded too. I really enjoyed just driving it, on and off road. Driving in the Sedona area was scenic and breathtaking, not to mention satisfying if in the right type of vehicle. As I was backing out of the garage I had to look at all of the gear and supplies that Miralani was planning on taking on our weekend trip. I was just hoping it would all fit in the Bronco. She would always go overboard when it came to camping out in the elements. If it was going to be a two or three-day trip she would pack for a week. She would always say, it's always better to have more of something than not enough and I guess in a way she's right. It's just the fact of having to carry everything in our packs, mostly mine that was a pain in the ass. I knew her friends Caitlin and Stacey would pack very light because they were not in the best of shape and would probably want to cut the weekend trip short when the batteries in their cell phones died or the signal strength from the cell towers were too weak to get on the internet, god forbid they wouldn't be able to post anything on Facebook for more than hour.

Once I got off the dirt section of the road and hit Highway 89 I decided to open the Bronco up, a few days ago I had adjusted the air to fuel ratio mix on the "Edlebrock" carburetor when combined with that ass kicking old school Paxton supercharger should give the Bronco an extra eighty horsepower when everything was tuned correctly. I really wanted to see if it had made a difference on the torque which I knew I would need this weekend on our off road camping trip. There was a very straight stretch of road right before coming in to the main town of Sedona and I knew this early in the morning it would be pretty safe to put the hammer down on this beast and see what she could do, not sure why guys always refer to their cars as females but it just seemed right. I pulled over to the side of the road to let this one car go by and then waited a few minutes for it to get down the road so I could have a pretty clear gap. I got back on to the pavement still in first gear and punched it while engaged in four-wheel drive to really feel the pull of this thing, when I shifted into second I was amazed by the length of the second gear tire chirp it made, the gear ratio in the rear end was set up for low to midrange pulling power but this acceleration was very impressive. I shifted into third gear at 45 miles per hour and still got a small tire chirp which I had never been able to achieve before. I got off the gas around 70 miles per hour because I was getting close to town and knew it wouldn't be safe to keep going any further at this speed and I was completely satisfied with the performance results from the adjustments I had made. There is nothing like the sound and feel of an early V-8 powered American made muscle car or truck, it is something everyone should experience in their lifetime, these types of vehicles are becoming quite scarce and expensive if you wanted to purchase one. The vehicles made today were much improved in many areas but lacked that feel and gratification you would get from doing a standing still burn out and then pushing the vehicle through all the gears to reach its top end.

I pulled up to Miralani's café and parked up front right under the sign for her business where I knew the Bronco would be safe from door dings, after all it had a five-thousand-dollar paint job and it was kind of my personal spot to park thanks to my relationship with the owner, I tried to get Miralani to put up a sign that read "Reserved for Park Ranger" or "Bronco Parking Only" but she wouldn't have any of it. I still think she is going to surprise me one day and have it done, maybe for my birthday or even Christmas. When I entered the café it was the usual locals and a few tourists, not bad for six in the morning. It normally picked up around eight or so when most of the visitors from out of town were just getting their day started, after all Sedona was a pretty laid back town and most people came here to relax and enjoy the beauty and serenity of the area. I headed over to my favorite booth where I could view the sunrise which made the hills burst with the colors of red and orange from the sun coming up from the east and it was always breath taking. As I sat down I looked for Miralani but couldn't see her anywhere. I guess she was running late or helping out in the kitchen. I ordered a cup of coffee from Jordyn, a wonderful young lady who was working as a waitress and going to school to become a lawyer. Jordyn and I we're always kidding around with each other and playing practical jokes on one another, she was a vegetarian and I would sometimes try to make her sick to her stomach by ordering some of the most, greasy meat meals I could think of, even if they were not on the menu and on this morning she was even wearing the t-shirt I had got her last year for her birthday, which said "Vegetarian is the Indian word for bad hunter." Remember I knew the owner and I used that perk as often as I could. I kept telling her she was too nice of a person to be a lawyer and she would always tell me, "Cole you just have to be a good actor to be a successful lawyer." Jordyn was very smart and only a year or so from taking her Bar exam. I knew that she would probably be here less than a year before leaving the café and we all would miss her dearly because she was so great with the staff and the customers.

A few minutes later Miralani walked through the front door and headed right over to my booth. She sat down, then spoke, "Cole I can't believe I overslept this morning, I think it must have been from the crazy dream I had." I then curiously asked, "Really, what was it about, do you remember any of it?" Miralani then looked into my eyes and said, "Cole I want you to be very careful today while investigating this case regarding the Escalade." My sister was always having these dreams of disastrous encounters for me ever since we were kids. I had always told her she watched too much television which in turn put those kind of thoughts in her head before going to sleep at night. I asked her what she had watched on television last night and she replied, "Cole this has nothing to do with any damn TV show that I may or may not have watched last night, and I wish you would take me more seriously sometimes." I could see that I had struck a nerve and that I had better apologize quickly. I then apologetically said, "Miralani, look I know you worry about me and the job hazards of my job but it isn't that dangerous and I am very careful all the time." She then gave me a serious look and said, "Cole, it's just that I've been having these horrible dreams lately of you getting hurt or being lost or stranded somewhere and your all alone and I can't do anything to help you." I knew that she was really upset at this point so I slid over from my side of the booth and put my arm around her and held her tight. Without saying a single word, I knew this would make the both of us feel better.

Miralani got up and stepped away from the booth, "I'll get your breakfast, I don't want you to starve to death out there on the job," she lovingly remarked. "Hey sis, don't forget the extra bacon," I quickly replied. She then turned around and said, "Cole, you eat too much damn bacon, by the time you hit fifty your arteries will be clogged worse than the men's room toilet here at the café." I laughed and then told her, "Don't worry, your biscuits and gravy will kill me before the bacon does." Miralani headed off to the kitchen to put my breakfast order in while laughing the whole way. My sister and I always kept things in perspective while trying to one up each other with humorous comments, it's just something we did as kids and never stopped. I think that's one of the reason's we have stayed so close throughout our lives and I was always grateful for that during the difficult times of our lives.

When Miralani returned with our breakfast I asked her if she and her friends were all ready for the weekend, she then replied, "I think so, I know I am." I then remarked to her, "Great, I'll be here in the morning around six-thirty or so and then we'll all eat some breakfast and then head out." I could tell she was really excited about this outing, she loved the outdoors but rarely got to enjoy it because of her busy schedule regarding her establishments here in Sedona. I was so proud of her and all of the accomplishments she had achieved in her life. Miralani then asked, "Cole are you planning on taking any guns with you on this trip?" and I replied, "You know I always pack at least a pistol and my trusty survival knife when I go out." My sister was not afraid of guns by any means, she actually had a few of her own. We both preferred the old west style pistols and rifles compared to the new era style of firearms, we both had several Winchester and Henry rifles in our collections. I preferred the Henry over the Winchester rifle's because the lever action was so much smoother and less likely to jam under rapid fire conditions and besides the Henry's were always the better looking rifle. I was not planning on taking anything that big on this weekend's trip but like I told my sister I always packed a sidearm just for protection from any threatening situations that may occur, it's always better to be prepared.

Halfway through our breakfast I received a call from Sam one of our local Sheriff's here in Sedona and he advised me that someone had broken into the impound yard last night and stole the Escalade and wanted to know if I could meet with him at the yard in thirty minutes or so. I told him, "I'm on my way now Sam." I wanted to check for any signs or items that may have been left behind like tools of some sort that might have been used for the break in and the later I waited the more difficult it would be to recognize. I still believed that this was a government owned vehicle and the fact that it was stolen out of the impound yard didn't change my mind one bit, all that really meant was the agency involved was not officially acknowledged by our government. I knew that this case was going to get much more difficult and demand more of my attention but I was not going to let it ruin my plans for the weekend. After the call from the Sheriff my sister looked at me and said, "Cole what's wrong?" I could see that look of worry in her eyes and knew she would be a little concerned over this new development regarding the Escalade. I told her, "Nothing serious, probably just some kids decided to break into are impound yard overnight and steal the Escalade for some joyriding." Miralani then looked at me with a hint of anger and said, "Really Cole, you think I can't tell when something has you worried or upset, now tell me what the hell is going on and does this mean you're working with the F.B.I. again and trying to keep it a secret." I could see that she was upset and worried about the events that had led up to this point concerning the Escalade and the fact that there were still no answers or leads, my sister new that this was going to consume me at some point in time and there was nothing she could do to stop it. I told her that this case was just taking some weird turns that didn't make any sense and I needed to get over to the impound yard as soon as possible before the crime scene got to contaminated from our own people. Miralani then replied, "Cole, I'm sorry I worry about you so much but I just don't trust some of our government agencies and I really don't like it when they pressure you to help them on some of their more difficult and dangerous cases." With that being said I got up from the booth gave her a kiss on the cheek, "I love you too sis but don't worry, I'm not working with the F.B.I. now or have been in quite some time," I reassuringly replied. She then said, "Okay Cole but please be careful today I still have this feeling that something strange is going on here and your caught up in the middle of it." I then remarked, "Okay I will but I have to get going, I'll stop by for lunch if I have time, if not, I'll make it for dinner so we can talk about our plans for the weekend and if we need to get any last minute items."

After leaving the café I couldn't stop thinking why in the hell it was so important to steal the Escalade out of our impound yard when it was just basically abandoned on a dirt road for the better part of a day, if it was government people and it was so important to get it back they would have had an emergency backup plan for just those types of situations. As I pulled up to the yard I could see that there was nobody else at the scene except Sheriff Jackson, he was pretty new at the job with only a few month's experience but he was highly motivated. I stepped out of the Jeep and said, "Hey Sam good morning, got any leads yet?" I figured he had gone over the entire area about forty-two times by now. Sam replied, "Good morning Cole, how was breakfast?" Sam was a good kid but I knew what he really meant, he wanted to know how was Miralani was but was afraid to ask, I knew that he was infatuated with her but was afraid to ever say anything to anyone because of their age difference which was about five years. Although Miralani was only twenty-nine years old she acted more like forty-nine at times. I guess that's why she's still single and didn't seem to get to much attention from the opposite sex. I've always believed age is only a mathematic number but sometimes seems to limit people from doing the things they really love or want to experience in life. I then asked Sam how was the yard broken into and did the video monitoring system pick anything up. Sam replied, "You know Cole, we haven't had a chance to review it yet." I suggested to Sam we can do that in a little bit but first I needed to check out the area of the break in and the spot where the Escalade was parked. Sam said he would go into the yard office and try to get the video going and find the timeline for the break in. I started to walk to where the Escalade had been parked when I glanced over at the main gate of the yard and noticed the chain hanging on the gate fence, it had a very funny look to it, even from the significant distance that I was from it. I headed over to the gate right away before someone could disturb the crime scene. As I got closer to the fence I could see that funny look I had noticed was actually the chain had been melted through on a couple of its links, not cut with any tools but actually melted and from something that put out a considerable amount of heat because there were at least four or five deformed chain links on the ground. I took a few pictures of the scene with my cell phone and asked myself what in the hell could melt through that chain fast enough without being noticed from any by-standers or people driving by, I mean even using a small torch of some sort would put up sparks like a fireworks display going off. I just hoped the video captured something that would shed some light to this whole thing.

I headed back over to where the Escalade had been parked and started to search the area for any clues that might help. I immediately noticed two sets of tracks one leading up to the driver's side and the other to the passenger side, both sets of shoe prints were some sort of smooth semi flat bottomed shoes that left no pattern of any sort like a tennis shoe would. That was either intentional or just dumb luck by the perpetrators because this type of shoe was nearly impossible to use as evidence in a court of law. I knew that the tracks did not belong to any of the employees at the yard because everyone that works here are required to wear a certain type of boot or shoe that had very distinctive tread designs on the soles for gripping purposes in regards to our job requirements of working outdoors and in all types of weather conditions. I was leaning towards the perps knew what they were doing and the type of shoes they wore was for that reason and that reason alone. There were absolutely no signs of broken glass or any other type of debris left on the ground but I did notice some sunflower seed shells around the area so I decided to see if they had a trail that might lead to any one direction or not. After a few minutes of searching I did indeed find a trail of shells that pointed back towards the main gate of the yard stopping short about ten feet from the break in point. This was finally some kind of a break and I now knew know that this was a professional job of some sort or even still government related somehow.

I continued my search of the main gate area hoping to find something that would confirm my suspicion of the fed's being involved in this. The two pair of footprints had led all the way to where the Escalade had been parked then their tracks stopped at that location confirming they entered the vehicle and left the crime scene. Upon further examination of the gate lock and chain I did notice something very strange about one of the melted pieces of the chain links on the ground, it looked as if it had landed on something other than the ground before its final resting place. There were a total of four melted droplets of chain link positioned on the ground of which three had formed a bond with the dirt compound of the yard before cooling off, the other in question here had some sort of foreign substance stuck to its surface meaning it had struck something else first before hitting the ground and I for one was about one hundred percent sure it was one of the perpetrators pant legs or shoe's and the droplet did have a slight smell of burnt rubber meaning it was more likely to be an area of a shoe. This could be the break I was looking for that might get this whole investigation headed down the right path and give me something to finally focus on. This is where all of my experiences with the F.B.I. and my tracking abilities were going to start to pay off. I sometimes thought that I was selling myself short by just being a park ranger and not using the knowledge and skills I possessed to better my career goals and help more people that were in need of help but I just could not find the strength or desire to leave the Sedona area which was my heritage and home, I was happy for now and I had Miralani close to me where I could always be there for her.

As I was just finishing my examination of the main gate area Sam came up to me then spoke, "Hey Cole, we've got the surveillance video ready if you want to see it," I quickly turned to Sam and said, "Great let's do it." We both walked into the tiny cramped security shack which was manned Monday through Friday eight to five but left unattended after five p.m. and Saturday and Sunday. Sam and I sat down in front of the video monitor and began to watch the feed from last night starting around five- thirty p.m. just to be sure we didn't miss anything. Sunset was usually around six p.m. during this time of year. I began to fast forward the video at 3X speed until something showed up on the screen. After a few minutes there it was, two individuals appeared at the main gate of the yard and began to attach some kind of device on the chain that secured the gate. I could tell that this was no ordinary break in right away. These two individuals were very relaxed and worked well together almost like they were dance partners or something. My attention was drawn back to the device that was attached to the chain when it started to put out a bright blueish glow around it, within seconds the chain collapsed and the two individuals entered the yard. I rewound the recording back to the point of where the device first started to glow to see if I could confirm my theory on the melted substance on one of the chain links. I started the recording again at the slowest speed possible and zoomed in as much as the system allowed focusing in on the one individual closest to the device. At the moment of the brightest blue glow Sam and I could both see the chain links give way and drop to the ground and at that point you could see one of the links had struck that individuals left shoe briefly sticking to it before falling off to ground when he started to enter the yard. After the two individuals had entered the yard they quickly headed over to the Escalade. I did notice that one of them was putting something in his mouth and spitting something out every few seconds, most likely the explanation for the trail of sunflower seeds.

Once the two individuals got to the Escalade they wasted no time getting in, it looked like they had a key which unlocked the vehicle by a remote system. This could only mean one thing, that they were the owners or working for the owners of the vehicle. I was now totally convinced that this vehicle was owned by the government and that these two individuals were government employees of some sort. There was no way of identifying either one of them due to their clothing which included hooded shirts that covered over half of their faces although one of them had a small slender shape like a woman. After spending most of the morning going over the recording Sam and I decided to call it quits and get some lunch at Miralani's. Sam could hardly hold back his emotions knowing he was going to get a chance to possibly spend his lunch with my sister. I asked Sam if he could leave the yard locked up for the rest of the day and to not let anyone else enter the yard until Monday morning when we could both further our investigation of this break in, I was going to only work half the day and head home after lunch to get everything squared away for our weekend camping trip. At this point I was really looking forward to this outing just so I could get away from this case and maybe clear my head a little bit. I know I was not too thrilled about my sister's friends coming along but I could deal with it for two days and hopefully they would enjoy the experience of Sedona's true beauty. All I knew is that I was going to have an enjoyable time driving the Bronco with the new added horsepower, even with the added weight of three more adults and all of the gear on the roof rack I knew it would be no problem at all.

Once Sam and I arrived at the café we made our way over to a booth and sat down. We had beat the normal lunch crowd and the tourists. Sam nervously looked around for Miralani while I decided to check the menu out and see if they had added anything new, I usually just ordered a couple of my favorite items on the menu which I hadn't looked at for some time. After a few minutes of searching I could tell it was still the same old menu so I just decided to get one of my favorite sandwiches. I then asked Sam, "Do you see anything you like, I mean on the menu." Sam replied, "Come on Cole, quit kidding me about your sister, you know I really like her, I'm just waiting for the right time to ask her out and besides I don't think she's even here right now." Just as Sam finished his comment Miralani approached our booth from the back area of the café where the storage and freezer were located and Sam didn't see her yet due to the fact that he was still trying to make me feel bad with his look of displeasure towards my earlier statement. When Miralani got to our booth she curiously asked, "Ask who out Sam?" Sam almost jumped out the booth he was so startled, "Yeah Sam, ask who out?" I quickly asked by piggy backing up on my sister's question. Even though Sam was a little younger than Miralani I thought that the two of them would be good for each other and make a great couple. Sam looked at Miralani and then replied very slowly and carefully by saying, "Oh just someone I have been thinking of asking out for some time but just don't know if she's even interested in me or not." At that point I thought I would save Sam from any more embarrassment by bringing up the menu, I then asked Miralani when she was going to add some new items. She then turned her attention to me and said, "I don't know Cole, I was thinking of turning this place into a Sushi bar and restaurant or maybe even a vegetarian only establishment, what do you think?" I looked at her and said, "Sorry sis, I'll keep my nose out of your business and I love the menu the way it is now." She gave me a smile then turned back to Sam and said, "Now back to you, if you don't ask this girl out you'll never know if she likes you or not, besides maybe she's just waiting for you to make the first move," Sam sat there completely silent for what seemed like eternity then replied back by saying, "You know Miralani your absolutely right, I am going to ask her out and I mean right now, Miralani would you like to have dinner with me next week, I know that you're busy this weekend but maybe one day next week I could take you to a nice steak house or wherever you would prefer, it would be totally up to you." Miralani looked at Sam and said, "Well it's about damn time you did this Sam, I have been hoping you might ask me out for some time now and yes I would love to have dinner with you any day next week and we both can decide where to go if that's okay with you as long as it's not here."

As I sat there in a total state of disbelief and still trying to figure out what just happened with these two people, I could not believe that Sam finally got the courage to ask my sister out and even more so I couldn't believe my sister was so anxious to go out with him and that I had no idea that she was even interested in him. I looked at the both of them and said, "Hey if you two are finished working out your dating schedule can I get something to eat now." Even though I was happy deep down inside I was not going to let them know that, at least not at this point, I didn't want to put any outside pressure on either one of them. Miralani looked at me and said, "Okay Cole what do you want?" I then ordered a grilled ham and cheese with fries which is one of my favorites here at the café. Sam then chimed in and said "Hey that sounds good to me also," Miralani then looked at the both of us and said, "Okay boy's coming right up." She turned and walked away towards the kitchen with a curious looking smile on her face. When she was out of hearing range I turned to Sam and asked him, "What the hell are you doing asking my sister out?" Sam looked absolutely terrified by the question and the tone of my voice, so I let him off the hook by saying, "I'm just kidding, I'm just finally glad you had the guts to ask her out but remember she is my sister and you had better treat her right." Without any hesitation Sam says, "You know by now how much I value our friendship Cole and that I have been interested in your sister for quite some time and you should also know that I would do anything for both of you." After those reassuring words from Sam I decided to change the subject by asking him to let me know if anything comes up regarding the theft of the Escalade while I was out camping over the weekend, he had my cell phone number and we both had police radios in our privately owned vehicles. Sam replied by saying, "Cole would you give this thing a rest just for a couple of days, nothing is going to change over the weekend and I already told you I will keep the yard locked up tighter than a drum." I then remarked to Sam, "Okay and thanks for always letting me stay so involved with these criminal cases here in Sedona, I really have no jurisdiction to do so." Sam then replied, "Jesus Cole would you stop already with the niceties, I'm not your brother in law yet and besides I probably wouldn't solve half of the cases around here without your help." I replied back by saying, "You know you're probably right Sam, maybe I should run for sheriff next year when your term is up." Before Sam could say anything about my comment Miralani showed up at the booth with our food and hers, which put a big smile on Sam's face. Miralani then said, "I thought I would eat lunch with you two, I hope you don't mind." Before Sam could spit anything out, I said, "Good, we can finalize our plans for the weekend." Miralani then replied, "Sounds good Cole, hey Sam I know it's a short notice and all but would you like to go with us this weekend?" Sam nearly choked on his first bite of his sandwich and I was a little stunned myself by my sister's response. Once Sam swallowed his food without choking he looked at Miralani and said, "I'm sorry Miralani I really wish I could but I have the weekend coverage this round of shifts and it's too late for me to try and switch with someone else, I really wish I could go." Miralani smiled then said, "No worries Sam, maybe next time we go I'll give you a better head's up so you can work it out with your schedule, we can plan something when we get together next week for dinner." I just sat there feeling like I was invisible or something, I couldn't believe how forward Miralani was being with Sam and trying to speed things up between them. I then said, "Sounds great you two but can we get back to the weekend plans and what time were meeting your friends here at the café in the morning Miralani." After that statement from me I think my sister got the message I was trying to send. She then replied, "Okay Cole how about I tell Caitlin and Stacey to meet us here around six-thirty or so, that should give us enough time to get something to eat for breakfast and get all of their gear loaded up in the Bronco." I then gave my sister a look of gratitude and said, "Great it's settled then, six thirty is perfect, by the time we eat, get loaded up and out on the trail the sun will be up and so should the temperature." The three of us then began to finish our lunch and talk about the wonderful sites and activities that our beautiful little town had to offer and how lucky we were to live and work in such a place.

Once our lunch was finished Sam and I headed off in different directions to go back to work. I told him I would see him bright and early on Monday morning to pick up where we left off on the break in at the impound yard. Miralani had already went back into the kitchen to help with a bunch of to go orders that had been called in at the same time making things a little hectic in the kitchen, she was great at settling people down when they would start to stress out. On my way back to the ranger station I stopped by the local hardware store and picked up a few things I needed for the weekend. As much as I hate to admit it I was really starting to get excited about this camping trip. I was really looking forward to getting the Bronco out on the trail and see what she could do and maybe teaching Caitlin and Stacey a little about camping and a few survival techniques that may come in handy someday if they ever decide they want to venture out on their own. The two of them came from very well off families and never really had to do much of anything they didn't want to, in other words they were pretty spoiled rotten from a very early age but they were my sister's best friends and I was going to do everything I could to make their weekend fun. After leaving the hardware store I then headed to the ranger station pick up a few of the newer maps which had GPS coordinates of all the local sites and vortexes on them which I thought was pretty cool and it would come in handy if there was ever some kind of emergency out there in middle of nowhere, I still didn't trust cell phones enough to be used in certain situations to where you had to give your location to someone for help. I also needed to pick up my required permits for the weekend and then I would call it a day and head home. After walking out the front door of the station I jumped in the Bronco and headed for home. On the way home I kept thinking about Sam and my sister finally going out and hoping that the two of them might start up a relationship because I thought they would really be good for each other, just the right amount of opposite between them for it to work.

When I got to the house I opened up the garage and decided to give a once over to all of the gear packed and staged in the back, I was still counting on Miralani's friends packing light and that everything would fit either in or on top of the Bronco's roof rack which could hold quite a bit of gear. I was pretty sure it would all fit, if not I would just leave some of her friend's gear behind. As I entered the house from the garage I turned on the TV to check out the latest weather report from the local news here in Sedona to get an update on this weekend's weather, I wanted to make sure there was no chance of any precipitation for the weekend, nothing worse than camping outside in the cold wet elements in just a tent, from a women's point of view that is. After a reassuring weather report from the news I opened up a few of the new maps I got at the station and decided to map out our route to our destination where we would make camp, I already knew where it was and how to get there but it would keep the girls from asking stupid questions if they had something to keep them busy while I was driving, you know like "How far is it?" and "Are we there yet?", I always liked to think ahead and be prepared. The time was flying by and I hadn't even started to load up Miralani's and my gear yet, I headed back into the garage to accomplish that task and to make sure the portable air compressor was working properly, once we hit the dirt part of our route I would drop about ten pounds of air pressure out of each tire to get a better tire footprint which resulted in better traction for where we were headed. After checking the compressor and loading up all of the gear it was after seven o'clock and I went back in the house to make myself a leftover steak sandwich along with a couple of beers. After dinner I hit the sack fairly early for me because I knew I would be up really early excited about the trip, kind of like how when you were a young kid and your parent's where taking the family to Disneyland or some other incredible place like that in the eyes of a young child. All I knew is that spending time out in the Sedona canyons and surroundings was like a day at Disneyland for me. I fell asleep with thoughts of Miralani and I at Disneyland when we were very young and how much fun we had with our parent's, I was just hoping these thoughts would bring me some very pleasant dreams.

3

COLD & HUNGRY

I t was early morning and I had a pretty good night's sleep, I slept with most of the windows open in the house because the night time temperatures were still pretty mild this time of year. I got up and took a very long shower knowing that I would not be taking one over the next few days, I know that there were a few places where we were going to make our camp that you could go skinny dipping if you needed to get refreshed or somewhat clean, not sure the girls would be too anxious to jump into the cold water which was pretty cold year-round. Miralani had called late last night and decided to come over here and wanted to leave her car in my garage instead of parked at the café, she said she would be here around five-thirty and it was now just a little past five and I was heading out to the garage to finish packing up the last minute items like the food, water and beer into the coolers with some dry ice. I wanted to get it all done before she got here. After the coolers were all loaded and packed away in the back of the Bronco I double checked all of the gear on the roof rack to make sure it was secure and that there would be enough room for Stacey and Caitlin's gear also. Again I had told them to pack light it was only going to be one night and two days of hiking. I already had most of Miralani's gear but I'm sure she was bringing a few extra items with her this morning. Once I was satisfied with the packing and the load positioning on the roof rack I gave the Bronco's engine compartment the once over checking all of the fluids and the output of the battery, it was only a year old but you never know these days because batteries are like politicians, you can't trust them to live up to their promises or guarantees. Everything looked good with the Bronco so I headed back into the house and made sure I had set the DVR to record the NFL games on Sunday, I loved football and my favorite team was the San Diego Chargers, mostly because it was about the only place in California that I like to visit and take some of my vacations. I had started watching Charger games at an early age and just always liked the offensive style of football they seem to play every year. Too bad it has never got them a Super Bowl ring but maybe someday when all of the planets are aligned and pigs can fly they might actually win a Super Bowl. After making sure the DVR was set properly I went to the kitchen to get a cup a coffee and get one ready for Miralani knowing she should get here any minute. One cup here and one at the café would be plenty, I didn't want a bladder full of coffee bouncing around out on the trail.

The doorbell rang and I said, "Its open sis," in walked my sister looking like she was right out of an Indiana Jones movie, I starred for a brief moment and that was enough for her to say, "What the hell are you looking at Cole, you don't like my outfit?" All I could do was say, "You look great, all you need is a bull whip," funny, she said with a little anger in her voice. Changing the subject very quickly I asked her if she had brought any other supplies or gear that we might need to load up before we headed to the café. She replied, "Just a few items us girls might need." Okay then I'll let you take care of that, I replied. After that brief discussion we both did a quick double check of everything that was already loaded and made sure that we had everything. "Looks good Cole, you did a great job getting everything packed." Miralani confidently remarked. I then replied, "Yeah but we still need to get Stacey's and Caitlin's gear loaded." Pausing for a second, she then spoke, "No problem Cole, I told them to pack light over and over again so they would get the message." Knowing her friends, I was only about fifty percent sure that they got the message. I then replied to her, "No worries sis, I can get all of their stuff up on the roof rack, even if they bring two full suitcases each, I can make it all fit." I was hoping and praying that would not be the case or I was in big trouble. There was probably just enough room for one small suitcase each but I was hoping they would bring soft travel bags that were much easier to load into tight places. After loading up the small items Miralani brought with her we headed back into the house so I could get everything locked up and she could get her cup of coffee I had ready for her, those K-cup coffee machines are fantastic, they're so fast and easy to use. It was just past six and I thought we had better get on our way if we were going to get to the café by six- thirty. Miralani had just finished her coffee and echoed my exact thoughts, so we headed out to the garage and jumped into the Bronco and I fired that beast up, "Jesus Cole, if I wasn't fully awake, I am now," she quickly remarked. I then said, "Come on sis, it's not that loud, besides it's always louder when the motor is cold, once it warms up a little bit it's a lot quieter." After closing the garage door and letting the Bronco warm up a few minutes we headed out to the café. Miralani called Stacey and Caitlin on her cell phone and let them know we were on our way to the café, the both of them lived pretty close to café and it would only take them a few minutes to get there. I knew we would get there on time around six thirty like we planned. The Bronco sounded great going down the canyon, I really loved those new mufflers.

We turned left off Highway 89A and onto Highway 179 towards "Gallery Row" where a lot of small businesses were located along with Miralani's café. Her cafe was located near the corner of the southwest portion of what the locals call the "Y" intersection, it is sort of the main hub of Sedona just south of "Uptown" the more touristy part of town. Most people use the "Y" as a reference for directions and where to meet up. As we pulled into the parking lot of the café Miralani said she saw Caitlin's car parked out front, she said the two of them were going to car pool to the café so there would be only one car taking up space at the cafés parking lot. As Miralani and I walked into the café we immediately saw Caitlin and Stacey sitting at our favorite booth, which was kind of always reserved for the owner depending on how busy it was. The two girls got up and bull rushed us before we could even sit down. They both seemed very excited about the trip and kept telling Miralani that they had been looking forward to going on a camping trip like this for quite some time. I politely interrupted the conversation and suggested we sit down and order are breakfast because the sooner we eat the sooner we could get started with the trip. Everyone agreed and once we sat down Caitlin asked, "Hey Cole how far is it to where were going to make camp?" Jesus, I thought to myself, we haven't even left the café yet and their already asking how long until we get there. I calmly answered Caitlin by saying, "Well Caitlin, it's a little confusing about trying to judge distance and time when it comes to off road trails." She then gave me a look of satisfaction and turned her attention back to Stacey and Miralani which was just fine with me, I really didn't want to have to explain the logistics and geography constraints that were involved when traveling off road trails to get to a specific destination.

Our breakfast arrived smelling absolutely wonderful as always, my sister definitely had two of the best cooks in town. I told everyone to enjoy this meal because it would be the last one that tasted this good for a few days. "Thanks Cole," Miralani said with a smile and a wink. Miralani and I both knew that our food supplies were pretty much all from her kitchen and had been prepared for us ahead of time and sealed in separate containers marked for breakfast, lunch and dinner. We told Stacey and Caitlin that we were going to take care of the food supplies because we knew what to get and where to get it. I'm sure they both thought they would be eating freeze dried foods out of bags that you just add water and heat. I figured we would keep that cat in the bag until lunch this afternoon. After going over a few things about basic survival skills in case Stacey or Caitlin were to get separated from us somehow when out hiking we were almost ready to get on our way and get this weekend outing started. I think everyone was very excited. As much as I was trying to find a way out of this trip the last few weeks I too was eager to get started and enjoy this time with my sister and her friends. Miralani grabbed the bill then spoke, "I've got this one guys, hope everything was good." Caitlin and Stacey said thanks and I suggested we should all make one last trip the restroom before heading out. All of the girls agreed with that one knowing this would be the last chance to use a toilet with plumbing.

As all of us headed out the front door of the café Stacey said, "Wow Cole, I just can't get over how beautiful your Bronco is." Caitlin chimed in by saying, "Yeah Cole, it really is nice, do you think Stacey and I might get to drive it out the trail a little bit?" After nearly swallowing my tongue I said, "Not in a million year's girls and not just because your girls but this vehicle is a very complicated machine and you have to know the gear range and how to drive it in all different types of terrain or you could end up doing some serious damage to the drivetrain, you know the motor and transmission." I wanted to make it clear what a drivetrain was to them and that they didn't think there was some kind of little train under the hood that drove the vehicle. Of course their response was "Okay Cole we get it but we're not stupid you know, I know a lot more about cars than you think," Caitlin said with a little anger in her voice. Stacey then agreed by saying, "Yeah Cole." After reconsidering my words to the girls I thought it best to apologize a little bit and offer a peace offering of some sort, so I said, "Hey girls you know I'm only teasing you two and maybe on the way back you girls could drive on some of the smoother parts of the trail and the street if you'd like." They both got very excited and said, "Great."

We then all piled into the Bronco with Caitlin and Stacey getting into the backseat, it's a good thing that the two of them were very small framed girls or they would have been a little uncomfortable because the backseat was quite small and did not have too much padding on the cushion sections. Hopefully they wouldn't complain too much when we got to the rough parts of the trail. The area that I had marked out on the map for our campsite would take about an hour and a half to get there if the trail was in good shape and there were no obstacles in the way or washouts in the trail. After about an hour in on the main trail it would get pretty rough and I hoped the girls would be okay with that. I was one hundred percent confident that the Bronco would have no problem no matter how bad the trail was. As we headed out from the café on highway 89A towards the west our route would take us towards the town of Cottonwood, we would turn off to the north around ten miles out of Sedona. The trail from that point would be pretty good for about an hour. As we were just leaving the outskirts of Sedona and passing the last gas station in town Caitlin asked, "Hey Cole are we going to have enough gas to get there and back?" while trying to keep a serious face I replied, "I think it will be close but we should make it." Miralani then looked at me from the passenger seat and gave me a smirk then saying, "I think Cole brought extra gas in those two gas cans on the back of the Bronco." Caitlin then said, "Great, because I don't think I could walk back to town." I just smiled and kept my eyes on the road. Miralani then asked the two girls if they had brought their mobile cell phone chargers with them. I was hoping that answer would be no but I was wrong. Stacey said, "Hey that's the first thing I made sure I packed in my bag." "Me too," said Caitlin.

As we passed mile marker ten I slowed down getting ready to turn off the main highway. If you didn't know the turnoff was there you would probably pass right by it. I progressively downshifted the Bronco into second gear as the turnoff approached. After making the turn we headed due north on what was basically a dry creek wash most of the year. We would be making our way back towards the northern part of the Sedona area where we would be making our camp about ten miles northwest of the "Boynton" vortex area. That was a pretty tough place to get too if you didn't have a very capable 4wd vehicle to traverse the challenging trails. I knew the Bronco would be quite capable and ready for anything that came our way. Stacey and Caitlin were chatting away in the back and Miralani and I were just enjoying the incredible scenery that was Sedona. It was now seven forty-five in the morning and the hills were still exploding with the bright red and orange colors from the sunrise over two hours ago. It was so majestic and peaceful as if it was all just a dream I was having, then reality reared up its ugly head when Stacey said, "Cole I need a restroom stop, if you know what I mean." I glanced up into the rearview mirror and said, "Sure no problem Stacey, I'll pull off the trail up ahead by those bushes." After she said sorry and that she had a small bladder I quickly remarked, "No worries, might be better to go now rather than later when we hit the rough part of the trail and a lot of bouncing around."

After taking care of Stacey's needs we were on our way again and almost to the roughest part of the trail. This part of the trail would be the slowest and take us another forty-five minutes or so to get to the camping area I had marked out for us. Miralani was texting her head cook back at the café to make sure things were okay and to let him know she would check in every couple of hours. My sister was a bit of a micro manager when it came to running her businesses and trusting other people when she was not there to oversee everything. Once the trail started to get rough I told everyone to hold onto the inside roof handles just in case things got a little too bumpy. I didn't want anyone banging their heads together in the back seat where it was a little cramped. I said to Miralani, "Hey sis you might want to put your phone in the glovebox so it doesn't fly out the window." She turned to me and asked, "It's not going to get that bad is it?" I reassuringly replied, "No I don't think so but I can't guarantee that the trail will be in good condition." Just as I made that comment the trail started to get really rough and gutted out. "Jesus Cole maybe we should have brought helmets." Caitlin quickly remarked. "No worries, I can see the end of this crap up ahead, then its smooth sailing after that," I confidently stated. At least that's what I was hoping for in my mind. It had been about six months since I had been on this trail and I didn't remember it being this bad. Within a few minutes the trail returned to being quite accessible and everyone relaxed a bit. I asked Stacey and Caitlin if they were okay and if they wanted to stop and stretch their legs. They both answered in unison by saying, "No that's okay Cole let's just get to our campsite."

Thirty minutes had passed and the girls were getting a little anxious to get to our destination so I decided to stop and tell the girls about a great photo spot up here on a nearby hill that overlooked our campsite location. "Wow, are we getting that close?" Caitlin asked. "Only about another ten or fifteen minutes and then the fun starts," I replied. Stacey then said, "I can hardly wait to get out and start hiking around some of these gorgeous hills and canyons." I told the girls that once we got there we still needed to get the camp all set up and that meant the tent which slept five to six people comfortably. This was going to be the worst part of the trip probably because the tent had an adjoining separate room where I would be sleeping. That meant it was probably going to be a nightmare putting the whole thing together and a nightmare trying to get some sleep with the three of them right next to me. Everyone agreed that would be the number one priority once we got there. After turning the engine off, we all got out of the Bronco and started up the small hill towards the location that I had told the girls about. The elevation was only about three hundred feet but it did look down into the canyon area that we would be calling home for the next couple of days. The weather was spectacular this time of year and the skies were filled with great big puffy white balls of cotton, it was truly post card beautiful. After a few minutes of walking to the top of the hill we reached the small clearing looking down onto the canyon. I didn't have to say anything at this point, the girls were absolutely in awe of the scenery. The best way to describe this little oasis in the middle of nowhere was simply to say that it was breathtaking. There were trees and brightly colored boulders the size of Volkswagens, there was a large creek nearby the campsite that provided a wonderful soothing sound in the evening which was very relaxing and hypnotic that would put you into a state of REM sleep almost immediately, unless there were three women in the tent with you.

After the girls had snapped all of the group photos they needed to post on "Facebook" we headed down the hill back to the Bronco. Once we were all in and buckled up we headed down into the canyon which I called "Cole's Canyon," I mean it didn't have an official name and I kind of discovered it I think, so what the heck, it's mine now. Of all the times that I had camped here before over the last few years I had never seen anyone else in the area. If you didn't know this area very well you would probably think you were lost while trying to get to another location of more commonly known campsites. Once we reached the bottom of the hill we entered a very small and narrow opening between some sagebrush that stood around five to six feet tall. "Cole where the hell are you going?" Miralani asked. "Trust me," I told Miralani. At this point Stacey and Caitlin were just enjoying the ride. As I turned off the trail there was an abrupt drop off that almost felt like the Bronco had achieved flight. The girls in the back were holding on like their lives depended on it. After a thirty-foot steep drop the Bronco had reached the lowest portion of the canyon and our destination was almost in sight. I made one final turn and the girls knew we had arrived. "Wow, my god this is amazing," Stacey said. "Brother you were right, this place is perfect," Miralani echoed. Caitlin still in a little shock from that last drop off just remained quiet and thrilled by the whole experience so far. I too was pretty entranced by the beauty of this place, no matter how many times I have come here before I still get the same reaction when making that last turn and everything comes into to view. It's just spectacular.

The unloading process was about halfway finished when the girls decided we needed to have another "Facebook" photo shoot in order to let all of their friends know what was going on in some kind of chronological order. Oh boy, I thought to myself. I really wish they would have forgot their damn cell phones. There were really only a few small items left to unpack and then we would tackle the challenge of putting up the tent. I was hoping with the four of us it wouldn't be too hard. I had never before used one of these portable mansions. Just to get a few laughs I asked, "Hey did anyone remember to bring toilet paper?" Stacey and Caitlin had a brief moment of terror on their faces before Miralani started to laugh, she then said, "Nice try Cole and yes I brought plenty." Changing the subject very quickly I asked the girls if they were ready to get started on the tent then we could cook up some lunch afterwards. We all agreed to hurry up and get the rest of the supplies out of the Bronco and proceed with the construction of our new home.

The tent came in a huge duffle bag that was the size of a person who might have been refused a membership from "Weight Watchers" by being classified as "Car Pool Legal." The thing only had two canvas straps on the top but the overall diameter had to have been four feet. In other words, when carrying it by the straps you almost had to bend ninety degrees to the left or right at the hips just to get the damn thing off the ground to carry it. Thank god it was only about twenty feet to get to the spot where we were going to set it up. After the four of us dragged the tent over to its final resting spot we began to unpack all of the set up hardware to make sure we had it everything, something I probably should have done already but forgot. Stacey was going to be the supervisor of this construction project by reading the instructions to the rest of us who would provide the labor. I was hoping it would take less than hour. Right then Stacey remarked, "Hey Cole these instructions are only in Chinese." Almost choking on the piece of gum I had been chewing for the last couple of hours it seemed, I then quickly gathered my composure, "What the hell, are you kidding me?" I replied. While giving me a wink and a chuckle Stacey said, "Got you, and yeah I brought toilet paper to." Caitlin was already laughing her ass off. "Way to go Stacey, not too many people get one over on Cole," Miralani commented. I guess I deserved that one.

An hour and a half had passed since the construction started of our tent and it was only half way done, the main area was complete where the girls were going to sleep but my separately attached room was not finished yet. I decided we should break for lunch and that I would finish my room afterwards by myself so the girls could start planning what they wanted to do first. We would still have plenty of daylight left after lunch if they wanted to go on a short hike of the surrounding area and get familiar with our compass directions in regards to finding their way back to camp in case if anyone got lost. As I opened up the main big cooler with all of the food I asked the girls what they preferred in regards to what type of sandwiches we had. They both responded by saying, "What," Stacey then said, "Cole I thought we would be eating freeze dried eggs or some god awful thing like that." I let the girls know at that point that Miralani had provided all of the food for our weekend. Caitlin then let out a sigh of relief by saying, "Thank god because I thought I would have to fast over the next couple days." Miralani started to laugh and then said, "Well you haven't seen what I packed yet, how do you know you'll even like it?" I told Miralani anything that comes from your café or anything you can make will always be fantastic because you're the best when it comes to making and creating great meals. She was truly gifted in that department. The girls both asked what kind of sandwiches we had. "On the menu for today we have turkey, chicken or roast beef all with cheddar cheese and the option of adding lettuce, tomatoes and onions if you like," I replied with the tone and expressions of a waiter.

After finishing our wonderful lunch, I quickly finished up with my tent construction of my room, then we all decided to go and hunt for some firewood and check out the camp surroundings. The temperature was right around seventy-five degrees and absolutely beautiful. The ground was mostly soft dirt and sand in this region of Arizona but there were a lot of areas of hard rock underneath the sand and dirt. Hiking the Sedona area was very easy on the feet unless you we're climbing around on the ever present rock formations. I was the only one here that was experienced in rock climbing and I had not intended to do any of that on this trip. We began our firewood gathering by heading north towards the creek which was flowing quite well this year because of an above average rainfall and the snowpack was very good up in the Flagstaff area. The girls were picking up small pieces of twigs and branches as I had asked them to do and I would get the big heavy stuff. We just needed enough for one night but it would have to burn all night and early morning so we could cook our breakfast. Caitlin slowly turned back towards our camp, "Hey Cole I have an arm full so I'm taking my load back." She remarked. "Okay," I replied. Stacey and Miralani we're just ahead of me and reaching their limit to what they could carry also. I knew I would have to make several trips to get enough of big pieces of wood in order to have a sufficient supply for our needs. The three of us then headed back to camp with our firewood.

When we got back to camp Caitlin had already got into the beer that I had brought and was lounging in one of the fold up chairs like she was done for the day and had no intention of ever leaving the campsite again. Her shoes were off, her shorts were rolled up and she had removed her shirt to work on her tan, luckily she had a bikini top on. "Sorry Cole I got thirsty and didn't feel like water, hope you don't mind," she said. "No worries, I must admit that beer looks really good but I have to go get some more wood, you girls relax and enjoy your time together and I'll be back in a bit." I reassuringly remarked. Stacey and Miralani stacked their piles of wood on top of Caitlin's then broke out the other chairs and the girls began to talk, I could still hear them laughing and giggling as I was heading out for more wood just a short distance from camp. After making two more trips I was satisfied that we had plenty of wood to keep us going all night and most of tomorrow morning if needed. I think the girls were on their third beer by the time I returned and it didn't look like any of them wanted to go out for a hike anytime soon. I decided to join in and just relax and talk about whatever they wanted to. Miralani then asked, "Hey Cole do we have enough wood or should we all go out together and get some more?" I then confidently replied, "Nope we have plenty sis, enough for all day tomorrow if need be." Miralani and I made sure that none of us would be cold and hungry this weekend.

4

THE FALL

After a few beers in and at a rapid pace I had almost caught up to the girls in that department. The temperature was starting to drop very quickly as it was approaching sunset. I decided to get the fire going so we could start cooking our dinner. We would be cooking steaks for dinner and making a few extra for the morning breakfast to be cut up in chunks and added with some eggs, onions and potatoes, which Miralani called Indian breakfast. It was a secret recipe passed down from our parents which also consisted of a special rub and other spices to be put on the meat. It was very good with tortillas that we also brought with us. I just hope the wildlife didn't get a whiff of it. The girls were still talking about life, boyfriends and clothes while I was stoking the fire to get it hot enough for the steaks. I asked Stacey and Caitlin how they liked their steaks and if they wanted to help cook them. Stacey said, "Well done for me Cole and no I trust your cooking skills." While Caitlin replied, "Well done for me too and I would love to come and help or at least watch." "Okay great," I said. Finally, I would get to show off my custom made campfire grill to some other people besides Miralani, I had designed it hoping to maybe sell one day on the open market. It was a reusable swivel based grill slash basket combination that would cook just about anything you could fit into it.

Miralani and Stacey moved their chairs closer to the fire once

Caitlin moved hers over to help with the steaks. Once the steaks were all cooked and we were eating our dinner by the fire I thought this would be a good time for some campfire stories. Everyone agreed we would take turns telling scary stories and the best one would eliminate that individual from having to help with cleaning up the dinner mess. The sun had set and the temperature had fallen to fifty-six degrees and would probably get down to around fifty overnight and that meant we would all be huddling around the fire until it was time to turn in. Stacey started out with her scary story which was pretty lame I must admit. Caitlin's was a little better but not much. It was now Miralani's turn and I knew hers would be pretty good because of the times we had spent with our parents and the stories they shared with us growing up. Hers was about an evil Indian spirit who roamed the Canyon lands of Arizona looking for any family ties related to the U.S. cavalry then he would haunt them till death. It was a good story but not as good as the one I had in mind. Before dinner I had put some premade little sacks of potassium perchlorate and aluminum powder in my pants pocket that were the size of chocolate "Hershey" kisses knowing if I could sneak them into the fire without the girls noticing it would really scare the hell out of them and I would win the story telling contest for sure, I just hoped that they would not blow up while in my pants pocket.

I started the story out by telling the girls a little about the history of the Sedona vortex's and all of the theories of what they really were and what they could do for someone who already possessed supernatural abilities such as psychic or telekinetic powers and if they came into physical contact with them. The main character in this story was a demon or an evil spirit who could change his shape to anything he wanted to. My story was about an old Navajo Indian man also known to be a "Yenaldooshi" who had the ability of shapeshifting or sometimes were called "Skin Walkers" and went by many names, he would only travel at night wearing coyote skins and primarily live in caves where they kept their collection of human heads. They are also known to be witches from other tales around the country. I could tell as I was setting the background of the story the girls were getting a little uneasy and restless moving closer towards the fire and I knew this was working out perfect for my little special effects finale. As I was nearing the end of the story I was one hundred percent sure that they would not notice me pulling out the small flash grenades that I had made. It would only take a few seconds for them to ignite once they hit the flames of the campfire. Miralani had heard the story before but had never experienced the flash grenades, this would be the first time I used them on her. After successfully planting the grenades in my hands it was almost time to end this story with a flash and a bang. I finished the story by saying, "The old Indian man was pushed into the burning pit where he let out a scream as he was descending into the bowels of hell," at this point I had just thrown the flash grenades into the fire a few seconds earlier and before Caitlin could finish saying, "Wow Cole that was some story," the flashes and pops scared the living crap out of all three of them. Right then I knew I had won the contest and I would not be doing any of the cleanup from dinner, I then remarked to the girls, "Well, you girls better get started with the dishes and start roasting some marsh mellows."

After the girls finished with all of the cleaning up they rejoined me at the campfire. I had already prepared some marsh mellow roasting forks made out of some hangers we brought along and they were loaded and ready for them to stick over the campfire. Caitlin was so excited to finally get to do something like this, she had led a pretty sheltered life and was not allowed to take part in any outdoor activities like camping and the special moments like these which were part of the whole experience, as she was gazing into the fire she turned and looked at Miralani and said, "How lucky you and Cole were to have parents to raise you in this way and experience the wonders of this beautiful area." I then replied, "I know we are but I want you to know that we can come out here anytime you want now because you have Miralani and I to share some of those experiences we had growing up and would love to consider you and Stacey part of our family now." Miralani looked at me and almost started to tear up. Caitlin was already misty eyed when she said, "Jesus Cole, I could just kiss you right now," she then scooted over closer to me and gave me a big hug and kiss on the cheek. I decided to break up this lovefest and talk about the stars and how old ancient tribes would navigate by them to find their way at night, one of the many things Miralani and I learned growing up out here in this part of the country. There is so much to learn from the study of the night skies when you're isolated from the mainstream city lights.

Stacey and Caitlin were both really enjoying the night skies, the astronomy lesson that Miralani and I were teaching them and the best part of the whole night so far was the meteor shower that had been going on over the past couple of nights, there was at least nine or ten big shooting stars every few minutes and hundreds of tiny ones sprinkled in with them, it was truly spectacular as they fell from the sky towards the background of the Sedona hills. My mind started to drift a little thinking about the case I had been working the past few days and I was still trying to make some kind of sense out of the whole thing. The theft of the Escalade was just driving me crazy and I was hoping that Sam would have some good news on that front when I got back on Monday. Sam was still a little green behind the ears when it came to these types of cases but he had the instinct of a bloodhound and was relentless when he had a lead to follow up on. At this point of my thoughts I turned to Miralani and asked her, "Hey sis so what's up with you and Sam?" She turned and looked at me knowing that I was just trying to embarrass her in front of her friends and to get Stacey and Caitlin back into some kind of conversation other than Indian heritage and ghost stories. Stacey jumped into the conversation saying, "Really Miralani, how long have you been seeing Sam?" Caitlin chimed in by saying "Yeah, tell us all about it."

With the light of the campfire you could tell that my sister's face had turned somewhat red and that she was a little irritated by the direction of this conversation but responding the way she always would when cornered she redirected the topic back to someone else which was me at the time by saying, "Okay girls, the truth of the matter is I haven't even gone out with Sam yet but I'm planning to next week, that is if he and Cole can solve this really interesting case their working on." Just like that the girls now focused on me and I knew what was coming next. Caitlin began by asking, "Yeah Cole, what kind of case is it you're working on, maybe we all could help by providing some outsider insight." I paused for a second to try to think of a way to answer without offending anyone's intelligence but I knew what ever my response was going to be it probably would. I turned to Caitlin and said, "I could really use some help on this case Caitlin but I can't say much about it at this point because it may have ties to the government and I wouldn't want to get anyone else connected to it and open themselves up for any federal investigative questioning from their agents." Stacey commented then by saying, "Well you can leave me out of this, I have no desire to have the government get involved in my life because I don't trust them one bit." I then replied, "I really do appreciate the offer of your help girls but it's better for now that I just keep quiet on this case."

We sat around the campfire for the next couple of hours talking about Sedona and how lucky we were to grow up here instead of some big city and all of the troubles that go along with them, such as the people, the crime, the job market situation of late and the lack of proper parenting when it comes to the number of children that end up in gangs and other criminal career paths that leads to a life of crime. It was quickly approaching midnight and I said to the girls, "Hey if we want to go on that hike I told you about in the morning we had better try to get some sleep so we can get up bright and early." The girls all agreed and retired to the tent, I would stay up a little bit longer and prepare the fire to burn for a couple of hours longer without needing any attention. I wanted to keep it burning through sunrise in order to try to keep the local wildlife away. I would have to get up a few times during early morning hours to keep it going but I wanted to make sure everyone stayed safe and mostly just to keep our food supplies safe. There are plenty of bobcats and coyotes out here that have honed their skills when it comes to locating and opening up coolers or any other types of food storage containers that you might think would be hard to get into for an animal. As I was positioning the wood around the fire I could already hear one of the girls snoring away through the tent walls. I'm pretty sure it was Caitlin because she had been so excited throughout the whole day. It was her first real camping trip and she was really taking it all in.

After being satisfied with the stacking of the wood on the fire it was time for me to hit the sack as well. I set my alarm on my watch for two a.m. so I could throw some more wood on the fire. I entered the side room of the tent through its own little door trying not to make too much noise so not to wake the girls. They were all in a deep sleep and the snoring was still pretty loud. I took my revolver a Navy Colt forty-five six-shooter out of my bag and put it next to my sleeping bag where I could get to it in a hurry if need be, again it's always better to be prepared for anything that might happen unexpectedly. Before zipping the door shut I took one more look at my baby parked nearby around twenty feet or so from the campfire. The reflections of the flames dancing off the red, white and blue parts of the paint job were absolutely magnificent and hypnotic. She had performed well today and I think the girls were very impressed by the off road capabilities this vehicle possessed. I zipped the door shut and climbed into my sleeping bag all the while staring at the light shadows flickering and dancing against the tent walls from the campfire. It seemed as only a few minutes had passed when my watch alarm went off. I shed my sleeping bag to go put some more wood on the fire and do a quick once over of the campsite. I returned to the privacy of my luxury suite and fell right back to sleep.

A few hours had passed when I was woken up by the giggling sounds of the girls in the adjoining room. The sun was just starting to rise and all I knew it was pretty damn cold in this tent, I had hoped the fire was still burning a little bit so it wouldn't be so much of a chore to get it burning strong again. I crawled over to the adjoining room zipper door and opened it up just enough to fit my head through and say good morning to the girls, they screamed of course and quickly tried to cover up with their sleeping bags. Miralani screamed out, "Damn it Cole, we're not even dressed." I simply said, "Don't worry the pictures probably won't come out anyways because I didn't have the flash on." Stacey and Caitlin both yelled out, "What," at the same time. I then suggested, "Hey let's get it in gear, we have a big day today and we need to get breakfast going sis!" I quickly pulled back into my side of the tent and zipped the door closed as fast as I could.

The campfire was at full steam and the girls came out of the tent with our breakfast supplies and cooking utensils. It would be my job to get everything cooked up. Miralani had prepared some ham, bacon, eggs, sausage, potatoes and even some biscuits that I was going to try to cook in the fire with my fancy grill slash basket. I was pretty sure it was going to work. We also had the leftover steaks from last night that I cooked, which Miralani had already chopped up into cubes. It sounded like a lot of food but we would need to eat a lot because of the long hike we had planned. I was pretty sure the girls could handle the physicality of it. On a scale of one to ten it would rank about a six. The temperature had finally started to rise some and it had got a little colder than I thought it would last night. That is one thing about this part of the country, the weather can change at a moment's notice this time of year. As I was cooking our breakfast the girls were huddled around the campfire talking about the upcoming hike and what they were hoping to see along the way. Miralani was acting like there big sister and trying to convince them that they would not be disappointed no matter what they saw or didn't see because Cole would make the hike very interesting and fun.

The smell of the bacon and sausage was absolutely mouthwatering and the Indian breakfast which had the chunks of steak, potatoes and green onions along with the spices that Miralani added to the meat could probably be smelt all the way back at the café. It was one of the favorites that the locals preferred at the café. I was preparing the tortillas to go on the fire next for a brief moment to warm them up, then we could enjoy this wonderfully smelling breakfast. Caitlin then remarked, "Wow Cole, I can't believe how good that smells, is it almost ready?" Taking the tortillas off the fire I replied, "It is now, so come and get it girls." They didn't have far to go since they were already sitting next to the fire but I just really enjoyed saying that, too bad I didn't have a dinner bell to ring. Caitlin and Stacey grabbed a couple tortillas and started to load them up with everything we had, I guess they were hungry. Miralani just sat back by the fire and watched with a big smile on her face. "Get in here and get some grub sis before it's all gone." I quickly remarked, "Don't worry Cole I will, just wanted to see if Caitlin and Stacey liked the Indian breakfast," she replied. At that moment both girls answered, "It's delicious." I then said, "Well I'm not waiting any longer, I've been cooking for the last thirty minutes and I'm starving." The smell of everything cooking on an open fire always made me so hungry, I guess that's the Indian in me again. By the time I got my meal prepared and sat down to eat the girls were nearly finished with theirs. I then said to them, "Hey there's still plenty left and it won't be any good by the time we get back from our hike, so eat up." Miralani and the girls said they were all stuffed and it was up to me to finish off what was left, so I did.

The sun had been up now for about an hour and it was starting to warm up. I knew it was going to be very nice for our hike, not too hot or cold, just right. We all had small half day backpacks with the insulated water bladders built into them, it was the only way to go when it came to storing and carrying cold water on a hike. I had just finished cleaning up the mess from breakfast when Caitlin asked, "Hey Cole should we take our cell phones with us?" Before I could answer, Stacey barked out, "Well I'm taking mine." I then told Caitlin, "Well if it's not too heavy I would take it, you never know what you might see for taking pictures and in case of an emergency you might need it." I had already told the girls that the cell phone reception wasn't very strong out here but if you had to make a call you could always make your way to high ground until you had enough bars on the signal to make a call. I'm sure that's probably why Caitlin asked if we should even take them, once again this was her first real camping trip so she is taking a lot in and having fun learning all the tidbits of information regarding camping and the limitations of your equipment and needs.

After securing the campsite the best we could and hiding my keys to the Bronco in the hidden compartment underneath the main frame section that only Miralani and I knew about we then grabbed our gear and headed out towards the northeast a couple of miles where we would traverse a large creek deep enough for everyone to get cleaned up if they wanted to. The water might be a little cold but it might feel pretty refreshing around the time we got there. I'm sure the girls would want to at least wash their faces and other demanding hygienic areas of the body, myself on the other hand would just go upstream a few hundred feet and strip down to my birthday suit and jump in with a bar of soap. Once the campsite was no longer visible from our position Caitlin started to get a little uneasy, I could tell she was somewhat uncomfortable about leaving the campsite with all of our belongings and the only mode of transportation to getting back to civilization. I turned to her and said, "No worries Caitlin, we'll be back before you know it and loading up the Bronco and then we'll be back to Miralani's for dinner." She then replied with a smile, "Thanks Cole, you're a sweetheart deep down inside and I like it, just wish we could see more of it."

We continued our trek to the north and had been walking now for about an hour and it was warming up really fast. It looked like it might get a lot hotter than it was supposed to. The water would be a welcomed site at this point in the hike, I could tell Stacey and Caitlin were out of shape and not used to walking very long distances especially on uneven trails and hills. I thought to myself when were they going to throw in the towel and say that they had enough and wanted to turn back. To my surprise they kept pushing on without even a whimper. Another fifteen minutes had passed when we finally reached the creek. The girls were already starting to shed their backpacks, once we got to the creeks edge the girls sat down on some rocks, took off their shoes and jumped into the shallow waters of the creeks edge and began to splash around and cool off. I said to Miralani, "Hey sis I'm heading upstream to take a swim in some of the deeper pools, I'll be back shortly." She replied by saying, "Okay Cole, maybe we'll head up there when we finish cooling down, don't worry we'll make a lot of noise so you can put your clothes back on." Caitlin then eagerly said, "Or maybe we won't, we might just sneak up on you." I just turned and smiled as I walked away.

I finally reached my secluded little spot that I had found the last time I was in this area, it had several cut outs along the banks and the water was close to seven or eight feet deep in those pools. They were almost like the size of a several small swimming pools and the water current flowed like a gentle whirlpool, I could hardly wait to jump in. Downstream I could still hear the girls frolicking around in the water, they were having fun and laughing so loud that all of the nearby wildlife had probably high tailed it out of the area. This would more than likely be the best part of the weekend for them, I on the other hand would be looking for new and interesting sites with the possibilities of discovering some new trails and sometimes even finding some old Indian artifacts that I usually gave to Miralani to display in her café.

I shed all of my clothes and all that remained was my cowboy hat and snakeskin boots, all I could think about was how funny it would look if the girls suddenly appeared at this moment. Off came the hat and boots and I quickly leaped into the creek letting out a howling yell before hitting the water, which I'm sure the girls heard. As I sank to the bottom I could see the wonderful rays of sunlight streaming through the depths of the water and creating a mystic underwater light show. There were several types of native trout in these waters around Sedona but I am pretty sure I had just scared the hell out of any that were nearby by executing my "Indian Cannonball" entrance into the water. My version of the traditional "Cannonball" was using only one arm to hold the knees in tight while the other arm was in the famous "Tomahawk" chop position prior to hitting the water all the while screaming or howling like a crazy Indian. After returning to the surface from my brief underwater experience I began to just float for a few minutes and enjoy the view, the sun and the serenity of it all. Even the girls had calmed down because I couldn't hear anything coming from downstream. I decided I had better get out and get dressed just in case they were heading my way.

After toweling myself off I thought I heard some noise coming from the scrub bushes behind me and just as I turned around to see what it was there stood all three girls with their cell phones out and snapping pictures as fast as they could. Caitlin yelled out, "Finally, I get a picture of some of the wildlife around here." Miralani was laughing her ass off and Stacey just stood there staring and taking as many pictures possible with her cell phone, I then yelled, "Stacey, stop with pictures already!" After a moment of silence, she said, "Sorry Cole but this is a new phone and I just wanted to see how good the pictures will come out." I quickly threw on my shorts and pants as the girls gave me a reprieve by turning around. "Wow Cole, this is a nice little spot, maybe we should all go skinny dipping here on the way back," Caitlin said with a grin from ear-to-ear. "Maybe, if there's enough time," I replied, still somewhat embarrassed. Caitlin's smile turned to a look of concern not knowing if I was joking or not. Now that I was fully dressed I suggested to the girls that we pick up where we left off on the trail. I figured from this point it would take about another hour or so to get to our planned destination where we could have a nice little lunch and roam around the area and look for some interesting sites and take some incredible pictures, it was one of the most beautiful areas near Sedona.

The trail was starting to get smaller and more challenging due to the tight terrain of the surrounding canyon, this was believed to be one of the canyons that the local Indian tribes traveled long ago. It was a very secluded trail and this whole area was quite easy to get lost in if you weren't familiar with the geography of the hills and rock formations. The girls were hanging in there and really pushing themselves and not a gripe or complaint from either Stacey or

Caitlin, I was very surprised and impressed by their toughness and drive, maybe I was wrong and too quick to judge them as spoiled yuppies who never had to work a day in their lives. They clearly had what it took to complete a goal or a desired achievement and I was going to let them know it before this day was over. As we trekked onward further into the canyon it started to open up and the trail split into three different directions. Having been down all three I knew the right one to take which would lead us to our destination.

After another ten minutes we made a sharp turn towards the south and we came up on a small mesa with an elevation around two hundred feet high and overlooking back towards Sedona, we had reached our destination. At that point Caitlin asked, "Hey Cole, where do we go from here?" I simply replied, "Nowhere girls, we're here and I am so proud of you, not once did you even show one sign of giving up or wanting to turn back, this is something you can be proud of." I knew that Miralani understood that I was talking to Stacey and Caitlin, my sister might have been in better shape than most of the other park rangers that I worked with and she was tough as nails when it came to the outdoors. I would put her up against anyone in a survival contest, she was that skilled and knowledgeable. In fact, when Caitlin asked about are exact location to post on Facebook Miralani answered, "Oh we're about ten miles west northwest of the end of the "Fay Canyon Trail" which is a much easier trail than the one you girls just did." I looked and smiled at my sister and said, "Wow, you never cease to amaze me Miralani." She just smiled back at me and then said, "Okay everyone, let's eat I'm starving."

The lunch was absolutely delicious and the view was spectacular, we were all just relaxing and taking in the fresh air and the soft sounds of the wind whistling through the surrounding sagebrush filled canyons. This truly was a spiritual place, the feeling of peace of mind was just overwhelming at times. I know the lore's and beliefs of the spiritual community here in Sedona are very committed to the vortex theories and beliefs of their healing powers and spiritual guidance but I personally have never experienced any of them but saying that, it does not mean that I'm a non-believer, in fact I do believe there is something out there in regards to the vortexes that has yet to be discovered. Stacey and Caitlin were taking more pictures to post on Facebook while Miralani was checking her phone for any messages. I then asked her, "Hey sis, everything okay back at the café?" Just fine, she said. I couldn't believe they could even get a signal on their phones, I guess the fact that we were a couple hundred feet up in elevation helped.

After wandering around for about an hour after lunch we all decided to start to head back to our camp, none of us found anything on our little treasure seeking hunts so it was probably a good idea that we head back now and take the extra time we would have to break the campsite down and get everything loaded back Into and on top of the Bronco. Hopefully we would all not be too tired from the return hike back to camp. As we were coming up on the creek area where I was caught skinny dipping by the girls, I immediately said, "Too bad we don't have time take another dip in the creek girls, I would have really enjoyed it." Caitlin laughed and said, "Sure Cole, we understand, you're still just a bit embarrassed from earlier this morning." Stacey then commented, "I don't think you have anything to be embarrassed about, I mean I'm just so glad I took a lot of pictures to remind me of the event." At that point I almost was ready to try anything to get that cell phone away from Stacey, she promised me she would not put any of those pictures on a social media site or email them to any of her friends. I could only hope she was telling the truth.

Passing the creek area, I could hear the girls giggling a bit and looking my way, I tried to ignore them by focusing on the surrounding hills and the beautiful skies above. It was at this point of the hike that I could hear a faint cry or whimper of an animal in distress or possibly injured. I looked back at the girls and said, "Hey girls hold up a minute, do you hear anything coming from that direction?" I was pointing towards the north and telling them to listen carefully for an animal in distress. We all stood perfectly still and listened for a few minutes and then we heard it, definitely it was coming from north of our location and not too far away but it did seem as if it was getting further away or just not as intense to when I first heard it. I told the girls to stay behind me and be as quite as possible as we headed off the main trail and began our way through the sagebrush, weeds and cactus. I knew as we were getting closer to the noise it was definitely a cry of distress and it was sounding a lot like a coyote or possibly a dog. All kind of thoughts were entering my mind right about now but there was one in particular and that was whatever this was I was hoping it was alone and not being watched over by a parent of some sorts. The smart thing probably would have been too stay on the main trail back to the campsite but I have a soft spot for animals, especially those that may need help.

We walked at a very slow pace for about ten minutes and the whimpering became much louder and I knew we were getting very close. The girls were getting a little nervous at this point so I told everyone to stop and then said, "Okay girls don't get scared, I'm only doing this just in case." I then slowly pulled out my pistol from its holster. I wanted to be prepared for anything that might present a danger to us. We were heading towards the base of a small hillside and I could see what looked like an opening or a sinkhole. I told the girls to be very careful because there were a lot of old abandoned mines in this area and you never know when the ground might give way to a cave in, that just about made them freeze in their tracks. I reminded them to stay right behind me if they wanted to continue or stay where they were and let me go and investigate the opening in the ground. They all answered, "Hell, we'll stay right here until you come back." Caitlin then said, "Pleases be careful Cole." Miralani then assured the girls of my safety by saying, "Don't worry Caitlin, he's the best there is at this kind of stuff, he's almost like a kid in a candy store when there's a little bit of risk involved in these types of situations." I turned towards Miralani and said, "Thanks sis, I think." I then continued towards the opening but I could barely hear the whimpering and whining, I hoped I was not too late to help whatever might be down in that sinkhole or cave.

As I got within a few feet of the opening the earlier sounds stopped all together but it did sound like something was digging or scratching the ground. I removed my hat and then decided to get on my belly and crawl up to the edge of the opening making sure not to disturb the surrounding ground and hopefully avoiding any type of collapse making the situation worse. I was only a couple of inches away from the edge when I heard a definite cry like a young dog or maybe a coyote, I was hoping for a dog, coyotes are a very nervous animal under normal conditions let alone being in some type of distress. I looked back at the girls who were still in sight and gave them a sign by putting my finger up against my lips to let them know to stay perfectly still and quiet. My next move was going to be tricky because I didn't want to frighten the animal to where he might injury himself if it was in danger from his surroundings. I gently pushed myself a few more inches to the edge and slowly looked down along the walls of the opening. To my surprise I could see the very distinct shape of a small or young pup that looked like a coyote but the light was pretty dim at the point where it was stuck on a ledge about ten feet down and the hole was more like a shaft of some sort, the walls were very smooth and the diameter was about six feet where the animal was trapped. I made the decision to let it know I was here to help. I then sat up on my knees and whispered softly to the animal, trying to get his attention and hopefully lower it's stress level.

I know the animal had already heard my crawling up to the opening but I wanted to make sure he saw me and that I meant it no harm. The sun was setting towards the west and the animal would soon be in the darkness of the shaft, I knew I didn't have much time to figure something out. The girls then started to throw some little pebbles at me to get my attention. I once again gave the sign for them to remain quiet, then looked at Miralani and began using some old Indian sign language to ask her to take the girls back to the camp and bring back my rope from the Bronco and that It was a young coyote pup stuck in the shaft. I just hoped she still remembered most of the signs I had just given her. When we were kids we would use this silent form of communication to talk to each other. Miralani then looked at me and gave me a sign that she understood the message and that she would return as soon as possible. I gave her a thumbs up and turned my attention back to the animal.

The time was going by too fast and the sun was only about two hours from setting. I knew the camp was only about twenty minutes away so the girls should be back within an hour hopefully. I decided to take one of my emergency light sticks out from my pants pocket and toss it down into the shaft in order to get an idea of how deep this thing was. I dropped it away from the ledge the pup was on so as not to scare it. I watched it all the way down to see if there were any more ledges or openings that might present a problem on the way down when I eventually would traverse down. The light stick came to its final resting spot about another ten feet down from the ledge the pup was on, so in all it was about twenty feet deep the best I could tell. The ledge was big enough for me to fit on with the pup as long as I took it slow. I decided to try to drop one more light stick down onto the ledge so the pup would have some kind of light and not be afraid of my descent, I just hoped he wouldn't decide to grab it with his mouth and chew it up or eat it because I had no idea how long this little guy had been down there.

It had now been over an hour and I was starting to wonder where the girls were and hoping they didn't get lost on their way back to the camp or back to my location, things look a lot different when the shadows hit the rocks and trails the closer it got to sundown. The second light stick landed just a few feet away from the pup and it was at this point I realized I was wrong about what it was, the pup was definitely not a coyote pup because of its head and body mass was much larger. I thought maybe it might be some kind of Husky mix and that meant it might not be so nervous about my presence. The pup was starting to settle down and accept me being there. I think it knew I was there to help. The sun was really getting close to setting so I figured I had better try to do something while I still had some light. I removed my survival knife from my belt and grabbed a nearby rock that was fairly good sized to use as a hammer. I then removed my belt and pounded the knife through the buckle portion and into the ground about a foot from the edge of the opening of the shaft. I then took out another light stick, activated it and sat it next to the knife. I was certain it would hold my weight for a short period of time, maybe just long enough to safely lower myself to the ledge where the pup was stranded.

I gave a quick look around for the girls and didn't see anything, I began to have second thoughts if this was the smart thing to do or just keep listening my heart and save this animal from certain injury and possibly starving to death. I leaned over the edge feet first and slowly continued to slide down to where the length of the belt was slack free and beginning to stretch and tug on the knife. I looked down towards the pup and it was totally calm to my surprise. I only had about another two feet to reach the ledge so I let go of the belt and tried to land as softly as I could. I landed quietly on the ledge and stood perfectly still for a few minutes just to give the pup its space and to reassure it I was not going to harm it. It only took me a few seconds to realize this was no ordinary dog and it was not a coyote, it was a full blown wolf cub about six to seven months old and very scared. I was pretty sure it had been here for quite some time because there were a couple spots on the ledge walls which showed signs of urination and there was a small pile of feces close to it.

I decided the sooner I tried to make a bond with the cub the sooner we could both be ready to get out of here, as long as the girls made it back soon. I guess the worst thing that could happen at this point was to have to spend the night down in this hole and wait for morning but was I definitely getting very worried why the girls were taking so long getting back. I knew the light stick at the top of the opening would shine bright for about four hours, after that it would start to dim very quickly and the girls would probably not be able to find my location. I would hope that they wouldn't even try to at that point. I began to crouch down on my knees to make myself seem less intimidating and much smaller looking to the cub,

I just wanted to reinforce the feeling that I wasn't there to do him any harm. When I got to the lowest position possible on my knees I could then tell the cub was a male from the light stick shinning on his underbelly. He was definitely some kind of Grey Timber wolf mix and absolutely a beautiful animal. As I offered my hand outward for him to smell he was totally quiet and still a little scared. I then began to talk to him in a very soft tone all the while moving my hand and body a little closer to his position on the ledge. He had been standing on all four legs since I slid down onto the ledge but he was now sitting down and his ears were totally upright and in a non-aggressive position, this was good news because I knew at that point he had accepted me being there with him and that I was not a threat. The fact that he was a very young cub also helped this situation from turning violent, if he would have been over a year old he more than likely would have been very aggressive. At this point I think we both were very happy that we had survived the fall into this shaft without any injuries. The next few minutes would determine how well this whole situation was going to turn out.

5

FIRST CONTACT

Ten minutes had passed since the cub had sat down and was totally okay with my presence so I decided to move even closer with my knees being only a few inches from his front paws. He then gave me a funny look like he wanted to play or something but what he did next was truly amazing, the cub starred at me for a few seconds then crouched down into a crawling position and shuffled his way up to my knees then put his head gently on my lap. I was shocked that he was so willing to basically submit to me as his alpha and so totally submissive and gentle. Another ten minutes had passed and it was almost totally dark in the shaft and up topside, I couldn't help wonder what the hell had happened to the girls, I just hoped they were okay and just got lost trying to find me on their way back from the campsite. I knew Miralani would have marked their trail outward from the camp when they came looking for me, she was quite good herself at tracking and marking trails in order to keep from getting lost and I knew she had a good supply of light sticks in her pack also. Speaking of light sticks it was time for me to crack open another one because it was beginning to look like the cub and I were going to spend the night on this ledge. I could tell the cub was very tired and still had not moved his head off my lap but I was going to have to shift my legs around and position myself a little tighter against the walls of the ledge to hopefully keep from rolling off if I happened to fall asleep. I carefully and very slowly lifted the cubs head off my lap just long enough for me to get to my desired position and that is when the cub decided he wanted to get a little closer to me by crawling up onto my lap and pushing his way forward onto my stomach. I knew the temperature would drop down below fifty degrees but at least we would be shielded from the wind.

As the light of the morning sunrise pierced through the shaft opening I looked down on my lap to see the cub sleeping soundly and snoring softly. I was totally convinced at this point that he trusted me completely. I started to move my body to keep him from sliding off my lap and he then began to wake up by moving his head and looking at me with the most gratifying look I had ever seen in my life, I knew we had formed a special bond that only could be described as very spiritual and calming to one's soul. I was starting to get a little hungry and I knew he was probably a lot hungrier than me. I remembered I had packed some beef jerky in my pack so I decided to see if he would take some from me. Without hesitation he took the first offering right out of my hand very gently and with those incredible yellow eyes of his I could tell he was very grateful. After eating half of what I had offered I decided I'd better save the rest in case we were stuck here for some time. I had two bottles of water which I poured some into my cupped hand and he lapped it up as fast as he could. I had already made up my mind that I was going to have to keep him as mine and take care of him because there was no sign of his mother or other siblings, I'm not sure what his story was but it probably was not a good one in regards to the rest of his pack or family. I figured I better give him a name as soon as possible in order to further the development of our bond and communication efforts. With our present location down in this shaft and all of the different shades of light reflecting his silhouette off the walls of the shaft from the light sticks I thought an appropriate name for him would be "Shadow" and also I had worked in the past for an Indian tracking group named "Shadow Wolves" run by the government that tracked smugglers, terrorist's and hardened criminals for the Homeland Security agency. I had thoughts over the last few months of getting a German shepherd from a rescue site so that I might have a partner to train and help me track but most of all just to keep me company when I was out on my calls. So "Shadow" it will be.

I thought to myself, what better tracking animal to have and train than a young wolf. Then reality set in, the two of us had better find a way to free ourselves from this damn shaft or there would be no future for the two of us. I took my cell phone out for the third time and still no reception signal, I guess this shaft was just too deep and even more bad news was the battery was down to thirty percent charge remaining. I looked at Shadow and said, "Hey Shadow, you got any bright ideas on how we can get out of here?" He simply snuggled up a little closer and moaned a bit. I reached into my pocket and gave him another piece of jerky. He seemed to chew this chunk a lot slower and savor the wonderful taste of something he had never tasted before. It was now just a few minutes before seven o'clock and the sun was starting to warm the shaft and it felt good. I took out another light stick and dropped it to the bottom of the shaft to see if I could spot anything that might help us get out. To my surprise I noticed another opening at the bottom along the side wall of the shaft that was definitely big enough for a man to get through. I knew that during the heavy rains the flood waters would sometimes create underground tunnels which usually lead to the surface eventually. I still had five light sticks in my pack and two in my pants pocket if I decided this was going to be our way out.

I had a smaller pocket knife in my pack so I felt somewhat at ease in case we ran into some type of threating wildlife. "Okay Shadow, let's do this," I said. My plan was to lower Shadow down by using my jeans as a form of rope and my shirt as a cargo basket to put him in and tie the sleeves around him so he could not slip out, it should work if he didn't panic when I wrapped him up. I would lower myself down the same way I used to get to the ledge we were currently stranded on. It was probably only about another ten to twelve feet to the bottom, I could almost just jump to the bottom but not knowing what the shaft floor consisted of I figured the lighter the landing the safer we would be. After removing my jeans and shirt it was time to get Shadow secured into my shirt. I gently started to pet him and move him into the shirt which was tied in a knot at the bottom of the shirt and buttoned halfway up. He definitely had accepted me as a friend and his alpha, he seemed to know what was about to happen and was okay with it, thank god because I really needed him to be okay with everything that was going to happen in the next few minutes. Once he was in the shirt I gave him more positive reinforcement by praising him and comforting him. I quickly tied the sleeves around his shoulders then looped them around his neck it was fairly tight but it needed to be, I didn't want him slipping out and falling in awkward position to the shaft floor. Once again he seemed to know what I was about to do and eager to get it done. I then took one end of my pant leg and looped it through the sleeves I had attached to him.

I gave him a great big hug and said, "Okay Shadow, let's see how brave you can be, I'm going to be right behind you my friend." After licking me on the cheek he gave me another look of approval from those piercing yellow eyes. I was still amazed at how fast he had created this strong emotional bond with me. There was no way now I was ever going to separate myself from him because my feelings for him were just as strong as his for me. I began to slowly lower him down towards the light stick so I could see him approach the floor. It only took thirty seconds or so and he was on the floor of the shaft. I then said, "Okay Shadow, good boy, now it's my turn." I slowly lowered myself over the edge to where I was just hanging about three feet from the bottom. I pushed myself away from the shaft wall and let go making sure not to land on Shadow. I landed pretty softly and immediately turned my attention to removing Shadow from the makeshift harness and putting my pants and shirt back on, it was still pretty chilly down here. Shadow responded by jumping up and down on my legs and seemed to be rejuvenated by the whole experience.

The next ten minutes were spent surveying the shaft floor for anything that might be useful once Shadow and I started our journey into the dark hole that stood before us. I did find a broken pick axe handle that was around three feet long that could be useful for all kinds of different situations. Shadow was staying right by my side but definitely interested by the dark opening in the shaft wall. Although he was probably only six to seven months old his nose was developed enough to pick up on any scents that may have passed this way recently and something had caught his attention already. After noticing Shadow's behavior, I decided to make some kind of spear out of my pocket knife and the pick axe handle. I tore one of my sleeves off of my shirt and cut it up into long skinny strips that I would use to secure the knife to the broken end of the axe handle, it was a bit crude but it would be affective in case I needed to use it for our safety, once again it never hurts to always be prepared but in this case I wish I had kept my pistol instead of giving it to Miralani. There were enough decent sized stones lying around in order to leave a sign, which was basically my name and an arrow pointing to the opening in the shaft wall just in case the girls found their way back to this location. The last light stick I dropped still had several hours of life left to it so I used the last remaining strip from my shirt sleeve to attach it to other end of the pick axe handle, hopefully at some point there would be some breaks of sunlight piercing through the ground from above.

I looked at Shadow and he was very anxious to get started and the fact that he already seemed to know what the plan was he really started to show the intelligence of the wolf species. I just hoped we could get through this ordeal quickly and I could get him back to my home which was soon to be his also. "Okay boy, stay close," I said, now was just as good as any to start Shadow's command training. As we passed through the opening it was a little tight for me having to crouch down some and Shadow followed me in staying as close as he could. The light stick was doing its job providing us with enough light to see how big this tunnel truly was. I could stand upright after passing through the opening from the shaft and it seemed to be getting bigger as we pushed forward. I couldn't quite tell what type of small cavern this may lead us to if any but the walls had a wet looking glimmer to them. I know that it hadn't rained for quite some time so I didn't think it was from flooding but it did feel and smell like water and underground water does have a certain smell to it. Going on the assumption it was water I was pretty sure we were heading towards or near an underground spring of some kind.

Four hours had now passed since Shadow and I entered this underground tunnel and still no signs of any possible routes to the surface. I decided to take a snack break and give Shadow a little more of the beef jerky and water, I knew he needed it more than myself. I could last a couple of days just on what little water we had in my pack but hopefully it wouldn't come down to that. Shadow was definitely a purebred wolf of some kind the longer I looked at him as we sat and ate our jerky, he was a stunning looking cub and sure to grow to be quite large. I was thinking what Miralani would say to the idea of me keeping and raising him to be my companion and working partner. I also was still a little worried about the girls being okay and wondering what happened in regards to them not being able to find their way back to me. A couple of crazy thoughts had entered my mind like maybe they didn't want to comeback or maybe they were out joyriding in my Bronco and it broke down on them or even worse they wrecked it and were stuck somewhere but I knew better than that, it had to be them not being able to find their way back and by now they have probably got the park rangers out here to help look for me. If the other rangers were to find me before Shadow and I could make our way out they would never let me live it down. All in all, it had just now been about twenty hours since I last saw the girls.

Our snack break was over and Shadow and I continued on our path through the tunnel which now was almost twenty feet high and the definite smell of water was getting stronger. The light stick on the axe handle was now starting to dim a little so I pulled another one out of my pack and activated it, then replaced the old one with it. I left the old one on the ground in case if anyone came this way looking for us, at least it would show that we were down here and pressing on. With the new light stick activated you could definitely see quite a bit more in front of us and compelling us to pick up the pace a bit to cover more ground all the while being cautious of unstable footing and moist ground conditions. Shadow was learning quickly to stay by my side and yet not get in the way or to make much noise. Wolves are a very stealthy animal even at a young age they adapt to their environment quite well and Shadow was no exception, I couldn't even hear his paws hitting the ground as we walked. After walking another hour or so I checked my watch for the time it was almost eleven o'clock so I knew the sun outside was almost directly overhead which meant if there were any more openings from the surface it should shine down through where we might be able to see them. Shadow was still full of energy and wanting to keep going at the current pace, hopefully the jerky was providing him with the needed nourishment for this journey we were undertaking. If we could find a snake or a large lizard it would provide us with some much needed protein and make for a tasty lunch or dinner. Hopefully the water source I was smelling was not too far away and it would be drinkable. That could make all the difference we needed to prolong our life expectancy if it came down to that.

The tunnel now at this point was more of a small cavern and had opened up into a large dome or pocket at our current location so I thought we should stop and check out the area for any possible food sources. I turned and looked at Shadow then spoke, "Hey Shadow want to look for some food?" Again he looked right at me with those big piercing yellow eyes as if too telepathically let me know that he understood what I was saying. We began to head towards the closest of the walls of the small cavern and looking directly at our feet to see if there were any animal or reptile tracks that might lead us to a source of food. Shadow was extremely excited and eager to help with the hunt, just in the short time we had been together I felt as if he was starting to meld with my mind and soul. I truly had respect for these animals because of their loyalty towards their packs and family members. The way that they would hunt together and plan their attacks on their prey was very coordinated and quite tactical from all the members of the pack, it was really very impressive. I was hopeful that the two of us could share our skills in tracking and form a great partnership which would in turn pay huge dividends for any future missing person's cases that I would be involved with.

Thirty minutes of scouring the cavern floor and there were still no signs or tracks of any life down here other than Shadow and myself. I decided to look for any small nooks or crevices in the shaft wall directly in front of us which might be a sanctuary for any type of small critters of some sort and just as I was getting close to the wall Shadow began to alert or show some kind of interest in something just to the right of our location. I then looked down at him and said, "Easy boy, let's not scare whatever it is away, it might be our only meal for a while." I slowly pointed the axe handle towards the direction that Shadow was staring at hopeful the light stick at the end would be just enough light to see something but not too bright to scare whatever it was away. As we both moved very slowly towards the right I could definitely here something moving about four to five feet directly in front of us, Shadow's senses even at their early stages of development were still better than mine and he was on to something alive and moving very slowly as if to match our pace of advancement. Suddenly the light stick exposed what was the last thing I wanted to see in this situation, there before me slithering towards us and picking up its pace was a massive Western Diamondback rattlesnake at least five feet in length from the exposed part I could see. I could tell Shadow was getting ready to pounce on it and I immediately tried to settle his nerves down along with mine. The snake was not backing down at this point and probably sensed that we were not going to just leave it alone. I knew that I would have to get within a couple of feet it in order to get my makeshift spear in range to kill this huge and very fat snake.

After going over my plan of attack in my mind several times I slowly reached down and pushed on Shadow's nose moving him backwards a little and telling him to "Stay" hoping he would understand. The last thing I wanted was for him to go after this poisonous reptile. He seemed to be a little cautious or afraid at this point which was good. I slowly moved a bit closer to the snake while rotating the axe handle around to get into position to strike it with my pocket knife attached at the other end but the problem with that was I had just lost most of my light directly in front of me thus giving the snake an advantage with his thermal reading capabilities of his tongue which could easily track my every move from my body heat signature. By now the snake was in a fully coiled position and ready to defend itself from any aggressive behavior towards it. Just as I was taking one more step to get a little closer I lost my footing on the slippery rock surface and fell to my knees only a couple feet away from the snake, I froze instantly and hoped to god Shadow was not going to advance on the snake. I very slowly turned my head around forty-five degrees or so to check on Shadow and to my surprise he was no longer there. I guess my sudden fall must have spooked him into hiding, I just hoped he had not run off somewhere in the dark but I had more important issues to worry about, like trying to avoid getting bit by this huge Diamondback all the while waiting for the right moment to pierce it behind its head with my spear.

After a few minutes of staying perfectly still I decided to make my move on the snake, even with temperature being pretty cool down below the surface I had started to sweat around my forehead and this was unusual for me because I had been around snakes all my life. I knew how to catch them, how to kill them and even how to cook them but this time and the circumstances involved had me very nervous. I began my assault by leaning forward ever so slowly waiting for the right second to lunge right into the snake just in case it decided to strike hoping to throw its distance judgement off by a bit. It only took a second before the snake started to rattle its tail giving me a warning sign to back off but I knew I was committed at this point. Tightening my knees up some to get a better lunge forward I quickly leaned back slightly then with the knife aimed near the back of the snake's head I made my attack move and at the same time the snake made his strike towards me, trying to avoid his bite my knees slipped again on the wet rocky surface exposing me for a deadly strike, I was just about to try to hit it with the axe handle as it made its second strike towards me when out of nowhere Shadow pounced on it while biting it a foot or so behind its head, the next noise I heard was horrifying, it was Shadow letting out a loud yelp. I moved the light stick close to him to reveal the dead snake still locked onto his right front leg. He was whimpering a little but more afraid of what had just happened then the actual pain from the bite. The good news was I had a snake bite kit in my backpack but had never tried to use one on an animal.

The next few minutes were going to be very critical if I was going to save Shadow's life, he being a very young cub meant that he only weighed around sixty pounds the equivalent of a small child. Most rattlesnake bites are not fatal to adult humans but the less weight you have the stronger the toxic poison becomes. Shadow was probably just trying to protect me thinking I was injured when I slipped the second time and exposing myself to danger from the snake. I was so glad he hadn't run off but I wish that he would have now because of his current situation. I quickly removed the snakebite kit and picked him up a little and then put his head and right front leg on my lap. He was very calm at this point and again seemed to know what was about to happen regarding the first aid I was getting ready to administer. I still had one small piece of my shirt sleeve that I could use as a tourniquet to stop the poison from spreading, I put it on and used another light stick to hold the tension in place after tying the knot of the strip of shirt sleeve. Shadow was so still and a perfect patient, I was so impressed with his bravery and loyalty I was praying that he would be okay. I quickly made a x-pattern cut on Shadow's leg all the while trying to keep him calm because that is the most important piece of the whole snakebite treating process, the blood flow remains at a slower rate when the patient is relaxed therefore enhancing the purpose of the tourniquet to restrict as much blood as possible from traveling too far from the bite area. After squeezing as hard as I could from the tourniquet down towards the bite and removing as much blood as

I could from the wound I quickly put some antiseptic cream on the bite area and bandaged the leg up. I would loosen the tourniquet once every fifteen minutes after this point of the treatment. All I could do now was sit with Shadow and keep him from moving around too much. I removed what was left of my shirt and made a small pillow for him to lie his head on hoping he would rest easy.

A couple of hours had passed and Shadow was resting comfortably by my side, his breathing was normal and that was a very good sign. I moved ever so slightly to move his head along with the pillow onto the ground. I needed to address the matter of cleaning the snake so all of this would not be for nothing. I slowly crawled over to the snake and stretched him out to expose what I thought was the biggest damn Diamondback I had ever seen in my life. It had to have been over eight feet in length and as fat as a brand new roll of toilet paper. This thing could feed about six people, it was huge. I had eaten rattlesnake before on many occasions and it was really pretty good. I figured Shadow needed to rest at least six to eight more hours to make sure all the toxin was out of his system and he was well enough to travel again and by the time he woke up I would have us a nice meal for us to feast on the rest of the day. I decided to cut the meat up into very small chunks because the only method of cooking it was two cans of "Sterno" in my pack, a gas fuel used for campsite cooking appliances. After cutting out a small wire from my backpack that was there for support of an additional compartment I then fabricated it into a couple of shish kebabs for Shadow and myself. The meat would cook up very quickly so I decided to wait for Shadow to slowly waken before cooking our dinner. I didn't want to take the chance of him smelling the food and waking him before his body had recovered enough for him to start moving around again.

As I sat and starred at Shadow I couldn't help to think if I had made a terrible mistake leaving the mine shaft and not waited longer hoping the girls would find us but life is about the choices we have to make and the tough ones can always be second guessed. My father always told me follow your heart and trust your instincts and that will get you through whatever life throws your way. I respected my father and his beliefs of our Indian heritage and the power of the spirits who watched over good men and provided spiritual guidance to those who respected the land and animals of this world. I was quite sure now that Shadow was going to be alright he just needed to get some rest and take it easy for a while and get some real food in him besides jerky. He had been asleep now for quite some time so I lit a can of "Sterno" and prepared our kebabs. Once on the fire they should cook up pretty fast since I cut the cubes of meat very small for Shadows benefit. After a few minutes of cooking on the fire Shadow began to wake up and his nose was moving around like some kind of bobble head toy. "Easy boy, you're going to be okay now, you just need to take it easy boy," I reassuringly remarked. He then looked at me and slowly crawled towards me as close as possible then laid his head on my lap. I looked down at him and said, "Just a few more minutes Shadow, then we're going to feast like kings." He then looked up at me and slowly oozed out a long and drawn out faint growl or moan. I sensed that he was giving me his approval of the meal we were about to eat. As I was slowly turning the kebabs over the fire the smell of the cooking meat was mouthwatering and the both of us were absolutely famished at this point of our adventure.

The first round of meat was ready and I quickly removed it from the fire and slid the chunks of meat off the kebabs and onto a guide map I had in my pack. That was going to be our dinner table for this fine meal we were about to eat. I quickly reloaded the kebabs with another round of meat cubes. I could see that Shadow was quite ready to eat. I turned to him and said, "You should be the first to eat my friend, since you made the kill and saved my life." Shadow responded by taking a sniff of the meat and then ate one bite and looked at me as if to be asking if he could have more, I looked him and said, "Go ahead boy, it's all for you." He then quickly turned his attention back to the meat and began slowly savoring each chunk of the snake meat. I slowly stroked the backside of his head and reassured him the food was for him. After a few minutes the last chunk of meat was gently chewed and swallowed by Shadow, the expression on his face was priceless. I figured now was a good time to see just how much affection I could give to Shadow so I leaned over towards him and slowly wrapped my arms around his upper body and then very gently pulled his head into my neck area then whispered in his ear, "Shadow my friend, I am forever grateful to you for saving my life and so honored to be your friend, we are now blood brothers." He slowly pulled his head back from me and just stared into my eyes, I could almost understand what he was trying to say with his mesmerizing eyes and I believe they were saying, "Thank you my friend for saving my life twice, by rescuing me from a long lonely death and from the snake bite."

After the second batch of meat cubes were ready to eat I placed the meat in two separate piles on our dinner table the guide map. Shadow watched my every move while keeping his distance and showing a great amount of discipline. I could tell the first batch of food had really given him some much needed strength. He was sitting up nice and straight and the affects from the snake bite were starting to fade away. My plan was for us to eat as much of this snake as possible over the next few hours then sleep here for the night. With plenty of rest for Shadow we would be able to push forward tomorrow morning. The speed of his recovery was telling me that I must have gotten most of the venom out from the aid I administered or the snake's venom sack had been near empty at the time of the bite, either way I was extremely happy with his rapid improvement. Moving one of the piles of meat closer to Shadow I said to him, "Okay Shadow, let's eat, dig in boy." I began to eat from my pile and Shadow began to slowly pick up pieces from his pile, the light stick I had placed in the center of the guide map kind of provided a candle lit dinner affect for the two us, it was very relaxing and quite nice. I had a very good feeling that tomorrow would be a much better day than today, I was confident that Shadow and I would find a way out of this underground maze.

Shadow and I had consumed as about as much snake meat as physically possible for our stomachs to hold. We were both getting a little sleepy and ready to turn in. It was getting pretty cold and the heat from the "Sterno" can was not enough to do either one of us any good. Shadow was already laying up against my side and with his head tucked away in my armpit. I knew that with his full belly that he should sleep very well tonight, me on the other hand probably not. I had all kinds of thoughts going through my mind concerning the whirlwind of events over the past week. The government Escalade that was stolen out of the impound yard, the lack of clues and leads to help identify who owned it or who wanted to steal it and if I had spoiled my sister's date with Sam. I wondered if Sam was out there right now looking for me and why they couldn't find my knife and belt I left to give them our location down the shaft. I also wondered how many rangers would be out looking for me, our station was understaffed to begin with and the fact that I was their friend and co-worker would not provide me with any special consideration but I also knew that Miralani had plenty of friends and people that worked for her that would be helpful when looking for missing persons. My sister would not quit looking until she had found me and that was very comforting at this point. Just as I was about to nod off Shadow began to snore and it was actually nice to hear knowing he would wake up refreshed and hopefully at full strength. I slowly began to drift off myself with my arm wrapped around Shadows body, the body heat from the two of us should keep us warm throughout the nighttime temperatures until the heat of the early morning sunrise would start to warm things up a bit.

I looked at my watch after waking up only after a few hours of sleep from what I thought I heard was the sound of a helicopters rotor wash. The sound was unmistakable for someone like me who had been in and around search and rescue helicopters for the last ten years of my life. Shadows eyes were already open from hearing the same thing, his ears were shifting back and forth towards the noise as it moved further away from our position. I wish I had some way of signaling it but we were too far below the ground and they would not be able to pick up our thermal heat wave signatures. I looked at Shadow and said, "Don't worry boy, they'll keep looking until they find us." I stroked his head and ears to try to get him to fall back to sleep. He looked up at me and with those yellow eyes of his with a very warm and content look and I knew he was just as confident as I was that we would make it out of here okay. I believed that tomorrow we would both be sitting around my back porch with Miralani and her friends going over the whole experience of the last few days and them getting to know Shadow and the story of how he took the snake bite while trying to protect me. Shadow had fallen back to sleep and now it was my turn to get some more sleep. I gently laid back down on the ground making as little movement as possible so not to wake up Shadow. I made sure I had another light stick ready by putting one in my pants pocket because I knew the one we had in front of us would go dim and finally out in a few more hours. I was starting to get a little concerned that I had only four left which was enough for about a day of continuous light if needed. Once again I drifted off to sleep as the noise from the helicopter faded away along with any hopes of being found for now but tomorrow was another day and even if Shadow and I had to dig our way to the surface, we were getting out.

I was dreaming about Shadow and I cruising the streets of Sedona in the Bronco when all of a sudden I was abruptly wakened by the wet tongue of Shadow licking the right side of my face. It was total darkness so I cracked open the light stick I had in my pants pocket. Shadow's head quickly came into focus and he looked wide eyed and raring to go. I knew that there was one thing I was going to have do before we got started and all I can say it was a good thing I had a small roll of toilet paper in my backpack and from the smell of things I believe that Shadow had already done his deed somewhere in the cavern. Once again it's always a good idea to be prepared for all types of situations and emergencies. After taking care of my personal needs I felt like a million dollars and I too was eager to get going. According to my watch the sun had been up for about an hour now and it was definitely starting to warm up a little in the cavern. I quickly loaded everything up that we needed and put it all back into my pack. I reattached the light stick to the end of the axe handle and we were on our way. Shadows tail was wagging like it had some kind of little engine powering it back and forth, he was full of energy. I looked down at him and said, "Okay big guy, let's find our way out of this hellhole."

There were three choices of exit tunnels from the main cavern we had just spent the night in and one of them had a pretty small opening to the entrance, almost too small for me to fit through. Shadow looked at me and I said, "Well which way do you think Shadow, left, right or the middle?" I let him sort of lead the way until I sensed which one he was heading towards then made my own evaluation of the three as we got closer. I could tell the one the middle definitely had more of a wet look to it walls. I looked down at Shadow and said, "Shadow, what about this one?" As I stared towards the middle tunnel. Once again he seemed to know what I was thinking and which tunnel I wanted to take. I moved the light stick forward into the middle tunnels opening and we pressed on, hopefully to reach our freedom from the underground maze we had called home for the past day and a half. I figured if we could just find a way that had an incline of some sort we could get close enough to the surface to find a weak spot in the soil and dig our way out. I estimated that we were probably around forty feet below the ground surface overhead. As Shadow and I continued to press forward the tunnel walls seemed to glisten once again as if they had been coated with some kind of foreign substance or a periodic flow of steam, the walls had no particular odor or color to them, they just had the appearance of looking wet. I was not aware of any underground springs in this area of Sedona so I was at a loss to where the steam might have originated from.

Twenty minutes had now passed and still no change to the geological conditions Shadow and I were passing through, we just kept going forward. The ground at our feet did seem to be getting a little more slippery from the moist conditions so we slowed our pace down a bit. As we continued on I could faintly hear what I thought sounded like the wind whistling and howling like you might hear on a stormy day. I checked out Shadows reaction and he definitely was hearing it also, his acute hearing even at his young age was ten times better than mine. We slowly moved forward all the while trying to fixate on a directional track of the sound which was very difficult with all of the nooks and crannies of this tunnel, most of which were too small to traverse through. There was something strange about the sounds that were now getting more pronounced, it almost seemed if as they were being produced by a machine because of the regular pulsing of the strength of the noise. It was starting to sound more like a big giant fan or vacuum of some sort. I knew that there was no machinery or underground factories of any type in the Sedona area, unless it was military and the government had done an unbelievable job on the secrecy of it. My mind was running wild now with all kind of crazy theories and thoughts all of which involved the federal government. I looked down at Shadow and said, "Shadow I'm not sure what lies ahead but we have to keep going and hopefully it will be our ticket out of here." He looked up at me and started to move forward on his own while letting out a faint whine. I was not quite sure how to read all of his different means of communication and body language but this is something that we both would become more familiar with over time.

With Shadow leading the way we moved even slower now to make sure we didn't pass up some kind of opening where the sounds might be originating from. He was doing a great job with his pace, his nose, his eyes and his ears, almost as if he was trying to tell me that he was better suited for this task and I was not going to interfere with him because this was an outstanding opportunity for us to build on our trust for one another. He was walking so proudly and tall and it was truly magnificent to watch one of gods most spectacular creatures exhibit some of its traits. Wolves are one of the world's best trackers and hunters and can hunt for days until they wear down their prey and Shadow was no exception to this, the more I studied him from a breed standpoint the more he looked like a purebred Timberwolf. I was hoping that this was the case because if he had any Alaskan Grey wolf in him he would grow to be much larger than a Timberwolf. We pressed on scanning the walls of the tunnel and carefully watching our footing as the ground was becoming very slick. Whatever was causing the moisture in this tunnel we were rapidly getting close to the source. The walls were now glistening like a slow flowing waterfall and the slight noise of droplets hitting the tunnel floor was increasing with every step Shadow and I took. I knew we were getting very close to a significant water source of some kind. Another ten minutes passed and to my surprise the tunnel was coming to a dead end about twenty feet ahead of us. I looked at Shadow and said, "Shadow stay, hold up boy, let me take the lead now." I knew that there had to be a source or an opening in the tunnel that could be dangerous if we didn't see it coming. I took the lead and we both moved at an extremely slow pace watching for any signs of cracks or small holes ahead of us, I just hoped that we hadn't already missed something.

We only had ten feet or so before we would reach the dead end of the tunnel, god I had hoped we hadn't come all this way for nothing. There had to be something here, it just didn't make any geological sense that this tunnel could come to a complete dead end, it had to have a source for all of the moisture up to this point and then we both saw it. Shadow stopped completely and began to make a faint whine and looked up at me. I said, "I know boy, I see it too," there before for us was an opening in the ground floor about five feet in length and a couple feet wide. I could hear the sound of water running slowly over the surface of the leading edge of the opening. It was definitely a decline from the surface Shadow and I were standing on. I turned to Shadow and said, "Okay Shadow, let's take this nice and easy, okay boy." I lowered and angled the light stick closer to the surface of the ground which now had a small layer of water about a quarter of an inch on it. This could get real slippery and dangerous now because of the unknown elements combined with the water, it could have moss or some other organic compound that could make walking like trying to ice skate uphill. Slowly Shadow and I moved forward and with every step checking our stance and grip on the surface looking like a couple of lost drunk snails.

After what seemed like an eternity Shadow and I reached the edge of the opening and it looked like a waterslide with a gradual decline that quickly became dark after ten to fifteen feet. The walls that lined the tube or shaft had a pretty steady flow of water dripping from it. I looked at Shadow and said, "Well boy, what do you think?" Shadow looked up at me and wagged his fluffy tail and gave me a look of approval, I think. It didn't really matter at this point because I had already made up my mind that we were going to turn around and head back to the small cavern we spent last night in and try another one of the other tunnels because this option of continuing down this opening just had to many unknown possibilities that could end up in a life threating situation. I slowly turned around and reached down to nudge Shadow to do the same so we could start our way back. He seemed to already know the decision I had made for the two of us. As I was about to take my first step there was a sudden loud mechanical turbine noise that actually vibrated the ground violently. Shadow immediately started to cry and act uneasy as if he had heard this sound before. I kneeled down onto my knees and held him tightly trying to reassure him it was going to be okay but it only took a few seconds to realize I was very wrong about that. The ground shook violently then all of a sudden the ground where we were sitting gave way and before we knew it Shadow and I were both going for a waterslide ride that we didn't want to be on. I held onto Shadow as tight as I could all the while trying to hold the light stick in front of us while we descended into the wet dark abyss. The loud noise had stopped but the flow of water had increased as we continued our faster descent to an unknown fate. Before I could think of what deadly possibilities awaited us we splashed down and came to a sudden stop.

Shadow and I now laid in a shallow pool of warm water about two feet deep and the size of a very large swimming pool you might find in a backyard. I looked at Shadow and asked, "Hey boy are you okay?" He seemed a little shook up from the ride but quite relieved the loud noise that was bothering him had stopped. After letting go of Shadow I started to wave the light stick around slowly in order to get my bearing and see what we had just fallen into. There was definitely dry ground all around the edge of the waterline. It looked as if the pool was draining out somewhere I just couldn't tell where. I turned my attention back to Shadow and said, "Okay Shadow my friend, let's get out of this cold water and get to dry ground." I knew that the water was probably very refreshing to him because wolves had triple coats which always kept them pretty warm. They were very well suited for extreme cold temperatures if needed, their coats could adjust to whatever their environment called for. We slowly made our way out of the pool of water where I quickly removed my shoes and squeezed the water out of my socks. I'm pretty sure they were going to stay wet for quite some time. I still had a couple of cans of "Sterno" if it got too cold for my feet, the same wire I used to cook the snake meat on I could use to hang dry my socks on.

Once I put my somewhat wet socks and shoes back on Shadow and I surveyed the area for any exits out of this water collection area and hopefully would get us headed upwards towards the surface and our freedom from this adventure that was turning into something out of the movie "Journey to the Center of the Earth." Shadow shook violently a couple of times to clear the water from his coat and then we both spotted a small opening about twenty feet to the right of us. It was definitely big enough for me to pass through thank god because I did not want to try to have to climb back up that waterslide we just experienced. We slowly headed towards the opening when the light stick started to fade quite a bit, I guess the water must have got inside it somehow when Shadow and I made our splashdown. I quickly grabbed another one from my pack and activated it, then attached it to the axe handle. We were back in business and we proceeded on. Once we reached the opening I stuck the light stick through the opening to get a glimpse of what was on the other side. It looked like another tunnel and the diameter was around fifteen feet or so, plenty large enough for us to traverse. I went first then Shadow followed only a couple feet behind, he wanted to stay very close since he heard that noise. I was beginning to think that the noise and earth shaking moment was something he had experienced before, maybe even the reason for his situation of being trapped alone in that shaft to begin with. I had a strong sense the both of us had not heard the last of it either.

We continued our trek moving through the tunnel not descending or ascending just staying level for the time being. The day seemed like it was passing by at a rapid pace and I did not want to stay another night down in the dark and cold abyss. We kept going as we didn't get too tired because there was no sense of actual night or day, it was always dark down here. I decided we would just take a short break when we needed it and then just keep pressing on. I figured the two of us could keep going strong for at least another twenty-four hours before we got to tired or hungry. Shadow had definitely shaken off the effects from the snake bite and was at full strength. The bond between the two of us had grown so strong over such a short period of time it was truly something special. I looked down at him then got on one knee and asked to come closer, when he did I put both of my arms around his neck and said, "Shadow, were going to make it out of here, I promise you that." He responded by pressing his long snout into my neck area and slowly groaned a little then licked my cheek. I patted him on his chest gently and said, "Okay boy, let's get going." Once again we pressed on towards our freedom and the life that awaited the two of us.

Another hour had passed when Shadow and I saw something that was totally out of place and almost made me think I was beginning to hallucinate from all of the snake meat we had ate but Shadow saw it too and immediately froze. There in front of us was what looked like and had to be a big manmade vent with faint traces of light filtering through on the surface we were walking on. I couldn't believe it, what in the hell had we stumbled onto. My heart was pounding about as fast as it ever had and my mind was racing with all kinds of secret government facilities that might be down here and what might happen if they found us trespassing here but on the other hand this could be our way out of here and back to the surface. There was no choice involved here, Shadow and I were going to have to find a way in through that vent. As the two of us got closer and closer to the vent the light extruding from it increased in intensity. I could tell it was about five feet by feet in size and it was designed to move a lot of air through it. Once Shadow and I got next to it I could see the task of getting through it just became more difficult, underneath the vent I could see fan blades. Well I guess whoever owned this could just bill me for the damage that was coming its way.

Shadow and I positioned ourselves almost on top of the vent and fan to get a better look at what was down beneath it. The fan blades were not moving which was a good thing, they would be a lot easier to deal with while stationary. I held the light stick closer to the edges of the vent to see if I could locate any mounting screws or other means of attachment and we were in luck, it looked like the vent louvers were just held into place by a few sheet metal screws from underneath the cover. With plenty of light to work with now beaming through the louvers I quickly removed the light stick from the one end of the axe handle then flipped it around to use the other end as a pry bar to loosen the whole assembly. I began to carefully work on one corner of the cover hoping to get enough clearance to be able to bend it back and forth enabling me to get enough leverage on it to pry it loose from the main support structure. After only five minutes or so the corner I had been working on gave way and the whole thing lifted right off on my first attempt to pry it up. I was ecstatic and so was Shadow knowing what we were planning to do. The good news at this point was I would only have to break or bend one of the fan blades in order for me to fit through. There were two main support beams that held the fan in place and hopefully would hold my weight just long enough for me to squeeze through and drop to the floor which was now in full sight and definitely a welcomed sight. I knew now that Shadow and I were going to get through this one way or another if it meant that the two of us got arrested for trespassing, I would gladly except that consequence in return for our safe return home.

I turned to Shadow and said, "Okay Shadow were going to have to go through the same routine of me lowering you down first then I will follow, my friend." He looked back at me and just wagged his tail with excitement. I sat as close as possible to the edge of the opening then with a couple of swift kicks I managed to break off one the blades from the fan motor and it made a horrific noise and echoed for quite some time. I removed my shirt and pants and quickly made the harness that worked so well before, Shadow just watched knowing what was about to happen and quite content with the whole plan. I carefully secured the harness to Shadow and began to slowly lower him through the opening I had just created. Shadow was enjoying his ride much better this time, his tail was wagging and his eyes were full of excitement. The floor below was about twelve feet so I would have to let him drop a couple of feet above it. I was sure he would be okay from that distance. Once Shadow was on the floor I dropped my backpack down next to him. Now came the fun part for me. I could tell the blades were fairly sharp and I would have to hold on to them for a brief second or two in order for me drop safely. I took the axe handle and laid it across the nearest support beam and ninety degrees across from the nearest blade that I broke off and would use it to secure my hold until I dropped to the floor. Without wasting any time because I didn't want that damn thing to turn on, I quickly executed my descent and dropped successfully to the floor next to Shadow. He was very excited and started to jump up and down on me. I turned to him and said, "Okay boy, I'm excited too." I grabbed my pack and tossed it up at the axe handle to knock it loose from the support beam, I didn't want to leave any of our supplies behind, including the axe handle, not telling how long it would take us to find someone down here or for someone to find us. With the second try the pack and the axe handle fell at our feet.

The next few minutes I spent putting my pants and shirt back on, then we tried to assess the situation to pick a direction to go in. What we were now in looked like something the government would construct and it had a definite military look about it. I started to think maybe I was wrong about the whole alien secret base thing, then a shock of reality set in when I saw the warning sign that was posted a few feet from our position that read "Warning High Pressure Steam Vent / Authorized Personal Only" and it made me nervous because Shadow and I could be in serious danger if we got caught in here when it went active again. I looked at Shadow and said, "Alright Shadow, lets double time it and find somebody," we began to run down the manmade tunnel at a steady pace making as much noise as we possibly could. I was dragging the one end of the axe handle along one side of the tunnel wall hoping it would create some kind of echoing noise that could be heard from a great distance hoping someone would hear it. After a few minutes the air seemed to be getting a little thin or I was just out of shape but I then realized Shadow was panting rapidly and looked lethargic, suddenly I felt dizzy and started to lose consciousness I looked down towards Shadow and he was lying on the floor completely passed out, I dropped to my knees then laid next to him before total darkness hit me.

I slowly opened my eyes to see a couple of fuzzy figures standing by my beside. I could tell I was in some kind of medical treatment room. I had an I.V. in my left arm and some heartbeat monitor sensors on my chest. My eyes were slowly coming in to focus and I could see the figures were two doctors or nurses and were talking about my condition. I was pretty groggy but I still had enough strength to yell out, "Where the hell am I and where's my wolf?" One of the men came over to me and said, "Take it easy Mr. Youngblood, you're just coming out of a week-long coma." I looked up at the individual who I presumed was a doctor and said, "You didn't answer my questions, now who are you and where is Shadow and where the hell am I?" I was awake enough to know that they went through my wallet and knew my name and I wanted the same. The man standing next to me said, "My name is Dr. Walters and you are under the care of our medical staff here just outside of Sedona," just at that point the other individual came over to the bed, "Mr. Youngblood my name is John Andrews and you can relax your dog or wolf is fine, we have been caring for him during your time of incapacitation and sense making first contact with the two of you," he said. I looked at the man and replied, "Thank you for that, I know I was probably trespassing on government property or something but Shadow and I had no choice but to enter through the vent in order to be found, we had been lost for a couple of days." The man named John then said, "Shadow, is that the name of your dog or should I say wolf?" Pausing for a second, I then said, "Yes, it is." John then said, "Well that is an interesting name." I then began to drift off a little when Dr. Walters said, "You should get a few more hours of rest Mr. Youngblood then we will answer all of your questions." The other man John then said, "We will bring Shadow to you at that time and don't worry, he is fine and eating like a horse, I'm sure he will be glad to see you." I slowly drifted off to sleep again, not knowing if I was being drugged or just tired from the length of the coma but I was glad to hear that Shadow was fine.

6

CHOICES

As I slowly began to wake up for the second time I could feel my senses and energy level almost at full strength. This time there was several more people in the room and one of them was a female, a very attractive female and she was holding a leash with Shadow sitting at the other end of it. I raised my voice a little and said, "Shadow, come here boy." All at once he broke free of the grip the lady had on the leash and jumped up on my bed, he began licking my face and whined a little. I could tell he was just as happy to see me as I was to see him. The room was silent for a few seconds, as the woman came closer to my bed she then spoke, "Well Mr. Youngblood, how are you feeling?" I looked up at her and replied, "I feel much better now than I did a few hours ago and seeing Shadow has made me feel even better, I want to thank you for taking care of him while I was out of it." The woman moved a little closer to my bedside and said, "You're quite welcome, he is a magnificent looking animal, so his name is Shadow, that's a great name, I'd like to hear the story behind that choice for a name sometime." I quickly responded by saying, "Yeah, I guess I have some explaining to do myself, I'm really sorry that Shadow and I had to trespass on your facility here but it was coming down to a matter of life and death for the two of us."

The very professional looking woman answered back with, "Don't worry about that now Mr. Youngblood, I can see already that this was a bit of a fault on both our behalves, I would like to debrief you on this whole situation and what our options are to get you back to your home and family." Almost interrupting her before she could finish I said, "Please tell me if you have notified my sister in Sedona and my employer, I mean I know that you know who I am and where I probably work so I just need to let everyone know I'm okay if you haven't already done so." The lady looked down at me with compassion and regret and said, "I'm sorry Mr. Youngblood my supervisor would not let me contact anyone from your family or employer until I reported back with the final assessment of your trespassing event." She then turned and walked away but before leaving the room she said, "I will try to close out this whole matter in the next few hours and hopefully we will have some good news to report to you, oh and I am sorry for not introducing myself earlier, my name is Sarah Cooper, I will leave Shadow in here with you from now on, please let us know if there is anything we can do to make the two of you more comfortable." I remained silent as she left the room, I was a little stunned and confused why the hell they had not contacted Miralani about the status of my condition. All I could do now was give as much attention to Shadow as possible, he was so happy he just kept trying lick my face and burry his head into my neck area. I guess that must be a sign of affection or bonding from the bread. The other gentlemen had followed Sarah Cooper out of the room and I could tell she was definitely the one in charge around this place.

After eating a very big and very tasty meal that was provided by another gentlemen Shadow and I kept each other company for the next few hours by moving around the room and getting up and down off the bed to in order to start exercising my muscles in my legs, they were very stiff and weak, I guess after being in a coma for a week the muscle atrophy sets in pretty fast. Shadow on the other hand looked as if he had grown taller by a couple of inches and put on about ten pounds, he had definitely been eating good unlike the I.V. bag I had been on for a week. I decided to see if I could poke my head out of the room just to get a glimpse of where

I might be, as I grabbed the door handle very slow and careful I tried to turn it slowly but it wouldn't turn at all, I guess I was locked in and for security measures they didn't want to take the chance of me seeing something I shouldn't. I was quite familiar with top secret security clearances and the precautions that certain agencies took to protect their secrecy of personal and the operations of their agency. The working relationships I had made over the last five years with the F.B.I. had provided the opportunity for me to receive a top level security clearance with our government. I was one hundred percent positive that these people here had already discovered that yet were still keeping me in the dark because my clearance was not high enough to know about this agency.

I kept thinking about what Sarah Cooper had said about not notifying anyone from my life to at least let them know I was alright. My mind again starting running crazy with all kinds of theories of how they may not let us go at all and just possibly get rid of us, I mean I know our government has ways to make people disappear if they thought it was necessary for national security reasons. I really needed to talk to the lady named Sarah again and make her understand that Shadow and I were not a threat to any part of their agency or operation they might have here. This whole situation was just act of survival on our part, nothing more. I had to convince her that we saw nothing before passing out, which was the truth. She seemed like a very reasonable and approachable person but then again if she was a highly trained agent of some kind she was probably able to put on any type of persona depending on the situation at hand. I was getting very nervous awaiting her return. I looked around the room for my clothes but there was no sight of the torn up, dirty grungy attire I had worn during this whole adventure. They probably burned them because of the stench and possible contamination that Shadow and I might had picked up along the way to get to this point of our travels. The doctor did say we both had a clean bill of health and that I just needed to rest a bit more to regain my strength.

Another hour passed by according to the clock on the wall and still no sign of Sarah Cooper. I was beginning to think something was wrong and that they didn't believe my story about how Shadow and I got here. They just had to know my past history with the F.B.I and why the hell haven't they vouched for me by now. They had my wallet with all of my identification and credit cards and pictures of Miralani, my park ranger I.D. for which they easily could obtain my service record from them if requested. Again I couldn't stop thinking about how my sister was coping with me being missing for over a week. These people here should have at least notified her I was still alive or something of that nature. The more I thought about it the angrier I became. The only thing that was keeping me from becoming too violent was Shadow's calmness and his company, at least I knew we had a future together now and nothing was going to change that, except the fact that I might go to jail. Shadow did look as if somebody might have given him a bath because he smelt better than me. I assume they could only give me sponge baths while I was in the coma. I decided I wanted to at least get cleaned up if it was possible, there was a bathroom adjacent to my room so I went to see if it had a shower or tub so I could get cleaned up. I was in luck, it had a shower and there were clean towels hanging on the wall, I presumed for me. I removed my gown and turned on the water, it was so nice to actually see and hear a shower, I know that seems a little weird but if you hadn't had one in over a week you'd know what I was talking about. Shadow had followed me into the bathroom and laid down on the floor next to the doorway as if he was standing guard. The water got hot very quickly and I wasted no time at all getting in.

It seemed like fifteen minutes had passed and I still couldn't put down the bar of soap, it was so refreshing to just wash and rinse over and over again. This was probably going to be the cleanest I had ever been in my life. It was just then I heard a knock on the bathroom wall and a female's voice say, "It's just me Mr. Youngblood, Sarah Cooper, I see you discovered the shower and please don't take this the wrong way but all of us here will appreciate the fact that you can now clean yourself." I replied, "Well I probably smelled worse than Shadow so I decided to do something about it and I'm glad you and your people are happy about it." The lady named Sarah quickly answered back, "One more thing before I leave and give you some privacy, I went ahead and got you some new clothes and shoes, there laying on your bed, I hope they fit, we did use the sizes off your discarded ones and oh yeah please call me Sarah if you'd like." I paused for a second thinking she really is a nice person, then said, "Okay, thanks a lot that's very kind of you and please call me Cole." She eagerly replied, "Okay Cole I will, I'll be back in a little bit and I'll answer all of your questions but I'm going to have to ask a few of my own." Somehow that last part of her statement sounded as if I was in some kind of trouble. Once again I paused a few seconds then replied, "Okay that sounds great Sarah," she then left the room and I finished up with my shower.

Shadow and I walked out of the bathroom to see one pair of knew jeans, a t-shirt, new socks, a button up long sleeve tan shirt, a belt, a pair of what looked like snake skin boots and the icing on the cake was a brand new black "Stetson" hat lying on the bed. I couldn't believe what I was looking at and how the hell did they know I liked black cowboy hats. This was starting to get really creepy and I began to wonder how much more did they know about my private life. I still wasn't sure who these people were but one thing was for certain, they were very thorough and probably had unlimited resources. I quickly got dressed and to my surprise everything fit like a glove, even the boots and hat. Shadow looked at me like I was a different person or something, I looked down at him and said, "It's okay boy, I'm still the same guy, don't be afraid." The clean smell of the soap probably had more to do with it than my attire. Although this was probably the first time he had ever seen a cowboy hat and he was definitely checking it out. As I was putting on my new belt there was a knock at the door, "Hey Cole, are you decent, can I come in?" The voice on the other side asked. I then replied, "Yes, come in please." Sarah walked in and slightly tripped on the carpet and then said, "Wow, you look like a totally different person cleaned up." I smiled a little and replied, "Was I that bad before?" Sarah laughed and then remarked, "I mean you look really nice and it looks like everything fit alright." I smiled again and said, "Yeah, thanks so much, I will repay you for whatever the cost was for all of this and my compliments to whoever picked it all out, they have great taste." Sarah looked at me for a few seconds and then said, "Yeah I do have great taste and don't worry about the tab, it's on the government." Once again she seemed so nice, "Okay, thanks again," is all I could think of saying at the time.

The room grew silent for a moment as we both just looked around avoiding any eye contact what so ever as if all of a sudden we were both embarrassed about something. Sarah was a very gorgeous woman and it was starting to cloud my judgement of what might be really going on here. I quickly snapped out of the trance that seemed to be taking over my thoughts and emotions just long enough to ask her when we might get to those questions. Sarah turned her full attention to me and said, "Okay Cole but first we need to get you something to eat and its passed my lunch time so let's go, oh yeah this will be my treat." I looked into her stunning blue eyes and said, "Yeah I am a little hungry, where will we be going to eat?" Hoping her answer would be somewhere in Sedona but I knew better, I wasn't going anywhere until I had my debriefing session with Sarah and even I wasn't sure what the outcome was going to be from that. "Just follow me and you'll see," she said.

The three of us headed out the door and made a right turn down a very long and quiet hallway, Sarah asked me to not talk to anyone else other than her for now due to security protocol. Without hesitation I agreed trying to make some brownie points with her. We continued to walk down the hallway side by side not seeing another individual, at least so far. I turned to Sarah and asked, "What kind of food will we be having for lunch?" Sarah replied, "Oh I don't know that depends on what's left over from yesterday." With a big smile she then said, "Just kidding, we have a great cafeteria here and they can serve just about anything you can think of." As we came to the end of the hallway with Shadow by my side I noticed that it split in two directions, we kept to the right and proceeded down another long hallway for a few more minutes before coming to some double doors on the right side which were labeled with some kind of a food and drink symbol on both doors. "Well here we are Cole, the finest eating establishment within fifteen miles and the only one within fifteen miles," Sarah said. "I assume that it's okay for Shadow to come in while we eat, you know if this place is no good I could take you to my sister's café, now that's some really good food and I know she wouldn't have a problem with Shadow," I slowly suggested. Sarah responded by saying, "Alright Cole, I might just hold you to that and you can pick up the tab on that one, just not today though." I wasn't quite sure what was happening here between Sarah and myself but there was definitely some kind of attraction between the two us and it had been affecting my thoughts and emotions since the moment we first met.

The two of us entered the cafeteria and headed towards the beginning of the food line, it looked more like something one would see at a Las Vegas style buffet. Once again Sarah reminded me to try to avoid talking with anyone at least for now, she said. As we made our way through the line I noticed all of the different types of employees around us, I mean the place looked like some type of manufacturing facility or some kind of giant medical research program that was being kept a secret by the government. For the most part they all looked like technicians of some kind and they were very clean looking hence the medical aspect of my theory. Sarah then noticed me looking around and asked, "See anything interesting Cole?" I quickly turned my attention back to the buffet offerings and said, "It all looks good to me." She smiled again and said, "That's not what I meant Cole, it's okay to look around I know it must be driving you crazy not knowing where you are." I stopped dead in my tracks and said, "Yes, it is Sarah, I just want to eat then we can go and start your interrogation of me and then maybe I can let my sister know that I'm alright." With her hypnotic eyes she looked at me and said, "Cole I'm really sorry about this whole keeping you in the dark thing but there won't be any interrogation because I have already checked you out and ran your security clearance through our agency and you passed with flying colors, now let's sit down and eat and I will tell you almost everything you want to know." Once again I was at a loss for words so I just said, "Okay thanks, I guess." She gave me another smile and we continued down the line.

The three of us proceeded to a nearby table where Sarah and I sat down with our food while Shadow laid down by my feet. I was very impressed at his demeanor being around all of these people, he was so mellow and calm as if he belonged here. "Amazing, isn't it?" Sarah said. I looked up at her and said, "What's amazing?" Sarah then looked down at Shadow and said, "You know the way he seems to always know what's expected of him." This lady was not only smart and gorgeous but her senses and intuition demonstrated her astuteness of her surroundings and the ability to read people or in Shadow's case, wolves. Once again I just seemed to be getting more and more drawn to her, there's just something about her outbursts of energy and yet the calmness of her voice that is so intriguing. I looked up from the plate of food I had sitting in front me and said, "Your absolutely right about Shadow and I can't explain it Sarah, ever since I rescued him from that ledge in the mine shaft that started this whole adventure he has been nothing short of amazing and understood everything that I have communicated to him, he is truly exceptional and now my best friend." Sarah just smiled and began to finish her meal.

Once we both finished our lunch Sarah scooted her chair around closer to where I was and leaned towards me and said, "Cole you're a very impressive man and your work the Parks and Recreation department has been amazing, also I know about your part time working relationship with the F.B.I. and all of the missing people you helped locate either alive or in some of the worst cases their bodies to at least bring some comfort and closure to the families of those victims." I sat there quietly for a few seconds then replied, "Wow Sarah you seem to know my whole life story, should I be worried or happy that this mess is near closure."

She quickly answered back, "Cole, I will be taking you and Shadow back to your sister's cafe in an hour or so but I need to, no I really want to ask you a very important life changing question for you to consider over the next few days and yes I've already contacted Miralani to let her know you're alive but that you just came out of a coma a short time ago and that I would be bringing you back into Sedona to meet at her café." At this point my eyes were already tearing up and I was so thankful for the words that Sarah just spoke, I slowly and thoughtfully said to Sarah, "Sarah, thank you so much for finally letting my sister know about my wellbeing and excepting the fact that Shadow and I were here by purely an accident and as far as what you want to ask me go right ahead." I then took a deep breath and a sigh of relief knowing that I would soon be home.

Sarah smiled and held her hand out to reach for mine then grasping the top of my left hand said, "Cole I'm really sorry I had to wait this long to notify your sister but protocol dictates my actions as a supervisor and an agent of this facility, which is what I want to tell you and ask you about the decision I want you to think over." Sarah then paused for a bit and for the first time since we met I sensed a lot of apprehension and nervousness about her, finally she looked deep into my eyes and asked, "Cole what would you say if you had an opportunity to save so many more lives by using your great tracking skills and all of the experience you have learned from the F.B.I could be put to even a better use by working with myself and joining our agency full time and as far as being an accident that you and Shadow are here now I tend to think it's more like destiny." I pondered for a brief moment then looked at Sarah and asked, "Are you really asking me to come work with you at some secret underground base outside of Sedona that nobody even knows exists and I'm just supposed to give up everything that I love doing in my life, is that what you're asking me Sarah, because if it is I am going to need a whole lot more than what you just told me to consider a career change at this point I my life." Sarah just smiled again and said, "Cole what I am offering you is a chance to make a difference in this world that you can't even imagine, all I can say up to this point is you would be doing what you love to do and would be coming on as my trainee at first then my partner, I'm a very good judge of character and I am one hundred percent sure you have what it takes Cole and most of all you have the heart and goodwill that makes you special and perfect for this job, please just think about it Cole." Once again staring into my eyes with almost a hypnotic trance.

I sat there again at a loss for words after Sarah made her pitch one more time. I was flattered and scared to death at the same time. This time I leaned in closer towards her and grasped her right hand and said, "Sarah I don't know what to say, I am very flattered by the things you just said to me but I don't think I can even consider it until I have returned home and had some time to get my mind clear and then maybe we could get together again in order for me to ask some very important questions about this offer, I will admit it has my curiosity going at full speed right now but you're absolutely correct in that I need time to think about it." Sarah then put her left hand on top of my left hand that was still holding and clinching on to her, then with great compassion she said, "Thank you Cole, that's all I can ask of you and I would definitely like to get together with you maybe in a few days to answer whatever questions I'm allowed to, oh yeah and this offer applies to Shadow as well, I think there could be some great advantages to having his skills to assist and aid in our cases." I then quickly and emotionally replied, "The offer just keeps getting more intriguing Sarah and I will think long and hard on it but for now can we get the hell out of here and head for my sister's café?" Sarah smiled then answered with, "Okay Cole, let's get your all of your stuff and a few little parting gifts that I have for you and Shadow then we'll be on our way." Finally, Shadow and I were about to head home.

The three of us left the cafeteria and headed back to my room and while we were walking down the hallway Sarah made a call to someone and all I heard her say was, "Cooper 1 requesting departure in fifteen." This whole thing just kept getting more and more like some kind of spy movie with me being the oddball character thrown into the mix. As we entered the room I could see a new looking backpack and my old one next to it, also there was a canvas bag with Shadow's name stitched on it. I looked at Sarah and said, "The parting gifts I presume, I wonder what's in Shadow's." Sarah laughed then replied, "I wanted to replace that old beat up backpack for you since it smelled like a dead animal, I assume you two ate the snake from the skin that was in it, also Cole you will find a computer tablet in the new pack that is preloaded with some of my personal information and phone number in order for you to get in touch with me if you decide you want to talk more about this offer. The tablet is yours to keep no matter what you decide, you may find it handy in helping you with some of your daily tasks and activities, I've preloaded it with all of our geographical 3-D satellite imaging maps consisting of the western states that you are so familiar with, I hope it will be of some use to you." For a brief moment I found myself thinking about staying here with Sarah and not wanting to leave just yet but then I came to my senses when Shadow started to push on my legs like he was ready to get the hell out of here.

I turned to Sarah and asked, "What's in Shadow's bag?" Sarah replied, "Oh just some dog stuff like toys, some rawhide chews and a harness for walking him that I'm sure he will outgrow it in a month or so." I walked over to the bag with Shadow's name on it and called him over, "Come here Shadow, look what Sarah got you, all kinds of cool stuff." As I opened it up he stuck his long snout in the bag and pulled out a stuffed animal that resembled a sheep or some kind of goat, perfect I thought for a wolf. I turned to Sarah and said, "Sarah I can't thank you enough for everything you have done for Shadow and I we really were so lucky to be found by someone like yourself, you probably saved both of our lives and we will always be so grateful for that, hopefully we will be able to repay you for all of the kindness you've shown the two of us." With what looked like a tear falling from her eye she said, "Okay Cole, enough with the goodbyes already I'm getting all choked up and you do realize that Shadow is the one I will miss the most around here anyway, he is the one I spent the most time with, I'm just kidding, I will miss the two of you, I just hope this is not a forever goodbye." I picked up the new backpack and asked Sarah if I could just leave the old one here to be thrown out, she said. "No problem Cole, we'll take care of it, are you ready to hit the road?" I nodded my head and said, "How about it Shadow, you ready to head to your new home, I know I am." The three of us then left the room.

After several more turns down some different hallways we finally came to a large roll up door and an adjacent normal sized door. Sarah then said, "Cole we are about to enter are motor pool area, try not to look around too much once we get inside, this is a highly top secret area and you don't quite have the clearance for everything that might be in here at any given time but I'm taking that responsibility for not blindfolding you, I think I can trust you at this point of our brief relationship." I just nodded my head again and said, "Okay Sarah, no problem." Shadow looked up at the two of us and made a faint whine and wagged his tail, as if to say me too. We entered through the smaller door and wow, I couldn't believe how big this area was.

The three of us slowly walked towards the right side of the immense garage that was filled with all types of normal looking cars and I thought to myself what the hell is so top secret about this, it's just probably all of the employee's cars that worked here, then Sarah said, "Cole when we enter this next garage please do not ask any of the technicians any questions about the cars, okay." I replied back, "No worries Sarah, Shadow and I will keep a tight lip." I actually couldn't wait to get through the next set of doors and see what exactly might be in there, once again the whole spy movie scenario was creeping back into my mind. Sarah walked up to a cipher lock and entered a code to activate the smaller door for us to gain entry. Once the three of us passed through the doorway I nearly had a heart attack, it looked like a vintage car collection and probably worth a fortune, I mean there was any and everything you could imagine here, it was unbelievable that something like this could exist out here in the middle of nowhere.

As we walked towards one corner of the garage which was about the size of a two football fields I noticed something that did catch my attention in a nervous way, there to my left at the other end of the enclosure were at least a dozen newer looking black Cadillac Escalades and it was at this moment I knew my life was going to change forever. Sarah then asked, "Everything okay Cole, you looked like you just saw a ghost?" I turned my full attention back to Sarah and said, "Sorry I just got lost in the moment, I'm a huge car fan and your collection is astonishing." She quickly replied, "We'll their not exactly mine but we can use them when needed for undercover purposes." I couldn't tell if Sarah knew about the stolen Escalade case of mine or not but now was not the time to bring it up. I was almost certain that the Escalade that I was involved with belonged to this agency or organization or whatever the hell this place was.

Sarah, Shadow and I headed towards a group of vehicles that looked like P.O.V.'s or at least civilian looking. Sarah pulled a set of keys out of her pants pocket and deactivated an alarm on a vehicle just ahead of us. To my surprise it was a fully restored black and white two tone Toyota Fj40 4X4 from the late sixties or early seventies. I thought to myself now I'm really starting to like this young lady. As we approached the vehicle I asked, "Sarah please tell me everyone that works here with you gets one of these." She just chuckled a bit then said, "No Cole this is all mine, it took me five years to restore it and I just got it back on the road a few weeks ago." As she opened up the back doors to let Shadow jump in I said, "This is so nice, whoever did the restoration did a fantastic job on it, I like the fact it was restored to its original condition from the factory except for the newer style rims and more aggressive tires." With a little anger in her voice Sarah said, "I did the restoration so what do think of that, I mean you don't think a woman is capable of doing such a task, well I'll have you know that I did everything on this Fj except for the paint job, I even rebuilt the motor myself." I then quickly interrupted, "I'm sorry Sarah, I didn't mean it like that and I certainly did not mean to offend you in any way, I just figured you didn't have the free time it takes to do such a project, believe me I know from firsthand experience when I did my Bronco." The two of us just looked at each other for a moment then she said, "No offense taken Cole, besides I'm just yanking your chain a little, hopefully you didn't take me too seriously but I am very proud of the job I did on my Fj." Once again she played my emotions like a pro, I then answered, "Sarah you should be proud of the job you did, I know for a fact it might be the most original and nicest looking one of these I've ever seen and I have seen a bunch of them," again she just smiled then we both jumped into the Fj.

Once the engine was warmed up and Sarah asked if we were ready to go I hesitated for a second thinking if I should ask the question that had been on my mind the last fifteen minutes or so, she then asked again, "Well, something wrong Cole, are you ready to go or not?" I quickly blurted out, "Don't you have to blindfold me or something like that?" Instantly Sarah began to laugh and replied, "No Cole I trust you, this is another one of those calls that I'm making on my strong belief that you will be a part of this someday even if it's just on a part time basis." Just at that point of the conversation when I was ready to thank Sarah for trusting me Shadow muscled his way from the back to almost getting up in the front seat with me. I immediately changed my focus to Shadow and said, "Hey Shadow, you have to stay back there my friend and please don't shed too much on Sarah's interior, I don't think she would like that." Sarah looked at Shadow and spoke, "That's okay boy, it's been dirty before and this won't be the last time I'm sure of that." Before we headed out I said to Sarah, "Hey Sarah I'm not sure how Shadow is going to handle being in a moving vehicle, I haven't had him long enough to train him for that, I just hope he doesn't get car sick." After a look of much concern she replied, "Me too." She put the Fj in gear and we were on our way.

Once Shadow had settled down in the back seat area we began to head out of the huge garage area slowly going through the secured area roll up doors and then back out into the main parking area of the underground structure. This place was quite impressive I couldn't even imagine how big the whole facility was. As we headed for what looked like the main entrance or exit we came to a small guard shack with a little old man in it. I tried to stop myself from asking but couldn't, I turned to Sarah and said, "Wow all this high level security and a facility the size of Rhode Island and all you got is this little old man standing guard, he must be a bad man." Sarah laughed a little then said, "Cole don't always trust what you see to make judgement on something or someone, looks can be deceiving and sometimes even be intentional." As we stopped at the guard shack the window slid open a bit and the old man stuck his head out and said, "Hi Coop, hey the old Fj sounds great, I told you the air to fuel ratio just needed a little adjustment." Sarah leaned a bit out her window and said, "I don't know what I would do without you Charlie, you're the best, hey don't forget I'm taking you out to lunch next month on your birthday." The old man smiled and said, "Are you kidding me, I've been looking forward to this since last year, I even went out and bought some new jeans and boots since last year, just so you wouldn't be too embarrassed to be seen with me." Sarah sat up straight and leaned even further out her window and with a stern voice she said, "Charles Anderson you're the handsomest man around this place and a perfect gentleman, and don't you forget it, hell Charlie you're the reason I come to work every day with a smile on my face." The old man just looked at Sarah for a moment then said, "Damn Coop, I wish I was thirty years younger." We slowly pulled away from the shack and proceeded towards another big roll up door.

After passing through what appeared to be the last hurdle in obtaining my freedom from this place I could actually see sunlight up ahead. I turned to Sarah and said, "He seemed like a very nice man, how long have you known each other?" Glowingly Sarah said, "Most of my life, I mean even going back to when I was just a kid I remember Charlie being around our family." I could tell Sarah had deep feelings for the old man and that he was a very special friend. As we came to the end of the tunnel the sunlight was beaming through the opening and it never looked so good. "Where does this come out Sarah?" I asked. She turned and said, "I could just give you the GPS coordinates Cole, that would be a whole lot easier for you when you try to find your way back but if you must know our facility is located eighteen point seven miles northwest of Sedona just off "Dry Creek Road" and down a small but passable dirt road that takes you to this point right here if you know where to look." Excited that she told me I quickly replied, "Just off "Dry Creek Road" you say, I'm pretty familiar with that area and don't remember seeing or hearing about any entrance to a huge government facility." Smiling then laughing she spoke, "Well, I guess you're just not as familiar as you thought you were, I will say it's a little hard to spot unless you know exactly where to look." I could tell she was playing some kind of game at this point but I knew that she trusted me completely because otherwise I would have blindfolded or something else to make sure I would not be able to find my way back. As we came out of the tunnel I quickly turned and looked behind us to get some sort of visual imprint on my mind to where the opening was and to my surprise there was no opening at all, nothing, just a steep wall of a canyon we were now in. Sarah again started to laugh then turned and winked at me.

With a bit of anger in my voice I said, "Okay what the hell is this place and where in god's name are we, really I need to know because it's driving me nuts Sarah." She turned towards me and said, "Cole there are some things I just can't tell you technology wise at this point but I will tell you we are in "Secret Canyon" just northwest of Sedona." I thought to myself for a second really "Secret Canyon" but the more I looked around it was starting to look familiar, the hills, the position of the sun reflecting off the gorgeous mountains, we had to be in "Secret Canyon." I somewhat confused replied back. "Secret Canyon, what kind of idiot hides a top secret government base in a place called "Secret Canyon", I mean isn't that a little stupid?" Sarah quickly answered by saying, "That idiot would be my father." After back peddling a little I quickly said, "You know what I mean, I'm sorry about the idiot remark but you have to admit that it's probably not the best idea in the world." Sarah then replied, "Cole that's exactly why it's the perfect place to hide a secret facility, it's because of the name that most everyone would be thinking exactly like you." I had nothing to comeback with because it did make sense, I looked at Sarah and said, "I guess I'll have to learn how to think like a spy if I decide to work with you Sarah, hell you might not want to even work with me because of my ignorance of the whole secret agent stuff, after all I'm just a park ranger." Sarah then pulled the Fj off the road a bit and came to a stop, then looked at me with those piercing eyes of hers and said, "Cole it's because of who you are that I'm offering you the job and besides there would be some indoctrination of our policies and procedures, not to mention some pretty intense physical training, by the looks of things you won't have any problems with that." I smiled then replied, "I guess I should say I'm flattered but I'm still more confused than ever about what I could possibly do that you can't already." Sarah just smiled, then put the Fj in gear and we started heading towards Sedona again.

It was just a short ride to reach "Dry Creek Road" where things really started to look familiar. Shadow had fallen asleep in the back of the Fj which was a relief because I so worried he would get car sick on the bumpy road but once again it seemed like he knew what was expected of him and was quite familiar with being in a vehicle which had to be impossible." Sarah was mastering the Fj over the bumpy road and the combination of her driving skills and the mechanical performance of this vehicle was quite impressive. It made me think about how my Bronco was doing and if the girls had even gotten it home for me or if it was still sitting in the middle of nowhere. I said to Sarah, "Hey you know this is a very impressive 4WD vehicle Sarah, you did a hell of job on the restoration." Sarah then spoke, "Why thanks Cole, that means a lot coming from you, I've seen your Bronco and it's beautiful, this Fj doesn't quite have the power of your Ford but it will get the job done." Quickly I asked, "You've seen it, where is it? Is it okay? Is it at Miralani's now?" Sarah interrupted me and replied, "Cole hold up a second, your Bronco is fine, I believe your sister returned it to your home shortly after your disappearance, as for as where it is now I can't answer that but we'll know soon enough." I let out a big sigh of relief, then asked Sarah, "When did you see my Bronco Sarah and where was it?" She then replied, "Remember Cole I had to do a pretty thorough background check on you once we figured out who you were, that investigation revealed just about everything pertaining to your life and personal belongings." I slowly responded with a little uneasiness in my voice "Wow I'm starting feel like I have just been audited by the I.R.S. and I really don't like those people, I believe that most of them are all crooks deep down inside." Sarah starting laughing really loud this time and said, "Cole, that makes two us I hate those people too, I'm really starting to like you, we pretty much think alike you know." This time I began to laugh and it had been some time.

We were just coming up to the outskirts of Sedona when Shadow began to wake up. Sarah quickly looked back at him, "Finally it's about time you woke up, sleepy head," she said. It would only be a few more minutes until we reached the pavement and back on a main road. I was getting nervous and excited about seeing Miralani again, I wondered how mad she might be with me thinking that I was somehow behind her not finding out I was okay until just recently. I know that Sarah told her I was in a coma for over a week but somehow she probably thought she should have been told a lot earlier and I tend to agree on that but we can't go back and change the past, all I know is that it will be good to give my sister one of the longest hugs ever. I would call her now but my cell phone was damaged from all of the water Shadow and experienced during our journey, I guess I could ask Sarah if I could use her phone but I was a little apprehensive about talking with her, I believe at this point seeing her in person was the best path for our reunion. As we got closer I asked Sarah if she knew where Miralani's was located, she said, "Yeah, I have eaten their many times, it's got to be the best café in town." I couldn't believe it, I then impatiently replied, "Wow, how the heck did I never see you in there, I definitely would remember your face, I mean you're a very attractive lady and one would definitely notice you in a public establishment." With her eyes focused on the road she just smiled.

As the three of us got closer and closer to the café I started to feel like I was almost going to get sick or something and Sarah must have known how nervous and anxious I was getting and said, "It's okay Cole, your sister is going to be so excited to see you and besides I'm here to take the heat if she is upset with how long it took to notify her about you, I've got your back big guy." I know this sounds crazy but I was really starting believe that Sarah could be trusted as a good friend even with the fact that I had only known her for less than a day, I looked at her and said, "Thanks Sarah, I really appreciate that especially since this whole situation is my fault and you did not ask for any of this to happen," she then said, "We'll talk about that later Cole, you just enjoy this reunion with your sister because nothing is more important than family." This lady was truly getting to me and I kept thinking how did I not run into her before. As we got within a few blocks from the café I reattached the leash to Shadow's harness, I wasn't sure how he would react to the crowd at the café not to mention the busy traffic in Sedona this time of year. I told Sarah she could park right up front in the spot that was usually open for me and she said, "Okay great, I always try to keep this old girl away from tight parking spots to avoid those nasty door dings, after all this is a very valuable classic vehicle and I'd like to keep it that way." Wow, another feather in her cap, not too many women give a damn about their vehicles when it comes to parking, they just want to get as close as possible to the front entrance of where there at. I then told Sarah, "You know you're absolutely right, I feel the same way about my Bronco, most people these days just don't give a shit about being careful not to damage someone else's vehicle by the simple act of opening a door." She just looked at me and nodded.

Miralani's was now in sight as we slowed down to turn into the driveway of the establishment. I could see my sisters BMW parked out front in its normal spot, this was really happening, it wasn't some dream I was having while still in the cavern with Shadow. I was home, well at least my home away from home. Sarah pulled into my spot after I showed her the location and she said, "I hope

I don't get a ticket, this looks illegal to me," I then remarked, "No worries Sarah, I know the Sheriff, he's a good friend of mine, hell he's probably inside right now." Before I could even get all the way out of my seat Miralani came bursting out the front door screaming and crying running up into my arms and clinching on to me like a bear climbing up a tree. I too was shedding a few tears which gently flowed down my face and dropped on to Miralani's neck. She finally after what seemed like ten minutes let go and stood back a couple of feet and said, "Jesus Cole, I don't know if I should hug you some more or slap the piss out you, what the hell happened to you, we came back and couldn't find any tracks or signs of where you had been, it was like you just disappeared." I slowly and gently reached out and put my arms around my sister and told her, "Sis listen I will explain everything to you but first there's someone I'd like you to meet, this is Sarah Cooper and the four-legged animal she is holding onto is Shadow, the reason for all of this, Sarah is the one who pretty much saved Shadow and I from being lost forever and what was almost certain to be our deaths." Miralani looked at Sarah for a few seconds then spoke, "Wait a minute I know you, I have seen you before in the café, you come here for breakfast with a couple of your friends from time to time, anyway I'm sorry for rambling on, I just want to say thank you so much for everything you've done for Cole, he's the only family I have left and I'm so happy you found him." Sarah then replied, "Why don't we all go inside and we can get to know one another and I can help answer some of the questions you must have for Cole and myself."

After another long hug Miralani finally stopped crying and replied, "Hey that sounds like a great idea, Cole I can see that Shadow is really made some kind of bond with you he keeps trying to pull away from Miss Cooper and get close to you, are you going to keep him?" I quickly answered back with, "Yeah sis, he's very special and we have been through a lot together, I'll tell you our story once we get inside, it's okay for him to come inside isn't it?" Without hesitation she said, "Hey he's family now, I can see that, he is so stunning, he's a wolf of some type right?" I eagerly replied back, "Yeah, he mostly definitely is and you're not even going to believe how smart he is." Like a child showing off a new toy I grabbed the leash from Sarah and we all walked into the café. Once through the doorway I was shocked to see all of Miralani's and my friends standing in front of us holding a big banner that read "Welcome Home Cole" I couldn't believe that all of these people were here just to welcome me back. I was sort of embarrassed and didn't even know what to say other than thank you all for this, I am so glad to be here and not stuck underground out in the middle of nowhere. Sarah turned to me and said, "Cole you have a lot of people that care about you, you're a very lucky man." Miralani then spoke, "Yes he does Miss Cooper and we all missed him dearly, everyone that is here wanted to show their appreciation for how much he has done for this community and the people who live here by having this welcome back celebration." I almost teared up when suddenly Shadow started to rub up against my leg as if he wanted something, I guess he wanted me to introduce him to everyone, I then said, "Hey everyone can I have your attention for a moment, I would like to introduce you to my newest and best friend "Shadow" he and I have been through quite an adventure over the last week and a half and I'm sure everyone will know the whole story soon enough." Sarah quickly leaned up to me and whispered into my ear and said, "Well maybe not the whole story Cole." This time it was my turn to look at her with a big smile and say nothing.

Once I made my way around the café to thank everyone personally and some of them wanting to pet Shadow I asked Sarah if she was going to stay and eat with us, she quickly replied, "Of course Cole, you got enough free meals out of me it's about time you started to pay me back." I was quite happy with her answer but didn't want to let on too much about how I was really starting to like her. I then said, "Great, let's go see what my sister set up on the buffet table, this place really does have really good food but then again you probably already know that." We slowly made our way to the buffet table with Shadow sticking close to my side but I could tell he was getting a little curious about the food on the table,

I then asked Miralani if she had any cooked hamburger back in the kitchen that I could give to shadow. I didn't think what was on the buffet menu would be very good for him. Miralani quickly replied, "Hell no Cole, you're not going to give him hamburger now, this is a special occasion, I'll have a big New York fillet cooked up for him right away, does that sound okay to you Shadow?" I could tell my sister was being taken by Shadow's allure, "Okay sis, I just hope he doesn't think he's going to get steak all the time, when we get home it's going to be a healthy diet for this guy." I quickly commented. She then quickly headed into the kitchen to have Shadow's meal prepared.

As Sarah and I made our way through the buffet line piling our plates full of chicken, pizza, egg rolls, garlic bread and salad I said to her, "Hey follow me and we'll head over to my favorite booth, you too Shadow, come on boy!" We made our way to the booth and to my surprise shadow jumped in on one side while Sarah and I sat together across from him. I thought for sure he would follow me in on my side but just maybe he was sensing my ever increasingly feelings towards Sarah. I looked at him and said, "That's a good boy Shadow, your food will be here shortly." Sarah turned to me and said, "You know Cole this is starting to feel like a first date or something." I almost spit out the water I had just sipped from my glass, then after taking a deep breath I replied, "Well I'm good with that as long as there's a second one in our future." I couldn't believe I had just said that. Waiting for some kind of a negative response from her I just sat there staring into my food. "Oh I think there may be a second and who knows maybe a lot more," she reassuringly remarked. I just kind of smiled again and began to eat to avoid any eye contact. Within a few minutes Miralani came out with Shadow's steak and moved in right beside him pushing him over a bit in order to join us at the booth. She began to cut the steak up into small pieces and put them on a separate plate in front him all the while Shadow was staring at the meat and gyrating his nose like a spinning top toy.

The four of us sat there eating our food while most of the people there had already finished and were starting to leave after saying welcome back to me one more time. Shadow had just about finished his cut up chunks of steak when Miralani had a bowl of water brought over to him. I then told her, "Jesus sis you're going to spoil him rotten, eating and drinking at the table." She then replied, "Well he's probably thirsty after all of that meat, everybody else here has water and besides like I said, Shadow is now family." It was at that point I realized that I would never have a problem finding a dog sitter, I just didn't know if I would get him back. Sarah then spoke, "You know I think Shadow is something really special, I have been around several breeds of hunting and working dogs most of my life and I can sense that he has a very strong desire to be loyal and obedient to his owner or pack in his case with him being a wolf and all." I turned to Sarah and said, "I couldn't agree more Sarah, he really is something special, he probably saved my life down in those underground caverns we were in, I had slipped when trying to kill this rattle snake for some food for the two of us when he lunged in front of the snake that was about to strike me, Shadow actually put himself between me and the snake and took the strike instead of me, then killed the snake before the a effects of the bite set in, I thought I was going to lose him at that point but his strong will to survive pulled him through the night." Miralani with tears starting to fall from her eyes said, "Oh my god Cole, he really is special and now that I know he saved your life I'll love him with all my heart," with her tears now flowing like a waterfall Miralani reached around Shadow with her arms and gave him the most affectionate hug I've ever seen from her.

Once the hug ended I noticed that Sarah too was starting to tear up a little and getting a bit emotional. I quickly remarked, "I guess I'd better not give any more details of that event since I know the two of you would probably breakdown and start balling." After getting a very dirty look from the both of them I then asked, "Well who's the lucky one that gets to give Shadow and I a ride home?" Miralani was the first to respond by saying, "We'll I know I just said how much I love him but I don't think I want Shadow in my BMW until he's at least had a bath." Sarah then spoke, "Actually Miralani,

Shadow had a bath a little over a week ago when we first found him along with Cole, I mean that Shadow had the bath and Cole didn't get one until this morning, I can vouch for Cole, I think he's clean enough to ride in your BMW. You could take Cole and I could take Shadow, I'm just kidding, I'll give them both a ride home because there are still a few things I would like to talk to Cole about, that's if you don't mind." Miralani then replied, "Not at all Miss Cooper, I don't mind one bit, besides I will probably be spending a lot of time over the next few days at Cole's helping him get his strength back by preparing and cooking all of his meals." Sarah then replied, "Great and Miralani please call me Sarah if you'd like." I was completely happy with both of those answers from the girls, I was hoping Sarah would take me home and getting my meals catered from Miralani was just the icing on the cake.

We finished up our meals not quite as fast as Shadow did but never the less we did all pretty much clean our plates and my plate was just as clean as his, not even a crumb was left to be eaten. I then asked Miralani if she had the Bronco towed home and if it was okay, she then replied, "Well I believe it's okay, Sam and I drove it all the way back to your place the next day after you disappeared and it never complained once to either of us about anything being wrong with it but then again I'm not very fluent in automotive dialect." Sarah started to laugh a bit then said, "Anytime you're ready and feel like leaving Cole just let me know." I then said, 'Hey sis speaking of Sam how did your date go with him and where the hell is he?" My sister then replied, "He wanted to be here Cole but when I told him the good news about you he had already been sent to Phoenix for some refresher training from the sheriff's department down there, as for our date went we sort of saw each other every day that you were gone, I mean if it wasn't for Sam helping me get through this whole thing I don't know what I would have done." Feeling relieved that my sister had someone here to help her through this mess I was very sorry that Sam was not here so I could thank him personally for what he did for Miralani during my absence. I then told Miralani, "Sam is a good man and I hope the two of you will pursue a relationship if you haven't already, well what I am trying to say is that you two are good for each other." My sister started to get a bit embarrassed and directed her attention back to Shadow by giving him another hug.

I looked at Sarah than asked, "Well what do you think Sarah, feel like heading out?" Without hesitation she said, "Heck yeah, this booth is getting a little uncomfortable, I think my ass has fallen asleep." Miralani loudly replied, "Hey I just had these things reupholstered a few months ago, maybe if you had a little more meat on those bones and your rear end you might appreciate it." Sarah started to laugh, then I said, "I don't know sis, I think her bones are perfect." Miralani then spoke, "Yeah Cole, we know what you mean." Shadow started to get a bit restless and wanted out from the booth so I figured it was time to get going, the three of us headed out to Sarah's Fj and Miralani said goodbye with one more hug for myself and one for Shadow and then said, "I'll stop by around lunch time tomorrow and bring you something to eat." I emotionally and thankfully replied, "Thanks sis, Shadow and I are just going to take it easy tomorrow and take a lot of naps, just give me a call when you're on the way to make sure were up or haven't gone to the store for something." She then replied, "Okay Cole I will but don't you go out in that garage of yours and start cleaning or messing around with the Bronco, it can wait a few days before you clean it up." I agreed, then Sarah, Shadow and I walked out the door of the café and got into her Fj.

After pulling out of the parking lot Sarah said, "Cole you'll have to give me directions once we get on the main road." I then replied, "I thought you knew everything about me Sarah, I'm sure you probably know the actual address but not the physical location, it can be tricky finding the turnoff from Highway 89, so yeah I'll give you directions and hopefully you'll find your way back the next time you come to visit." Again Sarah just smiled and kept driving. Shadow was sitting up in the back seat area which was quite unique due to the dual seats that ran parallel with the sides of the Fj, he was enjoying the fresh air coming in through the windows. This really was a fine vehicle and a pleasure to ride in considering its age. I then asked Sarah, "Hey what year is your Fj Sarah, they all kind of look the same from the late sixties all the way up through the seventies, is there a way to tell them apart?" I pretty much knew that the only changes on this vehicle through those years was the difference in the bumpers and the external lighting but I was trying to get her to open up a little and maybe eventually tell me some things about the underground base and exactly what the hell they did there. Sarah turned to me and said, "It's a nineteen seventy model Cole and Toyota kept the same body style all the way up to nineteen eighty-five, there are only subtle changes they made too exterior but for the most part they all look the same and I believe they were introduced in the USA in nineteen sixty." I was totally impressed again with this woman who just kept getting more and more interesting the longer I was with her.

Now that we were on a subject that we were both comfortable talking about I then said to Sarah, "Well it's the nicest one of these I've ever seen by far, if you have some time when we get to my place I can show you my Bronco if you'd like, I think you're the type of person that can really appreciate bringing an old vehicle back to life and then have the confidence to drive it as your daily driver." Sarah then replied, "Why thank you Cole, that's one of the nicest things anyone has ever said to me in regards to my cars that is and yes I would love to check out your Bronco, I almost bought one several years ago but I thought it had too much rust to be a good restoration candidate." I quickly replied, "Yeah, that's one of the main issues with the old Bronco's they are notorious for rusting out in certain spots of the fender wells and the firewall but if you can find a good one to start out with it's definitely worth the money to put into it, there appreciation value has just kept going up over the last fifteen years or so and doesn't look like it's going to slow down anytime soon." Sarah nodded her head and replied, "Well maybe I'll ask you for some help to find me one, I really would like to do another restoration project within the next year or so." I then happily replied, "Sure thing, I'd be love to." As we got closer to the turn off from the main road Shadow once again started to get a little restless so I asked Sarah if she would mind pulling over for a few minutes to see if Shadow had to do some business after all he did just eat a whole New York steak and probably needed to go." Sarah laughed and agreed whole heartedly.

After Shadow completed his needed business we all jumped back into the Fj and we were on our way, within the next few minutes we turned off the main road and I said to Sarah, "Were almost there, just a couple more miles and will be at your new home Shadow, you're going to love the huge backyard area for you to run around in and the house is very big also, it's just going to be us boy, two bachelors living the dream." Right then Sarah burst out loud laughing and shaking her head as if I were talking to college roommate or something. Sarah then spoke, "So what kind of parties are you and Shadow going throw in this wild bachelor pad of yours, I mean are you going to take Shadow down to local animal shelter to pick up girls for him or what?" I was the one who started to laugh this time and before you knew it we both were laughing our asses off, even Shadow was making some low toned growls and grunts from the back, I began to think this was a defining moment towards the beginning of a very special friendship between all of us and one that would last a lifetime. I quickly turned to Sarah and said, "There it is, my home, just pull right up front close to the garage door Sarah." She answered, "Okay Cole, wow what a beautiful home it's so big, how much property do you have here Cole, I mean is all of this yours even all the way down to the creek?" I then proudly replied, "Yeah, pretty much it is, I mean there are no fences out in front or on the sides of the house but it is over fifteen acres of choice land here in Sedona, I'm not even sure what it's all worth but I would never sell it, my father passed it down to me and hopefully someday I'll pass it down to my family." We all piled out the Fj and Sarah just kept looking around at all of the scenic views from the property, she then remarked, "This is really peaceful here Cole, so quiet except the sounds of mother nature, I can hear the birds, the wind flowing through the trees in the canyon and mostly the serenity of the soothing sound of the water cascading over the rocks from Oak Creek, I think you are a very lucky man Cole to have such a wonderful place to call home." I nodded my head and agreed with her then we headed to the front door.

A few steps from the front door Sarah quickly asked, "Hey do have your keys to get in?" I then replied, "No but I have an extra house key hidden here hidden in the backside of this Indian medicine man statue." Starring at the statue for a few seconds Sarah then said, "Medicine man, looks more like a burnt out hippie from the sixties if you ask me." I turned around to face Sarah all the while trying not to laugh and said, "Hey I paid a lot of money for that work of art, it's signed and numbered by the artist, it will probably be worth quite a bit someday." Sarah then replied, "If you say so Cole, I still think it looks like a hippie from the sixties, it's actually kind of creepy." I let out a chuckle and as we entered through the front door, Shadow made a quick burst and into the living room he went. Sarah stopped after her entrance and stood completely still and slowly scanned the entire room like some kind of security camera system at a bank, she then said, "Wow Cole I'm impressed, this is really nice, I take it you did all of the interior decorating yourself, I mean it sort of has that look and feel of you all over it." I almost didn't quite know how to respond to Sarah's compliment, she did just insult my medicine man out front but I'm pretty sure she was just trying to be funny. I quickly said, "Thanks, yeah I did most of it and Miralani has picked up a few things along the way for me, my sister really does have a good eye when it comes to most types of art, most of her expertise however lies in old and rare paintings, particularly southwestern art." Sarah said she would tend to agree with her expertise and then said, "Well if your sister picked out all of these paintings tell her I said they're absolutely beautiful." I quickly answered, "I will." Shadow was checking out every room of the house.

After giving Sarah a quick tour of the house I asked her if she would like something to drink, to my surprise she answered, "Yeah, I'll take a beer if you have any low calorie ones." I then replied, "You're in luck, I normally drink Miller lite and I should still have some in the fridge if my sister and her friends didn't stop by while

I was missing, would you like one of those?" She quickly answered, "Yes, that sounds great." I then asked if she would like to check out my Bronco, she impatiently replied, "Hell yeah, I've been looking forward to seeing this thing, I mean I've heard so much about it from you and other people you know." I quickly grabbed a couple of beers and we headed out to the garage. The garage was a three car garage but my Bronco was the only vehicle I owned presently, I used to have an old mustang that I was going to restore but somebody made me an offer I couldn't refuse and besides I used the extra money I got from it to help with the expensive paint job I had put on the Bronco. We approached the garage from the side of the house and Shadow was running around like crazy in the backyard area checking out his new domain. As Sarah and I approached the side door on the garage I pulled out my extra set of house keys from my jeans pocket that I had in the kitchen along with the keys to the Bronco. As we started to enter Shadow came up from behind us and was the first to go in, I then said, "Hold on boy, let me at least get the light," even though it was fairly dark without the garage light on I could see that Miralani must have put the car cover on the Bronco to protect the paint from the dirt and dust that's so bad here in the Sedona area.

The garage light illuminated the entire structure and the shape of the Bronco was now fully exposed. Sarah turned to me and said, "Well let's get the cover off, do you need my help Cole?" Shadow was running around doing laps around the entire garage with an occasional sniff of the tires on the Bronco. I turned to Sarah and said, "Okay Sarah, why don't you get up by the front and I'll start taking the cover off from the back which is the hardest to get up and over the roof rack without it getting caught." Sarah quickly positioned herself by the front custom brush guard bumper and I stepped up on the rear bumper and began to roll and throw the cover up and over the roof rack towards Sarah. Sarah then commented, "Jesus Cole this has to be the biggest car cover I've ever seen, just let me know what to do here, okay." I quickly answered, "Okay I'm just going to roll and throw this whole thing towards you, just kind of make sure it doesn't get caught up on the brush guard and I'll hop down and come and help you." Shadow was really getting excited maybe even more than Sarah was at this point. I then threw the whole clump of the cover towards Sarah and realized I probably threw it too hard, she was completely consumed by it and fell to the floor and if that wasn't bad enough Shadow then pounced on top of the cover thinking Sarah was playing some kind of game. As fast as I could I jumped down off the rear bumper and ran up to the cover with Sarah underneath it and Shadow on top of it and her. I shouted, "Hey you alright under there?" there was no response or even any movement.

I quickly pushed Shadow off the cover and told him to stay, my heart was pounding as fast as it ever had, I just hoped she was okay and hadn't hit her head or something. I slowly started to pull one side of the cover off where I thought her feet were when all of a sudden something grabbed and wrapped around my knees pulling me to the ground and on top of the cover then before I knew it I was on the floor on my back and Sarah was on top of me laughing her ass off. I shockingly and cowardly said, "Hey take it easy, I'm sorry I didn't mean to throw it that hard, really Sarah I'm sorry don't be mad." Sarah looked directly into my eyes and said, "Cole I'm not mad at you, if I was you would be unconscious right now, I just wanted to see how hard it would be to take you down but most of all I think I'm really starting to like you, would you like to get up?" I quickly replied, "Yeah I really like you too Sarah, you sort of caught me off guard, otherwise I don't think I would have gone down so easy and actually I'm not sure if I want to get up or not." Just then Shadow jumped in closer to us and started to lick the both of us to make sure we were all right I guess or maybe he just wanted to join in thinking we were still playing. Sarah quickly rolled off of me and as the two of us sat on the cover the Bronco came into full view, she then remarked, "Oh my god Cole, that's got to be the most beautiful truck I have ever seen." I too was thinking the same thing seeing Sarah from a whole new prospective, she was the most beautiful woman I had ever seen. Even Shadow had calmed down I guess because Sarah was not tossing me around on the floor anymore. I turned to Sarah and said, "Yeah, it really is beautiful and so are you." I couldn't believe I had just said that, my god what was I thinking, she is probably going to leave now as fast as she can.

After a few minutes sitting side by side and still on the garage floor Sarah finally leaned over towards me and softly said, "Thanks Cole, although you sort of caught me by surprise with that comment I'm not going to deny that I also have been hiding some strong feelings towards you, I just don't want to move to fast into a relationship with the possibility of you thinking I was only doing it to get you to come work with me or even maybe thinking I was too easy and some kind of tramp and I'm sorry Cole if I gave you the wrong impression by jumping on top of you like I did but sometimes I just do crazy stupid things." She then leaned a little closer and gave me a soft kiss on the lips. Totally stunned I remained quiet for a few seconds trying to gather myself and for the first time in a very long time I was getting butterflies in my stomach as if I was back in high school getting ready to ask a girl to the prom. I just decided to say what I was feeling and what was on my mind, so I calmly responded with, "Sarah since the first moment I met you I have been becoming more and more attracted to you and my feelings have grown immensely for you and as far as you coming across as cheap or manipulative that's absurd, you are the most interesting, exciting and warm hearted woman I think I have ever met and I've only known you for a day, my god you're amazing." Sarah was also quiet for a couple of seconds then deeply looked into my eyes and said, "Hey Cole lets go inside and talk, to hell with the rules and regulations of the agency I have to tell you, no I want to tell you everything there is about me and what I do and the opportunity that lies in front of you, please Cole lets go inside." I could see that a few tears were falling down Sarah's cheeks so I grabbed her hand and helped her up, we then headed back to the house.

Shadow lead the way back to the kitchen, Sarah then turned to me and said, "Here, let's sit here Cole." Standing next to the kitchen bar stools, I then replied, "Okay Sarah, you seem very upset about something, you know my father always told me the truth is always the quickest way to heal all matters, maybe not the easiest but definitely the best road to travel when dealing with life and the relationships we encounter." Sarah looked down towards the floor as if to hang her head because she was ashamed of something then slowly looked up into my eyes and said, "Cole you said we have only known each other for a day or so but I feel like I've known you all of my life, every day that you were in that coma I was there at your side hoping and praying that you would come out of it and be okay. The more background checks I ran on you the more I became intrigued with you and your career, I began to develop feelings for you without even having a conversation with you. Cole, my biggest concern and feeling of guilt was the fact that I'm the one who made the call to release the sleeping gas that put you and Shadow down in our ventilation tunnel and put you in an unexpected coma, I never thought we would have to use it, let alone anyone having a serious reaction from the use of it, I'm so very sorry Cole, I nearly killed you from my actions and following the damn protocol, can you ever forgive me?" I sat completely silent and motionless for a few seconds then said, "Sarah, there's nothing to forgive, I would have made the same decision if I were in your position, hey Shadow and I were trespassing and no matter what the reason for it, accident or on purpose you had no way of knowing what that reason was. Actually the way I look at it is you didn't almost kill me Sarah, you probably saved both of our lives and for that I will be forever grateful." Sarah began to cry and reached to embrace me, we both then stood up and wrapped our arms around each other and just held on.

Shadow was lying at our feet trying to get involved as much as he could in our emotional moment. I guess I couldn't blame him he too was probably very attached to Sarah as I was at this point. Sarah took my hand and lead me over to the living sofa and said, "Cole, please sit down there's so much more I need to tell you." Trying to get Sarah to relax a little and feel at ease I quickly replied, "Okay but should I get a box a "Kleenex" or something?" We both sat down on the sofa with Shadow hot on our trail, Sarah then spoke, "Cole what I'm about to tell you is highly classified and I could go to federal prison just for telling you without getting a sworn statement and an employment contract from you." I quickly interrupted her by saying, "Hey I don't want you to get into any trouble Sarah, you don't need to do this." She immediately replied, "No Cole, I need to tell you, I owe you that much." I then answered, "Okay but you know you can trust me and I would never do anything to put you at risk or harm you Sarah." We both moved closer to each other and Sarah grabbed both of my hands and held them fairly tight then said, "Cole I know this is going to sound a little crazy and you're probably not even going to believe what I'm about to tell you but it's the truth and after what we just shared I will always be truthful with you from now on." Again I told Sarah okay and I was really starting to get very nervous myself, I then said with a comforting tone, "It's okay Sarah, I trust you and will always be truthful with you too." Sarah sat silent for a few moments then took a deep breath and exhaled very slowly.

Gazing into to Sarah's big beautiful eyes and holding on to her hands she very emotionally spoke, "Cole what if I told you there was a way to save so many more lives of missing people many of them children before they ever were put in harm's way, I mean actually stopping horrible and heinous crimes before they ever happened. What if I told you our government agency the one which you and Shadow accidently stumbled upon is actually a highly scientific top secret project that has created a method for humans to travel in time forwards and most importantly backwards with extreme precision in order to change the destiny of certain chosen individuals that should have never died in the first place, most of these individuals are young children that go missing and are never found. Cole what I'm saying is we have the ability to stop and save these children and a few chosen adults before they become victims, this is the opportunity that I'm offering you, a chance to make a difference in changing the world from our actions." Totally stunned and a little worried that this whole thing may just be a dream I sat there staring at Sarah for a moment almost hoping that she would burst out laughing and say "I got you Cole" but that didn't happen.

Once I had processed everything that Sarah had just told me and still totally confused and a little shell shocked that the possibility that everything she just said might be true I responded to Sarah by saying, "So you're totally serious about everything you just said and this isn't the world's greatest prank that you are trying to scam me with right, I mean if it is you should win an academy award for your performance." Sarah then replied, "Cole I'm being totally honest with you, I know this sounds crazy and like some kind of a cheap science fiction storyline from a bad movie but it's the truth and it's real and I have personally experienced it, I need you to believe me Cole, I'd like you to be a part of it with me as my partner by enlisting as an agent in our organization." Again I just sat completely motionless and stunned. I tried to calm down as much as one could after hearing what I just did but I responded to Sarah by saying, "Sarah, I believe in you and I would trust you with my life after everything you have said and done for Shadow and me but I don't think I'm even remotely qualified to take on something like this or even should, I mean it sounds like you're playing god or something, what gives anyone the right to go back in time and change history, I mean isn't there a chance that it could cause an even worse affect by changing the destiny of certain individuals, I mean I'm not a science fiction geek but I've seen enough of those bad movies you just referenced and they all say changing history could be bad for the future." Sarah then paused for a brief moment then said, "Cole I know this all seems unbelievable and will take some time to process but with if all of those concerns you just talked about were taken in to consideration and accounted for and even if we knew we had the blessing from god how would you feel about it then?" Wow she seemed to have an answer for everything, I mean this was really the truth she was speaking here and she wanted me to be a part of it. I just remained quiet still trying to absorb everything she had just told me.

After a few moments had passed I couldn't help but think what my father told me about the choices we make in life and what we make of ourselves from those choices. Before I could even say another word Sarah began to speak again, "Cole just another bit of information you should know and this is about yourself, I think you're probably the most qualified individual for this endeavor that I've ever had the pleasure to know, I think you have the heart and compassion of an angel and the strength of warrior and that is so very hard to find in someone these days, you have a gift and all of the skills of someone who could make a huge difference in this troubled world we live in today, you're a very good person and I for one would do everything possible to help you on this journey if you decide to take it on." I paused a moment to take in all that Sarah had just said and I was quite flattered and embarrassed by it all to say the least. Shadow was still lying comfortably at our feet next to the sofa when suddenly I decided to give Sarah my answer, I told her, "Sarah I think I had already made up my mind when you first offered me this opportunity to work for you and your agency but I was just too scared to give you an answer at that point, I really love what I'm doing now as being a ranger and working in the great outdoors of Sedona but I've always felt like I have held myself back and missed out on a fulfilling career by not taking earlier opportunities to work fulltime with the F.B.I., so with that being said and throwing caution into the wind I accept your offer and would love to be your partner and hopefully I won't disappoint you, oh and on one condition that Shadow can be a member of our partnership." It only took a millisecond before Sarah jumped into my arms and most of my lap and then said, "Oh Cole you won't be sorry, I promise you, I'm so happy I could just scream." Shadow jumped up onto the sofa next to us and seemed just as excited as Sarah.

The seconds turned to minutes then what seemed like an hour had passed just talking with Sarah about our future working together and the basics of what to expect on a day to day basis when all of a sudden I had just remembered one more condition that I wanted to be added to the terms of accepting this position, I quickly made my request, "Hey Sarah there is one more condition I'd like to request if it's at all possible." She then replied, "Sure Cole what is it?" I looked deeply into her eyes with a look of great concern showing on my behalf and asked, "Do I have to wear a damn suit for this job because I really hate those monkey suits." Sarah began to laugh and then smiled before she answered, "No Cole you can wear whatever you'd like but I would highly recommend some comfortable jeans and long sleeve shirts because of the cool temperatures we encounter working underground most of the time." I let out of huge sigh of relief and then said, "Great because that could have been a deal breaker." Sarah quickly smiled and looked down at Shadow and said, "Okay Shadow, you're now employed with a very top secret government agency, I guess I'll have to get both you a badge now." I started to laugh at Sarah's comments to Shadow when it hit me, I'm going to work for an organization that I don't even the name of yet. I then hurriedly asked Sarah, "You know Sarah you've failed to mention what organization that I'll be working for, the F.B.I. or the C.I.A. or maybe N.S.A. or some offshoot of those, I mean I should at least know the name of the company that will be signing my checks," she quickly responded, "Actually Cole you kind of already know the name, you just don't know the connection yet, do you remember when I told you shortly after you came out of your coma of how I thought it might be destiny that you and Shadow were found in our ventilation tunnel, well before you came all the way out of your coma you had brief moments of speaking a word over and over at the times of your short durations of speech, you see Cole we didn't know that was the name of your wolf but it just so happened to also be the name of our very top secret organization and I had to make sure you weren't some kind of spy trying to infiltrate and steal our technology, so you see now why I couldn't notify any of your friends or Miralani until I was satisfied about who you really were, so to answer your question Cole you have just accepted a position from the agency called S.H.A.D.O.W. and I will explain later to you what exactly that means but it will be easier to just show you." I just sat and pondered the statement she just made.

Once again this situation just got a whole lot more interesting,

I then said, "Wow, I'll be working for a place that has the same name as my wolf and here all this time I thought I had the coolest name around town." Sarah began to laugh again and her smile was so beautiful, I could tell that she really was quite happy with my decision. It was getting late in the afternoon and closer towards dinner time. I asked Sarah if she wanted to get a bite to eat with me and that I needed to go out and get some supplies for Shadow and that I knew a place where we could bring Shadow with us to eat. Sarah quickly replied, "Sure Cole, that sounds great, I can drive if you'd like, I mean if your too tired, I know this has been a big day for you emotionally." I looked at Sarah and said, "You must be joking, will take my Bronco, I think she is probably dying to get out of the garage and go for a drive." Sarah gladly accepted my offer to drive and replied, "I'm excited to ride in that big American made beast of yours Cole, where did you have in mind to eat, your sisters place?" That was the last place I had in mind right now, not because I didn't want to eat there but I wanted some privacy for Sarah and I during our dinner so we could continue our conversations about my new career and I kind of just wanted to be alone with Sarah for a bit longer without any interruptions.

The three of us headed out to the garage with Shadow leading the way again, he was really getting familiar with the surroundings and the structures of the property. As we entered the garage I said to Sarah, "I hope there's gas in it, I'm sure Sam would have put some in it if it was low." Sarah then said, "If not we always take mine Cole." I got the passenger door for Sarah and the only way in for Shadow to get in the back other than my door or the tailgate, I called for him to jump in and he did right away, then Sarah jumped into the front seat and I closed the door for her and made my way around to the driver's side and hopped in. I put the key and turned it to the accessary position to check the fuel level and the status of all the other critical fluids before starting it up. Everything looked great with over a half tank of gas so we were good to go. I then looked over towards Sarah and said, "Hold on to your socks girl because this thing is going shake rattle and roll like you've probably never felt before." Sarah just smiled again, I then turned the key all the way to the right and the Bronco fired right up with a glorious thunder from the dual exhaust system and being in the garage made it even sound better. The idle was a little rough and low because it was probably a little cold and thirsty after sitting for over a week but it only took a few more seconds and it smoothed out just fine. Sarah was looking at all of the gauges on the dash and I could tell she was impressed with the display. I had spent quite a bit of money on having all the original housings modified with modern L.E.D. lights and the bezels were chrome plated to a brilliant shine. I backed out slowly and closed the garage door when she said, "Hey Cole let me hop out and lock up my Fj," I quickly answered, "Sure, it's probably not going to get bothered here but you never know with a rare vehicle like that, why don't you just pull it into the garage." After Sarah jumped out to pull her Fj I into the garage I quickly said, "Hey Shadow, what do you think of Sarah." He softly made a low moaning and whining sound while wagging his tail, I quickly responded, "Yeah, I like her too, I like her a lot." Sarah jumped back in and we were on our way.

7

TOGETHER

The wind coming through the windows of the Bronco mixed with sound of the mufflers echoing through the canyon was music to my ears and Shadow was loving it too. Just then Sarah commented, "Cole this thing sounds awesome, it sounds so powerful and mean, did you build the engine yourself?" I proudly replied, "Most of it, the heads I had professionally done down in Phoenix buy a friend of mine that owns a speed shop." Sarah then commented, "Well all I know is this has got to be the most enjoyable sound I have ever heard coming out of a combustion engine." Quickly I replied, "Thanks Sarah, I'm really proud of how this restoration and modification turned out, I think the money was well worth it." Right then another thought hit me, I never asked how much of a salary I would be earning on this new job. I decided to wait till we were eating and I could ask a lot of questions concerning this new path I was about to head down. Once again Sarah asked, "Where are we going Cole?" This time I answered with the location and name, "It's a place called "Squatter's" just north of town a bit, if you haven't been there before I think you're going to like it." She then replied, "No I haven't been there, I take it they allow dogs." I quickly answered, "Yeah and the place has an outside eating area if you'd prefer to eat outside, I really think you'll like it Sarah, it's set up to resemble an old mining camp eatery." Once again she cracked that beautiful smile of hers and said, "Sounds like fun." I couldn't stop thinking about what lied ahead for the two of us, I mean really, time travel, I kept hoping this wasn't some kind of dream and that I would wake up suddenly and there would be no S.H.A.D.O.W. organization and horribly most of all no Sarah, dreams can suck in a big way sometimes.

Twenty minutes later we were pulling into the parking lot of "Squatter's" the place wasn't too crowded yet but it would be very soon, so I think we got here just in time. Over the last couple of years, I kept suggesting to Miralani that she should make an offer to the owner of this establishment because it was a virtual gold mine, a money making machine, she was always quick to remind me that she had enough headaches and worries about when it came to running her current businesses she owns. After parking the Bronco, we all jumped out and headed towards the front door, I knew the owner Nick Trotter very well and was hoping he wouldn't make too much of a scene from seeing me back alive and well. Shadow was walking and behaving very well, even the crowd was not affecting him at all, I mean for a wolf who are known to be quite nervous and jittery, at least that's what the so called animal experts say. For not having worked with him on any training he sure seemed to know what was expected of him. Sarah walked through the door first then Shadow and I followed, the hostess immediately asked, "Three for dinner?" I quickly replied, "Yes, Sarah would you like to sit inside or out?" Sarah then answered, "Outside sounds good to me if you don't mind," I then replied, "Outside it is." The hostess then ushered us to the patio which sort of wrapped around the side of the building putting the gorgeous sunsets into perfect view for the customers.

Once seated at one the best tables outside to view the sunset, the waitress then came over and handed us a menu and asked if I needed to see a dog menu also. Although I had been here many times before I had never brought an animal with me. I then answered the waitress, "Yes please, Shadow has never eaten here before but I'm sure he will love it." Sarah started to chuckle a bit and I then said, "What's so funny?" She then replied, "Cole I think you and

Shadow are going to be very happy together, I mean you both seem to communicate to each other so well, probably better than most married couples." This lady definitely had a great sense of humor and quite witty. While we waited for Shadow's menu to arrive I asked Sarah if she saw anything on the menu that caught her eye and she replied, "I really like fish Cole and the Albacore tuna melt with seasoned fries sounds really good, too bad they don't have any Rattlesnake for you and Shadow." This time I began to chuckle, then replied, "Yeah a good Western Diamondback stew sounds really good about now, hey Shadow." Shadow just looked at me as if he knew what I had just said, like I was crazy or something. Sarah then said, "Damn Cole, I swear I think he really can understand the English language, I think he's going to be something special after you have spent time training him." I quickly replied, "He already is something special to me." Sarah again smiled and then agreed.

After placing our orders which consisted of Sarah's tuna melt, my big bowl of chili and Shadow's specially prepared chicken pot pie for dogs which almost sounded good enough to be on the human menu, Sarah and I then began to talk, Sarah started by saying, "Cole I know you must have a thousand questions for me so fire away." I had thought of several key questions on the way here and now I guess was the time to get some answers hopefully. I began with, "Sarah first of all let me just say that I'm really grateful for the opportunity you have afforded me and I hope you're not offended by any of the following questions I may ask." She quickly replied, "Hey Cole, I told you before that I will never lie to or hold anything back from you, as far as I'm concerned you have just as much right to know everything that I know." Again I was blown away by her sincerity and honesty with me. My first question was, "Sarah I'm still having a hard time with the fact of what we will be doing with changing history and all, I mean are you sure that this is actually changing the world for the better and how do you know for sure?" Sarah paused for a moment then simply said, "Yes Cole, ninety-nine point nine percent sure and when we get you started back at the base we will go over all of the past success cases from the past two years and you can judge for yourself." Without hesitation I said, "Well that certainly answered that question." I then asked, "How many time traveling agents are there actually, I mean I'm not sure if that's what you call them but how many are there, is it just you?" Sarah again smiled then said, "No Cole, it's not just me, there are eight teams of two agents each and four of those are made up of a male and female, and we are all just called S.H.A.D.O.W. agents." Again I couldn't believe how precise and truthful her answers sounded. My next question was going to probably be the one where she might hold back a little but I had to ask, "Sarah, just how dangerous is this time traveling technology, I mean has anyone ever died from it or not come back and just vanished into thin air, just how much of a risk is there to our lives?" I could see that this question got to Sarah and it was somewhat upsetting to her and I wondered if I had just crossed over the line or something.

I quickly tried to change the subject but Sarah then interrupted me by saying, "No Cole, let me answer your question I told you I wouldn't hold anything back from you." I quickly stopped her response and said, "Sarah I'm sorry, I didn't mean to touch on any personal or difficult situations for you to answer, it's okay you don't have to tell me anything you don't want to, so let's talk about how much money I'll be making." Hoping she would take the opening to change directions from previous question she sat there quiet for a few seconds then said, "Cole it's okay, I'll have to tell you about everything eventually it might as well be now, first of all yes there is always some danger when traveling in time because of the unknown factors of quantum physics and variables of space and time and yes we have lost one agent since going online with the device, it just so happened to be my ex-partner who disappeared seven months ago somewhere in the past and has yet to return, so are you having any second thoughts?" I couldn't believe what I just heard, the truth and the realization of this whole situation had just come to fruition. Sarah continued to sit and stare at me while I remained quiet for some time. I wasn't even sure how to respond to her answer, I mean she just told me her last partner disappeared in time and now I'm going to replace him, the only thing I could think of saying at the moment was, "Sarah I'm sorry about your partner, I know that must have been hard to tell me about the circumstances involving him, I won't ask you anymore questions and no I'm not having second thoughts." Just then the waitress brought all of our orders and it couldn't have come at a better time.

The three of us began to dig in and even Shadow had a special dinner set up for him on the ground next to the table. The food must have been quite good because there was total silence for what seemed like five minutes. Then Sarah spoke, "You'll be making at least five times what you're making now Cole and that's just to start but I guarantee after a few missions in you won't even care about the money." I then turned to Sarah and said, "You know Sarah, I don't even care about the money now, to be honest with you, I'm doing this because I believe in you and because you believe in me." She then said, "I do believe in you Cole and I believe together we can make a difference." We looked at each other for a brief moment with complete silence and then returned to eating our dinner. Shadow had devoured his pot pie in a matter of minutes, I almost wanted to taste it but thought he might take my arm off as fast as he was chowing it down. I asked Sarah how her sandwich was and if she was going to want dessert because this place had the best strawberry cheesecake I had ever tasted. She got very excited and said, "Oh yeah, I love strawberry cheesecake and I'm definitely going to have some." Shadow was out of luck of luck for dessert, they had nothing on his menu, besides sweets are not good for dogs.

Sarah and I finished our meals and then ordered dessert, still in awe over her beauty I had to ask the question that I had been holding back all day, "So Sarah is there someone special in your life, I mean is there a Mr. Cooper?" Sarah smiled a bit while turning a very light shade of red and replied, "Sorry Cole there is a Mr. Cooper and he is very special to me, he's my father." After that emotional elevator ride of an answer I quickly gathered my composure and said, "So you're not seeing anyone or in a relationship of some kind?" Sarah slowly replied, "No Cole, I'm not in any relationship right now, except maybe just the one with you." Quickly she then looked down at Shadow and started to fidget with her spoon while turning a brighter shade of red. I was overrun with emotions from her answer and hadn't had these types of feelings for some time now but they were definitely giving me a feeling of warmth and uneasiness at the same time. I looked at her and said, "Well that makes two of us Sarah, I haven't been in a relationship for quite some time." She then looked up at me and said, "Well, now you have Shadow and I and let's hope it's the beginning of a very long and happy one." We slowly gazed into each other's eyes without saying a word and feeling the overwhelming attraction between us.

Our desserts arrived at the table looking absolutely delicious, Sarah then eagerly commented, "Wow Cole, if that cheesecake tastes as good as it looks I might have to order another one to take home for breakfast with my morning coffee." I reassuringly replied, "I promise you Sarah you're going to love it." We both very slowly savored each bite while Shadow watched, at least he didn't seem to interested by the cheesecake, I guess because it had no smell of meat or anything else that would get his nose going. The sun was starting to set in the western sky of Sedona dropping down behind the beautiful mountains that entrenched the area. We were so blessed to live in such a place, truly one of God's gifts to mankind. Sarah slid her chair around next to mine and reached for my hand, then together we watched the setting sun's glorious finale and it was spectacular as always. As the sun disappeared behind the mountains Sarah looked at me then leaned closer as I did the same until our lips were close enough feel each other's breath, I knew what was about to happen and neither one of us made any effort to stop it, our lips slowly touched then gently began to become firmly pressed to one another, Sarah's other free hand reached up and around the back of my neck as she began to gently pull me closer and our lips even tighter together. For a few moments I lost all of my senses and awareness, my heart was pounding as fast as it ever had during this long and passionate kiss, then as we slowly pulled away from each other she looked into my eyes and said, "I've been wanting to do that for quite some time now." Her kiss had kindled a fire inside of me which had been dormant for many years.

After slowly trying to catch my breath I replied, "Just when I thought that cheesecake couldn't taste any better, you had to go and put some on your lips." After laughing a bit and then before she could respond I said, "Sarah, I hope you felt what I just did because I'm still feeling it, that's something I've also been thinking about doing but didn't want to be too aggressive or give you a bad impression of me and scare you off." Sarah then said, "Cole, I hope I didn't scare you off in any way but I've always felt a person should trust in their feelings and act on them and mine are telling me that I'm very attracted to you and that you're a special man with a huge heart and I believe there is something wonderful happening here with the chemistry between us and I think you have very similar feelings towards me." I quickly and emotionally replied, "No Sarah, everything but scared, I'm just wondering where do we go from here?" At that point the waitress brought the bill to the table, horrible timing on her part, I thought. I quickly grabbed the bill and said this one is on me. Sarah quickly changing the subject again then said, "Hey Cole we better get going if you're going to get those supplies for Shadow, I think the pet store closes at seven." Deciding not to pursue my previous question I replied, "Yeah you're right, I can't afford to feed him steak and pot pies all the time." After paying the bill Sarah, Shadow and I headed out to the parking lot but before getting into the Bronco I looked at Shadow and asked, "Hey boy do you have to do some business?" Shadow then looked up at me as if to say thanks and quickly made his way to an area just for the dogs who had eaten here, they even provided the plastic bags and a sanitation disposal container. Since I didn't see Nick the owner I would have to stop by in the next few days and thank him for the service Shadow received, he definitely made the dogs feel welcome at his establishment. Shadow finished his business and trotted over to the Bronco, then we all piled in and headed for the pet store. As we were driving Sarah asked, "What all our you going to get for Shadow Cole, I mean do you know what to feed a growing young pup?" I hadn't had a dog since Miralani and were kids, so I wasn't up to date on the different types of food and nourishment requirements for a young dog or wolf in my case. I told Sarah that I would have to ask someone there at the store for advice on that matter.

We arrived at the pet center just a few minutes later and pulled into the parking lot. We then all got out and headed into the store which was like a huge outlet just for animals. Once in Sarah commented, "Wow this place is huge." I quickly located a salesperson who had just finished with a customer and asked for some assistance with Shadow's needs. Right away the man, named Ron according to his name tag said, "My god is that a wolf?" I quickly replied, "Yes, it is and he's been enlisted as a working dog for the government so I need your help with all the needs in order for him to maintain a very healthy diet and maybe you can recommend a good training or walking harness of some type." Quickly and very nervously Ron said, "Why, why yes sir, I can do that." The three of us followed the man throughout the store as he made his sales pitch on several items ranging from puppy food to shampoo's. Sarah was trying to hold back her laughter as the man was clearly nervous from my possible government connection with Shadow, I guess he thought we were some pretty serious agents or spies of some sort, in a way he was correct I guess. Our cart was filling up rapidly, I turned to Sarah and said quietly, "I guess it's a good thing I'm making more money now because I have an extra mouth to feed." Sarah then replied, "Don't worry Cole, if you run a little short I can spot you some." Chuckling a little, I happily replied, "Sarah, you've got to be an angel or something, why couldn't I have met you ten years ago." She then answered, "Ten years ago I was in Switzerland living with my father doing research on a project with him for CERN." Confused a little by her answer and not knowing what the hell CERN was I decided to ask Ron if that just about did it, he then replied, "Almost sir, what you have in your cart is a very good start but as your wolf gets older his food requirements are going to change, I would recommend checking with your vet on those time frames and recommendation's." I thanked Ron for his help and we proceeded to check out.

After loading everything up in the Bronco we finally headed back to my house. I remarked to Sarah, "Ron was very helpful didn't you think?" Sarah nodded her head some and then replied, "Cole you had that poor man so nervous I thought he was going to pee his pants." I couldn't help but to laugh a little at the whole experience. Quickly responding to Sarah while still laughing some I slowly remarked, "Hey I'm not laughing at Ron, just at what I came up so fast when he asked about Shadow being a wolf, I just wasn't even sure if it's legally okay to own such an animal, I didn't want him reporting me to some kind of animal rights group or something like that." Sarah then replied, "Hey I thought your answer was pretty good and for the most part very true." We then both smiled as I kept driving. Shadow was resting in the back, I guess this day was quite a bit for him, I keep forgetting that he was pretty much wild and own his own when I found him but I'm still amazed at how quickly he has become accustomed to humans and their daily activities. I turned my attention back to Sarah and remarked, "Hey I'm really sorry for keeping you out late, I mean I don't know if you have to work tomorrow or not, I know the Parks and Recreation department gave me a few weeks off, I guess that's going to end up as a two-week's notice." Sarah then said, "No worries Cole, I pretty much make my own schedule, I'm kind of in charge out at the facility." I then replied, "Yeah I sort of picked up on that when we were out there earlier today." She just smiled again.

As we turned off the main road and headed towards the house it was pretty dark out even with the full moon tonight, so I turned on the off road "KC" lights on the roof rack to help light up the road. Once I turned into the main driveway in front of the house I could see Sarah's Fj out front as it was illuminated from the "KC" lights. I commented to her, "Damn Sarah, that really is a nice 4X4, I tell you what, I'll help you find a Bronco if you're seriously interested in one but only on one condition, you help to convince me to get an Fj similar to yours and help with the restoration." She quickly and reassuringly replied, "You got a deal my friend." The three of us jumped out of the Bronco as it came to a full stop in the garage. Shadow immediately headed for the backyard, I guess he wasn't quite done with his business back at "Squatter's", Sarah and I slowly walked to towards the back door to the kitchen when she said, "Cole it's getting late, I guess I should head home." I slowly turned to her and asked, "Hey you never told me what part of town you live in Sarah, you know if you don't feel like driving home you can stay here the night, I mean if you'd like." Damn I couldn't believe I just asked her to stay the night, I hope she didn't take it the wrong way, what am I talking about, of course I hoped she took it the wrong way, there wasn't anything more I ever wanted so bad then for her to stay the night with me and I mean all night, the two of us together, this woman was driving me crazy and I was falling hard for her.

Sarah and I stood there in silence looking at one another when all of a sudden Shadow who just finished off his deposit let out a loud blast of gas that sounded like someone letting air out of a balloon all at once, I can only assume it was from the doggie chicken pot pie from "Squatter's". Sarah and I both began to laugh so hard we started to tear up, she then slowly moved closer towards my chest, put her arms around me and whispered in my ear, "Do you really want me to stay Cole?" The warmth of her breath and the fact she was blowing in my ear between the words that she had just spoke almost made me collapse at the knees. Without saying a word, I put my right hand on her face and began to caress her cheek slowly, then moving my hand behind her neck I gently pulled the two of us closer until our lips met softly in the shadows of the moonlight. The two of us slowly walked into the house never letting go of each other in complete silence, only the scuffling from Shadow once he entered through the doorway broke the silence. Sarah and I knew our relationship was about to take a huge leap forward and neither one of us wanted to slow it down one bit, the sexual attraction between us had reached the point of no return. I knew Shadow was probably good for the night, at least I hoped he wouldn't have to go out again. Sarah and I headed to the master bedroom, somewhere along the way our clothes started to come off and left a trail down the hallway and to the bed. Our passion for each other had totally taken over command of our bodies and the heated intimacy that followed.

Several hours had passed when I woke up from Shadow's entrance into the bedroom, Sarah was still in my arms and sleeping like a baby, she looked like an angel, an angel who had just commented a crime of passion by stealing my heart. This was an incredible woman, full of life and full of love. I laid my head back down on to the pillow, thinking of all the wonderful things we were going to experience together, I still hardly knew that much about her, I mean little things like what kind of music she liked or what kind of outdoor activities she liked, if any. My mind was spinning with joy and excitement because I was finally in a relationship and I just hoped that it was the beginning to something special. Shadow fell back asleep at the foot of the bed and I was still looking at the most beautiful woman in the world curled up in my arms, it was only one o'clock in the morning and I knew that I needed to get some more sleep because tomorrow was going to be a big day. I was going to have put my notice in with the Parks and Recreation office, stop by the café and see Miralani to let her know about my career decision and I wasn't sure if Sarah wanted to let anyone know about our relationship at this point, I would agree with whatever decision she made. I know my sister would be absolutely ecstatic about the two of us if she knew, she had been trying to hook me up with some her friends for years with little or no success. It's been one hell of day and I'm starting to feel like a truck ran me over so I closed my eyes and slowly drifted off to sleep once again.

I suddenly awoke to the soft warm breath of Sarah whispering these words in my ear, "Hey ranger, good morning, I hope you slept as good as I did, Cole last night was amazing." She moved away a bit then said, "Please don't think of me as being a tramp or something, I've never done anything like that before, it's just that the feelings I have for you are so overwhelming and I think I have really fallen for you." I pulled her back into my arms and emotionally replied, "Sarah I feel the same way and I don't know what path this relationship is going to lead us down but I do know from here on out I will always be there for you and will never do anything to hurt you or let you down." She then buried her head into my chest again and said, "Cole, I think we have something very special here and I hope it lasts forever." Shadow then jumped up onto the bed and nudged his way in between us and Sarah then remarked, "Yeah and you too Shadow, you're very special to the both of us." I then looked at the two of them and thought how wonderful my life had just become, a little over a week ago I had nobody else in my life other than Miralani, now I sort of have a family of my own, at least that's how I saw it.

The sun was beaming through the bedroom window and the morning was in full swing now that it was approaching seven o'clock, Sarah then said, "Hey how about I take you out to breakfast at your sister's place if you'd like, then if you want to we can let her know together about our newly formed relationship, both professionally and personally but first I need to go home and get some clean clothes." I quickly agreed and replied, "Yeah that sounds great Sarah, I wasn't sure how you wanted to handle that, I don't know about you but I think I hear the shower calling to the two of us and it's saying you two are very dirty and need to be cleansed." Sarah then laughed and said, "Wow Cole, I think you might have a little preacher man in you, a shower does sound good but I'm not sure how clean we'll get." The two of us jumped out of bed and bull rushed the bathroom like the running of the bulls in Pamplona Spain. We both nearly tripped over our own clothes heading towards the bathroom door at the same time and I then said, "We'll ladies first, I'm going to go let Shadow out to do his business then I'll join you in a few minutes, keep the water running." Sarah quickly eagerly replied, "Hey Cole, don't take too long." I quickly called for Shadow to follow me out towards the patio door so he could take care of his needs. He seemed to know exactly what I wanted him to do and that I was in a hurry, what a good dog.

It only took a few minutes and Shadow was running back into

the house and I decided to give him one of his rawhide chews I picked up at the pet store last night, basically it was a rolled rawhide stick about six inches long and a couple inches thick and should keep him occupied for a bit. I quickly made my way back to the bathroom to join Sarah in the shower, hoping she had saved her backside for me to help soap up. I felt like a kid on Christmas day about to play with one of his new toy's and it was a feeling I hadn't had for a long time. As I got close to the bathroom I could hear the water running and saw a little steam slipping through the crack of the door, I don't think I had ever been this excited about taking a shower in my entire life, these were the moments that would make our relationship so special and memorable, at least that's I was I hoping for. I made my way into the bathroom and said, "Hey you need any help in there, hope so because I'm coming in." Sarah softly replied, "Yeah, hurry up there's a few spots I can't get to, I think I could use your help." After almost tripping on the bathroom rug I just about fell into the shower and into Sarah's arms, she began to laugh uncontrollably, I then joined in and started laughing my ass off. Thank god my shower was quite larger than most or one of us could have been injured, it had three shower heads from different directions and the spray pattern was almost like that of one of those automated car washes that you would drive through, it really was quite refreshing and soothing. I could tell that it had Sarah's approval. The two of us embraced as if we had become one and our passion took over once again.

After finishing up with what was probably the longest and most tiring showers of our lives we quickly dried off and got dressed to get a start on what was going to be an emotional day with a long list of actions that lied ahead from my personal life changing decisions I had made over the last twenty-four hours. Sarah reminded me that we needed to stop by her place so she could change and send a few emails to the agency that could not be sent via a mobile device. Sarah the asked, "Hey Cole you can leave your Bronco and I'll drive if you'd like." I thought about it for a second and replied, "Yeah, that's sounds good, I'd really like to bring Shadow though, I don't really want to leave him alone quite yet, maybe after a few weeks of him getting use to his new surroundings he'll be able to deal with me not being around some of the time and I will have to put in a tall fence that seals up the backyard area." Sarah quickly answered, "Yeah, sure Cole I wouldn't think of leaving him behind, after all he is a part of our team and the more we bond together the better off we'll all be." Sarah then walked over to Shadow and gave him a big hug and a kiss on top of his head. Shadow responded by wagging his tail and kneeling down on his front legs then stretching while letting out a very soft moan, I sort of knew how he felt from getting that kiss from Sarah.

After spending the next twenty minutes getting a few things in order the three of us headed out to Sarah's place first then on to Miralani's for breakfast. Shadow was comfortable in his spot on the back seat of the Fj as we approached the main road that heads in to Sedona. I still was having a hard time believing how much my life had changed overnight. I was now attached to one beautiful woman who I would get to spend my work days with and I finally had someone to share my time off with. After reaching the main part of town we headed due north weaving our way through some small housing areas and a few gated communities. Sarah said she had just moved into a small house on the furthest northern housing project that just opened up a few months ago. I then remarked, "That sounds nice, how many bedrooms and what's the square footage?" She quickly answered, "It's a little over two thousand square feet which is plenty big enough for me and there are three bedrooms with a three car garage." I quickly replied, "That's great, so I'll have a spot in the garage for the Bronco if I spend the night." Smiling Sarah replied, "Hold on a second ranger, now you're ready to move in, just kidding Cole, I think it will be fun having two different places to continue our relationship, moving forward with it I mean and besides if we end up carpooling to work we can take turns on where to stay, that might be kind of fun." Again this lady always seemed to be thinking ahead and wanted to be well organized for whatever might come our way.

We slowly made a right turn into a driveway in front of a very nice newer style looking home. I quickly stated, "Sarah this is nice, it's definitely you, just the right size and beautiful." She then said, "Thanks Cole, I'm really happy with it and very comfortable in it." We pulled into the garage and parked. We both got out of the Fj at the same time and Sarah then asked, "Well would you like the grand tour of "Casa de Cooper"? I men that's what I call it sometimes." I eagerly replied, "Hey I like it, "Casa de Cooper" it has a ring to it, Sarah you might want to save your bedroom for the last part of the tour because I'm not sure we'll make it out of there with our clothes still on." As we both grinned a little Shadow found his way to the backyard and proceeded to do his business again. I quickly said to Sarah, "Hey please don't be mad at me but I think Shadow is making himself right at home." Sarah then focused in on Shadow and saw what I was talking about then replied, "Hey this is going to be his home part time and he might as well break in the backyard and put his scent down now, maybe now I won't have so many gophers tearing up my yard." I then replied, "Yeah and any other types of small critters might just disappear altogether, after all hunting prey is what wolves like to do, I just hope your neighbors don't have cat's that like to trespass through your yard." Sarah quickly responded by saying, "No Cole I haven't seen any cat's around since I moved in." We made our way into the front of the house and immediately I was taken in by all of the American Indian art that engulfed the foyer of the home. It was filled with gorgeous paintings that lined the walls and small animal statues arranged in the corners of the adjoining living room. Sarah began to slowly take me through the house and the more I saw the more I began to see a side of her that was truly amazing and see just how wonderful this woman was and how lucky I was to be in her life.

Shadow was still surveying the backyard when the two of us reached the bedroom, we paused a moment and looked at each other with the same thought in mind but we both realized we had a lot to accomplish today and our desires for each other would have to wait for now. Sarah then said, "I'll just be a few minutes

Cole, I have to pick out an outfit and then send a couple of emails out to the agency and let them know I'm taking a few days off, I really think we should spend some time together and get to really know one another." I quickly replied, "I couldn't agree more Sarah, I have the two weeks Parks and Recreation gave me so I might as well spend as much of that as possible with you but I will have to spend a day or two to out process from the system and handoff my workload to the other rangers and I'm sure that you will have to prepare somewhat for my orientation into S.H.A.D.O.W. and resolve any security clearance issues that may be required from my background check." Sarah nodded her head and agreed. I then went out to the backyard to check up on Shadow while Sarah took care of her wardrobe change and email requirements.

When I got outside I couldn't believe what I saw, Shadow had a dug a whole about two feet deep and two feet wide. I quickly yelled, "Shadow stop that, what the hell are you doing boy," I ran over to see what had compelled him to do this act of digging his way to China. I guess he must have overheard Sarah telling me about her gopher problem because at the bottom of the hole was a small pocket that had two what I assumed were dead gophers lying there in the fetal position. I quickly pulled him off the hole and said stay, hoping he would understand that command. I turned towards the house and could see Sarah through the patio door, I then asked, "Hey Sarah could you come her for a second, I've got some good news and some bad news." She quickly stopped what she was doing and came outside. I then heard a slight gasp before she asked, "What the hell happened?" Shadow immediately did an about face and hide behind my legs, I then replied, "Well, the good news is that you now have two less gophers in your backyard, the bad news is that you also have a hole the size of a laundry basket in your yard." Sarah then replied, "Oh well, I was thinking of putting in a pool sooner or later, I guess I know now who I can get to dig the hole for it, I hope you didn't punish or yell at him Cole." I quickly answered, "Well I sort of yelled at him, a little, I just wanted him to stop digging when I came out here and caught him in the act."

Sarah then went over to Shadow and kneeled down to his eye level and said, "It's okay Shadow, but this is bad, the hole is bad, no more digging like this okay." It was at this point I began to understand what parents must go through trying to discipline their children when it came to some form of punishment. Shadow seemed to understand what Sarah was saying to him because he constantly stared at the evidence from his mining operation while he was being scolded to some degree.

Sarah then turned and headed back to the house with Shadow actually following by her side, then the two of them went back into the house. I then quickly located a shovel on the side of the house and began to fill in Shadow's handy work all the while he was at Sarah's side while she sent out her emails. I was beginning to think he was falling for her just as hard as I had, in other words he was moving in on my girl. At least she didn't seem to upset about the hole, I think she was pretty fond of him also. After spending the next twenty minutes completing the landscaping project I returned to the house to find Sarah just about ready to head out for breakfast. I then asked. "Are we ready?" Sarah replied, "Yeah Cole, I don't know about you but I'm pretty hungry." The three of us headed back out to the garage and piled into the Fj, for now Shadow had no problem getting through the passenger side door but I could tell it wouldn't be long before he would have to get in through the back of the vehicle, and the same could be said for the Bronco. I once again commented how nice Sarah's house was and how I was looking forward to spending more time with her in both of our homes.

As we backed out of her driveway she commented, "You know Cole, this prospect of living in two different locations has the potential to be quite exciting and fun for the two of us." I then replied, "Yeah, I think so too, you know I forgot to see how big your shower was, I mean that could have a lot to do with my decision to stay the night or not." Sarah grinned a little and then said, "Well you could always just take a shower by yourself Cole." I quickly answered, "I don't care if it's the size of a shoe box, I'm going in with you no matter what, I never want to shower alone again." Sarah reacted by laughing and saying, "Yeah, me too, maybe we could try a hot bath tonight Cole, I have a really big tub in the main bathroom." After almost choking on my tongue trying to spit out my answer I then replied, "A bath, how come I didn't think of that earlier, I mean I haven't taken a bath in a couple of years, I think." Sarah then replied, "Well I guess we'll have to take care of that tonight, I mean if you want to." I looked at her and said, "Are you kidding me, if I want to, hell I haven't stopped thinking about the shower we took this morning, so hell yes I want to, I wouldn't even care if it's a bubble bath with some kind of perfume in it." Sarah chuckled a bit then said, "Okay ranger, then it's settled, you're coming home with me tonight and we're taking a bubble bath." Jesus, I felt like that kid again at Christmas with another present I was about to unwrap. I just smiled and said, "Okay." We then continued on to Miralani's.

Shadow was resting comfortably in the back again as we got closer to my sister's café. I had just called her to let her know we were on our way and that I had some very exciting news to tell her, she said great and she would try to get my favorite booth set up for us. Sarah turned to me and said, "Cole you have a wonderful sister, she loves you a lot, I just wanted to say again how sorry I am that I couldn't let her know earlier about your welfare, I know that she may resent me for that but I will do my best to make it up to her." Without any hesitation I reassuringly replied, "Sarah please don't feel that way, I know for a fact that my sister would never feel that way towards you and I know she likes you already and depending on how much I'm allowed to tell her about what we're going to be doing and how your organization saves children's lives she is really going to like you even more." Sarah paused a moment then said, "Well I hope so Cole, I just don't want there to be any issues between us that may affect the relationship between you and I." I quickly replied, "I wouldn't worry about it Sarah, once we tell her about the two of us she is going to consider you to be family and trust me you're going to be smothered by attention from her." Sarah then smiled and I could sense some measure of relief from her as she became more at ease with our plans to tell my sister about the two of us.

A few minutes later we pulled into the driveway of the café and parked in my sort of reserved spot, I was still clinging to the idea that someday Miralani would put some kind of sign or marking that it was reserved for me, oh well maybe if I keep on bugging her enough about it she'll cave in on the matter. As the Fj's motor shut off Shadow immediately jumped up and wanted out, he was a little restless this morning, my guess is that meal he had last night was bothering his stomach a little. I asked Sarah to give us a moment over on the grass to see if he had to do some business or not. Sarah quickly replied, "Sure Cole, I need to call and check in with my father to see if he got my emails and find out when he wants to meet you." As Shadow and I headed to the little grass patch next to the café I turned back to Sarah and said, "It's only been a couple of days and I'm already meeting your dad, wow you do move fast." As she began to laugh she quickly replied, "Yeah ranger and I'm expecting a ring by tomorrow." I quickly turned back towards Shadow as if I didn't hear that remark and started talking to Shadow. I could see Miralani through the window and she hadn't seen me yet, so that was good, I didn't want her to run out and interrupt Shadow while he was trying to do his business, she really liked him and would probably go to him first before me which I was totally okay with but it wouldn't matter anymore because Shadow just finished up and I quickly removed his deposit with one of the bags I got I the pet store last night. Sarah then came over as she got off her cell phone and said, "Well are we ready?" I could tell she was still a bit nervous and reluctant for this encounter with my sister.

The three of us walked into the café and Miralani ran over to greet us and began with giving Shadow a big hug, then said hello to Sarah and finally embraced me with a hug and kiss on the cheek, she quickly remarked, "Wow Cole you look great, your color, your posture and most of all you look so happy, you really look so much better than yesterday brother." I then replied, "Thanks sis, I feel great and yeah this is the happiest I've been in quite some time." Sarah then said, "Well I don't know about anyone else but I'm starving." Miralani then replied, "Yeah Sarah, let's get seated and

The S.H.A.D.O.W.'s Of Sedona

order, I've got your favorite booth saved Cole, come on Shadow you too." After sitting down Miralani stated, "You know Cole, the three of you almost look like a family, I mean you guys look like you've been together for quite some time." Figuring this was as good as time as ever to drop the bombshell about Sarah and I quickly said, "You know sis that's funny that you should say that because that's one of the things that Sarah and I wanted to talk to you about, you see I think the reason you noticed right off the bat on how happy I looked was because that Sarah and I are now a couple, I mean seeing each other, dating, together or whatever they call it nowadays and I never been happier." Sarah quickly jumped in and said, "Yeah Miralani, I mean I know what you must be thinking but it just happened and we both think it was meant to be, our feelings for each other are true and honest and we both believe it's something special, please don't be upset or angry with me." I remained quiet while Miralani was speechless and stunned.

A few moments had passed with Sarah and I just waiting for some kind of response from my sister, then finally she spoke, "Sarah you must be one special lady, I mean I've been trying to fix my brother up for years with little or no success and you got him hooked after just a couple of days, hell I'm not mad or upset, I'm impressed and I couldn't be happier for the both of you, so tell me all the details, I'm so excited." I quickly jumped in by saying, "Okay sis but there's more, I have decided to put my resignation in with the Parks and Recreation department and start a new career with the agency that Sarah works for, a federal employment opportunity that was just to appealing to pass up, I mean it's something that I think I'll be able to have great satisfaction doing." Miralani still stunned a bit quickly replied, "Jesus Cole, when you said you had some exciting news to tell me you weren't kidding, I mean a job with the feds, I thought you didn't want an eight to five job and not to mention having to wear a monkey suit." Sarah quickly jumped in by saying, "He wouldn't have to wear a monkey suit, in fact he better not." I then replied, "Sis this job is very special, a once in a lifetime opportunity and I'm not going to let it pass me by." I could

141

then see the admiration in Sarah's eyes as she gazed upon me. I then stated, "I'll be working for an agency that specifically deals with saving the lives of children and the prevention of all these horrific crimes that you hear about on the news all the time, I mean we have a chance to make a difference here and to possibly stop these things from happening." My sister sat quietly for a few seconds then said, "Cole I love you and if this is what you want to do and Sarah is the one woman you have been looking for all of your life, then for God's sake don't let anyone get in your way or prevent you from pursuing and obtaining the happiness the both of you deserve, I for one will be there for the two of you if you ever need anything and oh yeah Sarah, welcome to the family." Sarah began to cry and moved around the booth to embrace Miralani and the two of them hugged for a moment, then Shadow jumped up in the booth between the two of them, Miralani then said, "Okay Shadow I'm sorry, you're also welcomed into the family and if Cole ever needs a babysitter for you I will always be there for you." Sarah quickly slid back around to me where she then gave me a long and passionate kiss.

After our brief moment of passion Miralani then remarked, "Now that's a sight I've been waiting to see for a long time, yep I think you two do have something special and I hope you'll will be very successful in your careers and that you'll make a huge difference in this messed up world we live in today." Sarah's cell phone then went off as all of us sat there beaming with happiness and joy. Sarah's call was very brief and just when I thought this day couldn't get any better she turned to me and gave me another kiss, only this was a quite a bit shorter, she then grinning from ear to ear said, "I got my vacation request approved Cole, you know what that means, I've got the next two weeks off and that means the two of us can spend some uninterrupted time together and really get to know one another, what do you think ranger, want to shack up for the next two weeks?" Miralani let out a very loud laugh and said, "Wow Cole this woman has really got her hooks into you, you'd better be careful." I began to laugh a little also, then slowly replied,

"Well I don't know Sarah, you see I had planned spending the next couple of weeks with someone very special to me, what do think Shadow, is it okay if Sarah joins us?" Shadow quickly looked up and began to whine and moan a little, I then said, "Sorry Sarah, Shadow says he'll think about it, he also says maybe if we stop by the pet store again and pick him up some chew toy's he would consider it." Both the girls chuckled some before Sarah replied. "Really Shadow, after I let you get away with digging a hole half way to China in my backyard, that's how it's going to be, well maybe I just won't let you ride in my Fj anymore." I quickly answered for Shadow, "Okay Sarah, he says he has changed his mind only if he can ride in the front seat once in a while." The three of us then began to laugh very loudly, just then Jordan came over to take are order, she commented on how good I looked and said it was so good to have me back and okay. I gratefully replied, "Thanks Jordan, I really missed you too and all of those greasy burgers you have served me and I'm looking forward to keep grossing you out with my orders." Jordan laughed and giggled, then took are orders and then left to the kitchen.

While waiting for our food I asked Miralani, "Hey sis what about you and Sam, when is he coming back from his training?" Miralani then replied, "I just talked to him last night and he said he would be back in a couple of days, he says he anxious to see you and talk about the case you two are working." I paused for a second, then remembered the case, yes the Escalade stolen right out from under our noses, I have been so occupied with Sarah I've totally put that case out of my mind, or at least on the back burner and then there was the fact that all of the government vehicles that I saw back at the S.H.A.D.O.W. base were black Escalades. I wasn't ready to bring this up with Sarah just yet so I simply replied, "That's great sis, you know when he gets back the four of us should go out to dinner during the next couple of weeks." Sarah then commented, "Yeah, that sounds like fun and I would very much like to meet Sam, Cole has mentioned him a few times and he sounds like a very nice man." Just then our food showed up and we began to dig in, I think Sarah and I were definitely quite hungry from all of the calories we must have burned off over the last twelve hours. The matter of the black Escalade would have to wait for now, I didn't want to risk putting any stress on this newly formed relationship between Sarah and I, the fact that I was now holding something back from her was already making feel horrible but I needed more information before I confronted her with what I knew.

Shadow ended up getting some scrambled eggs with chunks of ham mixed in. Sarah was quite happy with her western omelet, Miralani had her usual cup of coffee with burnt toast and I had my favorite, biscuits and gravy country style with chicken fried steak and hash browns and my sisters place made the best I've ever had. Once everyone was almost finished I asked Sarah if she wouldn't mind going with me when I put my resignation in with the Parks and Recreation department, she quickly replied, "Cole you're stuck with me for the next two weeks and after that we'll be working together, I'm not letting you out of my sight ranger." I quickly said, "Thanks Sarah, it will be a tough thing emotionally but if your there at my side I think it will make it easier and besides I want to introduce you to some of the guy's I work with, I mean worked with, in other words I'd like to show you off, there never going to believe that I could be in a relationship with such a gorgeous woman." Miralani then remarked, "Jesus Sarah, I don't know what kind of spell you've put on my brother but I have never heard him talk like this, I mean never, I'm beginning to think this might not even be my brother." Sarah chuckled a bit then said, "Cole you don't realize how lucky I am to have landed a guy like you, I feel like I just the won the man lottery or something, you're unbelievable and remarkable and I've only known you for a very short time, I can't wait to discover all the wonderful things about you and be a part of your life." Again I was floored by this woman and her honesty and compassion, I emotionally replied, "Sarah, call it destiny or just plain blind luck but I too feel I'm the luckiest man alive to suddenly and wonderfully have you become the most important part of my life, I truly have been blessed by your presence and I'm so thankful for whatever magical or heavenly intervention that brought us together, I've never felt this way about anyone before." I could see that Sarah was starting to tear up and so was Miralani, I decided to change the subject quickly since it was starting sound like a tear jerking chick flick movie inside our booth. My sister was quite right, the things that were coming out of my mouth didn't sound like me but since meeting Sarah I've become a different person.

I looked at Sarah and asked, "Hey gorgeous after taking care of my resignation paperwork would you like to watch the sunset from a very special place that I've found over the years of exploring the hills of Sedona, I think it's probably one the most magnificent places to watch the sun go down, the colors of the hills come alive, then quietly fade away revealing the stars of the heavens." Sarah just stared at me for a moment then said, "My God Cole, I think I would follow you to the ends of the earth, yes I would love to watch the sunset with you at your special place." Miralani looked at me and just smiled, knowing that this was a special moment between Sarah and I, she then said, "Hey you two, I've got to get back to running this business so thanks for breakfast and most of all thanks for the best news I've heard in a long time, I know you two are going to be very happy together, not mention all of the fun and excitement of your new career Cole, I'll see you two again soon, take care." As she left the booth she gave Sarah a big hug and Sarah looked at me with a face of unrelenting joy and pleasure, I then asked her, "What is it Sarah?" Sarah emotionally answered, "Cole your sister is so nice, I mean she doesn't hold any grudge or ill will towards me and I'm so happy for that because the last thing I wanted to do was to cause some kind of friction between you and your sister." I looked at Sarah and said, "See I told you she would like you, my sister has a heart of gold Sarah and I have a feeling that the two of you are going to become very close and best friends." Sarah then looked at me with her watery eyes and said, "Thanks Cole and I hope your right, I really don't have any close friends with the job and all but I think I'm going to start taking some time off every now and then." At last I think Sarah was at ease with the decisions she had made concerning her security protocol in regards to notifying Miralani during my coma.

After Sarah had paid the bill like she promised we made our way out of the café and loaded up into the Fj. Sarah then asked, "Hey Cole would you like to drive?" I quickly replied, "Maybe later when we go and watch the sunset." She then said, "Okay, that sounds good to me and maybe you can give me your opinion on how my Fj performs." I then replied, "Sure thing Sarah, it would be my pleasure but don't think I'm going to return the favor by letting you drive the Bronco." She quickly replied, "What the hell, you're kidding me right, I mean if you're not I guess I'll have to reconsider taking that bubble bath with you later tonight." I then reassuringly answered, "Of course I'm kidding, you should know by now how much I like teasing people, especially those I really like." Sarah started to laugh a bit then turned her attention back to the road and said, "Hey you'll have to give me directions on how to get to the ranger station because I've never been there before." Without hesitation I replied, "No problem, it's just a few blocks off the main road." Shadow was definitely liking Sarah's Fj, maybe even better than my Bronco, the back seat area actually had much more room with the dual parallel seating arrangement. The three of us had really bonded together quite well for only knowing each other such a short time.

As we got closer to the ranger station I could start to feel my stomach getting a few butterflies and I was definitely feeling some uneasiness about what I was about to do concerning my career. I felt pretty strongly that I was making the right decision resigning from being a ranger and joining Sarah's agency S.H.A.D.O.W. and that I was still young enough to make this change without feeling like I had just wasted all my time with the Parks and Recreation agency. Sarah could tell that I was getting nervous and said to me, "It's okay Cole, I know this a huge step for you, I want you to know I will be there by your side for this new and wonderful journey your about to embark on." Just then we pulled into the ranger station parking lot and I said, "Thanks, I sort of needed that, I never thought I would be leaving this job and it's just an emotional moment that is a bit tough." Myself, Sarah and Shadow slowly got out of the Fj and headed to the main entrance it almost felt like I was walking into a funeral home. Sarah grabbed my hand and together along with Shadow by my side we entered the structure. As we made our way towards my desk there was only a couple of employee's working, all of the other rangers were out on calls, I guess this was probably the best case scenario for me emotionally. The three of us made our way to my desk when one of the administrative assistants named Carol came over and said, "Cole, so good to see you back, how are you doing?" I turned and replied, "Hi Carol, I'm doing pretty good thanks for asking, hey Carol I'd like you to meet my girlfriend Sarah," Carol quickly asked, "Girlfriend, why Cole I didn't even know you had a girlfriend, I mean I thought you were single," I then answered, "Yeah, I was up until yesterday, anyway, Sarah this is Carol, she has worked here for about five years and this place wouldn't be able to function without her." Sarah then remarked, "Hello Carol, it's a pleasure to meet you." Carol then said, "Sarah I'm pleased to meet you and might I say you are one lucky girl to land this one, Cole is one in a million, he's got to be the nicest person I've ever worked with." Sarah smiled and said, "I couldn't agree with you more Carol." I just smiled feeling a little embarrassed.

As we stood and talked for a few more minutes I introduced Shadow to Carol so he wouldn't feel left out. I then left Sarah and Carol to talk a bit while I went over to the paper forms area and just hoped that they had a few copies of the official resignation forms, I was in luck because it's not every day that an employee decides to resign so the forms that were there had probably been there for quite some time, because this agency was lacking in the computer software area the online forms were very limited and quite crude, most of the important forms and documents were all still in paper form. I quickly grabbed a couple blank forms and returned to Sarah who was still talking to Carol who was on her knees getting licks on her face from Shadow. I said to Carol, "I see that you and Shadow have become good friends, I can tell he likes you Carol." She quickly replied, "Wow Cole he's such a beautiful animal, where did you get him, I mean he's a wolf of some type isn't he?" Sarah then responded by saying, "Yeah Carol he is and I think Cole found him out in the middle of nowhere when the two of them got lost for over a week, thank god both of them have pretty good survival skills or we wouldn't be here talking about it." I knew why Sarah had just jumped into to the conversation and the reasoning behind it, so I then said, "Yep Carol, Shadow actually saved my life out there when we were lost and I'm not really sure where he came from but's it's long story and I'm still looking for some more answers to help clear the whole thing up." Carol then replied, "Well I'm just glad you made it back okay and now I have another new friend, isn't that right Shadow." At that point I figured it was a good time to head out and pick up a few more things at the store since I would probably be staying at Sarah's tonight, at least I was hoping it would turn into all night. I looked at Carol and said, "Carol it was good to see again you but we have to get going, we have a lot more errands to run and little time to do them." We all said our goodbye's and the three of us headed back out to Sarah's Fj. Shadow was really liking all of this attention he had been getting over the last couple of days and I was still amazed at how friendly he was to everyone, I mean he wasn't nervous at all around people which goes against what most experts say about wolves and coyote's. He was truly exceptional and special.

Once we got loaded up we headed to the local grocery store to pick up the personal items I needed to get to take over to Sarah's place to keep for overnight stays and I was pretty sure there were going to be lots of them. As we were driving I turned to Sarah and said, "So gorgeous, what are we going to do over the next few weeks, I mean do you have anything in mind, would you like to go somewhere or do you just want to hang out here in Sedona?" I could see that she was thinking hard to come up with an answer so I helped her out by asking, "How about just you, Shadow and me head up to the Grand Canyon and do a little hiking and swimming, have you ever been to "Havasupai Falls" it's absolutely breath taking if you've never been there." Sarah then eagerly replied, "Cole, that's a fantastic idea, I've never been there and have always wanted to go but never had the time or anyone to go with for that matter."

I quickly answered back, "Well you do now sweetheart, I've even worked their part time as a guide when I was a teenager, so I know where all the hidden spots are that are truly magnificent and not to mention very secluded if we happen to forget our swimming suits and feel like skinny dipping." I could tell that Sarah was really excited about this idea and the experiences that we would encounter together, she then replied, "Cole you've got me so excited, I mean I think we should go as soon as possible if they have any openings at the lodge, what do you think?" As we pulled into the grocery store parking lot I replied to Sarah, "Hey I'll make a few phone calls in the morning and they will make room for us if they have to, I still know quite a few people that work and run the lodge and general store, so don't you worry, I'll get us a room."

I knew that I could get us a room at the lodge I just hoped Sarah wasn't expecting any fancy because these weren't really hotel rooms by any standard, they were more like single room dorms you would see at a college campus, I mean they had no phone or internet service and no televisions either but there were a couple of rooms they always kept on standby for employees and important tribal members and that's what I hoping for because they were a little nicer. Sarah then leaned over and gave me a great big kiss and said, "You really are one in a million." At that point the three of us piled out of the Fj and then Sarah said, "Hey Cole I'll stay out here with Shadow because I don't think animals are allowed in the store unless there working dogs, maybe I can get him a special badge and vest to wear when you need to take him into places like this." I looked down at Shadow and said, "Hey boy, Sarah's going to stay out here with you, I'll be back in a few minutes' okay." I quickly turned and headed towards the mass of humanity that was entering the store, I guess this was a bad time, I usually did my shopping very early in the morning on my days off, hopefully I could just pick up the few things I needed then get the hell out of there. Grocery shopping had to be right up there with going to the dentist or doctor for a checkup, it definitely was not on my top fun things to do list, that's for sure.

I grabbed a little hand basket upon entering the store and started to make my way up and down the aisles trying to remember where everything was from when I was in here the last time but I could never remember, I guess because I was always in such a hurry just to get done and get out. My best bet was to get what I needed and hit the express line which had very few people in it at the moment. The most important item on my list was a nice bottle of wine that Sarah and I could enjoy tonight and maybe some kids bubble bath soap. At times I still thought this whole thing might be just a dream and I was afraid I was going to wake up and there would be no Shadow and worst of all no Sarah, but before I could worry anymore about it being a dream a little old Indian lady hit me in the back of the ankle with her shopping cart which hurt like a son of a bitch which led me to believe that all of this was quite real and quite wonderful. I was now in a relationship with a very beautiful woman who was soon to be my working partner and together we were going to be saving people's lives, I was so happy even with the pain shooting upwards from my ankle that I looked at the little old who was extremely upset and apologetic and said, "It's okay mam, I shouldn't have been standing in the middle of the aisle." She quickly replied, "Oh young man, you're so sweet, I'm the one that can't hardly see anymore, are you okay?" I slowly approached her and replied, "I'm fine, is there anything I can do for you, do you need any help getting any items that may be out of reach for you?" She grabbed my hand very softly then paused for what seemed like a couple minutes and then said, "You can do one thing for me, just keep on being you and kind to people, I can tell there is something special about you and I have sort of a sense that has been with me all of my life and it's telling me you are destined for great things young man, you and another, will do these things together." The little old lady then let go of my hand and slowly walked away, my hand felt like it had been under a heat lamp or something, there was something very spiritual about that little old Indian lady and I had a feeling of calmness about me when she let go of my hand, oh well, back to my shopping, I know that Shadow was probably getting very anxious to leave the parking lot area.

I grabbed the last item I needed and headed for the express checkout line which only had a two customers in it, before I knew it I was out the door where I saw Shadow and Sarah sitting in the back of her Fj with the double doors swung wide open and a couple of kids petting Shadow, I could tell he was enjoying all of the attention. As I came up to them and put my two grocery bags in the back of the Fj one of the kids said, "Hey mister your dog is really nice, is he a wolf?" I slowly turned around to answer the young boy and said, "Yeah, he is and he's very smart and friendly." The smaller boy then responded, "Wow I think I'm going to ask my mom if we can get a wolf, there really cool." I smiled a bit then replied, "What's your name son?" The smaller boy answered, "Ben", I then said, "Well Ben, you see wolves aren't really meant to be pets, they belong in the wild to help keep mother nature balanced and I didn't go out and get Shadow, the two of us just sort of found each other and became very good friends and now we live together but if he ever wanted to return to the wild I wouldn't try to stop him." The young boy looked at me with a little sadness in his eyes and said, "Gee mister I never really thought about it like that, I guess it wouldn't be fair to animals like him to be kept locked in a backyard and never get to enjoy running free." I quickly replied, "You got it Ben, you're a pretty smart young man, most grownups don't even understand what you already do but I tell you what Ben, I'm going to give you a card with my name and phone number on it and if you check with your parents about really wanting to get a dog and they say it's okay you tell them to call me and I will help find you a great dog at our animal shelter here in Sedona, how's that sound?" The young man got really excited and said, "Thanks mister, I will, what's your name anyway, I mean so I can tell my parents who I was talking to today about wolves and maybe getting a dog," I looked at the boy and said, "It's Cole and It's on the card you have, you can tell your parents that I would be happy to help." The two boys said goodbye and ran off excited about the possibility of getting a dog and meeting Shadow, I just hope their parents wouldn't get to upset with me for being too forward with them about getting a dog.

As I turned my attention back to Sarah and Shadow I could see that Sarah was just staring at me kind of funny like, I then asked, "What is it Sarah, is something wrong?" Sarah slowly replied, "Cole you truly are an angel, the way you talked to that boy Ben, I mean you just gave him an education on mother nature and how people see things differently in the world, he probably learned more in that short talk with you than he has since he's been in school, the more time we spend together the more amazed and impressed I am with you, I think Carol was right, I really did land a very special guy." I leaned over towards Sarah and gave her a very long passionate kiss. Seeing Shadow through the corner of my eye I could almost read his mind as he was staring us, it was almost as if he was sending me a message through telepathy telling me thanks for my comments about wolves but also that Sarah and I should get a room. The one thing that I could see happening over the last day and a half was that he was becoming very taken with Sarah as much as I had. As the two of us pulled apart from our lip lock I turned to Shadow and said, "Hey boy, I know you're getting a little jealous but you're going to have to get one thing straight here, Sarah is my girl too and I think the two of us can share her without any problems as long as you realize she likes me more than you." Sarah started laughing uncontrollably after that comment then said, "Hold on boys, there's enough of me to go around for the both of you, you're just going to have to share fifty-fifty because I don't want to be the one to cause any problems between the two of you." Shadow then looked at Sarah then at me and I swear he understood every word she just said. The three of us then loaded up and we were on our way.

A few minutes had passed since leaving the grocery store parking lot as we were heading back to Sarah's place, when I asked, "Hey gorgeous how about for dinner we just take a small bucket of fried chicken and a nice bottle of wine up to that secret spot to watch the sunset and yes Shadow you're invited too." Again Sarah laughed loudly and then said, "Yeah Shadow I could never leave you behind, besides the three of us are partners and a soon to be an elite team of G men and chicken sounds great Cole." Now It was my turn to start laughing loudly, "G men." I said, it did have a nice ring to it even if it was a bit out of date. I then told Sarah, "G men" is okay but S.H.A.D.O.W. agent man is much cooler, don't you think?" Sarah smiled and replied, "Cole you're too funny, for the record we just call ourselves agents, we try to leave the S.H.A.D.O.W. part out of it when we can." I looked at her with a sad face and said, "How boring is that, I mean this is probably the coolest and most important government agency in the country and we don't have a nickname yet, we're going to have to work on that Sarah." She smiled and then rolled hers eyes a little. As we pulled into her driveway Shadow woke up from his short little nap, he really was getting quite comfortable riding in vehicles, which was great because we had quite a drive ahead of us if we did indeed go to Havasupai Falls in the next couple of days. The three of us then hopped out of the Fj and headed into Sarah's kitchen. Sarah then asked Shadow if he needed to go out and do his business, I then asked Sarah if I could use her phone to try to make those reservations at the Havasupai Falls lodge, after saying, "Sure Cole whatever you need," the two of them went out into the backyard to take care of Shadow's needs.

After spending a few minutes on hold I finally got to speak with someone, who's name and voice I recognized right away. It was an old friend of mine who basically hired me part time when I was a teenager right out of high school, he had somewhat of a drinking problem back then and I used to call him "Ten Beers" instead of his real "Ten Bears" I know that's the most common Indian name you always hear in all of the movies but that was his real name and he loved me for calling him that and the practical jokes we used to play on each other. Ten Bears must have been around thirty years older than me, he decided to change his Indian name and go by Billy Two Feather's a few years back, which was actually his first name. I think at times he thought of me as the son he lost in a climbing accident many years ago when I first started to work for him. He recognized my voice right away after asking him, "Hey do you know who this is?" The voice at the other end of the phone said, "Cole is that you, damn how are doing son, my god it seems like a couple of years since I last saw you, is everything okay?" I quickly replied, "Yeah it's me, I'm okay, how's everything down in the canyon and how are you doing Ten Bears?" There was a brief pause then he answered, "Damn Cole, you know I go by Billy Two Feather's now, hey it's sure is good to hear your voice again, I've missed you son, are you planning to come down to the canyon and see the falls, it would sure be nice to see you again," he quickly replied, "A matter a fact I'm thinking about coming down in a couple of days if I can get a room for me, my girlfriend and our dog, that's if you have anything available, I know it's really short notice but the two of us just got some time off together." It only took a couple of seconds before Billy Two Feather's answered, "Hell Cole I got two extra rooms available for V.I.P.'s and there both open for the rest of the month, you tell me what days you want and it will be on me son, no cost for you and your girlfriend, I can't wait to meet her." I quickly replied, "Thanks a lot my friend, you don't know how much this means to me, you're really going to like Sarah my girlfriend and I'll bring my animal friend who you are really going to be amazed with and happy to meet, if you have next Monday through Thursday open we'll take those days and should be on the canyon floor by midday on Monday." Billy Two Feather's then replied, "Cole, consider it done my friend, let me know if anything changes otherwise I'll expect to see you on Monday." I quickly and thankfully replied, "Thanks again and I can't wait to see you again too." We both said our goodbye's with great anticipation towards seeing each other once again.

Sarah and Shadow just then walked back into the house from the backyard and she could tell by the smile on my face that she was about to hear some really good news, she then said, "Well, what's with the big smile Cole, did you get the reservation, are we going or not?" I could tell the anticipation of my answer was the reason for her hopping up and down like a little kid that had to go to the bathroom, I then slowly replied, "I have good news and bad news, the good news is that they only had room for two of us and the bad news is I'm taking Shadow instead of you." Sarah then smiled and said, "You keep talking like that ranger and you'll be taking that bubble bath with Shadow instead of me." My grin quickly changed to a look of deep concern and I then replied, "Just kidding gorgeous, the three of us are booked for this Monday thru Thursday in one of the special V.I.P. rooms and my friend is picking up the tab, so that gives us the weekend to get our supplies for the trip and plan our activities and hikes." Sarah then leaped from almost five feet away into my arms and nearly tackled me to the floor, then softly said, "Cole we're going to have the time of our lives, hiking every day and finally getting to see all those beautiful waterfalls in the canyon, I'm so excited, I need to go out and get some new cargo shorts, new tank tops, new socks, new hiking boots, new sun glasses, new backpack and most of all of new bikini and you can help me pick that one out." Gasping for air after she had finally finished telling me her shopping list I then said, "Hey we're only going to be there three and half days but I will definitely help you pick out a bikini." Sarah gave me a kiss on the lips and then she headed off to her bedroom to see what she had and what she was going to have to get for the trip.

Shadow and I decided to turn on the TV and check out the forecast for the Havasupai area next week to help Sarah with her choices concerning her wardrobe. The two of us sat on the couch like we owned the place, I just hoped Sarah was really going to enjoy this trip, I still was not even sure how much she really liked hiking and the outdoors. I guess I had better tell her about the hike down to the canyon floor to get to the lodge, it was a pretty stout hike and not for the novice hiker, however there was another option to get down to the canyon floor which was a ten-minute helicopter flight service that ran several times a day from atop the canyon rim. The weather should be perfect this time of year consisting of cool mornings and topping out around eighty-five during the day, perfect for hiking early and then swimming in the pools of the falls and hanging out till later in the afternoon and hiking back to the lodge as it cools down. All of this I would run by Sarah once she returned from the bedroom. After watching the weather forecast over the next week it confirmed my expectations and it looked like it was going to be wonderful.

Sarah then snuck up behind me and said. "Close your eyes Cole, I want to get your approval for this outfit I'll be taking on our trip, now slowly turnaround and keep your eyes closed," I eagerly agreed all the while trying to turnaround without falling over the couch, I then said, "Okay but I hope it's something that shows off that cute butt of yours," Sarah then replied, "Okay ranger, open your eyes." I slowly opened my eyes and damn near fell forward over the couch trying contain myself, there in front of me on the other side of the couch was Sarah standing completely naked with a bottle of wine in one hand and two wine glasses in the other, she then said, "I thought we could take that bubble bath a little earlier than we planned if that's okay with you." Trying to climb over the couch as fast as I could and looking like a drunk Olympian hurdle racer I almost fell flat on my face. I couldn't hardly speak but finally after gathering myself I replied, "If that's all you bring on this trip, I will be a very happy man and hell yeah let's take that bath now." The two of us headed back to the master bathroom and Shadow stayed out on the couch seeming to enjoy watching the weather channel. Once we got to Sarah's bedroom Sarah she started to run the water and I peeled off my clothes as fast as I could like I had just fallen into an ant hill. Sarah was giggling the whole time watching me get undressed. This lady was putting me through some of the most emotional highs I've ever experienced.

As I stood in the bathroom doorway I just stared at this gorgeous woman who was running a bath completely naked and looking like a Michael Angelo statue as she was stirring the water while leaning over the edge of tub, my god I was such a lucky man. Sarah's tub was very large and custom shaped in the form of an oval. It was plenty big enough for the two of us. The water was full of the bubbles and getting close to the top, Sarah turned around and asked, "Do you think this is enough Cole?" I then replied, "I guess, I'm having a hard time taking my eyes off of you stirring all those bubbles around."

Sarah then placed the bottle of wine and the glasses on a little table next to one end of the tub, she then gently climbed into the bubbly abyss and disappeared up to her neck. I quickly moved closer to the edge of the tub and said, "Hey could you maybe put your knees up so I don't end up stepping on your legs and then busting my ass while falling out of the tub." She then laughed and said, "Don't worry Cole, there's plenty of room and I'll make sure you don't slip and fall." I slowly made my way into the hot bubbly water that seemed a bit slimy from all of the soap, I couldn't believe it but it felt so soothing and relaxing and as my ass hit the bottom of the tub I said to Sarah, "You know, this was a great idea, I don't remember my bubble baths as a kid feeling this wonderful, maybe it's because I've never had a beautiful woman in the tub with me before, you know all I can think about right now is how the hell are we going to have sex in here without creating a tidal wave and getting your floor all wet." Sarah then said, "Don't worry about the floor Cole, I do own a mop you know." With her beautiful smile that followed, I then slowly slithered my way up next to her as she handed me a glass of wine.

We began to talk about our plans for the trip to Havasupai Falls and who's vehicle we wanted to take. I recommended we take the Bronco because I would be more comfortable driving since I was familiar with the route and on the way back we might try some off roads trails for the last twenty-five miles or so. Sarah thought it was a fantastic idea and that she was really looking forward to this time together. Between the wine and the heat of the water in the tub it didn't take long for the both us to became very relaxed yet aroused at the same time, high tide was only a few moments away, I was totally on board with how fast this relationship was moving and how my feelings towards Sarah had grown over the last couple of days, she was my best friend and the woman who was quickly stealing my heart.

8

PARTNERS FOREVER

The wonderful bubble bath and the water activities Sarah and I had just performed led to a mop and bucket brigade for the two of us, it seemed as if almost every drop of water ended up outside the tub on the bathroom floor. The two of us couldn't hardly stop laughing, we paused to take a break from the mopping just so we could get our strength back and to check on Shadow, at this point wearing only our underwear when we headed out to the living room to relax on the sofa and talk some more about our trip, Shadow had joined us and was laying down on the rug next to the fireplace. We talked for about an hour on things like what our likes and dislikes were, from everything to food to our opinions on politics, we were really digging into our most inner feelings and opinions, the two of us were finally getting know each other in a way other than just the pure physical pleasure and the attraction that we shared for each other. The more we talked the more we found out how much alike the two of us were and maybe why this relationship had moved so fast up to this point. As it started to get later in the afternoon I asked Sarah, "Hey are you still wanting to go and see that sunset I promised you, I mean we don't have to if you'd rather stay here and just relax." She quickly replied, "Yeah Cole, of course I still want to see it, it sounds like it will be wonderful, especially if I'm with you." I looked at her and said, "Well I guess that means we should probably put some clothes on then."

Sarah then giggled a bit and remarked, "Well at least for the ride there, then we'll see what happens once we get there." I smiled, then replied, "Wow woman you have a one track mind and I love it, I just hope my physical stamina is going to be able to keep up with you, you agents must train pretty hard, I'm not sure I'm going to be able to handle the physical requirements of this job." Sarah laughed then said, "Oh believe me Cole, I think you're in better shape than you realize." After turning a little red I again suggested that we stop and get a bucket of chicken on the way to watch the sunset, Sarah agreed and we headed back into to the bedroom, I hoped to get dressed because I was pretty worn out from the bath.

Thirty minutes had passed and we were both now dressed and almost ready to head out the door. Shadow was done with his puppy nap and I was about ready for one myself but I knew that I would get my second wind if Sarah was going to let me drive her Fj to our destination just outside of town. The three of us loaded up into the Fj and I assumed the drivers position. Once we were all in Sarah said, "Hey don't be afraid to put this thing to the test Cole, I would really like to get some idea of how capable it is off road wise, I've always been a little worried it's not been built tough enough to handle some of the more challenging trails around Northern Arizona." I gladly replied, "I'll do my best without breaking anything sweetheart, I wouldn't want to get you mad at me." Sarah chuckled a little then said, "You'd better not break my baby, I put a lot of sweat and tears into the restoration but if you do break something you'll just have to spend more time with me in order to fix it." I smiled as we pulled out of her driveway and began our trip to my secret location where the sunsets are spectacular but first we needed to stop and get that bucket of chicken and something for Shadow to eat.

After a few minutes I pulled over and called Miralani on my cell phone to see if she was still at the café to see if she might be able to whip something up for Shadow for us take with us, she answered right away and said, "Hey Cole, what's up, everything okay?" I then asked, "Hey sis if your still at the café you think you could make

Shadow up a little to go box of food, Sarah and I are heading out to watch the sunset and were getting a bucket of chicken for us but I'm not going to give that crap to Shadow, can you help us out?" Miralani quickly replied, "Damn Cole, you really have fallen hard this woman and I'm glad, I really like Sarah and she's probably the best that's happened in your life for a long time, Cole I would love to help you out, if you want I can just watch Shadow for you and you can pick him up later tonight if you two want some alone time." I paused on the phone for a second wondering if Shadow was ready to be left with someone for a period of time. I was pretty sure he would be fine and not freak out or anything like that. After my brief pause I then said, "Okay sis you got a deal, I guess now is as good a time as any to see how he reacts to me not being around him all day and he needs to get used to seeing and being around other people as he grows into adulthood, are sure you want to, I mean you didn't have any plans for tonight did you, because if so it's no problem that he comes with us." I could hear the eagerness in Miralani's voice when she replied, "Cole you know that I fell in love with Shadow from the moment I first saw him, so hell no I don't mind, I'm really excited for the opportunity to spend some time with him and for the two of us to become close friends." I then told her, "Okay sis, thanks a lot, I really appreciate this and it will be nice to spend some time alone with Sarah, see you in a bit." I quickly ended the call and got back on the main road to head to Miralani's.

Sarah was looking at Shadow in the back when she said, "Hey Shadow you're going to get to spend some time Miralani and I bet she is going to spoil you rotten with food and love." I turned to Sarah for a brief second and said, "Yeah that's what I'm afraid of, he probably won't want to come back to us after spending some time with her." We reached the café in less than ten minutes and the three of us jumped out of the Fj and headed into the café where Miralani was waiting anxiously with her arms held out towards Shadow, she quickly motioned for him to come to her and then she said, "Come here Shadow, you're going to spend some time with aunt Miralani and were going to have such a great time but first let's see what we have to fix you for dinner." I got down on my knees and gave him a big hug and said, "Okay boy, Sarah and I are just going out for a few hours and we'll be back for you okay, I promise you, Miralani is going to take good care you my friend." Shadow then looked at me with those big yellow eyes and began to wag his tail as if to say it's okay, I'll be alright. This animal was so special and so smart I swear he could almost read my mind at times. Shadow then sprinted towards my sister and began to rub up against her legs showing his sign of approval. I could tell that Miralani was touched by the telling signs of emotion from him. Sarah and I turned around and slowly walked out the door. Sarah grabbed my hand and said, "He'll be okay Cole, he's in good hands with your sister." Sarah could tell I was a little upset with leaving Shadow, this was the first time we'd been apart since coming out of my coma and it was very emotional for me and probably as well for Shadow. As Sarah and I pulled out of the parking lot I really got this overwhelming feeling of peace and gratitude from the path that Sarah and I were heading down, the connection or bond the two of us were creating was truly becoming more than just physical, it was becoming spiritual as if we were destined to be together and I believed she felt that same sense of bliss that I did.

The sun was about two hours from setting when we pulled into the drive thru-chicken joint, we quickly picked up are order and then headed out to the hills of the southwestern portion of Sedona. This was a favorite area of mine due to the beauty of the surrounding mountains and hills that reflected the sunlight off the brightly colored landscapes of Sedona creating magnificent sunsets. It would take about thirty-five minutes to reach our destination then we would have enough time to enjoy our meal along with some wine, after all we really didn't drink that much or even have a chance to enjoy it during our bubble bath. The paved section of the road was about to run out and from then on it would get a little rougher the closer we got to the secret spot. I asked Sarah if it was okay to get the Fj a little dirty because there was a couple of little shallow creek crossings that were only a foot or two deep but it was going to be quite muddy in a few spots, she quickly replied, "Oh yeah, I want to see what this old thing can do and see just how to drive it in those conditions, I never really got educated on the proper techniques of four-wheel driving and ins and outs of using all of the different gear ranges." I then replied, "We'll you get a bit of an education on this little trip and maybe this weekend we can go out around the local area on some beginner trails and we'll get you up to speed on how to really fully experience the capabilities of this vehicle." Sarah bursting out with emotion then said, "Wow that would be great Cole." She then leaned over and planted a big kiss on my cheek.

The dirt road was definitely becoming more like a trail now and Sarah was really starting to enjoy the ride, she was getting to see what this great classic vehicle was made to do. I'm sure the brilliant black paint job was going to look more like an old big fat ripe avocado by the time we got back and especially when Sarah could see it in the morning. I then told Sarah, "Hey don't worry about how dirty it gets, I'll wash it in the morning for you." She quickly added, "You mean we'll wash it, it might be fun." I sort of had to agree with her, it probably would be a lot of fun, not to mention the two of us would more than likely be soaked afterwards. We were just about ten minutes away now from the spot and the trail was still pretty challenging, I knew it was about to open up and become much flatter as we neared our destination. Sarah was still smiling and having a great time observing her Fj perform wonderfully. As we continued on Sarah asked, "Hey Cole are you happy about how things have worked out so far and how fast our relationship has blossomed, I mean do you still think you made the right decision with your career change and all of the other choices you have had to make over the last few days." Totally surprised by the questions from Sarah I stopped the Fj and suggested we take a break from the trail and that we get out to stretch a bit and talk. Once we were out and leaning up against the back of the Fj I put my arms around her and said, "Sarah I want you to know this is the happiest I've ever been in my life, you're the most wonderful woman I have ever met and the most exciting, you've put some kind of charge into my life that makes me feel so great and now I have someone to share all of the fantastic things life has to offer, I really think we were destined to be together and as far as my career choice is concerned that's something I may not have an answer until I've been with you and the agency for some time but at this point I'm thinking yeah, I made the right decision and I couldn't be more happier than I am right now." Sarah looked into my eyes and gave me a long wonderful kiss that seemed to put both of us at ease with how fast things were going between us.

After spending a few more moments talking about our future and how happy the two of us were we then got back on the trail and pressed on. The sun was still about an hour from setting so we still had plenty of time to eat and watch the sun slowly descend and disappear towards the west. After a few more minutes had passed we reached the top of the flat mesa that overlooked all of Sedona and the surrounding hills. Sarah jumped out before I could even come to a complete stop, she was spinning around like a top just trying to take everything in, this spot was truly heavenly. I shut off the Fj and jumped out to join her, she quickly ran up to and said, "Jesus Cole, you weren't kidding about this spot, this view is like a real life postcard and we're smack dab in the middle of it. I have never seen Sedona like this before, it's amazing, thank you." I quickly replied, "I thought you would like it, I discovered this place about ten years ago and it's like no other, the views and tranquility are sometimes spiritual for me, I have never brought or told anyone else about this place, you're the first Sarah and now it's our spot." I slowly put my arms around her and she did the same, we just stood there holding each other for a moment taking in the beauty and wonder of this place called Sedona.

Our chicken was smelling pretty good and the two of us were pretty hungry and the sun was close to setting so we set up our makeshift dinner table which consisted of a very old looking thick Indian blanket that Sarah had along with a large lantern which was from the modern era that belonged to Sarah, it was very bright from the massive L.E.D. light source, not like my old style

"Coleman" lanterns that barely provided enough light to find your way out of a tent. During our meal we began to talk about all of the great things we would hopefully accomplish as partners working for the S.H.D.A.O.W. agency. The chicken went down very quickly and so did the wine, I told Sarah one glass was all I wanted because going back down the trail at night was a little more challenging and demanded all of my senses and attention, besides over the years I had seen so many horrible accidents concerning drunk drivers not to mention the horrible camping and hiking incidents that left people very badly injured or in some cases death. Sarah agreed with my feelings towards drinking and driving and then said, "Cole you're a very wise man for your age and I think that's one of the things that has really drawn me to you, not to mention your kindness, your big heart, your love for animals and mother nature and most of all ranger, I think you have the nicest butt I've ever seen on a man." She then busted out laughing uncontrollably and then quickly said to me, "No seriously Cole, I know this is going to sound kind of crazy and I've been holding back from saying this because we have only known each other for such a short time but seeing the effects of time firsthand like the past, the future the present, it's all connected the worst thing a person can do is to hold on to something believing there will always be time for it later, what I mean Cole is I'm trying to say that I have fallen in love with you and I want you to know that now in case there is no tomorrow, you're the man I want to spend the rest of my life with, however long that might be." I sat motionless for a second then looked into her eyes and said, "Sarah I feel the same way about you, I don't know what the future may bring us but I do know that the present has brought me so much happiness since I've been with you and can't even imagine ever not being with you, I am in love with you Sarah and I will always be there for you, even if it's somewhere else in time, you're the most precious part of my life and I'm so glad destiny brought us together." We both then turned just in time to see the sun finally set behind the hills of Sedona with a burst of red and orange light that was now reflecting off Sarah's beautiful face. I truly believed we were now soulmates and our spirits were connected.

The darkness consumed the area around us except for the bright glow of the lantern and the wonderful lights from Sedona piercing upwards towards the heavens. Having been in each other's arms for the last five minutes we decided to pack up and head back before it got too late to pick up Shadow at Miralani's. After a few minutes were on our way and could hardly keep our emotions in check, it would be a long wait till we got back to Sarah's and let our passion for each other take control once again. The lights on the Fj were the only thing that I could recommend to Sarah that should be upgraded or have an additional set of "KC Day-Lighters" added to her bumper, I did give her a full report on my opinion of the performance of her Fj and it was outstanding, the restoration she did was great and it performed terrific on all of the different types of terrain we covered on this trip. Sarah was quite pleased and asked, "I can't wait for you to teach me how to really drive this thing Cole, I just hope I don't break it learning." I quickly replied, "Don't worry sweetheart, what you might happen to break remember it can always be fixed and I can show you on how to do that also if you'd like, I mean I know you have mechanical skills regarding engines but if you need help with setting up or repairing any type of suspension parts I'm your man." Sarah smiled and then said, "So you're my man, I kind of like the sound of that." I could see the glow on her face and the brightness of her eyes even though it was dark inside the Fj, she truly was as happy as I was.

After reaching the pavement and now back on city streets I handed my phone to Sarah and asked her to call Miralani to let her know we were about fifteen minutes out from picking up Shadow, she said, "Okay, should I make sure she is still at the café or do you think she went home?" I looked at Sarah and said, "You don't know my sister that well yet, she practically lives at the café, she usually doesn't get out of there until around ten or eleven because she always does her daily totals and re-orders before the next day of business, she is a very dedicated business woman who has become quite successful so I'm not the one to question her approach on how to run a business." Sarah then replied, "I know that she is a very meticulous person who pays attention to details, I've noticed that about her in just the few times we've met, she's a really nice person and I hope that we can become good friends in time." Sarah made the call and Miralani was still at the café as I suspected, we were getting fairly close to the café now and I was getting excited to see Shadow again, it was nice to spend some time alone with Sarah but I must admit I really hated being away from him, the two of us had made quite a bond since our meeting in that shaft where I found him. I could tell that Sarah knew what I was feeling also and she then said, "I bet you can't wait to see him again, huh Cole." I nodded my head and smiled, then said, "He's my best friend Sarah, I mean he saved my life and the two of us have something special, not just the usual loyalty from a pet but something much more, like his ability to understand everything that's said to him, it's almost like he can understand the English language, you know I still don't even know how a wolf of his type was ended up down this far south from his normal range of habitats, I mean he shouldn't be any further south than Utah or Colorado or maybe parts of the northern rim of the Grand Canyon, there's still a lot I have to learn about my friend." Sarah then replied, "Give it time Cole, both of you will become even closer than you are now, with time and companionship your bond will probably be stronger than any human relationship could ever be." I looked at her and said, "You know, I don't think it will be as strong as the bond the two of us have but it might take a close second, thanks for being so understanding when it comes to Shadow and the feelings we have for each other." She simply smiled again and put her hand on mine.

After a few more minutes of silence we arrived at the café and we walked up slowly to the window of the café to see if we could see Miralani and Shadow and what they might be up to and to know surprise there sat my sister with Shadow in a booth and it looked like she was reading him a bedtime story or something of that nature. Sarah started to giggle and I said, "Yep, that's my sister, she's going to spoil him rotten, I can't believe she's reading to him." Sarah quickly defending Shadow said, "It's okay Cole, remember you're the one who told her he's part of the family now, so she's probably going to treat him so, I mean like a baby brother and why the hell not, Shadow is very special and deserves it." I knew Sarah was right and that I am probably spoiling him just as much but in a different way. The two of us walked up to the door and knocked because it was after business hours and she always locked the door after closing, she quickly came into view and Shadow had stayed in the booth until he saw Sarah and I, he then leaped out the booth with the grace of an acrobat, even at a young age he was already showing the gracefulness of the wolf breed who are known to be some of the most cunning and stealthy animals in the world, in other words they are very quiet and don't leave signs of their presence and are very difficult to track. After seeing Sarah and myself and successfully clearing the edge of the booth that he was sitting in, Shadow then sprinted over to greet us and almost took out my knees from his power slide on the tile floor. I quickly got down on my knees to avoid any ligament damage and to give him a great big hug, he was so excited to see Sarah and I, after all we were probably the parental figures in his life at this point and his loyalty and love for the two of us definitely showed.

After a few minutes of getting a tongue bath from Shadow Sarah then decided to join us on the floor and take part in the reunion. Sarah gave him a big hug and said, "You see Shadow, we came back for you and I'm sure you were in very good hands with Miralani and probably got lots of treats and love." Miralani then spoke, "Well we had a great time the two of us, we played out back for a bit, then we had a great dinner and then we had a fantastic after dinner snack, I think this has probably been the best date I've ever had with the male species ever, Cole like I said before if you ever need me to watch him all you have to do is ask." I stood up and gave my sister a hug and said, "You got a deal sis, I certainly will and I'm sure Shadow won't mind either." Sarah then stood up after her tongue thrashing from Shadow and said, "Thanks again Miralani, Cole and

I had a good long talk, a nice little dinner and it was so beautiful to watch the sunset from that location, it was very special and it will be a forever memory in my mind." Miralani quickly replied, "Sarah you know you are like family now and I can see that you two make such a great couple, the glow from both of your face's is absolutely magical, I don't think I've ever seen a more passionate and caring relationship blossom so fast between two people, both of you are so lucky in have something very special." I quickly interjected my thoughts and said, "Thanks sis, I told Sarah you were a very good person and the two of you really have a lot in common and I bet you guy's become very good friends." They both looked at each other, embraced and Miralani then spoke, "I think you're probably right on that Cole." Sarah smiled then turned to me and said, "Well we should probably be heading home we don't want to keep you from your business tasks Miralani, we've taken up enough of your time for tonight." I agreed with Sarah and gave Miralani a big hug and a kiss on the cheek then told her we'd probably see her sometime tomorrow, we then headed out the door and into the Fj.

Shadow again was resting in the back seat area of the Fj and I could tell he must have had a very good and tiring time with Miralani, Sarah was driving and I could tell she was a little tired also. We both had full stomachs from the chicken and we probably were going to hit the sack early in order to be refreshed for a big day of shopping tomorrow consisting of all of our needs for the trip to Havasupai. It was still a little weird knowing I was going to stay with her at her house as if it were our house, at least that's how she was treating the situation and I was really taken by how generous she was with her possessions. I suggested that we should maybe work out some kind of schedule on where to stay and that it might be kind of exciting and fun to just change it up once in a while when we were out and about. I think we both already knew that a serious commitment was going to come our way and we'd probably have to make some kind of permanent housing arrangement, at least that's what I was hoping for, I was convinced that she was the one I wanted to make a commitment to. Sarah looked at me and said, "Yeah, that's a great idea and it does sound like fun, it could work to our advantage when we didn't want anyone to know where we might be at any given time, the lack of traceability sounds intriguing." I then asked her, "Hey Sarah there's something I've been wanting to talk to you about but have been afraid to bring it up thinking it may lead you to think that I don't trust you or there's some kind of criminal accusation coming from me, when we get back to your place I'd really like to talk to you about because I don't want anything kept in the dark or to hold on to secrets that may harm our relationship in any way." Sarah turned to me looking very concerned and then replied, "Cole, you know you can trust me and that you can ask me anything that is on your mind, if I can help put any concerns or uneasiness you might have about our relationship or about the S.H.A.D.O.W agency I'll gladly answer anything to help put the issue to rest." After hearing that response from Sarah I was at peace with what I would be asking her when we got to her place.

It only took another ten minutes or so and we arrived at the house, the three of us piled out the Fj, Shadow was still a little tired and sluggish as he walked behind us, it seemed as if he already knew where to go and what he needed to do as he headed out to the side of the house then wanting to be let into the backyard, I'm sure he had quite a bit to eat back at the café and had to take of business. Sarah quickly called for him to come into the house and then proceeded to walk with him into the backyard, the two of them were bonding very quickly, the three of us were becoming our own little pack and quite loyal to each other, it was truly amazing the sense of love and devotion that Shadow was displaying towards Sarah and I, we were a family and very happy with our lives. The two of them returning from the backyard looked so content and happy I almost wished I had gone out with them but then I remembered how much food Shadow had probably eaten so it was probably better that I had stayed in the house. I'm sure I would get stuck with the clean up tomorrow morning. Sarah walked over to me and sat down as Shadow went over by the fireplace and laid down which was allowing some cooler air to filter in and cool him off. Sarah then asked, "Okay Cole, what's on your mind?" I paused for a second and thought carefully on how I would start this conversation of what was probably going to sound like some kind of interrogation from the police. I then spoke, "Sarah I don't want you to take any offense to what I'm about to ask you and you know that I love you and trust you one-hundred percent but something has been bugging since I first saw it back at the S.H.A.D.O.W facility, okay here it is, before my little mishap in the underground caves I was working a case that involved an abandoned vehicle with no trace of any ownership or missing persons for that matter but once I had it impounded and before we could run all of the proper checks and inspections to help lead us to the legally registered owners it was stolen from the Sedona impound yard." Sarah quickly interrupted by asking, "So what the heck does this have to do with me or the agency?" I quickly answered her, "We'll Sarah that's what I'm trying to get to, you see when you were walking Shadow and I through the garage and motor pool area of the underground base I happened to notice all of the black Escalades parked in the one area and I can't stop thinking that maybe one of them might have been reported missing and could be the one that I found abandoned just outside Sedona, I'm not accusing you or your agency of any wrong doing or anything like that I just wanted to bring it to your attention, that's all." Sarah sat there quiet for a brief moment then replied, "Cole I'm not mad or offended but this does raise my curiosity about a possible misuse of some of our government vehicles, you see Cole there only meant to be used as a transport of personnel or transportation of equipment." We both sat silent for next few minutes.

After thinking long and hard Sarah finally said, "Okay Cole, when we get back from our little trip to Havasupai Falls you and I as partners are going to look into this, consider it our first training module, I think we can learn a lot from each other and the different techniques in investigation methods, I definitely want to get to the bottom of this." I let out a little sigh of relief then replied, "Thanks Sarah, thanks for trusting me on this and believing in me, I can't wait to learn from you and I think I can teach you quite a bit about tracking and profiling when it comes to human tendencies and habits." Sarah looked at me and smiled then said, "From what I've read on you from the background check I had to do when you were out of it in the coma you're a very talented and gifted tracker, one of the best I was told by our people, so if we can teach our strong points to each other we should make one hell of a team." Without any hesitation I replied, "I totally agree with you, I can't wait to start learning all the ins and outs of this job and the satisfaction from the end results and I think you and I are already one hell of a team." The two of us made our way closer to each other and eventually in each other's arms once again. After one of the most intoxicating kisses I've experienced in my life the two of us headed over to her computer and desk to start planning and plotting out our daily schedules concerning the hikes and how many of the waterfalls we wanted to see during our stay. Since we both were on the same work schedule now we had plenty of time before we had to commit to returning to work so we could be quite flexible on how long our stay would be.

An hour had passed and the two of us had pretty much figured out our whole schedule for the stay and what we wanted to accomplish on this romantic getaway and hopefully experience some of the spiritual magnificence this wondrous creation of God had to offer. Sarah and I headed back to the bedroom to retire for the night while Shadow had passed out in front of the fireplace and was snoring like an old man with a cloths pin on his nose. It had been a very long and tiring day for all of us and I think we were all looking forward to a good night's sleep. Tomorrow would be a little less hectic and a lot easier going except for the shopping, I wasn't sure how Sarah was going to be when it came to shopping but I hoped she wasn't going to be like my sister, that woman could spend weeks in a mall. I knew that Sarah and I would have to pack fairly light for this trip because no matter what option we chose either the ten-minute helicopter ride or the 8-mile hike down to the lodge we wouldn't want anything more than a large backpack for each of us. I was looking forward to see how much outdoor knowledge

Sarah had when it came to hiking, camping and survival techniques, this was going to be a fun trip for us and I think an opportunity to learn a lot from each other and a good time to start Shadow's training in tracking and verbal commands for scent recognition and other techniques that search and rescue dogs learn. I'm pretty sure he was going to be a very quick study and be one amazing partner to have help Sarah and I from time to time. Sarah and I laid down on the bed wrapped up in a fetal position about as close as two bodies could get to one another and then quickly fell asleep.

The next morning, we were awakened by a pounce on the bed and a very wet and cold nose being shoved into our faces which was followed by a slobbery tongue slapping us around like something you'd see from an old "Three Stooges" TV show. Shadow had burrowed his way in between us and was not going to budge an inch, Sarah began to laugh then gave him a great big bear hug and said, "Hey boy, do you need to go out?" She then looked at me as if to say it was my turn, so I jumped out of the bed and Shadow then soon followed, "Come on boy, let's go take care of your business," I said, I knew after holding it all night he was probably quite anxious to relieve himself. Sarah quickly said, "Hey Cole aren't you forgetting something?" I stopped for a second then replied, "What, I can't go naked out into your backyard, okay I'll put my shorts on." Sarah giggled a bit then said, "I'm sorry Cole but I do have some nosey neighbors, I wouldn't want you to scare the hell out of them, they might think you're some kind of peeping Tom or something and call the police." I thought to myself for a second, does she think I look like a peeping Tom when I'm naked, no she's just trying to be funny, I hope. She started to laugh again, then said, "Jesus Cole, will you hurry up and take him out, he's doing the Texas two-step while you're trying to figure out whether or not you look like I peeping Tom, believe me I'm only kidding but I do have nosey neighbors." As I walked away with Shadow I turned and said, "Okay but I'm just putting my underwear on and that's it." She kept on laughing only now a little bit louder.

Shadow took care of his business then the two of us headed

back into the house, it was a good thing he was quick about it because it was a little chilly standing out there in just my underwear. After closing the patio door, I turned around to see Sarah standing in the kitchen with just a t-shirt on and looking as beautiful as ever, once again I couldn't believe how lucky I was to have met and fallen in love with this wonderful woman who was now my best friend, my partner, my lover, my spiritual mate and hopefully the woman I would spend the rest of my life with. Shadow returned to his now favorite place in Sarah's house, right in front of the fireplace where he promptly laid back down and assumed the nap position. I walked over to Sarah as she was just starting to cook some eggs on the stove and reached around her waist, then gave her a light bear hug and kissed her on the back of the neck, then said, "Good morning gorgeous, anything I can do to help?" Softly and seductively she said, "Yeah, you can take your arms off me or we'll end up back in the bedroom before you know it." I slowly squeezed her a bit tighter and said. "Oh I like the sound of that but I guess I should eat first to get my strength up and maybe some coffee so I can be wide awake to gaze upon your beauty." She shrugged for a second then turned around and softly said, "Oh your good ranger, that's got to be one of the smoothest lines I've ever heard from a man trying to get me into bed." Smiling from ear-to-ear I then kissed her on the nose and headed to the kitchen table to read the ads in the morning paper to see if there might be any good sales on some of the items we needed to get for the trip.

The smell of the bacon and salsa covered hash browns was making me quite hungry, I turned to observe Sarah's cooking talents and she looked like a woman possessed by a master chef or something, I mean she was so precise and orchestrated in her movements from side to side of the kitchen it was really impressive. I was under the impression that she knew her way around the kitchen and was probably a fantastic cook, this relationship just kept getting better and better. Shadow was wakened by the smell and had locked in on the stove area with his nose and I knew that he was getting quite hungry himself. "Hey Sarah, do you think we can put some of that bacon grease on Shadow's dry dog food," I said. Sarah then replied, "Sure no problem, do you think it's okay for him to eat?" I quickly answered, "The guy at the pet supply store said putting it on their food once a week was very good for their coats." Sarah looked at Shadow then said, "Hey boy, you feel like eating breakfast, I think you're going to like it, lamb and rice dog food with a bacon grease topping and I might throw in a tiny bit of scrambled eggs." I looked towards Sarah with a very sad face and said, "Wow, what am I going to get?" Chuckling somewhat she replied, "Don't worry, I'm going to take care of you too Cole, you're getting my special hash browns with some of my homemade salsa along with the bacon and eggs." Feeling quite special at this point I turned to Shadow and said, "You see boy, she likes me more than you but I'm pretty sure you're a very close second." Sarah quickly dropped to the floor and gave Shadow a great big hug and kiss, then spoke, "Don't you listen to him Shadow, I love the both of you just the same." Shadow went crazy licking her as if she was a human lollipop. "I swear Sarah, this wonderful creation of God knows what we are thinking and saying, it's as if he understands the English language or something." She just smiled and kept soaking up all the attention Shadow was giving her.

After our fantastic breakfast had been totally consumed by all, Sarah and I got our shower out of the way with just the act of cleansing in mind, in other words there was no extra physical water sports involved other than lending a hand to one another, which was actually was quite enjoyable. We needed to get an early start to our day because there were actually quite a few good sales going on today which met our needs for the trip and the quantities I'm sure were very limited which meant if you didn't get there when the store opened you didn't have much of a chance to take advantage of the good deals. After getting dressed and grabbing our list we headed out the door. I asked Sarah when we got finished we should head back to my place to drop off the supplies and maybe we could stay the night at my place tonight and tomorrow night, then get an early start to get on the road Monday morning. We were both getting really excited and looking forward to this trip. I think this was going to be a great learning experience for the three us. I was planning on teaching Sarah some basic tracking skills and maybe some training for Shadow as well. It would be interesting to see how Shadow would respond to other dogs being in the area, there were sure to be campers in the canyon who had brought their pets. Sarah then spoke, "Cole if I'm going to be spending the next two nights over at your place I'll have to go home and grab some personal items and my hiking boots, everything else that I'll need we can pick up today, it was time for a new wardrobe of outdoor attire anyway." Smiling a bit, I replied, "Remember we're back packing in so you might not want to get to much stuff." She then said, "Just because I might happen to buy quite a bit of clothes doesn't mean I'm taking it all with me, remember Cole us women really like to shop." Sarah just smiled at me as we were backing out of the driveway.

Sedona only had a few places that carried the gear we were looking for so we wouldn't have to drive all over of the place to check off the items on our list. For the most part we didn't need to get any freeze dried foods since we would be getting most of our meals out of the general store at Havasupai. I did however want to get about five pounds of beef jerky here and divide it up between our two packs. As we neared our first stop Sarah asked, "Cole, how much water do you think we need to pack in for the hike down to the canyon lodge?" Pausing for a second, "Oh probably just a canteen each for the two of us and maybe two bottles of water in each pack, that should be enough for the three of us." I reassuringly replied. "Oh good, that doesn't sound too bad, I know that water can get very heavy after a while," she said. I quickly added that Shadow was probably going to drink more water than the two us combined, because he was still fairly young and his stamina was not going to be anything like it would be when he became an adult, wolves have been known to hunt their prey for hours upon hours sometimes with little or no water. Shadow was probably around seven months old and had a long way to go before reaching adulthood.

After parking we quickly entered the place of business and

began to look around for the items we needed. Sarah headed right to the outdoor clothing area and I had a feeling she might be there for some time. Turning back and looking at me she then said, "Hey Cole I'll be over here if you need for me, I see something I already like." I quickly replied, "Okay, I'm going to check out some of the other gear we need and maybe a couple of new backpacks, you know they make these really light ones nowadays." Sarah quickly turned her attention back to the clothing area and disappeared as if she was consumed in a maze of clothes racks. Shadow and I headed over to the outfitters section which I hoped was going to have everything we needed for this trip. Shadow was behaving very well amongst the other customers that were gravitating towards him and inquiring about his pedigree and how old he was. He truly was special and had an attitude and spirit that was calming yet showed signs of a great warrior. The two of us finally made it to the camping section where we then headed towards the backpack area to see what they had to offer. As I was looking at a couple of particular backpacks I happened to notice a small animal pack for dogs that looked like it might fit Shadow, I quickly picked it off the shelf and fit it over Shadow's head and shoulders, it was a little loose but it had some adjustment straps that I tightly adjusted around his frame. It was a perfect fit and he seemed to be okay with it, well at least Shadow was finished shopping, now for Sarah and I.

I peeked around the corner to check on Sarah and it looked she already had quite a basket full of items. I knew she probably wasn't going to bring most of the stuff she was buying but she was just covering her bases in case she didn't like some of the items when she got home. That's just the way women shop when it comes to clothes. Men on the other hand usually wait until something wears out before we shop for a replacement or anything new and that's just the way we are. I knew that anything Sarah ended up buying she was going to look great in, she was such a beautiful woman and probably could have been a model if she had chosen that career path. I continued to grab all of the other items we needed as my cart began to fill up quite quickly, I must admit that I too was probably buying some items that I knew we wouldn't be taking with us but this place really did have some great deals going on this weekend. I made sure that I grabbed a new emergency first aid kit and a new fire starter stick because it was always a good idea to keep those types of things updated and within the dated codes. There was even a special type of canteen for dogs and it looked like it would fit in Shadows pack, so in the cart it went. I slowly made my way over towards Sarah where she was holding up a pair of cargo style shorts that really looked good, as I approached her I said, "Hey lady, you going to buy those or just keep holding them up in the air?" After a brief pause she turned around and replied, "I really don't know, what do you think sir, you think these shorts will make me look fat?" I smiled then said, "Sweetheart you'd look in a gunnysack, I would make a remark about your butt and legs and how nice they look but I'm afraid you might tell your boyfriend, then I'd be in big trouble." She then laughed and lunged at me wrapping her arms around me then spoke, "Oh mister, you let me worry about him, you just keep telling me how nice I look and I might just go home with you." We both began to laugh quite loudly then started to check out all of the items in each other's cart.

As we were checking out I grabbed an assortment of sun tan lotions and bug repellent, this time of year there could be a lot of mosquitos around the stagnant pools of water. I had a little bit of a natural deterrent when it came to insect bites, I guess they didn't much care for Indian blood but on the other hand they would probably be quite happy to feast on Sarah, since she was so sweet. We completed checking out and headed out to the Fj, "I hope all of this gear fits in my Fj," she said. "No worries, even with Shadow in the back you've got plenty of room," I replied. We pretty much got everything we needed except for some snacks to take along for the road trip which would be around four hours, it was just under two-hundred miles from Sedona to the "Havasupai Hilltop" parking area. Sarah was quite eager to find out what kind of physical shape she was in considering all of the training she had to complete to get hired in by the government, she had told me the eight-mile hike to the canyon basin should be no problem for her. I was hoping she was right, to be honest I was more concerned about Shadow not being in good enough shape because of his young age but then again he was a wolf and their stamina is known to be amazing. After completely loading up the Fj and with Shadow being squished in the back as if he were in a package of sardines, I guess I was wrong about the load capacity of her back cargo area, we then were ready to go. Shadow was still being content even though I know he had to be uncomfortable being in such a small confining space. I patted and stroked the top of his head and said, "It's okay boy, we'll get back home soon enough after we unload some of this stuff." He licked my forearm, then laid down and curled up into a tight little ball, after turning and looking at him very quickly Sarah said, "Yeah Shadow, that's a good little wolf, I'll give you a special treat when we get to my place, you just relax and I'm sorry my Fj isn't any bigger for you." She then looked my way and smiled.

It only took ten minutes to get back to Sarah's place and she only broke the speed limit nine of those minutes. The three of us headed into the house and Sarah went back to her bedroom to drop off some of the stuff she picked up today and to pack up for the trip. "Cole don't freak out by how much stuff I'm bringing, most of it will be for when I stay the night from time to time, if that's okay with you," she remarked. "Okay but you're not taking over my bedroom closet," I immediately replied. Sarah smirked, then continued on to her room. Shadow and I decided to hang out in the living room and watch some television, I was hoping there might be some "Top Gear" episodes showing on the BBC network, that was definitely one of my favorite shows, I could watch the reruns over and over because it was so damn funny, not to mention the great cars and trucks they showcased and test drove. Once the TV came and on I turned the channel to BBC and Shadow and I were in luck there were two more episodes to be shown over the next couple of hours, although I hoped we wouldn't still be here after that. I made one final yell back to Sarah to see if she needed my help for anything then turned my attention back to the show after she acknowledged by saying no. Shadow fell asleep very quickly and I had become entranced with the show, Sarah walked by a few times to grab some items out of her hall closet all the while being very quiet and sneaky, I guess she didn't want to wake up Shadow or bother me while I was watching the TV.

An hour had passed and Sarah came out of her bedroom towards the living room and said, "Well, I think that's about it, I'm all packed for the next week or so, maybe tomorrow you can help me pick out the stuff I should probably take on our trip, that would be helpful and kind of fun, I mean I could model some of the outfits for you that I bought today." Turning my attention away from the TV. "Hell yeah, I like the sound of that, we can always come back here before we leave if you think of anything you might need," I quickly stated. "Sounds good to me Cole," she replied. Shadow was still sawing logs by the fireplace which had definitely become his spot. I then asked Sarah, "You want to sit and talk a bit or just load up and head to my place?" She then sat down beside me and replied, "Sure, let's talk, at least until Shadow wakes up, what's on your mind?" I then looked deep into her eyes, "You are Sarah, you're on my mind, I can't stop thinking about how lucky I am to be with you and how wonderful my life has become and we haven't even started our working relationship yet, I know this trip is going to very helpful for the two of us to really get to know each other and answer all of our questions we might have towards one another but I think it's also going to a great learning experience that the two of us can benefit from." Leaning in towards me she slowly put her hand on my cheek then passionately kissed me, then spoke, "Cole you are with a doubt the most endearing man I have ever met, in the short time we've been together you've managed to capture my heart and soul and I think this is just the beginning of something very special for us, I believe in destiny when it comes to love and I believe that we will be partners forever." As my heart was feeling as warm as the Arizona sun from her response I put my hands behind her neck and gently pulled her close enough to see the sincerity and love in her eye's, then with the gentleness of a soft breeze our lips met in perfect harmony.

An hour had almost passed as we sat and talked about life, death and the spiritual world and its relationship to heaven. It was so amazing how close our feelings and beliefs were the same. Sarah was a very well educated woman and seemed to have such a vast knowledge of the human race and the differences in so many cultural behaviors and beliefs, just in the short time we had talked I had felt as if I were a student in a classroom listening to a college professor or a professional public speaker, she just projected so much self-confidence and wisdom it was so very comforting and educational at the same time, not only is she the most beautiful woman I've ever met but also the most intelligent. I was starting to think if I was going to be able to keep up with someone so gifted, I knew I was in for some pretty intense training once we returned from our little vacation. All I know is that I was totally committed one-hundred percent to this woman both emotionally and soon to be professionally and I knew that she felt the same towards me and that would be enough to get us through any rough times ahead.

Shadow began to wake up and we decided to load up and head to my place for the next couple of days before our trip. Sarah seemed to be at ease with the switching off between our two homes but eventually there would have to be some kind of permanent arrangement that worked for the two of us. After putting a stop mail slip on her mailbox we pulled out of her driveway and she then yelled, "Woohoo, I'm on vacation, see you later home sweet home." Chuckling some, I then replied, "Yeah woohoo, me too." I couldn't believe I had just said the word woohoo, she was starting to affect my proper use of the English language that I was so proud of by completing all of my Jr. college courses. I was already learning new things from her and I didn't mind one damn bit, even if it made me appear less manly or tough, after all I did have a pretty tough sounding name. Speaking of names, I then asked, "Hey Sarah do you have any nicknames like the one the security guard at S.H.A.D.O.W. called you, I think it he called you Coop, I kind of like that, is he the only one that calls you that?" Sarah paused, then smiled, "Pretty much Cole, I think everyone else is a little afraid to use that nickname for me, you see Charlie has been around me most of my life and is really good friends with my father and my father is the guy in charge at S.H.A.D.O.W., so you see kind of why he is pretty much the only one that has ever used that name for me." Smiling, I then replied, "Well I really like it, I mean it fits you like a glove, I think it's perfect for you and who you are and what you do," she then said, "If you like it Cole I don't mind if you want to call me that, or you can make one up if you want." Grinning like a little boy who just took the last slice of pie I quickly replied, "Yeah, I sort of have one in mind, how about Peaches?" Nearly running off the road she reached over and slapped my shoulder and began to laugh a bit, "Peaches huh, I bet you thought long and hard on that one, I guess I'll have to think of one for you taking in you being an Indian and all." I began to laugh also then changed the subject very quickly and asked if she wanted to stop on the way and just pick up some fast food for dinner, then we could just take it easy and relax the rest of the night, she agreed to the idea.

After getting our order from the Mexican take out place we headed on to my home. Shadow was really getting excited with the smell of the food that was filling the inside of the Fj. "Hold on boy, we'll be home in a few minutes, then I'll feed you your food, sorry no Mexican food for you buddy, maybe I'll cut up some leftovers from the other day and mix it up with your food." Sarah reached around her seat and stroked the top of his head and that seemed to calm him instantly, lucky guy, she hasn't done that to me but then again I don't think it would calm me down one bit. Sarah and Shadow had developed such a good relationship it was so wonderful how the three of us were getting along like a family and to him I guess we were members of his pack. I really believed that this special bond would play a huge roll in the training and the use of Shadow to work with Sarah and I once we became established and qualified to actually go on assignments for the S.H.A.D.O.W. agency. I knew that he would be an excellent candidate to train for tracking on scent recognition and the overall alertness of his species would definitely be useful when it came to our safety. The three of us together were going to be something special I felt, the good that we would be able to achieve in a world that was spiraling out of control gave me hope that we really could make a difference.

After pulling up in the driveway I asked to Sarah to hold on for a second and I would open the garage so that she would be able to park in the garage next to the Bronco, "Okay Cole, that sounds good to me, do you need me to park to the far right side of the garage in case we need to load something in from the passenger side of the Bronco?" she asked. "Good idea sweetheart, most of the big stuff will be on the roof so Shadow can have more room in the back but there is going to be some snacks and other stuff that we'll need inside with us." I said. Shadow stayed in with Sarah and I jumped to help guide her in. After Sarah parked she and Shadow got out of the Fj and we headed to the backside of the house where Shadow ran to the grass and did his business as usual, Sarah and I walked in through the kitchen door, putting the food down on the counter, she then asked, "Hey Cole do you have any cold beer in the fridge, nothing goes better with Mexican food than a nice cold beer." This was a woman that had all the right stuff, I mean she likes beer with her food over wine, how lucky I was. Shadow came running up to the patio door after he finished his business and wanted in, I'm sure because he had to smell the aroma of the food for about five miles and he was probably hungry on top of that.

Sarah had retrieved a couple of beers from the fridge and I was getting Shadows food out to mix up some steak and chopped up carrots, carrots are really good for dogs and the steak will provide a flavorful mix with his food. I was going to make sure he ate very healthy during his development stage which would be at least a year and a half. He would need to become strong and have great stamina for what he was going to be trained for. On the other hand, Sarah and I were already fully developed which meant the two burrito's and tacos with an extra side of refried beans would not affect us at all, except for maybe later in the evening and only in a weight aspect if we didn't work it off of course. I grabbed a bag a corn chips up on top of the fridge and opened it up, then took a container of homemade salsa out of the fridge that Miralani makes for me, the beans and the salsa along with the chips would almost be enough for a meal by themselves. Sarah and I sat down at the kitchen counter and Shadow was at the end on the floor, I gave him his food first, then Sarah and I dove into our Mexican style buffet. We each had a burrito and one taco, the damn burritos from this place that I frequent a lot are probably about the size of a half used roll of paper towels, in other words they were huge and very good. Sarah bit into hers and I could hardly keep from laughing as the burrito was almost bigger than her head, "Hey you might want to cut that thing in half if it's too heavy to lift up to your mouth," I jokingly said. Quickly she put the burrito down before it could cause any more carnage on her face, "Yeah, you may be right, I think I've got more on my face than in my mouth, my god these things are big." I finally couldn't hold it in any longer and let loose with loudest laugh I've had in quite some time. "I'm sorry sweetheart, it's just that you have beans and cheese all over your cheek, not to mention what's all over the backside of your hand," she broke down and began to laugh with me.

Shadow broke up the laughter by sticking his head up over the counter as if to say thanks and to see what was so funny. In his own way I believe that he was laughing also, at least his tail was wagging wildly. Sarah quickly grabbed a knife off the kitchen counter and sawed the thing in half, "There, I think I can handle this beast now, what do you think Cole, want to use the knife on yours?" Saying nothing I picked up my burrito and shoved it into my wide open mouth and took a bite off it like a grizzly bear would bite into a freshly caught salmon. "Wow, that's impressive Cole, better not choke, I would hate to have to make a mess all over your kitchen floor while trying to save your life," she said. Almost choking from that statement alone I swallowed my food quickly and replied, "Your concern for my wellbeing is touching sweetheart, I think I will need that knife though, that bite almost stopped my breathing, I guess I was just trying to impress my girl," smiling she then said, "Cole I already know you have a pretty big mouth, so you don't need to display acts of manhood by shoving a three-pound burrito down your pie-hole." Sarah was right, I was acting like a teenager on his first date but it was sort of fun and exciting, once again this woman was causing a dizzying and euphoric effect on my better judgement, maybe this is what true love feels like.

After finishing our dinner, Shadow included, the three of us headed to the living room to relax a bit and talk some more about the upcoming trip. We agreed that tomorrow we would take it easy and just relax as much as possible and get our newly acquired backpacks in order and that included Shadow's new pack and his load as well, he was going to carry his own load if possible. Most of his food would consist of dried food and beef jerky. Sarah and I had picked up some freeze dried packets of food but for the most part we would probably get all of our needs from the general store. On the subject of food, Sarah then asked, "Hey will we be cooking our own food or eating at the lodge, I mean when we're hiking our meals might have to be out on the trail or at a campground fire pit or something." Pausing for a second, "Probably a little of both Sarah, I think for the most part we can get by on a big meal for breakfast then hold out for dinner, you're probably not going to want to eat too much if we're hiking and swimming all day." I replied. "That sounds like a good plan to me, I'm not going to feel like doing much hiking if I overeat," she said. "Well if we get hungry out on the trail I can show you how to track a rattlesnake and cook him up, after all they really do taste like chicken," I quickly replied. Sarah gave me a funny look and then said, "I think I'd rather starve myself for a day or two instead of having to eat any kind of snake." I began to laugh then said, "Don't worry sweetheart I'll take care of you out there, we'll have plenty of food to snack on during the day." Sarah then leaned over and gave me a great big hug and kiss, "My hero, I know I'm in good hands with you watching over me, I just hope I don't let you down on keeping up with you, I know that I'm in good shape but nothing like you Cole, you are one fine representation of the human male species," she stated.

After the redness faded away from my face I said, "Why thank you Sarah and may I say the same could be said about you, except for the male part of course, I remember as a kid looking at the nude magazines like "Playboy" that belonged to my father and always wondered if I would ever get to have a girlfriend that looked like the models in those magazines and now I don't have to wonder any longer, I have you and you're even more gorgeous than any of those women that ever posed for those magazines." This time Sarah turned completely red and replied, "Why Cole Youngblood, that might be the sweetest and most sexist comment anyone has ever said to me, you really think I'm prettier than those girls, I don't think so, my hips are too wide, my legs are too long, my boobs aren't big enough and my ass is too small, other than that I'm just fine." I immediately burst out loud laughing for a second then said, "Are you kidding me, you're a super model and don't even know it, I mean come on Sarah, have you looked at yourself in the mirror at all, you've must have had guy's chasing after you all of your adult life," she paused for a moment, "Okay Cole, you can cut it out, I know you're just saying those things because you love me, look I really have never had the time to even notice if any guys have been chasing me or not, between my schooling and traveling with my father all over the world I just didn't have enough time to get involved with anyone seriously." I then looked and smiled at her, "Well you are now sweetheart and you are the prettiest woman I've ever met and I'm going to remind you of that as much as I can," she smiled and then kissed me on the cheek, "Thanks, it's been so long since I can even remember what it's supposed to feel like to be a woman and not just dressing up like one, Cole you've sparked a fire in my heart and I'm so lucky to have you in it, I truly love you with all my heart," she said.

After spending the next ten minutes just talking and holding each other tightly we decided to retire back to the bedroom and try to get a good nights sleep. The two of us were now in a totally committed relationship to each other and it felt absolutely wonderful, there was a peace and calmness that had come over us and something we both needed desperately and it was long overdue in my opinion.

Even Shadow was a big part in our feelings and the tranquility that he brought to our little pack could not be overlooked. He decided to follow us back to the bedroom and plop down on the floor near the end of the bed. It seemed as if he already knew that we were all planning to go on a big trip somewhere and he too was wanting to get some much needed rest, after all he was still just a pup and their energy levels can get depleted so very fast that they really do require a huge amount of sleep per day to insure a healthy development during their adolescence period. After a few minutes in the bathroom trying to wash off the layers of refried beans off her face Sarah emerged wearing just a tee-shirt with a yellow road hazard sign on the front and it said "Danger, Slippery When Wet" I was totally speechless for a second, "Jesus, how do you expect me to get any sleep tonight with you wearing that?" I nervously commented. Pausing for a second she replied, "Well, I could take it off it bothers you," I quickly sat up at the end of the bed, "Bother me, I love it but I'm not going to be able to keep my hands off you tonight if your wear that, don't you have like a onesie or whatever they call those pajamas with the feet sewn on them?" Laughing uncontrollably for a bit she finally gathered her composure and said, "I tell you what Cole, I'll put on a pair of gym shorts I brought with me." It's not that I didn't appreciate her nighttime attire but I was really looking forward to a full night's sleep, the morning on the other hand would be an entirely different matter. After returning to bed with her gym shorts and tee-shirt on Sarah quickly slithered over to my side and put a big bear hug around me and said, "Sweet dreams ranger," Then it was me laughing while she was rolled back over to her side of the bed.

We were both awakened by Shadow jumping on the bed around five-thirty in the morning, I guess he needed to go out and take of business. During the night Sarah and I had found our way back together and were knotted up like several strands of Christmas lights, it must have been comfortable because we both slept through the whole night. Shadow was trying to burrow his way between us and was succeeding in his task, finally the two of us gave in and let him muster his way in. Sarah started to rub behind his behind his ears and he immediately began to moan and groan like he was about to have some sort of climax or something. "Okay boy, Cole's going to take you outside so you can do your business and when you come back I'll finish with the massage," she said. At that point I gave them both a dirty look and jumped out of bed and said, "Come on boy, let's get it over with, I know it's a little chilly outside but you're the one with the fur coat." The two of us then hurried down the hallway towards the patio door, where I quickly opened the door and swooshed Shadow out, he immediately ran to a sunny part of the yard and relieved his bladder. I knew it must have been in the low forties or colder because there was steam coming off his pee, it was kind of funny actually but I didn't laugh because I didn't want to embarrass my friend. Once finished he quickly ran back towards me and the door so I opened it up all the way because his coordination was still a little suspect at his age and especially now since he was acting a little goofy and wanting to play. The two of us then went trouncing back towards the bedroom.

I was the first to dive back onto the bed and almost knocked Sarah completely off the bed, "Damn Cole, what the hell are you doing, there's plenty of room for both of us," she said. "I know sweetheart but I wanted to beat Shadow up here so I get a massage instead of him," I pleadingly replied. Sarah quickly rolled over and jumped on top of me, "I'll give you a massage alright but first I'm going to rough you up a bit," she said. At this point I knew I was in for an ass kicking, she was a very physical girl who liked proving how strong she was and I found that quite alluring and unique. Once we got to Havasupai I think I was going to have to show her the old Indian leg wrestling technique, I'm sure she would really like it, I'm also sure I would be able to embarrass her. I could tell our relationship was going to constantly grow with these challenging physical encounters but I believe that the two of us really enjoyed this type of behavior especially if it led to more intimate interactions. My next move was to lie still and take the beating or fight back, I decided to cover up and absorb the punishment for my swan dive onto the bed but I would have my revenge soon enough, Shadow watched in horror as the abuse continued from Sarah.

It was a beautiful Sunday morning as the sun was beaming through the windows of the house, the three of us now lying on the bed just relaxing and enjoying each other's company. I looked at Sarah and said, "Hey why I don't make breakfast for you and you just relax here in bed, it's going to be a lazy day why not start it out right," she grabbed my hand then pulled me close to her and said, "You're an angel Cole but I need to get up and get some coffee, then I can start modeling some of the outfit's I got yesterday, I want to make sure I don't look like Indiana Jones or something worse." I quickly replied, "I think you're more the "Laura Croft: Tomb Raider" type, only a hell of a lot better looking than that actress who played her. "Really, you think I'm prettier than her, I don't, I mean she's got to be one of the most beautiful in the world," I could tell Sarah was getting a little bit embarrassed at this point so I changed the focal point back to me, "Hey do you think I'm better looking than Indiana Jones?" I jokingly said. Sarah began to laugh again and couldn't seem to stop this time, she was grabbing her stomach and curling up into the fetal position, finally she said, "Cole, you're definitely no Indiana Jones," pausing for a second she then said, "He looks like an old man in all of his movies, you on the other hand look like a man in real life, a man who has swept me off my feet." She slowly and gently put her arms around me and then said, "I love you." I softly kissed her on the lips, "I love you too Sarah," I emotionally said, then gave her a great big bear hug.

The two of us finally got up out of bed while Shadow was sawing logs and had no great desire to get up anytime soon. Sarah and I headed down the hallway towards the kitchen seeking our first cup of coffee of the morning. "Hey I'm still making breakfast for you," I cheerfully said. "Okay but I'll make the coffee," she replied. I began to take out the ingredients to make my famous Indian breakfast, our parents made this for us growing up and it was always great, not to mention so easy to make. Miralani even made her own version of it and put it on the menu at her café. It was one of the favorites of the locals who were regulars for breakfast. The coffee was brewing and there was nothing better than the that aroma early in the morning. I had just started the scrambling the eggs when I heard Shadow slowly meandering down the hallway from the bedroom. I'm sure it was the smell or the sound of me chopping up all of the ingredients that woke him up. Once everything was all cooked up and mixed together I put it in the oven at a 250 degrees just to keep it nice and hot until I could get the bacon cooked up, this is where I believe Shadow's nose was going to come alive and he would be right at my feet begging for some, he will get a few pieces and some of the bacon grease poured over his food when everything was done. Sarah brought my coffee over to me and the feeling of my hand touching hers as she passed the mug to me was so incredibly sensual and heartwarming at the same time, I truly was so in love this woman it was almost like a fairytale or something, she was so perfect.

After the bacon was finished I immediately gave Shadow a slice then put everything on the table. As Sarah sat down I went to the fridge and got the orange juice, jelly and butter for the toast. The last task before I could sit down to eat was to pour some of the cooled down bacon grease onto Shadow's food and give it to him and hope he would stay preoccupied for a bit while Sarah and I our breakfast. I made enough to feed a small army but then again I usually could eat two or three helpings of this stuff, it was that good. Sarah began to dig in and the expression on her face was priceless, "Damn Cole, this is fantastic, it looks so simple but the combination of onions, potatoes, steak and eggs with the salsa on top is absolutely mouthwatering," she quickly said after her first bite. I just nodded and kept eating. The coffee and juice were the perfect match to this meal it all just went together so well, each ingredient just brought out the flavors of all the others. "I'm so glad you like it sweetheart, thanks for being here to enjoy it with me, I just wanted to do something nice for you and show how happy I am that you're in my life and I love you, you're an incredible woman Sarah. Turning somewhat red in the face she almost started to cry, then said, "Cole, you and I have something special here and it's only going to get better, we're so fortunate to have found one another in this crazy world of ours I'm just so happy that we did, I love you too." For the next ten minutes we just kept looking at each other with an occasional bite of food in between and Shadow had laid back down by the fireplace to take a nap, it was quite peaceful.

After finishing our breakfast Sarah and I headed off to the shower and god only knows what might happen once we got there. The shower was refreshing and exhilarating as I expected it to be, afterwards I asked Sarah, "Hey, do you think we're really saving water by showering together?" Again she burst out with an uncontrollable laugh and then said, "Well I don't know about the water savings but I think the two of us our getting one hell of a cardiovascular workout that's got to be beneficial to our health." Laughing somewhat myself I then smiled and said, "Yeah, it's a lot better than jogging around the neighborhood." Laughing together the two of us finished getting dressed and began to get all of our stuff staged in the living room so we could decide what to take with us on our trip. Mine was pretty much ready to go I just needed to pack it up in the backpack but Sarah would have quite a few decisions to make on her wardrobe after buying so much yesterday. Sarah was staring at her backpack when I said, "What's wrong?" Slowly she turned towards me, "I don't think this pack is going to be big enough Cole, how many days are we planning on being there?" Cautiously I replied, "Don't worry sweetheart, that pack will hold everything you need and some, we probably will only be there four days maybe five if we decide to take a couple of hikes off the beaten path." She slowly turned her focus towards the backpack on the floor again, "Well if you say so but it sure looks awfully small to me," she said.

An hour had almost passed but we finally got all of our gear staged and separated by needs and wants, now came the hard part for Sarah and especially for me because she was about to start the modeling fashion show that I would ultimately have to pick which outfit's looked the best on her. At least I would get to see her undressing and dressing over and over as long as I kept saying I was undecided but I think she would catch on to that pretty quickly and then I would be in for another ass beating. My pack was already loaded up except for the snacks and water I wanted to take down along the hike to the canyon floor but that would only take a few minutes to load up in the morning. Sarah on the other hand was still going back and forth trying to figure out the actual size of the backpack and if she might have missed any more hidden compartments that might hold a few smaller items of clothing. Finally, the modelling show started and we were on our way to finishing up with the backpacks then we could move onto the garage and get the Bronco ready for the trip, mostly just checking all of the fluids and washing it. I knew it was in tiptop condition as always but one should check everything out before a long trip. The long drive would be good for the engine and for me, it had been sometime since my last vacation and I was really looking forward to this one because I had Sarah with me now to share in all of the wonderful sites this part of the country has to offer.

Shadow had now started to move around a bit with all of the commotion going on in the living room and Sarah then said, "Hey Shadow, you want to help Cole pick out some of my outfits too." He looked at her for a moment then laid his head back down as if he were saying "Hell no, I'd rather go back to sleep" at least that's how I interpreted his body language. Sarah on the other hand just said, "Okay boy, I know your still tired, that's alright because I think Cole will do a good job by himself." Sarah started to take off her jeans and tee-shirt then picked out a really nice looking pair of light brown cargo shorts that had more pockets than a pool table, she then put on a darker brown colored button up shirt with almost as many pockets but I have to admit it looked fantastic on her, as almost anything would. I quickly remarked, "Wow, you look great, I mean you look like someone you'd see on TV on one of those survivor shows or something, I definitely like that outfit for starters, okay let's see the next one," she smiled and began to strip down to her underwear again, this might be fun after all. The outfits kept coming and I was really getting into this whole thing, I mean I was truly enjoying watching and interacting with the woman I love and I know she appreciated all of my input and suggestions, even the smartass ones. We really were great partner's and would be forever.

9

HEAVEN ON EARTH

After the fashion show had ended and only taking a couple of hours we headed out to the garage and even Shadow finally woke up to help with the chores of getting the Bronco ready for the trip. Sarah and I entered the garage and Shadow followed. Sarah started to get the washing materials needed for the job, the bucket, sponge, wash mitts and the squeegee for the windows, she then asked, "Hey Cole, do have some kind a special soap for this fancy paint of yours?" After poking my head up and around the corner of the hood I replied, "Yeah, I sure do, it's in the big white cabinet on the wall, along with all of the other cleaners, this should only take a few minutes then I'll be done with checking everything out and I'll give you a hand." After turning her attention towards Shadow who had grabbed one of the wash mitts and took off with it she yelled while chasing after him, "Hey Shadow, come back here you little monster, Hey Cole your wolf is attacking that wash mitt." Laughing a bit and watching her chase him was pretty funny, "Hey Sarah you better just let him have it until he drops it, he probably thinks it's some kind of sheep or something, after all that's what it is supposed to be made of," I jokingly remarked. Quickly she stopped running after him and he immediately stopped and then lied down about ten feet or so away from Sarah. I then asked Sarah to keep an eye on him as I backed the Bronco out of the garage and onto the driveway, she replied, "Okay, I don't think he's going anywhere right now I must have run him down pretty good like he did too me." I smiled then closed the hood.

It always felt so good just to sit in this vehicle and look at the beautiful Bald Eagle with stars and stripes in the feathers of its wings that was painted on the hood, it was truly a work of art and definitely fit the personality of its owner, I loved my country and was proud to be an American. The next feeling that was almost as good was the turning of the key to start the powerful V-8 that sat underneath that beautiful eagle. The garage erupted with a thunderous fury bellowing out of the dual exhaust tips just under the back bumper, it was music to my ears. I did notice Sarah and Shadow jump a bit when it turned over, I pushed the clutch in and shifted into reverse the just letting the clutch out ever so lightly without any gas just letting the idle of the engine propel it backwards out of the garage, once out I'd let it warm up a little to avoid any carbon deposits on the cylinder walls. Most people don't realize that if you shut off an engine frequently when it's not warmed up enough there's a good chance you're scaring the cylinder walls with carbon build ups which will shorten the life of an engine. After a few minutes and seeing the temperature gage get to where I was comfortable I turned the Bronco off, making sure all of the windows were completely closed, I jumped out and went over to the side of the house and drug the hose over. Sarah had picked up the wash mitt that Shadow had got bored with and walked away from and was now checking out my activity with the hose, I'm pretty sure he may have not ever seen one yet and didn't know what was about to happen, my mind started racing on who I should spray first with the water, it was a no brainer, I was about to get my revenge for the ass beating that Sarah gave me earlier this morning and like they say, "Revenge is a dish that is best served cold" and I'm pretty sure that the water coming out of the hose was going be quite cold.

After the thorough drenching I gave Sarah with the hose the two of us began to wash the Bronco, with me climbing up on the bumpers and rock rails in order to get the roof clean, I asked Sarah if we weren't too tired after washing it I'd kind of like to get a fresh coat of wax on it, I mean it was going to probably sit out in the sun for almost a week and that's never an ideal situation for any paint job even with a car cover the sun could do some heat damage on the paint if it weren't protected with a good coat of wax. "I think we can do that ranger, if you promise to help me wax my Fj when we get back," she remarked. I quickly and reassuringly replied, "You got a deal lady, you know you might want to come up with a new nickname for me since I'm not really a ranger anymore, I mean I really don't mind." Sarah then said, "Okay but I'll have to take some time to think of one that's worthy for you." We both smiled then got back to washing, I did find one thing out for sure, it's much quicker to wash this beast with two people going at it. While Sarah and I slaved over the chore of washing and drying the Bronco Shadow had made himself comfortable lying down in front of the house, he really had become a great companion and part of our little family. After an hour of drying and cleaning the windows I finished up with the custom wheels I had put on a six months ago, they were spectacular looking, a five spoke design with a touch a red paint mixed in with the polished aluminum set them apart from any I had ever seen before and they accented the paint job quite nicely.

After the Bronco was dry enough to my satisfaction in order to put the wax on I pulled it back into the garage to avoid another cardinal sin where automobiles are concerned, never wax a vehicle in direct sunlight, it will ruin a paint job. Sarah applied the wax and I was in charge of taking it off, I always did it by hand and never used a power buffer or anything like that, it was not worth the risk of possibly burning through the paint and ruining the paint job. Shadow had moved into the garage to join us but then immediately laid down on the car cover in the corner of the garage, I was hoping he wouldn't get to attached to that, I guess I was going to have to buy him a couple of those big round dog beds, one for the house and one for the garage. Sarah and I were moving pretty fast as a team and this wasn't going to take as long as I thought. The afternoon was passing by quickly and we still needed to get everything loaded in the Bronco and I wanted to spend the rest of the afternoon and evening just relaxing with her. We finally finished around three o'clock and the Bronco was looked fantastic, Sarah turned to me and said, "You know Cole, I think I'm going to try to find one of these for myself, it's absolutely gorgeous, I mean in a patriotic way and it's so beastly looking with all of the extras you have put on it." Staring at her standing next to the Bronco I replied, "Wow, I don't know which one of you is actually more gorgeous, you or the Bronco but I think I'm going to have to go with you sweetheart." I quickly moved towards Sarah then suddenly put both of my arms across the hood then kissed the emblem on the side fender and said, "I love you so much sweetheart, never forget that." In the corner of my eye I could see Sarah coming at me full speed and not saying a word, maybe I had gone a little too far with that comment, she had to know I was only teasing her, well I guess I was about to find out.

Stopping just short of my chest and sticking her face right into mine she softly said, "Well I guess I'm going to have to work on stealing you away from your sweetheart, turning her attention towards the Bronco she put her hands on the hood and leaned in within a couple inches of the fender and with the most seductive soft voice I've ever heard come out of a woman's mouth, she softly whispered, "That's too bad you'll be stuck up on that lonely parking lot by yourself while Cole and I are skinny dipping down in the pools of the falls, don't worry though, when we get back I think I'm going to start staying over a lot more and parking my Toyota in the garage right next to you just so you won't get lonely." Totally blown away from the tone of her voice and the descriptive nature of her passion for me I slowly replied, "Jesus Sarah, that was downright mean and yet really sexy at the same time, I think we should go into the house before a fight breaks out." Slowly she lifted her hands off the hood and turned towards me with a smile that quickly became a grin followed by a huge laugh, "Cole you better say you're sorry or I'm going home right now," she said. Then she quickly added, "Hey I'm only fooling around with you, now let's get in the house and make up." She then chased me all around the backyard before we finally made it back into the house.

The two of us wrestled around on the couch which led to a series of long passionate kisses that got my heart rate beating out of control. I then said, "Hey sweetheart, why don't we save this for later this evening, because if we go any further here I'm not going to feel much like doing anything except maybe going right to sleep and we still have a few more things to take care before we head out tomorrow." Hoping I didn't get her upset, she then replied, "Okay Cole but you're going to have to make it up to me for putting me behind your beloved Bronco, Mr. ranger man." I looked into her big beautiful eyes then paused, "Sarah, I will definitely make it up to you even if it takes all night, you know I was only kidding about the Bronco thing, right," I quickly remarked, she then moved in closer and planted one more long sensuous kiss that almost made me lose control of my emotions, then softly spoke, "I know you were just teasing but maybe I just want to play along with you so you can make it up to me." This was a side of Sarah that was starting to come out more and more and I found it quite appealing and alluring. After a few more minutes we went to neutral corners of the couch and began to finish the planning of our trip concerning the activities once we had checked into the lodge. We needed to plot out the day hikes to the main waterfalls and the hikes to the lesser known falls that were pretty hard to find if you didn't know the area well. Also how many meals we would be eating at the lodge and how many we would be eating out on the trail. The trail meals would be light and prepackaged freeze dried meals and some of them are actually pretty good nowadays. I could see the excitement in Sarah's eyes again as we talked about the hikes and the adventures we might encounter.

As the afternoon grew late both of our stomach's began to talk to each other and they were saying the same thing, "I'm getting Hungry", Sarah turned to me and said, "Hey do you have any more bacon left, I can make us a couple of BLT sandwiches with pickles and chips if you'd like," quickly I replied, "Yeah, that sounds really good, I don't know about you but I'm starving." The two of us went into the kitchen to finish up talking about the trip and get our dinner going. I quickly refilled Shadow's bowl with his food in case he got going again with the smell of the bacon. He was probably the one that had the most relaxing day out of all of us. Sarah and I were pretty tired from the washing and the waxing of the Bronco, it was a pretty big vehicle and all of the attention to detail with the trim and chrome made it a little more difficult than most of the newer cars and trucks these days, mostly because everything was made out of plastic. I then began to cut up some tomatoes for our BLT's and Sarah had the bacon cooking and Shadow was just watching the whole show from the corner of the kitchen. I knew I was going to have to give him a little more bacon while Sarah and I ate. The lettuce was chopped and the tomatoes were sliced and finally the bacon was now ready to be stacked on the toast, we both agreed that BLT's were one of our favorite lite meals and quite refreshing to eat when you're just too tired to cook a big meal. After chopping up a slice of bacon into very small pieces and putting them into Shadow's bowl Sarah and I sat down at the kitchen counter and began to eat our fantastic meal.

Forty-five minutes had passed and we were both stuffed from the BLT's, the chips and pickles, we finished up with our planned activities and retired back to the couch to just sit and relax. Shadow had already assumed his favorite spot by the fireplace and was ready for another nap. Sarah and I began to talk about what it was going to be like to work together and the unbelievable times that lied ahead for the two of us, "You know Cole technically I'm going to be your boss once we get back from our trip and you're sworn in as a S.H.A.D.O.W. agent, after that you'll be trained and supervised by myself, then we will be assigned a team letter or number and maybe even a nickname," she said. After hearing all of that my mood of being relaxed just tensed up a bit and somewhat worried, I then remarked, "Wow Sarah, thanks for scaring the hell out of me and are you sure the agency is going to be okay with us working together while being in a relationship also." With an expression of absolute lack of concern, she then replied, "Hey don't worry about that Cole, I'm very tight with the guy that makes all of the decisions and he just happens to be my father." Feeling a little more at ease over this subject I quickly asked, "Hey what do you think your father will think of me and our relationship, I mean he doesn't have anything against Indians does he?" Sarah began to laugh uncontrollably again, then slowly snuggled up almost on top of me and said, "Hey, my father doesn't have a mean bone in him, I think the two of you are going to get along great, in some ways he's kind of like you Cole, I mean the way you value all life and respect the planet and all of Gods creations." Quickly with a sigh of relief and a big smile I simply said, "I really hope so." We then both wrapped ourselves up in each other's arms resembling a giant soft pretzel or something, I kissed her on the forehead, then the two of nodded off on the couch.

We were both awakened by the sounds of coyotes howling and yipping outside of the house, I had forgot that tomorrow was garbage day and actually when I looked at the clock tomorrow was right now, it was just after midnight and Sarah and I had totally crashed on the couch, if not for the coyotes during their weekly garbage run on all of the trash cans Sarah and I would probably would have slept the whole night on the couch. Shadow was just starting to alert on the sounds coming from the coyote's and didn't quite know what to make of it. I'm sure if I were to let him out back right now he would be drawn to them and probably want to play or join in their ruckus of knocking over trash cans to get some food scraps. If he were full grown, he would probably be very aggressive towards them in order to protect his property and the members of his pack. Sarah half asleep turned to me and said, "Hey Cole, what's going on, is it late, did we totally fall asleep here?" Rubbing my eyes, I replied, "Yeah, I guess we did sweetheart, a bunch of coyote's woke Shadow and I up." I then noticed he started to pace back and forth by the patio door, "I think he wants out," Sarah remarked. I made my way to the kitchen closet and grabbed his harness then slid it over his head, "Sorry boy but if you need to go out and do some business, I'm going to have to go with you as long as those coyotes are running around." I said while rubbing his ears.

Sarah got up slowly, "Hey I'm going to go get into to bed, you two be careful out there," she said softly.

As Shadow was sniffing around all over the backyard looking for any scent from a wild animal to alert on I could still hear the pack of coyote's traveling down the road. This is something Shadow will learn as he matures, when to use his keen sense of smell or his highly acute hearing and vision to help him track something or alert on a possible dangerous situation or harmful event that may be prevalent. Finally, after a few minutes he gave up on the exciting drama of the evening and relieved himself completely, another load for me to pick up in the morning. Praising him passionately I quickly said, "Okay boy, let's get back inside and go to bed." He leaped from his position and sprinted to the patio door almost pulling my arm out of the socket. The two of us quickly got back inside the house and I removed his harness, slowly we both made our way back to the bedroom to find Sarah already sleeping like a baby and snoring like a bear. Shadow made his way over to the end of the bed on the floor and I slowly pulled back the covers carefully not to wake her up and climbed in beside her. Her body was radiating heat like an old space heater and it felt good. I had set the alarm for four-thirty so we could at least try to get on the road by seven and that took in to account if we stopped at Miralani's for breakfast. Shadow now began to snore and I wondered if it might be better to go back out to the couch, between the two of them it sounded like something coming out of an old sawmill, I just put my pillow over my head and shut it all out, finally after a few minutes of listening to my own heartbeat I dozed off thinking about how much fun we were all going to have on this short little vacation, even Shadow should have a great time.

The morning came quickly, I jumped up out of bed and let Shadow out into the backyard, Sarah had quickly headed to the bathroom and began to run the shower. We both new that this morning's shower was to be again for cleansing purposes only. Shadow finished up and quickly wanted back inside, I headed off down the hallway to join Sarah and then we would load up the little supplies we had left in the kitchen and then finally we could get this show on the road. The two of us finished our shower in record time at least for the short time we've been together. We quickly got dressed and put the finishing touches on our packs, then we preceded to the garage to put the last bit of items needed for the trip into the Bronco. Shadow was running around and quite excited, he seemed to recognize how Sarah and I were acting and that something good was happening and that he was a part of it. It took about an hour for us to finally get all loaded up into the Bronco and ready to roll. I fired up the Bronco and backed it out, then closed the garage door and we and were on our way, first stop Miralani's for breakfast. Sarah looked over towards me then grabbed my hand, "Cole I'm so excited and happy right now I haven't been on a real vacation since my parents and I went to see the Grand Canyon when I was fifteen years old, thank you so much for suggesting this," she said with joy. I then looked at her and smiled.

We arrived at Miralani's in what seemed like only a few minutes, maybe I might have been speeding a bit but I think I just wanted to be on our way towards Havasupai more than anything. We all piled out of the Bronco as fast as we could, seeming to be on the same page about wanting to get on the road to get this vacation started. As we went through the front door my sister quickly came up to greet us, then hugged Sarah and then me, "Wow, you guys look so happy and excited, even Shadow looks extremely happy, come on and sit down, I've got your booth all ready, let's get your orders in so you can be on your way, I can see that you guys can't wait to get going," she said with some urgency and a smile. Sarah quickly replied, "Thanks so much for feeding us before we head out, I know Cole and I both appreciate it." I then remarked, "Yeah sis, besides it will be the last free meal we get for the next five days or so." She then started to laugh a bit, "Yeah, that figures my brother the cheapskate, it's probably the only reason you've been coming here to eat every day for the past five years I bet," she said with a grin on her face. Sarah then joined in on the laughing and jokingly remarked, "Yeah, come to think of it, he did tell me he liked the breakfast menu better at the place down the street on the corner, what was the name of that place Cole?" Choking somewhat and then smiling, I said, "Okay, that's pretty good Sarah, you got me again but my sister knows she has the best place in Sedona when it comes to serving breakfast." Miralani smiled at Sarah then the we sat down at the booth including Shadow, there would be a time very soon where he was going to be too big to fit in the seating area of the booth but I guess we'll deal with it when that days comes, for now he was quite content to sit in between Sarah and I.

After our orders showed up the three of us began to eat quickly, probably to quickly but never the less we pushed forward. Miralani had made Shadow some scrambled eggs and just a small amount of chopped up bacon because of the long trip that lied ahead for us, the last thing we needed was a dog that needed to stop and go to the bathroom every twenty miles or so, likewise Sarah and I limited our coffee intake to just one cup each. I looked at Sarah as we were nearly finished with breakfast and asked, "So what do want to do for the three-hour ride there, I mean do we want to get into to some serious dialog concerning our upcoming working relationship or time travel experiences although that might be pretty one sided or do you just want to listen to some music, I do have a very nice stereo in the Bronco, I just don't use it much because it drowns out the beautiful sound of the motor." Sarah then replied, "Well we could do a little of each of those things or just wing it and see what comes our way, I would though like to tell you about some of the secrets that I eventually am going to have tell you and maybe this might be a good time to do so, I just want to warn you ahead of time it could get very religious and spiritual once we head down that path, I hope that doesn't scare you off in any way." After paying the bill, I turned and looked at Sarah with great intensity, "Sweetheart there's nothing you could ever do or say that would scare me away from you because I love you." She reached for my hand and said, "Cole, I want you to know that I will always be there for you too and the love that I feel for you gets stronger with every day, I'm not sure where this relationship will end up but I will be at your side always because I love you." We both smiled and held our hands together tightly for a minute then slid out of the booth along with Shadow and headed over to Miralani to say our goodbye's.

After a few minutes of my sister tearing up and squeezing the life out of Sarah, Shadow and myself we finally headed out the door and were kicking off the start of this vacation. Sarah and Shadow were jumping up and down on their way to the Bronco like a couple of kids who just got out of school and beginning their summer vacation, it was pretty funny but heartwarming at the same time because this was my family and I loved them dearly. We piled into the Bronco and I fired it up, the tank was almost full so I would only need to stop once maybe twice depending on the availability of gas stations on the way there, I wasn't sure how many bathroom stops there might be but I knew we were getting a nice early start so stopping shouldn't be too much of a problem concerning our overall time allotted for the hike down into the canyon and reaching the lodge. As we pulled out of Miralani's we were finally on our way, the windows were down, Shadow was happy sticking his head out of Sarah's window behind her head and the two of them were smiling. The Bronco was gleaming as the early morning sun was showcasing it as we drove through the heart of Sedona, it truly was a magnificent looking vehicle and very patriotic, which caught the eye of any true blooded American. The great big Bald Eagle on the hood was the icing on the cake when it came to the paint job, people would just stop and stare at it when it was parked out in public. I think it brought out the patriotic spirit that had maybe been dormant in so many people.

As we got clear of Sedona heading west northwest on highway 89A I believe Sarah and I were really getting excited now because there was nothing that was going to stop us from reaching our canyon paradise vacation spot. Our route would take us from 89A to Hwy 89 then to Route 40 then to Arizona state Route 64 and finally to IR18 which would take us to the Hilltop parking area above the canyon. The trip would take at least three hours depending on how many times we stopped but like I said before we left early enough that a few stops wouldn't hurt our hiking time down to the lodge. I reached for my cd case in the glove box and then asked Sarah if she wanted to pick out some music to get us in the vacation mood, "Okay Cole, let's see what you got in here," she quickly replied. I then said, "You might see a few in there that you've never heard of before but it's all really good easy listening music, my favorite group is "One Republic" and my favorite song by them is called "Counting Stars" but they're all really good, I'm not trying to pressure you or anything on which one to pick but why don't you put that one in." Sarah busted out laughing, then said, "Okay Cole, I know that group and they're one of my favorite's also but I'm picking the next one." The two of us laughed together as she put the cd in the player.

The weather was warming up really nice as we were well out of Sedona and the scenic serenity of the landscapes kept the drive exciting and refreshing. An hour or so had passed when Sarah suddenly turned to me with those big beautiful eyes and said, "So, got any questions you want to ask, like about S.H.A.D.O.W. or about what it's going to be like working for this agency, I mean I was going to wait till your first day on the job but I think it might be a little overwhelming more than it already is, so fire away Cole, I'm ready to spill the beans about anything you want to know." Pausing for a few seconds then reaching for and turning the music down I carefully and slowly asked, "Okay first off, what the hell does S.H.A.D.O.W. stand for anyway?" Sarah smiled and giggled a bit then replied, "Well you may want to write this one down later because it's a mouthful, like I said before my father was the driving force of this project over the last fifteen years or so and basically named the organization after the scientific breakthrough and process which he discovered that allows a human being or for that matter any carbon based lifeform to travel in time with extreme accuracy and safety, so to answer your question the S.H.A.D.O.W. agency name stands for Synchronized, Hadron, Atomizing, Directional, Orthogonal, Wormhole, which basically means a process that takes a full body scan of your anatomy then loads it into the main system where it saves it in a file, kind of like a medical file your doctor would have, only this one breaks down every cell in your body and saves it as a re-constructible platform and the great thing about that is even if you were to get injured on a mission when time traveling back to S.H.A.D.O.W. this process would put you back together in the state you were in when you left on the mission, it's really fantastic and the medical possibilities alone are limitless, so how's that for an answer." I slowly reached for the cd player and turned the volume back up and then turned to Sarah with a look of total confusion, "Sorry I asked, I think I may be getting in over my head here, that's enough questions for now I think," smiling I turned my attention back to the road.

Another hour passed as we got closer to our destination, Sarah then asked if we could pull over to stretch our legs and take a few selfie pictures, it sounded like a great idea mostly because I would get to hold her in my arms again, I couldn't believe how quickly I yearned the need for her compassion and the feeling of wanting to physically hold her body next to mine, just driving this distance to the falls was going to be tougher than I thought it would be. After pulling over to a small turnout just for viewing and with an unbelievable backdrop the three of us jumped out and began to take some shots with our cell phones, even Shadow seemed to know what was going on and calmly posed with us, of course Sarah had a selfie stick, that thing must have had an outward telescopic extension of at least six feet, it could have been used as a fishing pole. Sarah quickly took over the photo shoot and directed us into several positions to obtain the best picture she could possibly take, "Hey you two, you've got hold still or they will all be blurry, Shadow you're doing better than Cole but both of you are too fidgety, I can't hold this stick up forever waiting for you to hold still, I want these pictures of our first vacation together to turn out good because this is a special time for us," she said with a raised tone in her voice. Shadow and I remained silent and bowed our heads as if to say we were sorry, we then made an extra effort to remain still for next the couple of minutes to show Sarah that these pictures were important to us as well.

Upon completion of what was probably going to be many photo shoots on this trip we were back on way and only a little over an hour away from our destination. Sarah was quite pleased with the photo's she took and had already sent them to her dad and Miralani, she and my sister were fast becoming very good friends, which was great, we were all becoming a family. Shadow was resting comfortably in the back after giving him a rawhide chew that he savored for at least five minutes, I guess he needed a nap after that and the stress of the photo shoot. There was one more stop we would need to make about twenty miles ahead for gas and whatever else we decided that we might need as far as snacks or drinks to accomplish the hike down to the lodge. I had brought my two old style canteen's that my father had given me a long time ago, they were still in excellent shape and kept the water much colder and longer than any of the newer ones on the market, I think the reason they showed no signs of wear on the inside was because of the fact that I only used them to contain water and nothing else. Sarah was now actually nodding off a bit until I would hit a bump in the road, "Hey do you want a pillow, I have a small one tucked way under the backseat in a big zip lock bag, it's clean and quite comfortable, I keep seeing your head bouncing around and hitting the side of the window pillar," I remarked. "Yeah, that sounds great, I'll climb back and grab it, I just hope Shadow doesn't get any ideas that I'm getting it for him," she replied. "I think he's quite happy with his little doggy bed stuffed down and on the floor, although it won't be too long before he's not going to fit back there to comfortably without some kind of modification to the backseat," I quickly stated.

After stopping for gas and picking up some fresh water and snacks we were only about thirty minutes away from the hilltop parking and helicopter staging area for the canyon lodge. Sarah had got a nice little nap in before we stopped and looked quite refreshed and eager to begin the hike down to the lodge, I also was getting pretty restless from the drive and was looking forward to the challenging hike. Shadow was up and looking out Sarah's window again enjoying the fresh air and the spectacular views of this beautiful area of Arizona, I guess he was probably thinking about his own kind and where were all of his brothers and sisters and if he would ever see them again, I promised him I would find out what happened and how it was that the two of us crossed paths and that I would try to locate his family somehow if they were alive, I don't think it would be wise to release him back into the wild after being somewhat domesticated after our newly formed bond and the friendship that has grown between Sarah, myself and him. We had become a family, not to mention the relationship he and Miralani had developed, I believe he was destined to be part of my life and Sarah's, maybe he would become a great factor in helping the S.H.A.D.O.W. agency complete their missions and become one their most important agents. He did indeed possess a special kind of gentle and wise spirit that projected outwards that you could feel immediately upon close contact. Sarah and I were blessed to have him in our lives.

The hilltop parking area was coming into view and only a few minutes away, I could tell Sarah was really starting to get excited now along with Shadow, the two of them had definitely formed some kind of spiritual connection already and they both looked so stunning, her with her hair blowing from the open window and Shadow's beautiful coat waving alongside her face all the while with the landscape of northern Arizona as a backdrop, it would forever be a picture in my mind and heart. Sarah then turned to me and said, "Cole this place is amazing, it's so breathtaking and peaceful." I then reached over, grabbed her hand and replied, "It truly is and wait till you see the falls and the beautiful turquoise pools that lie beneath them, the serenity and beauty of it all will change your life forever and give you a whole new outlook on life and how lucky we are to live here and call this place home." Sarah then squeezed my hand gently and said, "I know how close you are to mother nature and the vast knowledge you have of everything concerning your heritage and the appreciation of all life, that's what I think I love about you the most, you have such a calming effect on all things around you and you have already made me change my outlook about everything especially life." I returned the smile still holding her hand tightly, "I feel the exact same way, I mean since I met you my life has changed like I could never have imagined in a million years, I didn't think I was ever going to have these feelings I now have for you, you've changed my outlook for humanity and the given me hope that people can make a difference in making this world of ours a better place, if they believe in each other and the power of hope and faith," I emotionally replied.

As the hilltop parking area was now just a couple hundred feet away we were all so ready to get this hike started. There were only five cars parked so it looked like it was not going to be too crowded with people camping or just day hikers, the helicopter was parked which meant it was available if we wanted to change our minds about how we got to the bottom of the canyon. The Bronco came to a full stop where I positioned it somewhat in a very tough area to park unless you had four-wheel drive, my thinking was it would be safe from people getting too curious about what was under the car cover once it was tied down to the Bronco. Hopefully it would be safe, for the most part this tribal owned parking lot had a very safe reputation in regards to theft of personal items and car theft. Sarah and Shadow jumped out as soon as I turned the engine off, it would only take a few minutes to unload since most of everything was in our backpacks, I just had to take a few minutes to adjust Shadow's properly so it wouldn't rub under his front legs and give him a burn from the straps. The car cover would probably take the longest amount of time before we could start heading down the trail. Sarah and I were both in very good shape so the hike shouldn't take us more than a four hours even with some breaks along the way. I decided that I would take this opportunity to teach Sarah a little about tracking and how to read the signs of mother nature and how to use this knowledge to possibly benefit her in any of the challenging situations that she had to deal with concerning her missions at S.H.A.D.O.W. and maybe even in her personal life.

After securing the car cover over the Bronco and making sure

Shadow's little backpack was adjusted right we set off down the main trail and started our journey. I led the way with Shadow behind me being held onto by Sarah, that's what she wanted and I didn't argue because I pretty much new Shadow would keep her safe from any possible surprise encounters on the trail by unfriendly wildlife. A few minutes in to the hike which was mostly a slow decline all the way the lodge I asked Sarah, "Hey sweetheart, how's your tracking skills, I know you probably have been taught some by the government because I used to teach to quite a few agencies basic and advanced tracking techniques, you feel like getting a crash course on some old passed down secret Indian methods and knowledge of the land?" Quickly she replied, "Sure Cole, I know a little like you said but for the most part it's pretty basic stuff I learned at the F.B.I. academy, I would love to learn from someone with your knowledge and skills, I mean I know a little about your background and the stuff you've done with the F.B.I. after all I did do a pretty thorough security check on you remember." I stopped walking for a second, turned around and said, "Yeah but you don't know everything about me, there are a few jobs I performed for our government that included training a certain "Black Ops" organization that was responsible for tracking and capturing high level targets like certain terrorists and I bet you didn't know that I belong to an organization called, get this, are you ready for it? "It's called the "Shadow Wolves" and they only request my services on very special situations and circumstances." Looking a bit shocked and offended by my response she then replied, "Hey Cole, you're still not upset with me from when I had to dig into your background are you? Smiling and moving in a bit closer to her, then making eye contact she acknowledged the seriousness of my approach, "Hey sweetheart, I could never be mad at you but I just wanted to let you know that there are probably a few things your background didn't pick up on regarding some of my previous work for the United States Government," I said with a firm and proud tone. "We definitely need to talk more about this Cole, I don't want there to be any secret's or misguided discontent between us either and I do have some things I want to share with you on this little vacation of ours, now's the perfect time for us to get everything out in the open and I love you too much to let something fester to the point of being unpleasant or afraid to talk about," she said with great emotion.

After the brief conversation was over and coming to a complete agreement on getting anything we wanted out in the open to talk about we then began to head down the trail once again, the descent would be around two thousand feet and get a little steep towards the end but I was sure we could both easily handle the challenge, after all the most difficult part of this hike was the first three-quarters of a mile, however I wasn't quite so sure about Shadow being able to keep up, he still had a lot of puppy left in him and would tire more quickly and likely be needing a few more breaks than Sarah and I. He was actually doing very well so far, even with his little backpack probably weighing close to seven or eight pounds, but that would get lighter the further we went because he was carrying his own water supply. The sun was almost directly overhead as it got close to noon and it was definitely warming up. I double checked with Sarah about her putting on some sunscreen before we started out and she said she had, she was at quite a disadvantage because of her fair skin when it came to sun protection, myself on the other hand had sort of built-in sunscreen protection from the dark pigmented skin of my American Indian race, even so I always still used some level of additional sun screen protection. Our pace had now picked up quite a bit and we had been on our downward trek for about an hour and half. I decided we should probably take a little break and check everyone's pack, primarily Shadow's since his was the most difficult to get fitted properly. I also wanted to get Sarah started on some tracking techniques since I had pick up on some shoe tracks ahead of us.

After checking Shadow's pack, I then turned my attention to Sarah, "Hey you ready for your first tracking lesson," I asked. "Sure but what are we going track out here?" She replied. "Well I noticed a couple of hikers in front us and their tracks are pretty fresh, probably from earlier this morning," I said. Sarah then said with nervousness and excitement, "Okay great, it will be fun." We started out again on the trail at a slower pace so I could stop and explain and show her the simple little things to watch out for when examining foot prints or tracks from shoe's, or in this case two pairs of hiking boots that belonged to a male and female most likely due to the size and depth of the tracks they were leaving in the soft sand that lined the outer edges of the trail. The middle of the trail was pretty work hardened by the continuous mule service provided for riders and their luggage when preferred. Sarah was digesting everything that I threw her way pertaining to the tracking tips and the knowledge I was feeding her, she really was a spectacular woman, so smart and so beautiful and most of all causing me to be so enamored with her that I still had a hard time focusing and controlling my emotions when I was with her. With less than an hour to go to reach our destination I asked, "Hey you want to take a short break up ahead, there is a little rest area before we hit a dry streambed, from there it's pretty easy the rest of the way, after we cross a small bridge the village of "Supai" we be in our sights." We then agreed to take a short break.

We reached the rest area and then began to talk some more about the agency and what to expect when I start my training. "Hey Cole how much do you know about antique weapons, specifically small arms like old revolvers dating back to the thirties to say the sixties and seventies, the reason I ask is that part of your extensive training is going to include your ability to learn and become proficient with these types of firearms," she asked. Quickly and confidently I answered, "Well I think I know quite a bit about the old west style revolvers if that's what you mean." Sarah then slowly replied, "Well not exactly cowboy, I meant more like the old police revolvers, you know like the ones they use in all the movies from those time periods, you'll have no problem with this Cole, I know you can shoot and you have a great interest in old firearms so don't worry too much about it, besides I'm an expert marksman with these old guns and I can teach you everything about them." Pausing for a few seconds I then remarked, "Well I'll take all the help I can get, especially if it's coming from you sweetheart." I then asked Sarah a question, "Hey Sarah there's still one thing that's really stuck in my mind, I know I already asked you about this earlier but can you shed any light on that matter about the black Escalade. I just can't help thinking that you might have some kind of security problem at the agency or even worse, you know like some kind of rogue agent that might be conducting illegal activities on his own and behind the agencies back." Sarah then slowly answered, "I can Cole, I told you that I would not keep any secrets from you and like I said before now's the time to ask and get everything out in the open, so yeah I do know that we might have some sort of bad agent or other employee or employee's at S.H.A.D.O.W that's been doing things against the rules of our agency, my father and I are the only ones that have this suspicion and are the only ones trying to expose the individual or individuals and now my dear you are part of this internal investigation, to tell you the truth I think we can finally solve this mystery with your help and insight Cole." I looked at her for a moment with great appreciation, "Hey, thanks for being honest Sarah and yeah I would love to help you and your father put this issue to rest," I said with confidence.

After checking Shadow's pack again and putting the finishing touches on our conversation about the agency the three of us headed back out on the trail. Shadow was doing great and Sarah was really in great shape as I suspected. As we walked I said to Sarah, "Hey sweetheart we're getting really close now, once we cross a little bridge up ahead it will just be a bit further then we'll be in the main part of the village and there will see the lodge, the general store and some of the other little public buildings." She then replied, "Great, I can't wait, I think the first thing I want to do once we get our room is take a shower and get all of this dust off of me, I must look like a kid that's been playing outside all day." Slowing down some in order to get a view from behind her, "Hey I think you look fantastic, I wish I had a friend like you when I was growing up to play with," I said jokingly. "Yeah and I know what kind of playing you would've had in mind," she softly remarked. Shadow then came up in between us as he alerted on some people coming up the trail probably headed out of the canyon and back up to the hilltop parking area, quickly I secured Shadow's leash just in case, I knew he didn't have any problems with strangers but these hikers did look a little intimidating with their big packs and walking sticks. I could see that Sarah was on the same page as I and started to calm Shadow by petting him and seeing if he wanted any water, "Hey Shadow, you look thirsty boy, I know I am, how about we both take a little drink," she said as she gently stroked the top of his head. The hikers approached and immediately wanted to stop and pet Shadow, it was a young couple who were taken in by Shadow's beauty, "Is that a wolf puppy mister?" the young man asked. "Yes, it is and he's very friendly so don't be afraid, he won't bite, he might lick you to death if you get close enough though," I said. "His name is Shadow and he's an "Alaskan Grey" and "Timber" wolf mix we think," Sarah said with the admiration and love of a proud parent. After a few minutes of chatting with the young couple and being thanked for letting them show their affection for Shadow we continued down the trail where the village finally came in to sight.

Sarah, Shadow and I walked through the village as many tribal members and visitors gazed upon us, primarily staring at Shadow knowing that he was some sort of wolf breed, the American Indians hold the wolf as a very sacred part of their beliefs and as spiritual protectors. Shadow seemed to be almost parading himself as walked proud past the bystanders, I just think he's a bit of a ham myself, he loves the attention. The lodge was now in plain sight and I think the three of us were totally ready for a little rest. My friend "Billy Two Feathers" at least that's what he always wanted to be called now, was expecting us just around noon, so we were right on time or maybe just a little behind schedule. The three of us piled in through the front door of the registration office and there was Billy Two Feathers watching an old John Wayne movie on a TV that had to be older than him and Billy had to be in his late sixties by now. He suddenly turned around very quickly as if we had scared him, "Jesus, is that you Cole, you scared the crap out of me, you look great son, come on in and who's your friends you got there with you?" he said with a loud and stern voice, "Ten Bears, sorry I mean Two Feathers you old scalp hunter, it's good to see you, I'm sorry if we barged in like a herd of buffalo but the city life has turned me into somewhat of a klutz, you look great my friend, this is my girlfriend Sarah Cooper and the young wolf cub likes to be called Shadow," I replied with a bit of a laugh. "It's a pleasure to meet someone with such beauty Cole and your girlfriend is not bad either, just kidding, my name is Billy "Two Feathers" but you can call just me Two Feathers if you'd like, Cole was definitely right about you, you're absolutely stunning Miss Cooper," once again speaking loudly.

After a brief laugh and getting to know one another for a while Sarah, Shadow and I headed out towards our room. I turned back when I heard, "Hey Cole if you guys don't like that room for any reason let me know, I have a couple others that are vacant," Two Feathers said. Before I could say anything Sarah blurted out, "Okay, thanks One Feather, we will." I could see the reaction from Two Feathers as he began to laugh his ass off, "Cole, you're a lucky man," he said all the while trying to keep his composure from Sarah's remark. "Don't I know it," replying very quickly. "One Feather, you can call me Sarah if you'd like," as Sarah got one more jab in. I could tell right away the two of them were going to get along great. The three of us then trekked off to our room, Sarah was still giggling a bit, I'm sure from the "One Feather" statement. "That was pretty good sweetheart, I think he really liked that and that he really likes you," I cheerfully stated. As we swung the door open to the room Sarah said, "Wow, this is really pretty nice Cole, I mean it's big and it's clean and what a view, I think your friend Two Feathers took care of us very nicely, he seemed like a nice man and I could tell how good of a friends the two of you are." After a quick sweep of the room I turned to Sarah and replied, "Yeah it looks like they have done a lot of upgrades since the last time I was here, I think it will do just fine for the four days we have planned to be here." I quickly pulled off Shadow's pack and then Sarah and I hit the shower to get all of the trail dust off our bodies. As the two of us entered the bathroom I could see a look of concern on Sarah's face, "Hey I don't think this shower is big enough for both us," she said. Without hesitation I turned the water on, waited for it to get hot, wrapped my arms around her, gently picked her up, then squeezed the two of our bodies into the shower stall, "You see we fit, just don't drop the soap," I said with a smile.

After knocking the shower doors off their tracks several times we finally finished with our shower, we both agreed it might be better and safer to shower alone for the rest of our stay. When we came out of the bathroom Shadow was already sound asleep on the bed, I guess the hike down was a bit exhausting for him. "Hey Sarah, we should probably get to the general store before they close and pick up the stuff we're going to need for the next four days and decide what we want to eat for dinner tonight," I eagerly suggested. "Sounds good to me, I hope they have some kind of dog food there," she then replied. "I already asked Two Feathers when I made the reservations if he could make sure they had some for our stay when I told him we were bringing Shadow," I remarked while finishing getting dressed. I wasn't sure if I wanted to leave Shadow alone in the room or not while we went to the store, I mean I hadn't left him alone by himself anywhere since the two of us had been together, just as Sarah asked about Shadow he started to wake up and knew right away that Sarah and I were headed out. He jumped off the bed and looked like he was totally rejuvenated, "Hey I think he's trying to tell us something," Sarah remarked. I went over to his backpack and pulled out his leash, "Yeah, I think you're right Sarah, hey boy want to go with us to the store, we're going to get your food there because I didn't feel like packing a four-day supply of your food to bring down that trail," speaking to the both of them. After Sarah and I were finished getting ready the three of us headed out the door and made our way over to the general store.

Once we were in the store we picked up all of the little personal items we needed then planned out a few meals for the next couple of days. We had decided we would try to eat little lite meals or snacks during the day and only one main meal in the late afternoon hours. Most of the daylight hours would be consumed by the hikes and swimming in the pools below the various falls that Havasupai had to offer. After picking up all the supplies we needed for now we headed back to our room to drop everything off then we would head out to watch the sunset against the canyon walls and the wonderful sounds of the falls. For our meal tonight we just picked up a couple of sandwiches to take with us while we sat at the picnic table near our room. As we approached the table and sat down to eat our dinner the peacefulness and tranquility of this place was really starting to set in for Sarah and I. Shadow was even more calm than usual and seemed to be enjoying this place as much as Sarah and I. As we ate Sarah asked, "So what's on the agenda for tomorrow Cole?" Slowly I slid over very close to her then put my arm over her shoulder, "Well I thought we would shoot for two waterfalls each day and that should leave plenty of time for swimming and just relaxing next to the beautiful turquoise pools that surround them," I suggested. "Great, that sounds terrific, I can't wait to swim in those beautiful pools we saw coming in on the trail," she said with youthful exuberance. As we finished our dinner we could see a slight rainbow settling over the canyon rim from what must have been the mist of the waterfall's, it was almost totally orange from the sun setting and the reflections from the colors of the canyon. Sarah was cuddled up close next to me and Shadow was lying on the grass next to our picnic table only a few feet away, it was so quiet I could almost hear all our heartbeats. "You know I may see if "Two Feathers" wouldn't mind watching Shadow one of the days we're going to be here so we might be able to reach a couple hard to get secluded spots I know, I mean he wouldn't be able to traverse some of the terrain, these trails have several steep climbs and drop offs that might be a little dangerous for him," I said.

The view of the canyon walls and the soft noise of the water falling from nearby "Mooney" falls from our table was breathtaking and quite serene, Sarah and I just remained silent while looking around at all of the beauty this place had to offer. The village looked as if it had been trapped in time itself, there were no motor vehicles only beasts of burden to do the labor needed by the tribal people who were so lucky to live in such a majestic place. As the sun finally came to rest Sarah and I began to look at the stars and each other, our eyes kept meeting at certain points of the heavens, we both embraced the spiritual and heavenly feelings that had overcome us. "Sarah, I promise I will always love you and protect you from any evil or harm that comes our way, I have truly found my soulmate," I softly said with all my heart. With tears running down her cheeks and her hands clasping mine she replied, "You have brought out feelings in me that I have never felt before and I know you are the one I want to spend the rest of my life with, it was destiny that brought us together I believe, I mean just think about it, you spent time working for and training a government agency called "Shadow Wolves", you almost died trying to save a wolf cub that you named "Shadow" and now you are here with me and about to start a career saving lives from the past to change destiny to better the world in doing so, you have already saved mine and made it wonderful by being the man I will love and follow anywhere our paths may lead, call it fate or God's wisdom that the two of us are together and I do believe it's for a reason Cole, we we're meant to be soulmates." We both wrapped ourselves up in each other's arms and turned our attention back to the star riddled skies above.

An hour had passed and it started to get a little chilly so we decided to head back to the room and retire early because tomorrow would be full of physical challenges and satisfying rewards. After Shadow had finished doing his business he too was ready for a good night's sleep. The three of us now stripped down to our underwear except Shadow who was pretty much always in the buff, we were then finally ready to hit the sack. I left the windows cracked some so we could fall to sleep with the faint sounds of the canyon waterfalls off in the distance. Sarah and I were again clinched in each other's arms in the middle of the queen sized bed, Shadow was on the floor by my side of the bed already beginning to snore. Sarah cuddled up close, then softly said, "Thank you for bringing me here Cole, this place is so peaceful and beautiful and I know we're going to make some lasting memories while we're here, I love you." Looking deeply into her eyes then pausing for a second, "I love you too sweetheart and I feel the same way about the time we'll be spending together here, I know we're both going to become even much closer than we are now and that's the wonderful thing about two people who want to be together and share their lives with each other, if it is destiny that has brought us together then I am forever in debt to those forces that made it happen, goodnight sweetheart," passionately I replied, then slowly we both fell asleep wrapped and entwined together like a human ball of yarn.

I woke up early in the morning around four a.m. from one of the best dreams I've ever had in my life, of course it was about Sarah and I, we were skinny dipping in the pools beneath the waterfalls which eventually led to a mad passionate lovemaking session behind one of the waterfalls in total seclusion, it was a dream that I hoped might come true on one of our day hikes over the next couple of days. As I was headed for the shower Sarah was just starting to wake up and Shadow was still snoozing pretty good. "I'll only be about ten-minutes sweetheart, then the bathroom will be yours," I said, half asleep. Smiling and turning back over in bed she muddled, "Okay Cole, take your time, I'll take Shadow out if he wakes up before you finish up in there." I could tell the serenity of the place really made for some heavy sleeping and that it was going to be a little harder than normal to get up and out of bed. The ending of my intense dream was the only reason I woke up so early, otherwise I'd still be in bed with Sarah. The water from the shower was now hot and ready to fully wake me up for today's challenges. When I came out of the bathroom completely finished with taking care of all my needs I saw Sarah and Shadow on the bed together, she was eating her cereal and Shadow was eating a rawhide chew. "Sorry I took a little longer than I said but I'm totally finished and it's all yours now," I quickly remarked. "Oh no worries, Shadow and I were just finishing up our breakfast, I already fed him and took him outside, I think he is ready to hit the trails, it shouldn't take me more than an hour or so to get ready Cole, just kidding, you can start breathing again," Laughing a bit I then began to stare at Sarah's sleep attire which consisted of just a t-shirt, "Say, you know we could just stay in the room for a couple more hours if you'd like," Jumping out the bed as fast as she could, "No way ranger, if we did that neither one of us would have enough energy to even hike to the general store," she replied.

As I finished getting dressed Sarah had just got out of the shower, I then quickly fixed my breakfast and began to eat my cereal, I was hoping we could get started by six-thirty or so as the sun would be just be coming up. Once finished with my cereal I started to prepare Shadow's backpack for our hike today, mostly it would just carry his water and a few dog treats, that was enough for him. Sarah and I would carry some of his food for when we stopped and had our lunch at the falls. He could go with us today but probably not the next day which would consist of the more challenging trails which included wooden ladders to ascend and small caves with tight little steps to descend down to the pools and there was no way he would be able to traverse any of those obstacles. I'm sure Two Feathers wasn't going to mind watching him, I could tell that he was very taken by him and probably wanted to show him off to some of the tribal members that lived here. I was totally okay with that because I knew that Shadow would love to be showered with all of the attention, he was really becoming somewhat of a ham when it came to being around other people which is very strange and rare for his breed but then again I still had a lot of unanswered questions regarding his past and how exactly he ended up in that shaft in the first place, what I did know is that he and Sarah and I had become a very tightly bonded pack and I was so happy the three of us had found each other.

It was now six-thirty and we were almost ready to get this first day's hike started, I couldn't tell who was more excited Sarah or Shadow, "Hey you two about ready to hit the trail?" I asked. "I know I am Cole and I think Shadow has been ready since he woke up," she said with the energy of a hummingbird. "Great, let's hit it, we're burning daylight," I quickly replied. Our plan for the day was to hike to "Beaver Falls" first then head back towards the lodge and stop at "Havasu Falls" till mid to late afternoon then head back for dinner and some relaxation. These falls would be no problem for Shadow and would start out easy for all of us in a physical aspect. I shut the front door to our room and we were on our way. Sarah had her cargo shorts on with all the pockets and a big floppy tan canvas hiking hat, "Hey sweetheart, have I told you how great you look this morning, you're gorgeous," I remarked. "Stop it Cole, I look like I should be planting potatoes in a field or something," she replied. After gathering my composure from that statement I reassuringly remarked, "Hey you would look terrific in anything, even a burlap sack." I don't even know why I said that but it drew a very strange look from her, "Burlap sack! Are you trying to say something, do you think I look like a burlap sack in this get up?" She asked. Quickly, I looked at Shadow as if he could help get me out of this mess, I then leaned down and started to fidget with his pack, "Looks like this came a little loose boy," I said. As I started to stand up I could see Sarah laughing and trying to be mad at the same time, "I'm only kidding Cole, I knew what you meant and thanks for the compliment," she softly remarked.

After ten minutes of walking on flat ground and out of sight from the lodge we finally started to hit a few rises and drops in the trail. I had already told Sarah that I would try to keep us at a fast pace to take advantage of this easy trail and that way we would have more time to swim and relax by the falls. It should take us less than an hour to get to "Beaver Falls" and by then it would have started to warm up quite a bit, the water temperature was a constant seventy-degrees year-round and once you were in it, it wasn't bad at all, especially when the air temperature was above eighty degrees like it was supposed to be today. I continued to lead the way still moving at a good pace, Shadow was pretty much behind me and Sarah was bringing up the rear. I was a bit curious on how Shadow was going to react to the falls, I mean I'm sure he had never seen anything like them before and would be just as overwhelmed as a human seeing them for the first time. The sound of the water pounding the pools below the falls could be felt through your body when you got close enough to them and that's when I might be a little concerned about his response, hopefully he would embrace them and jump in the water with Sarah and I when the time came. "Beaver Falls" was a very active place for all types of ages because of the various heights of the falls most of which were under forty-feet and quite a few spots where kids could enjoy some much smaller areas of the falls to jump in and swim.

After thirty minutes of hiking at a pretty good pace we could see "Havasu Falls" up head, "Wow, you've got to be kidding me, this place looks just like a post card picture, it's absolutely breathtaking Cole," Sarah said with a stunned look. 'Yeah, it most certainly is, I knew you'd be impressed by this little piece of heaven on Earth," eagerly I stated. As we came up to the falls I could see that Sarah was probably thinking about just stopping here for the rest of the day, "I know what you're thinking sweetheart and it is tempting just to stay here all day but I'd like for you to experience as many of these gorgeous creations of God we can see over the few days, I promise you it will be worth it," I quickly remarked. "I know Cole, it's just hard to keep walking by something that's so beautiful and enticing," she reluctantly stated. I thought this might be a good time to take a couple of pictures to try to send out to Miralani if we had good cell phone reception. I took one of Sarah and Shadow with the falls in the background, then managed to wedge the cell phone in between two skinny branches on a nearby tree to get a picture of all three of us, it's amazing what these smart phones can do nowadays. "Okay everyone, hold still, I set the timer for thirty seconds, come on Shadow smile," I said with a chuckle. Sarah then quickly reached up towards my nose with her right index finger and placed it in my left nostril just as the picture clicked, "How's that for a memorable photo," she quickly said. We both began to laugh so loud that it started to echo through the canyon. Shadow was jumping up and down on Sarah's leg as if he was giving his approval of the little photo stunt that Sarah had just pulled on me, this wonderful animal most definitely had a great sense of humor.

After the short photo shoot we continued our trek towards

"Beaver Falls" which should only take us another half hour or so to get there. The trail was fairly easy just a little slippery from the loose gravel around the rocky portions of the trail, at least Sarah and I had the right type of hiking boots for this terrain. Shadow was starting to position himself right by my side as we walked, I was almost to the point of unhooking his leash to see what kind of reaction he would have out here in the wide open areas of this canyon, I was pretty sure he wouldn't take off or anything like that, I just wasn't sure about the possibility of encountering other hikers or even some sort of wildlife he might go after. He was pretty much domesticated by now but there may still be a little wild side to him if the right situation presented itself. "Hey can you two slow down a bit, I'd like to look around and enjoy some of this scenery as we're hiking, besides I'm starting to have a little trouble keeping up with you two," Sarah said with a little shortness of breath. "I'm sorry sweetheart, I guess I was just trying to keep pace with Shadow, I have to remember he has four legs and we don't, I'll pull him back a little, I think he would have made a great sled dog up in Alaska," I quickly remarked.

As we continued at a little slower pace but normal for most two legged creatures we began to hear the sounds of "Beaver Falls" and a lite mist filled the skies in front of us. This was the beginning of what appeared to a very beautiful day. The temperature was warming up nicely and we were all very eager now to relax and enjoy this mystical place, it's almost as if the water calls to you to jump in and become one with it. I could see that Sarah was feeling the same urge as I, which was to just jump in the water at the first opportunity that came upon us. It would be only another ten minutes or so now, "Hey sweetheart, we're almost there, can't hardly wait to see you in that bikini you bought," I remarked full of excitement. "Who said I was going to wear anything, I might just go skinny dipping if that's alright with you," she replied, while somewhat teasing me with a wink. "Hey I've got no issues with you wanting to skinny dip, let's just make sure we're pretty much alone and there are no children around, I guess that goes for old men too, wouldn't want you to be responsible for causing some old guy to have a heart attack upon seeing you naked, hell I can barely keep myself from having one," I nervously stated. She began to smile and laugh a bit just as the falls came into full sight. "Damn Cole, this is unbelievable, all these years I've lived so close to this beautiful place and never took the time to come here and experience this wonder of mother nature, the water is so pristine and the color is magnificent," she said as she reacted to the sheer brilliance of the turquoise colored pools of water above and below the falls. "Beaver Falls" were no more than thirty to forty feet tall at their highest spots but the pools above and below looked like stepping stones which had naturally made diving platforms around their edges, it was like a fun water park made by mother nature.

We quickly made up a small little camp by one of the nearby picnic tables and began to layout some of our stuff in order to lay claim to the spot, it was the closest one to the water and luckily nobody else was here. Shadow had already homesteaded his spot under the picnic table. "Hey ranger you coming in or what?" Sarah blurted out. As I turned towards her my jaw almost hit the ground, there standing only a few feet away was the most beautiful and totally naked woman I had ever seen in my life, the mist of the falls and the light from the sun reflecting off her body along with the backdrop of the falls was absolutely breathtaking and almost heart stopping as I had thought. "Jesus Sarah, you're definitely the most stunning, gorgeous, exciting and spirited woman I've ever met," I slowly said while still quivering from the awe of her beauty. I then quickly stripped out of my hiking boots, shorts and shirt, then together we jumped into a pool that was only a few feet away. The water was just a tad bit cold because it was still kind of early in the morning which probably explained the lack of any other people but it didn't take long for it to become quite comfortable as Sarah and I quickly embraced in the shallow part of the pool, it was only four to five feet deep in most spots unless you were very close to where the falls hit the pools. As Sarah wrapped her arms around my neck I could feel our bodies almost become one, "Cole I love you, never doubt these feelings I have for you and never doubt my commitment to you, I'm yours forever," she softly spoke as her lips came to rest upon mine. A complete feeling of warmth now consumed our two bodies as we stood half in and half out of the water, "I too have committed myself to make you the happiest woman on earth because I know I love you more than anything on this earth and I will always love you, now and forever, that includes the spiritual world where I believe we will spend eternity together," I replied after gently separating our lips from a long passionate kiss. After spending a few minutes of just holding and kissing each other in the pool we both were overcome with emotion and the sexual arousal that took control of what was about to happen, the two of us swam over to an area of rocks that were concealed behind some of the bigger falls and once there it only took a few seconds to become totally engaged in an unbelievable passionate act of love making, the two of us becoming one.

As we emerged from the behind the falls we decided we had better put our suits on as we were approaching mid-morning and there was sure to be some people showing up. As we got close to the picnic table I just realized we had both totally forgot about Shadow during our mating ritual under the falls, I was quite relived to see him still under the table just relaxing and taking in the serenity of this beautiful place. "Shadow, good boy, you didn't wonder off, for that bit of loyalty I have a surprise for you, how about a nice big rawhide chew," I said to him. He reacted with excitement and once again seemed to know exactly why he was being rewarded. As Sarah was drying off and getting her bikini out of her backpack she turned to me and said, "Hey can we just sit and talk a bit Cole, there's some more I'd like to tell you about the S.H.A.D.O.W. agency and I think we should talk some about our families, past and present." Giving her my full attention and just finishing putting my shorts back on I quickly replied, "Yeah, sure there's still a few things I'd like to tell you also, mostly concerning my parents and most definitely I would love to hear more about the agency I'm planning on working for and enticed me to make the career decision I did." In the back of my mind I still had a hard time grasping what I was about to get myself into, I mean the whole time traveling thing was just incredible to even think that it was possible and the that it had been going on for some time.

The three of us were now all huddled around the picnic table and enjoying the warmth of the sun as it was now fully over the canyon walls and warming up nicely. "So Cole, I wanted to let you know how happy I've been since we met and how wonderful it's going to be working you as well as being in love with you at the same time but I have to warn you once we get started and involved with your training there might be some rough times between us and you might think things have changed between us, I just wanted to let you know that I'm not going to be able to show any favoritism towards you and knowing you pretty well by now I think that's how you would want to be treated, just like all of the other agents, I hope you're not going to have any second thoughts once we get you started in the program, remember I will always be there to help you if you have any problems, that goes for people, training or anything that you might have concerns about," she said after taking a long breath. Taking in all that she had just said I paused for a few seconds, "Sarah I would expect nothing less from you, I know how good of a person you are and don't worry about me being able to handle the ups and downs of whatever training you throw my way, I will endure it because at the end of the day I know I'll be going home with you and you're the most important part of my life and I will do anything to keep it that way," I then replied being very direct and with all my heart. "Damn, I love you, we're going to do great things you and I, the world is going to be a much better place because of it," she said with tears slowly falling down her cheeks. "Cole I'd like to tell you a little something about my father and maybe that will answer some of your questions you may have concerning the whole time travel thing, I know it's still probably a little hard to grasp at this point but the main thing that you should know is that my father is pretty much the reason this technology is even in existence, he is more or less the creator of the equipment and all of the quantum physics involved," she quickly said. "So I guess he's the guy I need to impress the most, I mean professionally and personally because of our relationship," I impatiently remarked. "Don't worry about that Cole, he probably knows more about you than you know about yourself and I think he knows how much I love you, I'm still his little girl and he knows that I know that," she quickly replied.

The two of us kept talking for another twenty minutes or so when we decided to breakout some snacks and take a few more selfie picture's for Miralani and Sarah's father. We weren't able to send out any of the pictures so far because of the crappy cell phone reception. We took several shots of the three of us and the beautiful backdrops of the waterfalls, Shadow almost looked as if he belonged here as part of the surroundings, he was truly a magnificent looking animal and I think he was getting a little bit of big head when it came to taking picture's, in other words he was becoming quite the ham. He and Sarah were almost fighting to get in the center of all the pictures, the two of them had become very close. We sat eating our beef jerky, crackers and cheese and drinking some cold lemonade packs, it was a great meal, the surroundings made everything taste that much better. Shadow was still working on the rawhide I had given him earlier, it looked like he had finally lost the last of his puppy teeth, now he would begin to grow those famous big teeth that made all wolves so scary looking when they bared them. I figured that Shadow was now somewhere around six to seven months old and it would still be at least three more months before his teeth would become scary looking, although I'm not going to tell him that, I wouldn't want to hurt his self-esteem or feelings.

As we neared the end of our snacks Sarah asked, "Hey Cole tell me a little about your father, I mean was he a ranger like you or did he do something else for a living." Swallowing the last piece of jerky I had left in my mouth I then replied, "No he wasn't a ranger, he actually did some work for the government on the side but mostly he was a Navajo tribal elder who made important decisions and worked with government in regards to reservation policies and land management issues, he was also the best tracker I've ever known and taught me everything I know." Sarah paused for a second and had a look of great admiration from my statement, "I can tell you had a lot of respect for him Cole, you two must have been close, I know that he passed away a few years ago from what your sister has told me and I know about the tragic loss of your mother due to post op complications from her surgery, I'm so sorry for both of your losses Cole, my mother passed away when I was very young so it's pretty much been my father who raised me," she said with sadness in her eyes. "It's unfortunate that we have that aspect of our lives in common sweetheart, I'm sure your mother was just as beautiful as you Sarah and I'm sure she is very proud of what you're doing by saving so many lives and making a difference in the world," I replied. As more tears began to fall down her cheeks she decided to change the subject, "So let's talk some more about S.H.A.D.O.W and how it operates as a unit," she quickly said. "Okay but just don't overload me with too much technical mumbo jumbo, remember I'm not a scientist," I quickly replied. "You got it ranger man, first of all there are eight teams of two individual agents and half are male and female teams. I'll give you their name's when I introduce you to them all, it always leaves a lasting impression when you meet someone face to face for the first time." She stated with extreme professionalism.

We talked for at least another hour when I made the suggestion we should take one more swim then head back so we could stop at "Havasu Falls" and enjoy some of the pools there. Sarah quickly agreed and the two of us ran into the water until we were both totally submerged, by now there were several other couples in the water and some of them were jumping off the upper falls area by using the bigger rocks as diving platforms. Shadow had moved to the edge of the pool to watch us swim, all the while making sure he didn't get wet, I know that wolves are not supposed to be afraid of the water but he seemed to be a little timid by the rushing water coming off the base of the falls. I then asked Sarah, "Hey you want to try to diving off of those rocks over there?" Pausing and seeming a little scared I could tell she had no intention of doing any diving on this trip. "You know Cole I'm not a big fan of jumping off anything that could do me bodily harm, no matter how small it may seem," she replied. I smiled some then gave her a big kiss and asked, "Hey try to get a picture of me in midair, I'm going to dive a couple of times before we head back." She quickly turned and made her way back to dry ground then retrieved her cell phone. "Hey Cole, I'm going to climb up on these rocks over here to get a better shot of you jumping into the water," she yelled. "Okay, give me a few minutes to get up to the highest spot," I loudly replied.

After reaching a spot I thought would be good and safe for me to dive off of and making my entry point into the deepest part of water I then steadied myself on a rock platform sticking out a couple of feet from the edge of the falls, "Hey sweetheart, are you ready because I can't balance myself here much longer," I yelled out across the mist of the turbulent waters below. "Anytime you're ready, ranger man," she yelled back. With that response from Sarah I jumped out as far as I could, then tucked my feet in and hit the water perfect. As I surfaced above the water I could see Sarah clapping and Shadow jumping up and down as if to say nice dive, "Wow, you must have been on the dive team when you were in High school, that was beautiful Cole, come on over and check out the picture," she said with joy. Shadow's tail started to wag like crazy as I got closer to them, he almost looked like he wanted to jump in the water but didn't. As I reached dry land Sarah shoved her cell phone in front of my face, "Take a look, it came out great, I got you just a couple feet above the water, right before your entry, what form, I think maybe you missed your calling Cole," she remarked with a gleam in her eyes. "Yeah, that did turn out good, you are one hell of a photographer, are you sure you don't want to try a jump, we could go over to one of the smaller falls on the other side just over there, I could even try see if one of these other couples would take a picture of us jumping together," I softly spoke while begging. Pausing and then working up enough courage she gently grabbed my hand, "Okay Cole, as long we jump together and you tell me how to hit the water because I don't want to do a belly flop by accident, I'm just not very coordinated when it comes to diving," she said nervously.

When we reached the spot where we were going to jump from I signaled the couple who so graciously agreed to take our picture while we jumped. Holding Sarah's hand very tightly I then looked at her and said, "Okay sweetheart are you ready, you got this, I'll be right beside you the whole way down." Still looking very nervous and wide eyed she replied, "Yeah but don't let go of me until we hit the water," we then leaped off the edge and began our freefall to the beautiful turquoise colored pool. We both popped our heads above the water at the same time and Sarah was ecstatic, "Wow, can we do that again, that was great, I want to go a little higher, I mean I'm not scared anymore Cole," she said with a slightly raised voice. "Sure, we'll do a few more here, then start our way back towards "Havasu Falls" where the jumps are really high, not sure if you're going to want to try any of those but if you do I'll be right there beside you," I reassuringly replied. The two of us then began to make our way to a higher spot for the next couple of jumps. Shadow was still at the shoreline keeping the couple that agreed to take more pictures entertained and soaking up all of the attention he was getting from the young lady who was absolutely falling in love with him. The young couple was so gracious to take time out their day to help us out with taking some fantastic shots of Sarah and I jumping off the falls edge over the next thirty minutes. After we made our way back to the shoreline I asked the couple if they would like to join us later this afternoon back at the lodge and join us for dinner which was basically going to be barbequed hamburgers and hot dogs. They both said thanks but they were heading back up the trail to the hilltop parking area after swimming a bit longer here at "Beaver Falls". I said thanks for taking the picture's and gave them a state park business card with my cell phone number on it and told them if they were ever in Sedona to give me a call and Sarah and I would take them out to dinner. We then parted ways and Sarah, Shadow and I headed for "Havasu Falls" which was only about thirty minutes away.

The morning was rapidly coming to an end as we arrived at the falls, it was a little crowded for being a weekday but then again this place always had a lot of hikers and campers year-round. We quickly set up a little area on top of some big rocks because all of the picnic tables were taken. It really didn't make too much of a difference because we would be in the water for most of the time spent here. Sarah was the first to jump in off a small natural diving platform which consisted of some big boulders, it was at least fifteen feet from the surface of the water, she was becoming very comfortable with diving now and was getting braver with each dive. "Hey Cole, hurry up, the water is even warmer now and it's much deeper here," she said as her head surfaced from her dive. "Okay, just give me a few minutes, I think I'm going to climb to the highest platform to jump from," I yelled back. I quickly made sure Shadow had a nice spot to watch from and that I could see him also, once again he seemed as if to know what was expected of him and he nestled down on the rocks and laid his head down. I gave him a gentle pat on the head and said, "Good boy, you keep an eye on Sarah for me while I climb to the top of the falls." He slowly raised his head and looked deeply into my eyes and the two of us seemed to understand each other at that point.

I reached the top of the falls after a ten-minute hike and climb that was pretty challenging and not for the faint hearted, Sarah had already got out of the water and was on the shoreline with her cell phone ready to take a picture of me and my anticipated swan dive I told her I was planning to attempt. "Hey ranger, what are you waiting for, come on already, you're not scared or going to chicken out on me are you?" she yelled at the top of her voice, which I was sure everybody within five miles probably heard. I had done this jump many times before when I was quite a bit younger and somehow it seemed a lot higher up now but there was no way I was turning around to go back down a little lower, she would never let me live it down. "Okay, I'm going to count to three and then jump, so be ready to take the picture sweetheart," I yelled back down towards her. I got set, then closed my eyes and leaped off the edge, the sensation of free flight was instant and incredible, it seemed like only a second had gone by before hitting the water perfect. After surfacing from about twenty feet below I yelled out, "Yeah, how's that, did you get it, I think I hit that about as perfect as an Olympian diver," looking shocked and stunned then messing around with her phone she slowly said, "Sorry Cole I missed it, the damn phone timed out and shut off right when I was ready to take the shot, I guess you'll have to do it again." It only took her a few seconds of seeing my face before she broke out in a gut busting laugh, "Just kidding baby, I got it and it looks fantastic, I think you could be an Olympian diver, Shadow say's that was really brave but don't do it again," she said with concern, then jumped in the water to join me. After swimming and relaxing for a couple of hours we headed off towards the lodge.

Once we arrived back to our room we cleaned up a little then headed out to the picnic table outside our room and I began to prepare the barbeque for our dinner. "Hey Cole is there something I can do to help, I mean I can slice up the tomatoes, pickles and onions, I just don't want you to get too tired out," she remarked with a hint of a smile. "Don't worry about me sweetheart, once I get a couple of burgers in me I'll be full of energy for whatever you have in mind," I confidently replied with a big smile on my face. The three of us sat beside the fire waiting for it to reach its full cooking potential, Shadow was at the end of the table just lying on the grass watching the fire and relaxing, he almost looked as if he was hypnotized by the flames. The sun was almost ready to set behind the canyon walls and the beauty of the Grand Canyon once again showed its colors. Sarah and I began to talk some more about S.H.A.D.O.W. and the scope of the agency. Sarah described the teams in more detail by explaining the male, female partnerships of half of the teams and the cohesion that was needed to develop between them in order for the teams to be successful under pressure situations during the time save missions. It was all still pretty mind boggling for me but I was now coming to terms with it and fully realizing that this technology that man had created could indeed help change humanity and save the lives of so many and prevent the senseless murders and abductions of so many children. I was still in the dark about how this organization was so sure it was not changing the future for the worse in some cases by changing destinies but I believed in Sarah and I knew she believed what she was doing was for the good of humanity.

As we began to eat our dinner the sun had just fully set and the fire from the barbeque was glowing a bright orange and red, Shadow was still intrigued by the burning crackling sounds and the bright glow of the fire and the smell coming from the cooked burgers. Sarah had just fed him his dinner but his nose was definitely working overtime from the aroma of the burgers Sarah and I were eating. After we finished eating we began to talk some more about the whole time technology thing that her father had pretty much developed by himself and once again I felt like a first grader in a college classroom. Sarah gave me a funny look and said, "Don't worry Cole, there are people that have worked there for years and still don't understand how the technology works, trust me once you have experienced the actual movement through time you will understand it much better." I then returned the funny look, "If you say so but right now it's still way over my head," I said with some embarrassment. "I tell you what Cole, I can draw you a little diagram on how this technology works and I think you'll have a better understanding of what Sedona's vortex's actually have to do with manipulating time and space if you'd like or we can wait till you can actually see it in person," she remarked. "Hey that sounds too much like homework, I think I'll just wait until I can see it in person and actually maybe touch some of the equipment if your father will allow it," I quickly replied. Laughing somewhat deviously and then followed by a very serious look, she spoke, "Hey don't think you're going to get out of homework that easy my friend, once we get back and you start your training I'm not going to show you any mercy." I sat there frozen for a second waiting for her to crack a smile or bust out laughing but there was nothing, she remained very serious looking and I was getting a little worried, "What do you mean homework, I thought you said you were going to help me out and watch my back, I mean really, homework?" I slowly asked with a shaky voice. Her intense look finally gave way to a little smile, she then replied, "Well maybe not home work but there will be a ton of procedures and government policies that you're going to have to learn and know them like the back of your hand, I will help you like I promised Cole, I will do everything in power to help you learn everything that's going to be required and yes I will always have your back, never doubt that for a second." I then let out a sigh of relief and put my arm around her then pulled her in tight and closer to my body, she looked into my eyes and slowly pressed her sweet lips against mine.

The fire was now beginning to fade in the barbeque and the bright orange glow was looking more like a faded red road flare with spots of burning ash. Sarah and I cleaned up our mess and made sure all of the garbage was properly disposed of, the tribal members here were very adamant about liter removal and always enforcing the picking up and disposing of your trash. I motioned to Shadow to come and the three of us headed back inside our room to relax and then get some much needed sleep for tomorrows hikes. I had decided not to leave Shadow alone with Two Feathers because Sarah had already told me she wasn't planning on doing anything too dangerous as far as the trails we would be traveling on, besides I still wasn't quite sure about how Shadow would do being away from Sarah and I all day. For next couple of hours Sarah and I continued to talk some more about the agency, family, friends and last but not least how we would try to handle our working relationship in order to keep it professional and productive for everyone concerned. I made a very strong argument that it was going to be hard to keep my hands off her for most of the day while we were working together but I promised to do my best, she also made a similar comment. We both agreed that we would channel our affection and feelings towards each through Shadow as much as possible when we were working, I'm sure he was going to love that. The two of us gently faded off to sleep while Shadow had already called it a night much earlier.

The morning came quite fast as we all slept through the night without any interruptions. The next couple of days were a carbon copy of the first, lots of swimming, hiking and love making which was my favorite part of this vacation so far. We were now on our fourth day here and decided we would head back tomorrow, we were both quite anxious to get my new career started and we both began to actually miss our family, my sister was all I had and the two of us rarely separated for more than a couple of days at one time. Sarah was also missing her father and wondering how things were going back at S.H.A.D.O.W. mostly because of some of the things we had talked about over the last few days, for instance she said she was anxious to get this whole Escalade incident thoroughly investigated in order to get the bottom of it. The three of us had just got back from a long day of hikes and saw three more waterfalls, we were all pretty beat, I had saved the best for last in regards to our final dinner here. I had arranged for Two Feathers to bring in some steaks and lobsters for Sarah and I to celebrate our first vacation together, I had kept it a surprise until now, "Hey sweetheart can you grab that package of meat out of the fridge so I can start to get it ready for the barbeque," I asked. "Sure, what are we having tonight, I thought we were all out of meat to cook and we needed to go to the general store," she curiously commented. "Oh I saved something special for our last dinner here, go ahead and open it up and see for yourself," I quickly remarked. She quickly made her way back from the fridge and slowly opened the brown wrapping paper to expose two of the biggest lobster tails and two of the nicest looking New York steaks I had ever seen, Two Feathers had outdone himself for sure and I would definitely have to return the favor somehow. "Jesus Cole, steak and lobster, how in the hell did you manage this, I mean they don't sell this here, do they?" she asked after the shock of seeing our soon to be dinner. "I had Two Feathers fly it in from a secret source of his, I know you like lobster and I thought it would be a great way for us to celebrate our real first vacation together as a couple in this wonderful place, now let me get the steaks going because the fire is almost ready, oh yeah and you better get used to this kind of treatment from me because I'm going to love spoiling the woman of my dreams for the rest of time," I eagerly stated. "Cole, I love you," she softly and emotionally replied.

After the two of us separated from our long embrace and passionate kiss we headed outside to cook our fantastic meal. I even had Two Feathers get a New York fillet for Shadow. This was going to be a great meal and a great celebration for the three of us, maybe the start of a family tradition every time we take a vacation since the three of us were now a family, an opinion I'm sure the three of us shared. The bond between all of us was now greater than you could possibly imagine, we seemed to share not only a physical bond but a mental one as well, as if we could all understand each other with just an act or a look, it was truly a spiritual blessing that had been bestowed upon us. I knew that Sarah felt the same way just by her expressions and actions towards myself and Shadow, we were a pack, a team and most of all a family connected by the love we had for each other. As the steaks cooked we sat and stared at the stars which were now as bright as the fire that burned only a few feet from us. "Do you think he knows how wonderful you have made my life," I asked Sarah, as I stared into the heavens. "Of course he does Cole, I'm sure he is the reason that our lives crossed paths and started us on this journey, I believe he is the reason and is in total approval of what we do at S.H.A.D.O.W. and I believe he will watch out for our well-being," she passionately replied. "Well someday when the time comes I will personally thank him for bringing you and Shadow into my life, I will forever be in his debt," I emotionally remarked. "I'm sure he feels the same way about you Cole," she replied as she began to tear up.

As we began to enjoy the wonderful meal that was in front of us there was a peaceful calm which was accompanied by the soft sounds of the nearby falls that made this meal exceptionally gratifying and would leave another one of those lasting memories which the three of us would have forever. Our last evening here was by far the best, as I gazed into Sarah's eyes I felt such a warmth and completeness to my life I almost wished we could just stay here forever. We curled up and sat on the grass by the fire on a blanket with Shadow at our side and watched the shooting stars perform a fantastic show that could have only been orchestrated by the hand of God himself. Sarah and I continued to talk about our relationship and how well we had got to really know each other on this trip and how lucky we both were to be together in this world of so many lonely and unhappy people. I expressed my feelings on the whole social media craze that had consumed our world and taken over people's ability to do and think on their own, people were even relying on websites in order to find the so called perfect mate, it was a scary thought to let a computer pick and choose who was compatible with whom. All I know is, when the world didn't have computers to rely on, men and women did okay in finding long lasting relationships and the divorce rate was much lower also. Those days are long gone and part of the trade off and price humanity pays for the advancement of technology that in most other areas of life is a definite improvement. The evening grew late and we had a big day ahead of us tomorrow, we would be saying goodbye to this magnificent place and the people who live here. We cleaned up the remaining garbage from our meal and then we headed back into our room for our last night's sleep here, which I'm sure we were going to miss tremendously.

The night passed without any interruptions once again, the light of day was slipping past the curtains on the windows and our day was about to get started. We would say our goodbye's to Two Feathers and the very friendly staff that provided us with a feeling of friendship and family atmosphere. Sarah was double checking her pack after her shower and I was helping with Shadows rig. We would be packing a lot lighter for the hike back up to the hilltop parking area. Once everything was packed and ready there was a knock on the door, it was Two Feathers, "Hey my friend, you weren't going to leave without saying goodbye were you, hey I have a very special departing gift for you three and I won't take no for an answer, I have arranged a very special helicopter tour for you, Sarah and Shadow and then a return flight to the parking lot on the canyon rim, it's the least I can do for my favorite couple and new friends Sarah and Shadow, that should save you some time on your return trip to Sedona Cole," he graciously said. I was a little caught off guard by his offer but quickly grabbed his hand and replied, "Thank you my friend, we gladly accept your offer, I just hope Shadow will be okay with the ride," Sarah quickly added, "Thanks so much Two Feathers, you're so kind, the next time we come here Cole and I are going to do something special for you, or when you come to visit us in Sedona." Sarah then reached for my friend and gave him a great big hug, "Cole, you better take care of this woman, she is something special, I wish the best for the both of you," he remarked as he stepped back and knelt down on one knee to say his goodbye to Shadow. "Shadow, I wish we could have spent more time together, I know you will look after Sarah and Cole and protect them from all that is evil, I see this in you my friend, you will become a great warrior and protector of all things that are good, may the spirits and the four elements, earth, wind, fire and water guide you on your journeys, goodbye my friend," he said with great emotion and heart.

After saying all of our goodbye's Sarah, Shadow and I followed Two Feathers over towards the small helicopter that was parked and with the pilot inside waiting for us, this really was a very nice thing that my friend had set up for us, sure to provide more of those everlasting memories that Sarah and I would cherish for the rest of our lives. Shadow seemed to be okay as we got close to the copter, the pilot then stepped out and helped us with our backpacks and asked if either one of us wanted to sit in the front, I suggested that the three of us would sit in the back if that was okay with him. Shadow was now wagging his tail and seemed to be excited to get in the back seat area, Sarah climbed in first then Shadow and then I followed them in. Once everyone was secured and ready the pilot started the engine and the copter began to shake a little, Sarah gave me a little wink then said, "Wow this is going to be so cool to see all of the beautiful falls we visited from the air." I nodded my head then put my arms around her and Shadow and gave them both a gentle hug as the rotor blades began to lift us off the ground. Immediately Shadow's head began to move from side to side and he as he was scanning the terrain below as it got smaller and smaller, it must have been an unbelievable sensation for him, his first flight and that it was coming from a helicopter. It only took a few seconds and "Havasu Falls" came into sight, "Wow, it's even more beautiful from the air, you were right Cole when you said this place is like heaven on earth," she said with excitement. Holding on to her hand I gently leaned over and kissed her, then replied, "Yes, it is and you're my angel, I love you sweetheart." The scenic bliss that lied below us was truly spiritual.

10

BECOMING A PACK

After an hour flight of touring all of the falls and most of the surrounding Grand Canyon area we were about to land at the Hilltop parking area and I immediately noticed my baby parked in the lot with an unbelievable shine and glimmer to it, right away I knew that Two Feathers must have had someone remove the car cover and wash it for our trip home, again my friend had totally surprised me with his kindness. When we touched down on the ground Sarah turned to me and said, "That was unbelievable Cole, something I'll never forget, it was spiritually lifting and so breathtaking, I may never see anything as beautiful as long as I live." I quickly added, "Yeah, every time I see this place it somehow brings me back to my youth and the spiritual guidance I received from Two Feathers and his people, I'm so fortunate to have him as a friend and now you and Shadow have that same fortune." Sarah smiled and kissed me on the cheek and then the three of us exited the helicopter and then thanked the pilot for his flying skills and the knowledge of the Grand Canyon he was very impressive and quite good as a tour guide. We then headed over to the Bronco and began to load up our gear, we now had plenty of water and snacks for the drive back since we didn't have to use any of it because of the free ride from the helicopter. The car cover had been neatly folded and tucked up on the roof rack, another act from an old friend who really made this whole vacation happen for Sarah, Shadow and I, I would never be able to thank him enough but I would try.

After a short while we were all packed up and ready to hit the road, we took one last picture of the three of us at the canyon's edge overlooking the Havasupai land and made a promise we would come back at least once a year. Shadow jumped into the backseat and assumed his favorite spot. As Sarah and I were about to get in she asked, "Hey Cole, you want me to drive a bit, I mean if you're tired or just want to take it easy for a while I don't mind." Feeling a bit surprised, I replied, "Okay, I'll take you up on that offer, maybe I'll try to resend all of the pictures we took now that we should have good enough cell phone coverage." Sarah quickly headed for the driver's side door, "Great, I finally get to drive this beast, I promise I'll go easy on her," she said while acting a bit giddy. "Just know that it has a few more horses under the hood than your Fj-40 but knowing you I'm sure you'll be able to handle it," I reassuringly commented. Turning towards me and giving me a crazy look with her eyes crossed which was something I just saw for the first time made me freeze for a second then we both busted out laughing at the same time, god how I love this woman. I kept my mouth shut as we departed the parking area knowing she knew how to drive a four-wheel drive vehicle and before you knew it we were on our way back to Sedona.

As I sat on the passenger side of my Bronco which took some time getting used to, I had just resent the last of our pictures to Miralani because the cell phone coverage was pretty bad back at the lodge. I'm sure I would get a response back very quickly, I even took a picture of Sarah driving just to show her how much I loved this woman, I couldn't wait for her smart ass remark on that one, I love my sister but I sometimes think she's a bigger practical joker and kidder than me. I was now starting to get a little worried that I might not be able to get back behind the wheel of my own vehicle ever again, Sarah was having such a good time on the dirt road part of the return trip she almost looked like she was possessed or something. "Hey, you going to let me take over anytime soon sweetheart?" I sadly asked. "I don't know ranger, I really like this thing, I think I'm going to have to get one, that is if you can find me a good one," she replied. I began to chuckle some then said, "We can find you one, don't worry about that, hell I might just give you this one and build another for me, that is if you have something good in trade "Kemosabe", maybe you have something I like." Taking her eyes off the dirt road for a second and looking at me with a big smile, she then winked, "Oh I think I've got plenty to trade ranger, we'll have to discuss this further down the road in our relationship but I do know I have what you want," she seductively and convincingly replied. I quickly changed the subject, "It's going to be good to see Miralani and everyone back at the cafe, how about you Sarah, I know you probably missed your dad but any other people back at S.H.A.D.O.W. besides Charlie?" I quickly asked. "Way to switch gears ranger, no just my dad and Charlie are the only two people I'm close to there and that's the way I need to keep it, oh and I guess now's there's three counting you but you're a little more special," she replied.

We decided to stop and grab lunch and stretch our legs and hopefully maybe make a driver change. The eating establishment welcomed dogs so that was good, otherwise we would have just got something to go, I'm not a big believer of locking up animals in vehicle's while their owners are out and about, Sarah also shared the same opinion. Once seated and waiting for are meals the response came back from Miralani and she seemed ecstatic over all of the pictures from Havasupai Falls. "Hey Sarah, my sister loves the pictures, she really liked the one where you're driving the Bronco and wants to know what did you have to do in order for that to happen, she also said the one you took of me jumping off the big falls was great and the one of you, Shadow and me she was going to have that one blown up some and hang it in the café because we looked so happy and like a family," proudly and gratefully I remarked. "That's because the three of us are a family Cole, now and forever," she quickly stated. Our little pack was a family, filled with the love of each other and the trust that comes from a very close spiritual bond. I then reached for Sarah's hand and grasped it tightly, "I agree sweetheart, we are a family and I promise you nothing will ever come between us or break the bond we have formed," reassuringly I said. She gently squeezed my hand back a little and then gave me that beautiful smile that I have come to love so much from this kind and wonderful woman. Our lunch finally arrived and we enjoyed our meal as a family, it was another one of those moments that would provide more forever memories that were coming much more frequent with time and as our relationships grew.

As we got back on the road to Sedona after our lunch I had made my way back to the driver's seat and Shadow was putting his head right behind Sarah's trying to stick his nose out the window, "Hey boy, let me move my seat up some, then you can stick your whole head out and get all of that wonderful fresh air blowing by," she suggested. He was wide awake now, especially since he had finished up his lunch by doing his business before we got back on the road, he was becoming very accustomed to traveling in a vehicle which was fantastic, mostly because of his soon to be large size and a big dog that didn't like to travel would be a major pain in the ass. The more I saw him in the back seat area the more I thought about converting the back area of the Bronco into something with a little more room and comfortable for him as he was sure to grow to be around one hundred and twenty pounds or so, a far cry from the seventy pounds he was at now. Sarah was whispering into his left ear as he now had most of his head out the window, the two of them were sharing a special moment. I too was sharing a special moment with the beast that lied underneath the hood, I began to open it up some as we were now on a pretty good paved road, the supercharger seemed to be screaming to me "Thanks God, finally someone with a lead foot" as the Bronco reached ninety miles per hour.

An hour and a half passed and we all looked like we needed to take a pit stop and stretch our legs a bit. I stopped at a roadside gas station that had a minimart and a nice place to walk dogs. Sarah grabbed the leash and took Shadow for a walk and to take care of any leftover unfinished business from lunch as I began fill up the Bronco, this would be the last stop hopefully before reaching Sedona. This was a great trip, the three of us I know had a fantastic time and had some much needed conversations to clear the air of any concerns or apprehension about our soon to be working relationship. I was quite eager to get my new career started and open my eyes to this fantastic technology of time travel and how Sarah and I were going to play a major part in saving people's lives, I felt a special honor to have been chosen to join this organization and I was going to do my best to make Sarah proud of me and Shadow too. I was still a little worried about her father excepting me, not towards joining the agency but more of being in a relationship with his daughter, Sarah kept assuring me he would like me and not to worry but still I knew it was going to feel like taking someone's daughter to prom night upon our first meeting. The gas pump handle clicked and my baby now had a full tank which meant I could stay on the throttle pretty hard and get us home a little sooner as long as the traffic wasn't too heavy. Sarah and Shadow were still enjoying their little walk so I decided to stretch my legs some and join them after parking the Bronco in the rest area lot. The three of us walked some and Sarah and talked some more about the wonderful time we had over the past week and that we would definitely get back there again real soon. We both agreed that it had such a great calming effect on us and the spiritual cleansing the falls seemed to provide was just so peaceful and relaxing, we both felt it had changed our lives forever.

After our short stop we were back on our way towards Sedona, the beautiful place we called home, "Hey sweetheart do you want to stop by your place first or just head to Miralani's for a quick stop just to say hi and then we can head home from there, if you'd like," I asked. "Home, I like the way you said that, it has a nice ring to it, only which home did you mean, yours or mine?" she replied. Thinking I might have just put my foot in my mouth I doubled back really quick and said, "Well your place of course, I mean it's the closest to Miralani's but if you'd rather just head to my place we can do that too." Looking somewhat perplexed and perturbed she quickly answered, "I guess we're going to have to work out some kind of schedule or something once we start working together, I mean we'll probably figure it out and besides it will be fun living in two homes, at least for a while." We both just smiled at that point but I'm pretty sure the wheels were spinning in her mind just as fast as mine on this issue, we both knew sooner or later it would make more sense to live in just one home. Changing the subject Sarah said, "Cole there is still one more thing I really want to tell you about the S.H.A.D.O.W. agency but my father made me promise that he would be the one to tell you this secret about the organization that only he and I know, I want to honor my promise to my father but I also don't want to keep anything from you, what should I do Cole?" I slowly pulled over and stopped on the side of the road, "Sarah sweetheart, I would never ask you to break any promise you've made to your father, nor would I want you to, the time will present itself soon enough and when your father thinks it's right," I softly and understandably replied. "Cole, you're the most understanding person I've ever met, I will keep my promise to him and honor your opinion because I love you both and would never want to do anything to hurt either one of you.

Once we were back on our way I began to think about what Sarah had just told me and what could possibly be so secret that she hasn't already told me, anyways I hoped that I made it perfectly clear that I would never ask her to break a promise to her father or anyone else for that matter. Sedona was getting quite close now and I couldn't wait to see my sister and tell her how much Sarah and I enjoyed this trip, I'm sure she would be able to tell just by how we both looked, happy and peaceful. Shadow had finally settled down and was sleeping on the back seat, he just barely fit, one of my first priorities when I had some free time was going to build that padded floor with a quick release seat option for increased room and a special enclosure for him that would also be safe for him if we were to ever get in some kind of accident, god forbid. Sarah was actually starting to nod off a bit also, she looked so beautiful with the wind blowing and the sun streaming through her golden brown hair, I was such a lucky man. My mind began to wonder what I might be in for at S.H.A.D.O.W. in regards to the type of training I was headed for and how long of training program it was, I mean physically I was in very good shape and I think I could handle anything they could throw at me but I was more concerned about any possible mental or emotional stress testing like what I went through at the F.B.I. for my contract work I do for them and it was not fun.

Miralani's was only a few minutes away now and Sarah and Shadow were just starting to wake up, "Good, you're up sleepy head, we're almost there, hey you may want to drag a comb through your hair before we get there, you look like an old school female country western singer who slept on one side of her hair all night," I said with a slight chuckle and then waited for the slap or punch from her. "Hey thanks for the tip, maybe I'll just leave it this way so I can really impress everyone at the café," she replied with a glare in her eyes. Shadow was one hundred percent awake now and looked like he needed to do some business, I turned around and said, "Hold on boy, just a few more minutes and we'll stop." Again he looked like he understood every word I said, he was so receptive to voice commands especially at such an early age and the fact that I've hardly worked with him at all was amazing, he was truly gifted with great intelligence and awareness. I couldn't help to wonder how great it was going to be to work with him on the job, there's not too many careers out there that will let you work with your pet. I guess he will have to be classified as a service dog, the good news was at least it was a government job and he should get some kind of pension. Sarah then also turned and looked back at him, "Are you sure he can hold it Cole?" she asked. "Of course he can because I asked him to and he can understand everything we say to him, I'm almost sure of that, he's special Sarah and I know you see it too," I quickly replied with the look and pride of a proud parent. Sarah smiled as we turned the final corner to see Miralani's in front of us.

Once we parked I let Shadow out to do his business and it didn't take long, I praised and thanked him for holding it until now and then the three of us headed into the café. After only a few feet inside Miralani came running up to us, "Oh my god you guys, I didn't expect you back so early, you two look fantastic and I must say totally joined at the hip, Cole you really lucked out with this woman, I mean Sarah you're the best thing that's ever happened to my brother and you two look like the perfect couple, kind of like a match made in heaven," she very emotionally blurted out for the whole café to hear. Before either one of us could respond Shadow made his way over to my sister and began to rub his head up and down on her thigh's, "Oh Shadow I'm sorry, I didn't mean to leave you out boy, you are part of the perfect match too, let me give you a big hug," she said as she knelt down to give him a big bear hug. Shadow quickly began to give her a bath with his tongue. "So Miralani, what did you think of the pictures we sent, I'm convinced that this was the most beautiful place I've ever been in my life," Sarah stated. "Yeah sis, it's even more beautiful than the I remembered, mostly because I was with such a beautiful woman," I quickly added. "Nice one Cole, really smooth, all this time I thought I knew my own brother and didn't even realize that he was a ladies' man, oh and I agree Sarah, the few times I've been there I've felt the same way, there is something definitely spiritual and heavenly about it," Miralani somewhat jokingly replied.

The three of us and Shadow headed over to our booth, which was now Sarah's booth as well, "Hey sweetheart you know that this is your booth as well as mine, I mean it's our booth now," I stated as we began to sit down. We ordered lunch then the three of us talked for the next hour or so as we slowly ate our lunch, as the table was getting cleared of our finished plates my sister asked, "So Cole, when do you start this new job of yours?" I turned towards my sister and replied, "Well since it's Friday I imagine on Monday but I'll have to check with my new boss, well what do think boss, Monday sound good to you?" As I looked at Sarah waiting for a response. "Yeah, Monday sounds good to me, that'll give us enough time to find a nice suit for your interview," she replied. "Interview! I thought I already had the job, I mean I put my notice in with the Parks and Recreation department, what if I don't get the job?" I nervously asked. "Oh I'm not talking about an interview for the job, you've got that locked up, I'm talking about the interview you're going to have with my father," she firmly remarked. The look on my face must have been one of total fright and panic because Sarah and Miralani both burst out laughing at the same time, "Very funny sweetheart, you duped me into that quite nicely," I slowly remarked with a show a relief by exhaling loudly. "That's for the hair comment, I really think we're going to have a lot of fun together ranger man but I'm going to have to quit calling you ranger man I guess, I'll come up with something soon enough once we start working together," she said with a warm glow on her face.

As we stood up and began to step away from the booth Sam walked into the café, "Hey Cole welcome back, hey I need to talk to you for a second," he yelled. As he approached us and got closer he said, "Hey good to see you two back, how are you Sarah, hope you had a great time on your vacation, hey Cole I finally got a small break on that Escalade case, I can fill you later if you want," as he looked briefly towards Sarah. "It's okay Sam, she's going to try to help us figure this one out, mostly because she's got some inside information of a possible suspect in her own agency," I quickly remarked. "Sorry Sarah, I meant no offense, I just wasn't sure about releasing information in regards to this case," Sam replied somewhat embarrassed. "None taken Sam, no worries, I know how close you and Cole are and I want to help as much as I can once I get back to the agency, I'll dig as deep as I can without kicking up too much dirt or drawing any attention to myself," she said. "Well the break we finally got was a street cam shot of the Escalade leaving Sedona towards the west and it had two male individuals dressed in dark clothing and a partial match on the plate we had run," Sam explained. "Sam you got the complete plate number when you had it in the impound yard I'm sure so I'll just need to see if it matches any of our company vehicles we have registered back at our motor pool," Sarah stated. "Alright then, sounds like a plan to me, Sam as soon as we find anything out on this we'll contact you with whatever information we dig up," I said. "Okay Cole, that sounds good to me, you two have a great weekend and let me know if there's anything I can do for you two," Sam quickly replied. We gave my sister a hug and said our goodbye's then headed back to Sarah's to drop off her stuff and pick up a fresh wardrobe in order for her to stay the weekend at my place.

It only took ten minutes or so and we were pulling up into her driveway, as she hopped out to open up the front door and Shadow wanted out with her, "Hey I think he wants to take care of some more business, better keep him out in the backyard until I get everything unloaded," I eagerly said. "Okay Cole, I'll be right out to help with the unloading," she replied. "That's okay sweetheart, it's really not that much stuff, I'll get it all," I quickly replied. The two of them then disappeared through the front door as I was opening up the back tailgate to the Bronco. It only took two trips and everything of hers was now in her bedroom where she was already almost finished packing a small suitcase to spend the next couple of days at my house, we would leave from my house for my first day on the job Monday morning. I knew the closer it got to Monday morning the more nervous I was going to get. I was counting on Sarah to help calm me down on that upcoming issue. "Hey I did tell you it's a pretty casual dress code at S.H.A.D.O.W. didn't I, I mean you can pretty much wear whatever you want with the exception of shorts or sandals," she commented as she was putting a couple of pairs of nice jeans into the suitcase. "Well that's good because I never cared much for the white shirt and tie look, I mean that's okay for a funeral director but to have to wear that getup every damn day would be horrible," I replied. I could hear Shadow scratching at the patio door so I went to let him in, Sarah said she was almost done and we could get going after she checked her messages on the phone. Once Shadow was in I sat down on the couch and waited for her to finish up with her messages.

After five minutes or so she had finished, I then asked, "Hey do we need to drive your Fj on Monday in order to gain access to the parking structure at S.H.A.D.O.W. I mean maybe you should follow me home." Sarah headed towards the kitchen then turned back to say, "Yeah, it would probably be easier to take mine, Monday we can get you signed up with your Bronco, they just need a photo of you and a copy of your current registration and the agency will take care of the rest." The security at this place must be pretty good I thought, then that damn Escalade matter creeped into the back of my mind, if it was from S.H.A.D.O.W. how in the hell did it go missing for a couple of days without anyone alerting on it. Oh well, hopefully Sarah and I will get to the bottom of this matter once the two of us look into it. "Okay that sounds good to me, my old girl probably needs a bit of a rest after that road trip," I finally replied after regaining my thoughts of the events on hand. Sarah loaded up her stuff into the Fj and Shadow and I jumped back into the Bronco, "Hey sweetheart you just want to follow me home or do you need to stop somewhere else?" I asked. "No I'm good but due we need to stop and pick something up for dinner or do you have something we can defrost?" She then asked. "Hey why don't we just order a pizza and have a nice bottle of wine with it, something easy and quick and no mess to clean up afterwards," I quickly suggested. "Cole that sounds perfect, that will also give us more time to just relax and enjoy the evening," she remarked. "Okay sweetheart, that sounds better and better the more I think about it, hey when we get there I'll open up the garage for you and do me a favor by parking on the right side of the garage, I'm going to do a little tune up on the Bronco over the weekend and my air compressor and tool box is on the left side, we can tune up yours too if you'd like," I asked. "Okay, I will, I'll follow you and try to keep it under the speed limit, I don't want to get a ticket, besides my little old Land-Cruiser just doesn't have the ponies your Bronco has," she quickly remarked. The two of us then began our little caravan to my house.

I took it easy like Sarah suggested so it took a little longer than normal but we both arrived in my driveway at the same time, as the garage door opened Sarah slowly made her way in on the right side. I decided to leave the Bronco in the driveway for now until we were done unloading everything, Shadow had made his way up to the front seat as soon as we left Sarah's place, I think he definitely liked the front seat better because of the increased airflow he was able to get when sticking his head out the window. The three of us then began to unload the Bronco, even Shadow did his part by taking his backpack into the house. We dropped our backpacks off by the washer and dryer which we would come back to and take out the dirty laundry, I wanted to make sure we first got all of the leftover food back into the fridge to avoid any spoilage. It only took about an hour and everything was done, the Bronco was back in the garage next to Sarah's Fj and I must admit they looked good together, like it was meant to be, I guess kind of like how I felt about Sarah and I, as if it was destiny that brought us together, and I know we looked pretty good together. Just then Sarah stepped into the garage, "Hey Cole, what time do you want to order the pizza, it may be a little busy tonight because it's Friday," she stated. "Yeah your probably right but I won't be hungry for at least a couple of hours, why don't we order it around four-thirty and that way even if it takes an hour or so to deliver it we'll probably be hungry by then," I suggested. "Okay, hey I'm going to go take a shower, want to join me?" she seductively asked. After being restricted from any his and her showers at Havasupai because of the small shower, I quickly stopped what I was doing and turned towards her, "Hell yeah, let me check on Shadow first then I'll be right there," I replied after tripping over some of the gear I had just put in front of me on the garage floor.

Shadow had just completed doing his business and I put him in the house knowing that Sarah and I might be in for a long shower, after all we were pretty dirty, both physically and mentally. As I got close to the master bathroom I could hear the water running from the shower, I began to feel like that kid again at Christmas or like going into a candy store. The sweetest and most beautiful woman in the world was waiting for me in my shower, life doesn't get any better than this. I quickly shed my clothes and walked into the steamy enclosure to find her waiting for me with a bar of soap in her hand, "Hey ranger, why don't you let me clean you up before we get dirty again," Standing next to her and in total awe of her beauty and unable to speak I just nodded my head up and down like a frightened little boy. The next fifteen minutes were physically demanding and yet quite satisfying. As we stepped out of the shower I said, "I think after that sweetheart you should pretty much know the state of my physical conditioning and exclude me from any physical training I might have to go through at S.H.A.D.O.W. or wasn't that satisfying for you?" I confidently asked. She quickly took her wet towel and snapped it really hard on my ass, I almost jumped two feet straight up in the air. "Damn woman what's that for," I yelled out. "Oh I just wanted to see your reaction to a little pain, I must say, I'm very disappointed and you failed miserably on this little pain suppression test of mine," she stated, then she began to laugh. I quickly grabbed her towel and wrapped it around her waist and pulled her in close to me, "Sarah Cooper, my love for you gets stronger with every day but you should know I'll get you back for that," I remarked with all my heart. "I'll be looking forward to that," she softly replied. I dropped the towel and put my arms around her and the two of us gently engaged in a very long and heated passionate kiss.

We were both finally dressed and began to finish up with getting all of the gear put up and starting the laundry, Sarah really wanted to get her cargo shorts with all the pocket's washed so she could wear them around this weekend, she really loved those shorts, I still thought she looked like a zookeeper or something when she had those on but I sure as hell wasn't going to say anything, besides she looked like a gorgeous zookeeper and there's nothing wrong with that. We ended up back in the kitchen when after the last of the gear had been packed away in the garage cabinets, "Hey you ready to order that pizza, I'm actually starting to get a little hungry," she said. "Yeah, I am too, what do you want on it, the only thing I don't like on pizza are those damn little smelly fish," I replied. "Okay, let's get a supreme," she then stated. I agreed and called the pizza joint I've been ordering from for years, it's family owned and the owner moved out from New York many years ago to get away from the rat race of the big city. I told Sarah this place was definitely on the list of places I wanted to take her for a nice sit down dinner. "Hey Cole what about Shadow does he have any food left, I didn't see any out in the garage," she asked. "Well I know one thing, he's not going to get any pizza, I don't think it would be very good for him, I'll check in this one cabinet, I know I had a half a bag of off dry food for him somewhere, I just have to find it," I replied.

After finding Shadow's food Sarah and I began to talk some more about S.H.A.D.O.W. and the other team members of the agency. "You know Cole, if this theory about a rogue agent turns out to be true we're going to have a hard time flushing him out and getting him to incriminate himself, I mean these people are very smart and have been trained to deceive and to hide their intentions when they want to, I'm just saying we're going to have be careful on how we approach this," she said with great concern. "I'll definitely follow your lead on this because I know you probably know all of these team members quite well and I'm going to be a little of an outcast until I can get to establish some kind of working relationship with them," I strongly suggested. "I think you're right on the mark Cole, we'll take it slow and easy on this investigation, besides I have some pretty good relationships with a few people at S.H.A.D.O.W. that can definitely help us with solving this issue, you just have to remember Cole we can't have any outside investigation of S.H.A.D.O.W. pertaining to this case until we're one-hundred percent sure about who this person might be, that means keeping Sam sort of in the dark, are you going to be okay with that, I know he's a very close friend but that's the way it has to be due to the highly top secret status of S.H.A.D.O.W. and it's advanced technical capabilities," she said with a stern voice. "I fully understand that sweetheart but it's just going to be hard to start keeping secrets from my friends and family, I've never done that before," I slowly replied. "Cole, you know I love you and I'm telling you this now but I don't want it to sound like I don't give a damn about your feelings for all of those who you care about but this is the way it's going to have to be for now on because our secrecy directly concerns the safety of everyone you care for and love," again she said with even more of a stern voice filled with emotion. "I know that Sarah, I came to terms with that when I first agreed to take this new career on, I knew there would be some very demanding and personal sacrifices on my part but it will take some time for me to get comfortable with them," I slowly responded as I grabbed her hands and held them tightly.

The knock on the door could only mean one thing, our delicious pizza had arrived, I went to the door and opened it to the wonderful smell of the Italian masterpiece that awaited Sarah and I, quickly I paid the young man and gave him a ten-dollar tip since it was quite a way for him to deliver out this far from town. Sarah grabbed some plates and I grabbed my pie spatula in order to get those wonderful slices of Italian bliss from the box. Sarah's eyes got huge as I lifted the first slice out and plopped it on her plate, "Holy cow, that's a big slice, it smells great, I don't think I'll be able to eat more than one slice though," she said reluctantly. "Oh I bet once you taste it you're going to want another and another until your stomach feels like it's going to explode, it's that good sweetheart, let me grab a couple of cold beers to help wash those slices down," I said with great anticipation. "Sounds great, I'm going to feed Shadow, I think I'll mix in some of the leftover beef jerky from our trip with his food, that might be enough to distract him from our pizza for a while," she said. Sarah returned to her slice of pizza after feeding Shadow and I returned to the dining room table with our beers where Sarah was already enjoying her first bite. "Damn, that's good pizza Cole, you were right, it's absolutely delicious and I'm already thinking about how many more slices I'm going to be able to eat," she mumbled with a mouth full of Italian pie. Smiling I just sat down and dove into my first slice. We sat there for the next twenty minutes seeming to be in some kind of eating contest to see who could put down the most slices of the Italian masterpiece that was rapidly disappearing, "Hey I thought you said you were only going to eat one slice," I reminded her. "I guess we could stop now and save the rest for breakfast, I mean this might be pretty good with some eggs," she suggested. I nodded my head and closed the lid on the box then put it in the fridge where it would be waiting for us in the morning.

After five minutes of burping beer and pizza Sarah and I retired to the couch to relax and watch an old movie from my collection. "Hey what do you feel like watching, an old western, maybe a sci-fi classic or an old hot rod movie?" I asked. "How about an old western, you know one where the U.S. cavalierly kicks all of the Indian's ass," she said with a chuckle. "Okay woman, that one hurt, how about we watch the "Quiet Man", you know the one where a bunch of drunk Irishman beat the crap out of each other throughout the whole movie," firing right back at her and then smiling. The two of us laughing so hard we were almost crying, we then finally agreed on an old hot rod movie, one of my all-time favorites "The Lively Set" which had a lot of young up and coming stars in it, it also had some really cool hot rods and classic cars that just made it a great movie if you were a car guy like me. Shadow had curled up in his favorite spot next to the fireplace just like at Sarah's and seemed to be waiting for the movie to start and then probably fall right to sleep, I wondered how much more he was going to like that spot once winter came and I would be burning firewood almost every night, I'm sure the sounds of the wood crackling would be quite relaxing to him but the heat it would be putting out would more than likely be too much for him with his thick fur coat.

Once the movie started Sarah and I remained curled up together on the couch and began to dig into the popcorn I had just made, Sarah had given Shadow a rawhide chew to keep him busy for some time, I knew he was still pretty worn out the trip and would fall asleep quickly once he was finished with his chew. After thirty minutes or so Shadow was passed out and beginning to snore and to my surprise Sarah had also nodded off with head buried into my chest and shoulder. I didn't want to disturb either one of them so I just kept watching the movie and besides there was now more popcorn for me. I guess the trip was a little more exhausting for her and Shadow than I thought it would be. The two of them were now snoring in unison, I wish I could have reached my cell phone to take a video of this duet, it would have been hilarious to show it to her. Even with her snoring and a slight bit of drool oozing out of the corner of her mouth she still looked like the most beautiful woman in the world. At least I would have a slightly wet shirt as evidence to prove to her that she indeed was drooling, I was pretty sure I was going to get slapped again. After another hour and a half, the movie was finally over and the two of them were still sound asleep, at that point I just decided to try to gently roll over and let her stay sleeping on the couch for a bit longer, I still needed to finish up the laundry and a couple of other items that needed to be addressed before we went to bed. Slowly I rolled off the couch and stood up without disturbing either one of them, then headed off to the garage where the laundry awaited.

After folding the last bit of laundry and putting it in the basket I slowly turned and looked at the Bronco, "Goodnight sweetheart, thanks for getting us home safely," I thoughtfully remarked. I then picked up the laundry and slowly closed the door after turning the lights out, I would be back in the garage early in the morning to do a slight tune up on the Bronco then wash and wax my baby to get all of the dust and bug guts off the paint, you don't want to let that junk stay on there too long because it can destroy a paint job, especially a really nice one. When I returned to the living room Sarah was no longer on the couch, Shadow was still sound asleep but she was nowhere in sight. I started down the hallway towards the bedroom and I could hear the buzz saw of Sarah's mouth and nose, she was out cold and in bed, I quietly got undressed and gently slid into the bed next to her being careful not to disturb her, hopefully she would get a good night's sleep in because I think she really needed it. I quickly faded off into a deep sleep which was surprising with all of the racket she was making, I guess I was pretty tired too.

The morning came quickly as we both slept through the night without any disturbances. Sarah had rolled over and again buried her head into my chest, damn, I could really get used to this. This woman was now in complete possession of my heart and I would do everything in my power to make her happy and keep her safe. "Hey sleepyhead, how are you feeling?" I asked after seeing her eyes open briefly. "Oh Cole, I'm sorry for falling asleep on you last night but I just couldn't stay up any longer, I don't know what it was, I usually stay up pretty late every night," she softly replied. "It's okay sweetheart, I know you were tired and you needed the sleep, I finished up the laundry then I went to bed shortly after you did," I said after giving her a kiss on the head. "I guess you're right, I was pretty tired and worn down from everything from the trip to being nervous about your first day on Monday and introducing you to my father, I know he's going to like you but I just hope he doesn't think we both moved a little too fast in this relationship, you have nothing to worry about Cole, it's me that he'll give a little look of concern, just remember Cole, he's never met you but does know everything about you and your qualifications for justifying the need to hire you on as an agent," she stated. I then pulled her tightly into my chest and said, "You let me worry about convincing your father how much we both love each other, I will be respectful of his opinions but I will stand on firm ground about our relationship make it perfectly clear to him how happy the two of us are." Shadow then jumped up onto the bed and pushed his way up to our faces and began to lick us like we were some kind of lollipops, I guess he wanted to put his two cents in also.

After playing with Shadow on the bed for twenty minutes or so Sarah and took a quick shower. Once we were clean and had finished getting dressed we made our way to the kitchen for breakfast, "Hey you ready to try some leftover pizza chopped up and put into an omelet, I know I am," she quickly remarked. "Sounds great to me, can I help with anything?" I asked. "No I've got it under control, why don't you and Shadow go out and play some more in the backyard or something and leave the cooking to me, I'll let you know when everything is done," she replied. Agreeing with her Shadow and I made our way to the backyard, I thought maybe now would be a good time to work some more on his training and hand signal commands, I wanted him to learn some very important hand signals that we would be using out in the field, it's very important to establish a silent method of communication between a tracker and his service dog, or in my case a service wolf who was also becoming my best friend. We worked on his training for a bit then I would alternate with some play time then go back for more training. This was a proven method of keeping the attention of the animal during the training periods. Shadow was an extremely fast learner and had an amazing sense and feel of speech patterns coming from his handler, which in this case was me. Sarah would eventually have to spend some more time with him too just to make sure he was comfortable with her giving and using the same commands as I.

I could smell the eggs and the last night's pizza getting fried up together in a skillet and it smelled delicious, I didn't think it was going to be a great combination for a breakfast food even though I told Sarah it sounded good, I just hoped that it was going to taste as good as it smelled. Shadow and I finished up with our brief training and play session and headed back towards the kitchen just as Sarah yelled out, "Come and get it boy's" the two of us were already moving at a fast pace almost broke out into a sprint, hoping to be the first to try out this new breakfast recipe. "We're coming sweetheart," I yelled back her way. Once Shadow and I made it through the patio door I could see the wonderful looking spread on the table, "Wow, how the heck did you make all of this so fast, I mean it looks like a buffet at Vegas or something," I quickly remarked. "Well nothing's too good for my boys, only I think you better go easy on the eggs and pizza Shadow, I made some special bacon and eggs just for you Shadow so you wouldn't feel left out big guy," she lovingly replied. His ears perked straight up after her remark and hearing his name, he then headed over towards the kitchen counter area and began to scan the entire area with his long snout, wolves were known to have an incredible sense of smell and I'm sure in this case he was just trying to savor every delicious smelling item up on the counter.

The three of us were almost finished devouring the wonderful meal that Sarah had prepared and served us, "Sweetheart this has got to be the best omelet I've ever had in my life, just don't tell my sister that, I know Shadow liked his special breakfast, so what can we do for you today?" I graciously asked. "Oh I don't know, maybe just the three of us hang out here all day and do stuff that a family would do, you know like play in the backyard, due some yardwork, maybe wash and wax our vehicles, then have a nice barbeque at the end of the day and just relax out back and enjoy each other's company, I know it sounds corny Cole but I really never got to have moments like that when I was growing up with my family and I would really like to have those with you and Shadow because I love the two of you so much and besides we are a family now," she said with a tear falling down the side of her cheek. It was at this point in time of our relationship that I came to realize how much of Sarah's childhood must have been sacrificed due to her father's research and commitment towards building the S.H.A.D.O.W. technology. "Hey Sarah, it doesn't sound corny at all, it sounds exactly like what's coming from your heart and I for one would love to spend the day doing all of that as long as it's with you, I'm sure Shadow would agree if he could speak, okay then it's settled, let Shadow and I clean up the kitchen then we'll head outside to get started on the yardwork and cleaning the Fj and Bronco," I suggested. "You got a deal ranger," she quickly replied with one of the brightest smiles I've ever seen on her beautiful face.

After Shadow and I finished with the dishes, he helping with a few of the leftovers and I cleaned up all of the dirty pots and pans. The two of us along with Sarah were definitely going to make a great working team at S.H.A.D.O.W. as long as she and I didn't spoil him too much. We headed out to the garage where Sarah had already backed her Fj into the driveway, "Hey I didn't know if you wanted me to back your Bronco out too, we could maybe wash them together, it might be easier and quicker that way," she suggested. "Yeah, sounds good to me, hey you could've backed it out, remember what's mine is also yours now sweetheart, I'll get the bucket and the soap, there should already be a nozzle on the hose out front," I quickly replied. Looking a bit stunned by my statement she turned and said, "Wow Cole, your too much, I can't believe how sweet and kind you really are, I know you kid and tease quite a bit but deep down you've got to be the kindest and most thoughtful person I've had the pleasure to know. I guess that's a few of the reasons why I've fallen so hard and fast for you." I slowly walked up to her and put my arms around her waist and whispered into her ear, "I love you too but don't tell anyone else that I'm a softie, it's taken many years to build up this tough guy reputation of mine and I for one don't want to lose it." She quickly kissed me on the cheek and remarked, "Okay ranger, your secret is safe with me." Turning away she then went to get the hose while I jumped into the Bronco and backed it out of the garage, within a few minutes Sarah and Shadow were playing around by chasing me with the hose and gave me quite a dousing.

Thirty minutes had passed and after good round of playtime with the hose we finally finished up by drying the two vehicles. Sarah and I quickly pulled them both back into the garage where we might wax them a bit later. After closing her door on the Fj she asked, "Hey Cole where's all of your lawn and gardening stuff, I feel like pulling some weeds and trimming up the bushes alongside the driveway." After working my way over towards her I then motioned to her to follow me, "I'll show you my little homebuilt shed that my father and I built many years ago, I keep all of the tools and equipment in it for keeping up the landscape around the house, not to mention the big fire break further out from the house," I quickly mentioned. "Okay great," she replied. I gave her an extension cord and the heavy duty electric trimmer to take on the thick shrubbery and bushes that outlined most of the driveway. I on the other hand went back to cleaning the Bronco and Fj, they both needed to be vacuumed and the inside of the windows were absolutely filthy on the Bronco, I guess sitting up on that mesa parking area at Havasupai was enough to get the inside dirty, there must have been some strong winds one of the days we were there.

The rest of the afternoon went buy pretty fast and before you knew it we were all on the back patio eating burgers I had just barbequed. Sarah looked really tired from the yardwork but at the same time looked very happy and had a wonderful glow about her, "Hey ranger, thanks for today, I had a great time with you and Shadow and all of the work we got accomplished around here today was quite rewarding, I think tomorrow we'll just take it easy and talk about what you can expect on your first day on Monday," she softly remarked. "No worries sweetheart, I'll always do whatever it takes to make you happy and to keep our relationship strong, it makes me feel good to see you so happy and enjoying life together with Shadow and I, my life has become so much more amazing since you've come into it, I truly love you," heartfelt I emotionally replied. The two of us then curled up together on the swing and gazed into the stars. Shadow had fallen asleep on one of the other patio chairs that was more like a loveseat than a chair and he had made himself pretty comfortable in the thing. As the evening grew late the three of us finally called it a night and headed back into the house.

Shadow again curling up by the fireplace which had now became his personally claimed domain was falling fast asleep, I guess the rapid growth rate that dogs experience through their first year and a half of life can be pretty exhausting, not to mention all of the mental training and commands I was now teaching him. I was still amazed on how fast he picked everything up, the wolf species is a very special and gifted breed of animal and should be treated with appreciation and respect. Since the beginning of Indian culture, the wolf and the bear have been revered as great protectors of our people. He was getting so big and strong, I could hardly wait to see how spectacular he was going to be when he was full grown, I just hoped he wasn't going to get too large where it would be uncomfortable to travel in the Bronco for him. Sarah and I sat on the couch curled up in each other's arms and were just grateful for what we had and the closeness the three of us had developed, I guess you could say we had become a very close and loyal pack, a family pack of our own.

11

DAY ONE

The next morning Sarah and I found ourselves waking up on the couch wrapped up together again like a giant pretzel and Shadow still snoring away in his favorite spot. Sarah and I had agreed that today would be a lazy day and not to go overboard with any crazy plans or activities, we both wanted to be refreshed and energized for my first day tomorrow. As the two of us had just finished getting dressed and headed towards the kitchen the doorbell rang and Shadow jumped up and began to growl softly, I quickly put him at ease and slowly we walked over to the door together, I wanted to assure him there was no danger or need to be protective at this point. I didn't want him to be one of those annoying dogs that would absolutely go bonkers every time someone came to the front door and rang the doorbell or knocked, I would have to work with him on this. I slowly opened the door to reveal my sister and Sam standing there together, "Hey, what a surprise, what are you two doing here, everything okay?" I asked. "Yeah Cole everything is great, Sam and I were just in the area and I know I should have called but we kind of have something important to tell you and couldn't wait any longer," she replied. "Oh hi Sarah, good to see you again," she said as Sarah popped her head from around the corner of the hallway, "I hope we aren't interrupting you two or any plans you might have made but Sam and I have something very important to tell the both of you," she said as she closed the front door. "Hell no

Miralani, you're not interrupting anything, we got up a little while ago and we were just going to relax and take it easy today, we have no plans to do anything, hey why don't you two come on in and I'll whip up some breakfast for all of us," she quickly remarked. "Okay, that sounds good but Sam and I wanted to take you guy's out after you hear what we're about to tell you," she replied.

After a brief moment of total silence and the slow walk out to the living room we all sat down. "Hey Shadow, how are boy, I have really missed you," she stated as Shadow was licking her knees and lower legs. "Well what's so important that you and Sam had to drive over here and tell us sis?" I eagerly asked. "Yeah Miralani, what's up?" Sarah then asked. "Cole, I would like to ask you for your approval in your sister's hand in marriage, I know that you're the only family she really has and I wanted to make sure you didn't have any problems with me or anything else that might harbor any bad feelings towards this happening," Sam nervously and emotionally asked. After almost falling off the couch combined with the loud outburst from Sarah sitting next me I then turned and looked at Miralani, "Sam I've been hoping for so long for someone to sweep her off her feet and that she would settle down and be happy and even though I'm not her father I will put my two cents in on this matter, I've wanted the two of you to get together for a long time now and I couldn't be any happier, you two are perfect for each other and this is wonderful news," I quickly and thoughtfully remarked. "Oh my god Miralani, I'm so happy for you two, Sam you're a terrific guy and I agree with Cole, I think you two were meant for each other," as Sarah added her opinion to the conversation. Miralani just sat and cried a bit then looked up and leaned over to me and kissed me on the cheek, "Brother I love you so much, you've always been there for me whenever I needed a shoulder to cry on or just a big happy hug, Sam and I are so happy together and I know it's kind of sudden but I guess there must be something in the air lately, you've found the love of your life and now I have found mine," she emotionally said.

Ten minutes of nothing but hugs and a lot of tears of joy went by and even Shadow seemed to be moved by the whole experience, "Hey sis, I think Shadow wants to give his blessing too," cheerfully I remarked. Miralani then got down on her knees and gave him a huge bear hug and then kissed him on top of his very long snout. "Thanks Shadow, don't worry, you're still going to be a very special man in life, I will never stop loving you," tearful but with a bright glow of happiness on her face she emotionally replied. "Don't worry Shadow, there's plenty of love to go around in this house for you and you will still get to spend plenty of time with Miralani when I need her to watch you from time to time," I assured him. He then returned a look of gratitude towards Miralani and then almost knocked her completely down to the floor with one big last lick on her face, he then jumped up on the couch next to Sarah. "Well thank you Shadow, Cole he's getting very strong and not to mention growing like a weed, how big do you think he'll get?" she asked while getting up off the floor. "Well his particular breed of wolf which I believe is perhaps a Grey wolf or a mix of Grey and Timber could reach a weight of one-hundred and fifty pounds depending on the genes passed down from his bloodline, let's put it this way, I don't think he'll be under one-hundred and twenty pounds just because of the size of his feet and because of how big he already is," as I confidently expressed my opinion to her.

After the shock and joy of my sister's announcement Sarah headed out to the kitchen and asked everyone what they felt like eating for breakfast. "Hey sweetheart, I've got those four really nice New York strips I just bought the other day and steak and eggs sounds like a perfect way to celebrate this great news, I'll come out and help get them ready," impatiently I replied. "Yeah, that sounds terrific and it's perfect for the occasion," she quickly remarked. Sam and Miralani nodded their heads then gave their voice of approval. The next half hour or so went by very quickly and before you knew it we were all finishing up the wonderful breakfast that Sarah had made, Shadow even got some chopped up cubes of steak mixed in with his dog food, he was in heaven, the smell and taste of beef was definitely a favorite of his. The four of us sat around the dining room table and talked about relationships and how lucky we all were to have been blessed in finding the perfect partners in life, I believe our pack just got bigger, I know it sounds crazy but in the back of my mind all I could think about was how all of these new relationships were going to affect how much effort it was now going to take to complete my Christmas shopping.

Before we knew it the day was already growing into the late afternoon, Sam and Miralani decided to get going because they knew it was going to be a big day for me tomorrow with starting my new job and all, deep down inside I really wanted to tell them about S.H.A.D.O.W. but I had already come to the realization that I would probably never get to tell them the truth about the type of work I'd be doing. "Okay Cole, I hope your first day goes well, I'm pretty sure it will, besides it will be much easier to handle with Sarah as working partner, promise you'll take it easy on him Sarah, okay, I love you both and I'll call you early in the week to see how things are going Cole, enjoy the rest of the day, see you later," she said as we all walked out into the front yard. Sam was driving his new Sherriff's vehicle which was a hopped up Ford Explorer, "Hey Sam how do you like that thing?" I asked while looking at the Explorer. "You mean your sister or the Explorer, just kidding Miralani, actually Cole I love them both," he replied jokingly then took a defensive posture waiting for the slap from my sister. "Yeah you better cover up or I'll knock that smile right off your face," Miralani remarked with a little humor in her voice. Sarah and I both laughed then said our goodbyes. As we walked backed into the house Sarah commented, "Wow, they kind of act like they've already been married for a while," I laughed a bit then agreed with her. After that huge breakfast we both agreed that a light snack would suffice for dinner, the evening had arrived and we decided to hit the sack early, even Shadow seemed to know that we were expecting a big day tomorrow. The lights soon went out in the bedroom and it didn't take long for the two of us to fall asleep, Shadow too.

The alarm clock blew us both out of bed at four-thirty in the morning, Shadow got up and began to moan and softly growl as if to say "What the hell, why are we getting up so early, oh well I might as well go out and pee since I'm up." He usually sleeps through the whole night and doesn't want to get up until around six o'clock, so this was a little early for him. Sarah was first to make it to the shower while I let Shadow out to take care of his business. I quickly made my way back to the bathroom after letting Shadow back in the house and jumped into the shower with Sarah. We finished up with our shower and were getting dressed when Sarah asked, "Hey ranger you a little nervous or what, you forgot to put deodorant on and I think your missed a belt loop on your jeans, better check your underwear too, they might be inside out." Looking a bit flustered I'm sure, I then opened up to her by my remark, "No sweetheart, I'm not a little nervous I'm a lot nervous and I can't think straight, I mean I shouldn't be, hell you've told me pretty much everything to expect today and I've gone over everything in my head a thousand times to what I'm going to say to your father about our relationship but it keeps getting more muddled the closer we get to actually being there." Sarah then approached me and put her arms around my shoulders and looked into my eyes, "Listen Cole, my father is going to absolutely love you like the son he never had and always wanted, he probably knows more about you than you, I mean he's a very thorough and meticulous man who always does his homework on everything or anyone who he is involved with personally and professionally, so you can put your mind at rest honey, he's going to like you," she reassuringly said.

An hour had passed and we were almost ready to hit the road, Shadow almost seemed as excited and nervous as me. Sarah had already talked with her father yesterday and confirmed that we would be getting in this morning to start my indoctrination and complete all of the paperwork required to become an agent and most of importantly put me on the payroll, Shadow made one more trip to the backyard to take care of any unfinished business from earlier this morning then we all headed to the garage to load up in Sarah's Fj. We weren't going to stop at Miralani's this morning because there wasn't going to be enough time and I didn't really want to eat too much anyway, my stomach was still a little upset from all the anticipation of what I was going to go through today. The drive to S.H.A.D.O.W. would take us about forty-five minutes or so depending on the traffic in downtown Sedona, it was probably going to be the longest forty-five minutes of my life. Sarah was doing everything she could to try and make me feel more at ease but it just wasn't working, as we were pulling out of the driveway and watching the garage door close a crazy thought popped into my head, "Hey let's call in sick today and just stay home in bed, we can do this tomorrow, can't we?" I nervously asked. I then looked towards her and said, "Just kidding, sort of." She then put her hand on my leg and smiled, "You're going to get through this Cole, don't worry, trust me after the first week or so you're going to be so excited to be working at S.H.A.D.O.W. you won't want to even come home at the end of the day," she reassuringly remarked. "I hope your right sweetheart, I hope you're right," I softly replied.

We were just getting out of the city and the sun was starting to rise, at least the beautiful sunrise would put me somewhat in a calming state. All these crazy thoughts and worries just kept creeping into to my mind, I mean the thought of traveling back in time and the worry of getting trapped somewhere in time where you didn't belong was to say the least, quite concerning. If there was one comforting thought, it was that Sarah seemed to be at ease with the whole thing and believed it to be quite safe and reliable and I'm sure her father wouldn't let her do what she does if it wasn't safe or believed it wasn't the right thing to do. As we headed out of Sedona on the main dirt road towards "Secret Canyon" I knew it was only another twenty minutes or so before we reached the S.H.A.D.O.W base that was completely hidden from the public right under their noses, including mine which was sort of embarrassing for me because of how I considered myself such an expert of the local area. Whoever was in charge of the development and bringing this facility to fruition did an outstanding and unbelievable job of keep it concealed and hidden during its construction, it kind of made me wonder what other unbelievable secret facilities and technology might possibly exist that has been kept out of the public's eye and for how long.

Soon we were off the main dirt road and back on the dry creek bed which ran the length of "Secret Canyon", which became are main thorough way to the facility. Shadow seemed to be familiar with the surroundings of the landscape and acted if he was starting to remember this trip from the opposite direction. Sarah was concentrating on the trail and I was concentrating on her, suddenly all of my worries seemed to disappear as I watched this magnificent woman handle the creek bed in her Fj without any concerns or apprehension, with every passing day I became more and more impressed with this lovely lady. "Hey Cole, how you doing over there?" she suddenly asked. "Oh I'm alright now, I've just been watching the most beautiful woman in the world handle a four-wheel drive vehicle like it was a toy or something, you're amazing Sarah," I quickly replied. "It's just a dry creek bed Cole, not the "Baja One-Thousand", anything more than this I don't think I could get through it without some more training and experience in off road driving," she honestly remarked. "Well you have me for that now, I'd be more than happy to teach you everything I know and you can help teach me the science and technology of the time travel system and how it works," I eagerly suggested. Just then we pulled up on the secret hidden entrance that looked like something out of a high budget science fiction movie. The side of the hill opened slowly as Sarah activated some sort of remote switch on the dash of the Fj. We slowly pulled up and into the opening and proceeded through the tunnel for a hundred yards or so until we came up on the guard shack.

Sarah's friend Charlie was at the post. Sarah quickly rolled down her window, "Hey Charlie, how's the love of my life, I missed you, anything I should know about before I head in?" Charlie looked at Sarah smiled then said, "I missed you too, I see you brought him back, is he going to be a regular here and by that I mean your new partner, nothing much going on around here other than I still think someone is playing games with me and moving some of Escalades around and putting them in different parking spots." Sarah smiled back at him, "I'm sorry to hear that, I'm going to look into that, I promise and yeah Cole is my new partner and this is his first day, you're going to like him Charlie, he's a bigtime car guy like you, I bet within a couple of weeks you two are going to be the best of friends," reassuringly she said. Charlie waived us on through, "See you later Coop," he said. Sarah waived back outside her window and we headed for her parking spot. "I don't think that man likes me sweetheart, I guess he's a little jealous, I wonder if he knows about us or if he's just fishing for some kind of a response from me," I suspiciously remarked. "Oh Charlie's okay, he's just a little grumpy early in the morning, I guess if you sat in that little shack for most of the day it would eventually wear on your personality and attitude," she replied. Quickly turning my attention to the group of Escalade's that we were passing on the right side of the parking structure I began to wonder, "Hey sweetheart, you know when Charlie mentioned something about the Escalade's being moved around on him, what if it wasn't a joke but actually had something to do with my case in Sedona," I asked with some reserve. "I'm already on it Cole, I thought the same thing, remember I promised you we will get to the bottom of your case which is probably related to the rogue agent theory, while you're going through your initial in processing and lab work I'll start looking in to it and running some checks on the logs for all of the Escalades," she quickly stated.

Once parked, Shadow seemed to be anxious to get out and stretch, he seemed to be very excited to be back here. I'm assuming he probably made a few friends around here while I was in my coma. The three of us jumped out of the Fj and began walking towards the big double steel doors which looked like they belonged at NORAD or something. Shadow was prancing and running three-sixties around Sarah and I, he hadn't been this excited since the moment he was brought into my room after coming out of my coma. "Hey Shadow settle down boy, it's okay this is going to be your second home as well as ours too," Sarah remarked while petting his head and rubbing his belly. "Hey I'm getting the impression that he really likes this place Sarah, you guys must have spoiled him rotten while I was in my coma," I suggestively stated. "Well he did make a few friends here while you were catatonic," she replied. "I bet he did, his personality and demeanor are just so alluring it's hard to resist, kind of like a vampire you see in the movies," I remarked. Sarah nodded her head and we continued to walk towards the last set of security doors between us and the main facility, the butterflies in my stomach were starting to make a strong comeback the closer we got.

Shadow seemed to have calmed down once the three of us passed through the final doors to the facility, he was finally acting normal and at ease with his surroundings. "Hey Shadow, do you remember this place, I bet you remember all of the chopped up steaks I brought to you during your stay here," Sarah remarked. "So that's where he gets his love of steaks from, it's all your fault, no wonder he got so excited to see this place again," impatiently I said. "Uh oh Shadow, we're busted, sorry Cole but we didn't have any dog food around here when I took care him during your coma," she quickly replied. We both laughed a bit which seemed to loosen me up some and Shadow gave me a look of shame as if he were asking me to forgive himself and Sarah. "It's okay boy, I'm not mad at you or Sarah, I would have done the same thing, besides who could've resisted your sad and depressed look you probably had knowing that I was on my death bed," I sadly remarked. "Oh my god Cole, you really know how to spin a story, death bed, really?" Sarah asked as if to question the validity of my story. "What, I could have been near death, I mean nobody really knows, I did see some bright lights I think," I replied with some uncertainty and deep concern. "Okay Cole, we'll talk about it later, another few minutes and you're finally going to get to meet my father and remember just relax I guarantee he already likes you even if he tries to play like a tough guy or a jerk about us being in a relationship, I guess his sense of humor and pranking sort of reminds me of you," she reassuringly remarked. I then remained completely silent as we walked down the hallway, I was really hoping Sarah was right about him going to like me.

As the three of us came up to a set of stainless steel double security doors Sarah quickly extended out her right hand out towards a small box mounted adjacent to the doors. After she placed her hand completely flat on the scanner portion of the box she then swiped her I.D. badge through a side slot, within seconds the doors opened up to reveal another hallway that disappeared to the right. Shadow was the first to quickly jump ahead of us through the doors and then slowed his pace once he realized he had put some distance between Sarah and I. Again he seemed as if he knew the way, "Hey boy do you remember this area, Sarah has he been down this hallway before?" I curiously asked. "I'm sure he has Cole, he and my father became pretty good friends in the short time he was here during your coma," she replied. "I guess that explains it, it's as if he knows where we're heading and what or who waits ahead," I remarked. We then continued down the highly secured and private hallway for another few minutes until we came up to a small railway system complete with a passenger loading platform, it really looked like something you'd see at Disneyland or some other major amusement park, "Wow, what the hell is this?" I asked with total amazement and surprise. "This is our ride to my father's work lab and then to the collider central core control room, this is where it's probably going to get a little overwhelming for you Cole but I promise you you're going to love the shuttle ride, it's pretty scenic for being underground and all," she quickly stated. Just then a small and completely empty six-person vehicle of some sort came quietly down the tracks towards us, "Here comes our ride now Cole," she said with excitement. "This place just keeps getting more amazing by the minute, how far do these tracks go Sarah?" I then asked. "Well including all of the maintenance lines we have I'd say we have just over fifty-miles presently but we're expanding all the time," she confidently replied. I just stood there in amazement with my jaw almost touching the ground after that, I hadn't even seen much of anything yet but I already was in a state of shock over the sheer size this facility must be. Sarah then reached for the small handle on the side of the shuttle and entered a numerical sequence into the cipher lock keypad next to the handle. The door then opened in two different sections and the three of us piled in, there were two rows of three seats so we sat in the front row and Shadow was now becoming more and more excited with every minute that passed.

The door closed and made a sound like an air seal had been completed, we then began to move slowly away from the small loading platform. Shadow's tail was now wagging like crazy, he was surely very excited about what was happening. "Relax and enjoy the ride Cole, it should only take about five minutes or so to reach my father's lab," she quickly stated as our speed began to increase. We were probably only going around thirty miles per hour but it seemed a lot faster because of the closeness of the walls of the tunnel we were now in. After a minute or so the walls began to open up some and the beauty of the underground caverns began to light up from the exterior lighting that lined the tracks, it was stunning, the colors of this underground dwelling were truly breathtaking, "Wow Sarah, you didn't say anything about this before, why not?" I suspiciously asked. She paused for a second then began to pet Shadow to calm him down some, she then replied, "I know Cole and I'm sorry for that, there was just no way for me to describe it and I thought it would be a better experience for you not knowing what to expect, believe me you've only seen the tip of the iceberg." Not saying a word, I just smiled and continued to observe and admire the shear brilliance of this spectacular place. The shuttle was extremely quiet and smooth, "Hey sweetheart, how does this thing move along, I mean I don't hear any engine noise," I curiously asked. "I wondered how long it would take before you asked me that question, well it's like this Cole, the basic system runs off the technology of those high speed "Maglev" trains you see running all over the world now but this one is a little more advanced and was another one of my father's creations," she proudly replied.

After a few more minutes of spectacular underground scenery we began to slow down, "Well we're almost there, I can't wait to see my father, this is the longest I've been away from him in quite some time," she said with great anticipation. "God I'm nervous as hell

Sarah, do I look nervous sweetheart, I mean I'm not sweating am I, maybe he'll pay more attention to Shadow than me," I nervously remarked. As the shuttle came to a complete stop Shadow pushed his way towards the front of the door, "Relax boy, I know you're excited to see my father too just be careful getting out of this thing," she said holding Shadow back from the door as it began to open slowly. The three of us then carefully stepped out onto the platform which lead to a small staircase. As we began our descent down the stairs I felt a sudden wave of calmness and confidence consume my body and soul almost as if all of my worries had been lifted from me spiritually, it was something I had never felt before, "What's wrong Cole, are you okay, you look like you just woke up from a long sleep or something," she asked. "I don't know what it is Sarah but this place is starting to make me feel great, I mean I'm at ease with this whole situation that I'm about to encounter and I've never felt better in my life, I can't explain it," I happily replied. "I knew my father was going to like you," she quickly and softly remarked. A bit confused by her comment I just kept going down the stairs which was almost at its end, I could now see three different hallways that headed off into opposite directions. As the three of us came up to a small circular area centrally located between the three hallways Sarah turned and said, "This way guys, only a few more minutes and we'll be there." At this point I should have been jumping out of my skin but I was still feeling that complete calmness and total serenity of my surroundings, even Shadow had calmed down to a slow pace and gentle stride to his walk.

Our journey came to an end at another set of double security doors with another type of cypher lock that looked like something from a science fiction movie, then Sarah placed her hand up against the scanner of the device which then shot out some type of soft green beam of light which she then leaned into and it immediately began to scan her entire face while another beam of light this time red and much sharper and smaller in width began to scan her right eye, I then thought to myself "Holy shit, I think I just signed up to work for some kind of super spy agency", I couldn't help to wonder how much more elaborate this place was going to get just then the two beams shut off and the doors split down the middle and began to open at a very slow pace, at least to me it seemed slow but then again everything had seemed to slow down once we got off that shuttle platform and began down those stairs. "Here we go Cole, my father is expecting us, I can hardly wait to give him a great big hug," she said as a few tears of joy began to flow down her cheeks. I could really see how close Sarah and her father must be and it was obvious the two of them must have a great relationship. The doors closed behind us and as we took a few steps in, I could see the outline of a man wearing some sort of lab coat and standing proudly in front of a huge desk piled high with books and papers, he was very young and fit looking and not what I expected for a man of what I presumed his age was. "Dad, I'm so glad to see you, I've missed you terribly, I've been looking forward so much to introducing Cole to you, Cole come on over here," she said as the two embraced in a very strong hug. I slowly approached making sure not to interfere or shorten their emotional brace, "Hello sir, I'm Cole Youngblood and it's a pleasure to finally meet you," I strongly stated and greeted him with a very strong handshake. Just then Shadow made his way to the front of the desk and squeezed in between Sarah and her father. "Hey Shadow, I know boy, you're just as happy as I am to see him," she quickly remarked. "Dad, he is the one I've been telling you about for some time now, I know everything has happened so fast but we our very much in love and our souls have become one, we are committed to each other forever and we both feel we've found something very special between us and I think it's our destiny to be together," she emotionally and firmly said. The proud father stood before me and checking me out like the scanner I had just witnessed outside the doors of this office, "Well Mr. Youngblood I must say you're exactly the way I pictured you after Sarah's description, it's a pleasure to meet the man that has totally swept my daughter off her feet, you must have really impressed her son, she has always been so tied up with her work she has never made time to meet anyone, I'm extremely happy that you have come into her life and mine as well, please call me John and I already know this guy, I had a brief working relationship with Shadow here, I must say you picked out a great name for him, he's a very special animal Mr. Youngblood if you haven't figured that out already," he said with a voice that was chilling yet soothing at the same time. "Thank you John, please call me Cole if you'd like, I want you to know I love your daughter more than anything in life and that I will cherish every moment we spend together, I would give my life to protect her and do everything I can to make her happy and yes I do know how special Shadow is, I love him like a family member because he is," I calmly replied.

After fifteen minutes of breaking the ice and getting acquainted Sarah's father then remarked, "Cole you ready to get started with day one, I'd like to show you around and give you the grand tour and try to explain exactly what we do here and how everything works, of course Sarah and Shadow are invited as well, I'm sure you're going to have a million questions and Sarah can help with many of them." Sarah and Shadow lead the way towards the door as I walked with John, the two of us began to talk about the facility and the overall size of the place, "John this place is amazing, how long did it take to construct, I mean from what I've seen so far it looks like it probably took decades," I inquired, all the while feeling as if I've known the man my whole life, it was so easy to talk to this great man who I had only just met a very short time ago who also seemed at peace with the relationship Sarah and I have. I could tell he was a man with great intelligence and compassion, there was a certain warmth and glow about him, I guess that's where Sarah gets it from. "Well, to tell you the truth Cole this started out as a dream of mine when I was much younger than you are now but I never really had the financial support to get serious with the research until oh I'd say about twenty-five years ago when I convinced the government to give me a research grant, that's when things really took off in the right direction and culminated into what I'm about to show you today," he thoroughly explained.

As the four of us including Shadow who was now walking along side of John headed back towards the shuttle platform Sarah then asked, "Dad did you have a chance to look into the information I gave you that Cole provided about the Escalade?" The tall man gently spoke but with the first sign of what I would call an irritated or slightly aggressive voice, "Yes and we will all talk about it at a later time when I have gone over all of the data concerning that time frame, thanks for your help and information on this issue Cole, it has been quite illuminating." I remained quiet for a few seconds wondering if I should pursue this topic or let it go as he suggested, I chose the latter, "Your welcome sir, I think we both would like to get to the bottom of this issue," I strongly remarked. "Hey dad how's all of the other team members doing, did you give them the heads up on Cole or is this going to be a complete surprise to them, I know Charlie knows but would never blab to anyone else," inquisitively she asked. "They all know you're getting a new partner but that's as far as I went with informative heads up," he replied. As we all made are way up the stairs and to the awaiting shuttle I began to see and realize the special relationship Sarah and her father had and how lucky she was to have a man like this to watch over her and protect her. He reminded me a lot of my own father when Miralani and I were growing up. "Thanks dad, I really appreciate that, I think it's best that I brief them on the entire situation with Cole and myself, I'm sure everyone will be comfortable with our relationship as long as we keep it professional while on the job," as she quickly added her opinion on the matter.

The four of us quickly entered the shuttle as we reached the loading platform and within seconds we were all loaded on the shuttle which began to move forward at the same slow pace as before, I guess to ensure all of its passengers are safely seated and secured. "Okay Cole there are four more stops after this one and will take us probably till lunch to stop and show you all of them, I really think this will be quite interesting and unbelievable what you're about to see this morning, remember to fire away on any questions right away that might pop up in your mind because you're going to get an information overload today and will probably forget most of what I explain to you by the end of day but don't worry, sometimes even I forget how all of this technology works," he reassuringly remarked. "Alright John, that makes me feel much better, I just want you to know ahead of time I didn't really have any interest in science when I was growing up, all of my time was spent learning tracking, hunting, fishing, learning survival techniques and the spiritual knowledge of the Navajo people from my father who was an expert at all of them, he made me the man I am today and I will always be grateful for that," I proudly stated. "It sounds like your father was a great man Cole, I'm sure he is very proud of you and your accomplishments, I know I would be," he remarked, again with that soothing and calming tone in his voice, it was almost spiritual. Sarah looked at me and just smiled as if to say "I told you he would like you" as the shuttle now began to pick up speed.

The underground scenery was starting to change somewhat now with more man-made lit structures beginning to pierce through the openings of the cavern walls and shuttle tunnel. We began to slow some as we made a sharp turn and then a large cavern opened up with several structures that quickly came into view, "Well this will be our first stop Cole, these are the vortex monitoring stations that collect and provide live streaming data of the six main vortex's of the Sedona area," John explained before I could ask my first question. "Okay but what do they exactly monitor, is it some kind of energy source or something?" I then asked. John slowly turned towards me and said, "Sort of something like that Cole, it will be easier to explain most of it when we get down there, I can tell you that the six vortex's help create the critical link to the whole time travel operation and its success." I responded simply by nodding my head and acting as if I understood what the hell he was talking about. Sarah could see the look on my face and I'm pretty sure she knew what I was thinking, she kept her silence so not to embarrass me and I was thankful for that. As we disembarked from the shuttle and began our descent down the stairs I began to finally grasp what the overall size of this facility must be, I mean my god, it must be at least twenty-five miles in diameter from the underground parking area, or at least that was my best guess.

We reached the bottom of the stairs and John lead the way towards the structure that was directly in front of us about fifty yards or so. "How you holding up ranger, everything okay?" Sarah asked. "I'm okay sweetheart, just a little overwhelmed of the size of this place," I slowly replied. "Well just remember this is only the tip of the iceberg, it only gets bigger and more impressive the further we go on this little field trip," she remarked. After that remark I began to feel like a kid on the first day of school, afraid that I wouldn't be able to learn or remember anything that I saw or heard today. "Well I'll try to take in as much as possible sweetheart, I'm just glad I've got you to help me with my homework," I said with encouragement. John continued to lead the way with Shadow at his side. I was having just a little bit of jealously beginning to creep into my thoughts and emotions concerning Shadow and how well he seemed to know John and the fact that he was so comfortable by his side. I guess the two of them must have really bonded while I was in my coma here at the facility. As we made our way down the stone path towards the first structure I could see a big set of double security doors quickly come into view. As soon as we got to the entrance John leaned forward and activated another type of scanner that scanned his entire facial features with a type of green lit sweep. Once the scan was complete the doors opened to reveal a highly technical advanced looking room about the size of a theater lobby and laid out about the same way, there were people working on both sides of the room with more computers than I'd ever seen before in one place.

After a slow walk around the room John began to introduce me to everyone as Sarah's new partner and this was my first day of indoctrination, they were all introduced to me as technicians and had all been here at least five years. "Cole the main purpose of everyone's job in here is to keep an eye on and track all of the positive and negative energy flows of vortex's one through three and the other structure next door does exactly the same thing only it monitors vortex's four through six," John remarked as we continued our slow walk around the room. The amount of numbers and diagrams that were being displayed on the computers were absolutely overwhelming and totally written in Greek to me. "Okay sir, if you say so, I mean it looks like a lot of numbers to me," I slowly replied. "Don't worry Cole, this part of the job you really don't have to be an expert in, just sort know the theory on how everything relates to each other," Sarah then remarked, trying to make me feel a little less intimidated by the vast amount of computer data illuminating from all of the glowing screens in the room. After an hour or had passed by and the look on my face of absolute information overload John suggested we head back to the shuttle and proceed to the "agent only" medical facility that was next on our tour or field trip as Sarah called it.

Once we reached the shuttle platform and boarded we were on our way again. My mind was still trying to process most of everything I had just seen but it just wasn't happening, I guess it really was going to take some homework on my part to learn this highly technical time travel process and the overall operation of this advanced facility. "Cole the next stop will be our medical facility for our agents and only our agents, because of security reasons and the advanced medical screening that all of our agents must complete before going out in the field it is highly classified and requires a K-8 level clearance which you will obtain in a few days Cole, I have been running all the checks on you over the last few weeks and everything looks good," John explained as the shuttle was now at full speed. "Well I hope I can pass the physical and security requirements sir, I don't want to let my partner down," I quickly replied. "Cole there are no requirements really, it's more of a screening and medical profile we need to keep on every individual to be used in conjunction with the time travel process itself, don't worry there's nothing that's going to keep you from becoming an agent unless you just decide not to go through with it," John reassuringly stated. "So I guess this is the place we come to if we get injured out in the field," I carefully and slowly remarked. "No Cole, this the place that will actually provide the information for your treatment or recovery process but let's not get too deep into that subject just yet," he said.

"Well I did have a physical back three or four years ago from the F.B.I. when I was working on a missing persons case, maybe I could get all of the medical records they have on file and provide them to you," I eagerly remarked. "That's okay Cole, we won't need any previous medical history concerning your medical screening here at S.H.A.D.O.W we will create a new profile just for you and it will be the most advanced medical physical evaluation you could imagine and I promise it will be painless," John spoke with that calmness and peacefulness again. He voice was truly hypnotic.

The shuttle began to slow down as we neared our next stop, Sarah was sitting quietly with Shadow next to her, "Oh yeah Cole, my father forgot to tell you or remind you that you've already met our doctor, I'm sure you remember him, he was there when you first came out of your coma, his name is Dr. Walters," she said. "I do remember him, he was very nice to Shadow and me, I hope he remembers me because I would like to think he might have been the reason I came out of that coma and I consider him a friend," I quickly remarked. "Oh I'm pretty sure he does," she replied. Then turning her focus on her father she remarked, "It's all in a day's work for him Cole, he's done some pretty amazing things here at S.H.A.D.O.W. working in conjunction with my father." John smiled some then sat down on the small bench in between Sarah and Shadow, "Well the most amazing thing he's done recently was to save you and Shadow after we found you in our ventilation shaft half dead from malnutrition and dehydration, he gets all the credit on that one, we're just very lucky to have him here at our facility," expressing his opinion on the doctor. "Well, all I know is that Shadow and I were very lucky to be found by you guys and even luckier to have such a great doctor provide us with the quality of medical care that we received," I strongly remarked. "I'm quite glad too, you and Shadow have become a huge part of my life and I'm so glad the way things just seemed to be destined for us and fall into place perfectly," Sarah emotionally said.

The shuttle came to a complete stop and we headed out onto the platform where there were no stairs this time, just a small ramp,

I figured it must have been made for large shipments of medical supplies and things or maybe even for human transporting like injured employees on stretchers, at least that's what was I thinking. Again the walkways and paths were cut out of the stone base of the underground cavern, this place was just overwhelming and I had lost all aspect of the size and scope of this amazing facility, I couldn't even get my bearings down, I mean I didn't know what direction we had been traveling in, it was a bit unsettling for me. I quickly changed my focus onto the ramp that we were walking down and again Shadow seemed to know his way around this area, "Hey John, excuse me for asking sir but how much of this place has Shadow seen before, I mean he seems to be right at home with every step we make, was he treated here in this medical facility while I was in my coma?" I carefully asked. "As a matter of fact he was Cole, he knows the doctor just as well as he knows me, I'm sure he will be excited to see him also," John replied. "The doctor did a great job realizing that Shadow was not a hundred percent over his snakebite and that he had a blood infection that needed immediate attention," Sarah then remarked. "Well then this man really is a friend of mine and I must thank him properly," I reassuringly replied.

Again we found ourselves at a very secure looking set of stainless steel double doors with the same type of security scanner that would be granting our access. I began to wonder how long it would take for me to get clearance for all of these highly secure facilities and the secrets they held, this was really beginning to feel more and more like I was in the middle of a spy movie or something. The doors quickly opened after John's face and eyes were scanned and recognized, I guess it would be pretty much impossible for someone to gain an unauthorized entry into any of these facilities I had seen so far. As we entered the room or medical lab as I would prefer to call it we approached a man that became more and more familiar looking as we got closer, it was the doctor I met after waking from my coma, "Hello Mr. Youngblood, welcome back, I must say you look a lot healthier than the last time I saw you, hello Shadow, how are big man, you too look better and bigger, I think you've doubled in size my friend," the man remarked. "Hello, doctor Walters right, I never forget a name or face, especially that of someone who probably saved my life, I'd like to properly thank you and say how much I appreciate what you did for Shadow and I, please call me Cole, I now consider you a great friend and a great medicine man in my culture," I emotionally replied. "You're quite welcome Cole, I'm just glad you've decided to join us here at S.H.A.D.O.W., I believe that you will find this to be one of the most rewarding choices you've ever made in your life, so welcome to the family Cole, you too Shadow but I think you have a been a member since we first found you my friend and Cole, please call me Ben if you'd like," he said as he knelt down to give Shadow a big hug and kiss on top of his nose.

Sarah, her father and Ben then began to give me a personal guided tour of the facility and Shadow seemed to be right at home again just walking next to Sarah's father with the occasional brush up against Ben's trousers, he was quite comfortable in this environment. The place was very impressive with equipment I'd never seen before or could recognize as being medically related for treatment of patients or anything else you might see at a doctor's office, there was only a couple technicians working and looked to be running some sort of blood tests, at least that was my best guess. "Hey Cole, feel like giving a small blood sample while were here, if not that's okay but we'll have to get one sooner or later over the next couple of days," Sarah asked. "Sure no problem but I would've thought you guys already had run some blood tests on me while I was in my coma," I quickly commented. "We did Cole but your blood was tainted with some toxins from the knockout gas we used on you and Shadow, sorry about that by the way, the thing is your blood has had ample time to filter all of those toxins by now and we need to get a clean sample for our blood data regeneration system, so basically in a nut shell Cole we can reproduce blood in a matter of minutes for every agent here at S.H.A.D.O.W. in case of injury or any illness that may occur," Ben quickly informed me. "Wow that's crazy, I've never heard of anything like that, I'm still a little concerned about the toxins that was in that knockout gas that kept me in that coma for so long but I do trust you Ben and I would be more than glad to give you a sample now if you'd like," I then firmly agreed to the blood test. "Great, it will only take a few seconds and we only need a couple of drops, not a quart like what most hospitals take," Ben remarked. "Alright ranger, way to step up to the plate, you're not going to pass out or anything like that are you?" Sarah jokingly asked. "Don't worry about me Agent Cooper, I think I can handle it," I reassuringly replied.

A few minutes later and after a very small amount of blood that was so gingerly removed from my body we concluded with the tour of the medical facility and once again I personally thanked Ben for saving our lives from dehydration and the exposure we suffered during our time lost underground, he concluded the tour with, "Just doing my job Cole, I'm sure you and Shadow will become a regular site around our fantastic facility and I mean that in a positive way of course, once you receive your high level security clearance authorization and it's enabled into the access system you and Shadow will be free to come and visit any time you'd like," he remarked. "You can count on it doc, hopefully it won't be for any medical needs just a friendly visit," I happily replied. John, Sarah, Shadow and I then headed back to the shuttle loading platform where I began to think what's next, John must be saving the best for last, hopefully he trusts me enough to not hold back on anything or to keep any secrets at this point in our relationship, after all I think he knows and senses how much I really love his daughter. Once the shuttle began to move forward again John and Sarah looked at each other for a brief moment then seemed to agree on something without even saying a word, "Cole my daughter believes and thinks it's time for you to see the most top secret secure facility and highly advanced technology that has ever existed for mankind since the beginning of time and I am in total agreement with her, I have only known you in a physical presence for a short time Cole and I know that you are a honest and trustworthy man who would always follow his beliefs and trust in his heart and soul, what you're about to see is a gateway to humanities most evil and unthinkable deeds that mankind has bestowed upon itself over time, for that reason alone was the driving force behind the development of this highly technical and heavenly organization, please keep an open mind for what you are about to witness and experience, one more thing I must tell you before we reach our final destination, welcome to the family and please watch over Sarah, she can get a little hotheaded and reckless at times but she is the best S.H.A.D.O.W. has and this place would not be here if it weren't for here," John spoke, with the voice and tone of a very religious man, again it almost felt as if his words touched my soul and had some kind of soothing or calming effect, maybe he was just trying to put me in the right frame of mind for what awaited Shadow and I.

After the uplifting yet soothing heads up from John I was quite ready to finally get to see and try to understand what the hell this whole time travel thing was about and hopefully understand how it worked and why it was so important to travel back into the past. Sarah had come over and sat next to me while her father was keeping Shadow occupied by rubbing his belly and scratching his chin. Once the shuttle reached cruising speed Sarah grasped my hand and held it tightly, I guess she was just trying to be comforting, "I'm okay sweetheart, really, I'm ready for this and the most important thing to me now is that your father believes I'm ready also, he's a great man Sarah, I can tell by his words and the wisdom he speaks, nothing is wasted, everything he says has a meaning and a reason, it's an honor to meet and know someone like him," I softly remarked. "I'm so glad you two have such admiration for each other, he thinks the same of you Cole, even before he met you he was very impressed with your background and love for nature and the respect you have for all living things," she expressed with deep sincerity. The shuttle began to slow down as we approached the last stop, at least on this tour, I wasn't sure how many other stops or underground facilities might possibly exist down here. As we were approaching the shuttle platform for this stop I could tell this area was quite a bit more encapsulated with human technology and futuristic structures and tunnels of all sorts heading off in different directions.

The doors opened on the shuttle then we disembarked onto the loading platform, Sarah still holding onto my hand firmly started to lead the way which I thought was a bit surprising until I saw her father was busy typing some kind of information into the top of a small podium with a very bright green lit circular screen about the size of a small pizza, "Hey sweetheart, what's your father doing if you don't mind me asking," I quietly asked. "He's activating a new agent recognition program from this point on and will automatically process and store all of your physical attributes and abnormalities that you might have, don't worry Cole you won't even know it's happening," she confidently replied. "I'm not quite sure what you just said but it definitely sounds above my pay grade," I slowly replied with some confusion and bewilderment in my voice. "It's really quite simple Cole, what the recognition program does is record all of your physical movements, such as walking or gesturing when talking to another person or your what you might call your telltales if you're a poker player, even your breathing patterns are recorded, so the reason for this Cole is that is impossible for someone to gain entry to this part of the agency unless they are who they are supposed to be, it's the first and last line of defense in regards to security, there are still the standard methods of identification but this physical recognition program cannot be fooled, it would take years of study to try to impersonate one of our agents," as John explained his actions after leaving the podium. "Well I just hope I can remember to act like me the next time I come this way, I wouldn't want to trigger some kind of alarm or something," joking somewhat, I then remarked. Sarah began to laugh and then so did her father, then all of us proceeded towards one of the illuminated tunnels with John leading the way, this time Shadow stayed at my side, I guess he had never been this far before.

The walk down the tunnel was long and cold, I began to wonder how far down we actually were, I did notice that this tunnel or corridor looked a lot like the one Shadow and I were found in, mostly because of the vents on the ceiling looked very familiar, I guess when you break into a secure facility like we did you have a tendency to remember the details. After ten minutes or so of walking at a steady pace we finally came upon a different looking type of doors from all of the previous ones I had seen up till now, these were more like part of the stone walls that surrounded them. John approached the scanner on the wall, and again activated the it which then engulfed his facial features with a scan then followed by the tighter beam that focused on his eyes. It took only a few seconds then the doors began to separate but not fully open and before I could ask what was happening both of the door segments disappeared into the base of the floor right in front of us, it was like something out of "Star Trek" or some other sci-fi show, it was very impressive and quite secure looking actually. "Remember Cole, try to keep an open mind for what you are about to see and experience today, it will be quite remarkable and yet so simplistic once you grasp the basics of the process," John stated. "I will sir, as long as you don't go too fast or in depth on the science parts because I never went to college, all of my expertise or college major if you prefer is in what my father taught me, that is mother nature our heritage and the knowledge and skills of tracking and survival techniques and I'm quite proud of the time and education he provided for me," I strongly expressed. "I know Cole and I believe that's why you're here, this organization has needed someone like you for some time now and I believe what you know and the skills you possess are far more valuable than any college degree, never sell yourself short young man of what and who you are, I for one am so grateful for your decision to join us," emotionally John remarked.

Once all of us entered the massive room which seemed to disappear in all directions the doors rapidly closed behind us. "Well are you impressed ranger?" Sarah asked. Standing there in somewhat of a daze all I could think of was Disneyland, "It's kind of funny sweetheart that you should ask that," with a look of enchantment I replied, "I don't know why but all I can think of right now are the memories of my childhood with Miralani at Disneyland, mostly the "Pirates of the Caribbean" underground ride with the stone walled tunnels and that wonderful feel and smell of the cold mist coming off the waterfalls from the ride, crazy isn't it, I guess I'm just missing my sister or something," I remarked. "No Cole, you're just recalling some of the most precious memories of your life, that's what sights, smells and sounds can due to our subconscious, those senses can extract long forgotten memories, most of the time they're pleasant ones but in some occasions can bring back deep dark memories that our minds have kept locked away for years," John quickly explained as if I were sitting on a couch in a psychiatrist's office. "Okay daddy, quit trying to get into Cole's head, you've got plenty of time for that later," Sarah remarked. "Sorry Cole, it's a bad habit of mine, it won't happen again unless you ask me for some advice on such matters," John reassuringly said. "No worries sir, I could probably use a little help in that area or at least I will soon, especially after today," I replied. "Okay then, let's get this tour started, come on over here next to me as I will explain the whole time travel process here at S.H.A.D.O.W. and maybe even give you a brief demonstration on how it works," John stated.

Standing next to John with Sarah and Shadow standing a short distance behind us John began to explain his lifelong passion and amazing accomplishment, "Cole what you are about to see is a combination of a miracle from heaven and the amazing advancement of technology and science that has taken a lifetime of research and not to mention a little help from our government over the past fifteen years," remarking with his introduction of the facility. From what I could see it looked like there were six perfectly cylindrical tunnels coming in from the stone walls that surrounded the facility which all focused and ended on a fairly good sized octagonal platform about the size of helicopter landing pad you might see on a roof of a skyscraper. As we walked closer down towards the platform I could see what looked like several control rooms embedded into the stone walls, the size of this place was coming into full view and it was quite overwhelming. "So Cole I'm sure you have noticed all of the tunnels that are leading up to the platform just ahead of us, those are the main induction ports from the various vortex's that surround the Sedona area, what they do is bring the positive and negative magnetic energy flows into a central focal point which is underneath and above the platform and then basically how it works is the six vortex energy ports combine with our two artificially made energy sources that are brought in from our energy source and focused above and below the platform creating what we call an orthogonal wormhole, an eight-sided vortex or wormhole to be more precise which is the main source of the time travel process," "are you with me so far?" John asked. Pausing for a brief second and actually understanding what he had just explained I then asked, "John, where does the energy source come from that produces the two artificial vortexes, I mean I don't see any big power sources here or anything that looks like a nuclear reactor thank god." John looked at with me with a certain admiration I think for asking a question, "Cole, that's a great question, you're right about the nuclear reactor, those things absolutely scare the hell out of me and you won't find any of that here at S.H.A.D.O.W. I promise you," "what we use for a power source is my version of a particle collider, you know that big thing they have over in Switzerland that spins atom particles around in a giant circle under magnetic control then introduces various particles in the opposite direction to collide and create some kind of new particle or energy source," John proudly replied. "That's amazing sir but where is it, I don't see anything in here that looks like what you just described," I curiously asked. "Actually ranger you've already walked over and by some of it," Sarah chimed in. "Let's head up to the main control room, I'll be able to explain much easier with some of the visual aids from the controls and the boards that are there," John then added.

After a brief walk up an inclined path we arrived at what I guess was the main control room, it had an identifying plate above the door which read "Hadron I.C." I wasn't sure what the hell that meant but I had a strong feeling I was about to find out. As the four of us entered the room all I could see were computer and gauge monitors of some type and it looked like something you might see in a control room of a nuclear power plant. "Cole this is what we call the "Hadron Instrument Control" room and basically these gauges and computer controls monitor and adjust the influx of power coming from our Hadron power source, if you step over here I can show you on this screen exactly how we use these power source," John quickly suggested. "Okay sir but remember take it slow, my science background is pretty much knowing how to make gun powder and that's it," I hesitantly replied. "Okay Cole but I think you're a lot smarter than you let on to be, anyway what you see in front of you is the overall monitoring screen for the Hadron influx to the vortex intermix chamber were everything comes together and then is directed and adjusted to the correct input to the orthogonal platform which encompasses all of the vortexes including the two artificially created ones from here and when fully activated together we can create a space time warp field to where we can move object's or organic material through time and successfully return them," John then explained. "That's pretty amazing sir but I'm still pretty fuzzy on how it actually can send a human back into time then retrieve that person back to the present," I quickly asked. "Another great question Cole, the best way to answer that is to show you a couple of medical scans of some of our agents stored here in one of the data bases, step up to this screen here Cole and take a look at what we call our "Reconstruct files", what you're looking at is the DNA and carbon blueprint to a couple of our agents, these are the building blocks the atomizing processer which we use to reconstruct every living thing or inorganic object that travels through time, the atomizing processor also is the main piece of equipment that deconstructs all living matter and enables the ability to travel through time," John confidently replied. "Sure, I get it, no problem, is it lunch time yet, I'm getting hungry," I jokingly remarked. "It's okay Cole, I know it's a lot to throw at you so fast but we need to get you up to speed as soon as possible, don't worry it will make more sense to you once you accept the facts and realize it actually works and that probably won't be until you experience it first hand," Sarah quickly added.

Thirty minutes or so had passed with more tidbits of information being thrown my way via courtesy of John and Sarah. Finally, John suggested that I watch a little short recorded video of the actual time travel process of two agents being sent back in time. "I think this will help with the overwhelming amount of unbelievable information your mind is trying to process right now Cole, this video clip is from last year showing one of our teams going back to the late seventies to help solve and change a missing child's abduction case, I'm glad to say the mission was a complete success, once the video starts pay close attention to the platform where the agents are standing, it will give you a good perspective on what the process actually does to the human body during the atom deconstruction and transmission process," John remarked. I then stood directly over the brightly lit led screen that was as sharp as my TV at home, I began to watch as John requested, focusing on the platform that the two individuals were standing on, a man and a woman dressed in some kind of one-piece jump suits that looked like some old school jogging outfits from the seventies that were way out of style. It only took a few seconds into the viewing that I began to see the two individuals become totally encapsulated in two brightly lit bubbles that originated from where they were standing, then in a matter of seconds the bubble's that contained each of them instantly were gone like turning out a light, there was nothing there except for the image that had been burned into my mind, it was truly fantastic. "Now watch closely Cole after I speed the video up a few minutes, one week of time in the past only represents a few days of time in the present," John explained. As he slowed the video down to resume normal playback I stepped in closer towards the screen and focused on the platform as John had previously suggested, all of a sudden two separate bubble's began to appear in the exact same spot within seconds I could see the outline of each body residing in their bubble, another few seconds passed then the bubbles disappeared and the two individuals re-appeared and looked to be perfectly fine. "What did I just witness John, did those two people actually travel back in time and come back," I somewhat frantically asked. "I know it's confusing Cole, sometimes I even have a hard time trying to grasp and understand the whole time space calculations and theories, what I can tell you is that actual time passes by at a slower speed the further we go back thus giving us the appearance that it only took several days to complete an assignment but in actuality it usually takes weeks for the agents who are working the case back in the past," as John tried to simplify the whole time travel experience and the science behind it.

After standing totally still and quiet for a few minutes I finally broke my silence and asked again, "Can we possibly now please go to lunch, I need some time to process everything I've seen here and to clear my mind of everything and just think about food or something that'll free up my mind for a short time," I exhaustingly suggested. "Daddy I think Cole is right, he's had enough brain overload for one day, let's go eat and then I can help Cole with some of the administrative paperwork that he needs to fill out," "Cole that will probably take us till the end of the day and then we can go home and unwind and talk about today if you'd like," Sarah firmly remarked. "You're absolutely right, we should go and eat, Cole I think you have survived the crash course on most of our time travel processes and with just a little preparation and training provided by Sarah you should be good to go very soon," John reassuringly remarked. The four of us then headed back out the way we came and I couldn't wait to get back on the shuttle as I was now feeling a little light headed and dizzy, probably just nerves and anxiety over everything I just witnessed, not to mention I would soon be in one of those bubbles that would send me back in time, I almost started to have second thoughts about making this decision but just then Sarah put her arms around my waist and looked at me and smiled, all of a sudden everything was right in my world again and I got my second wind, I felt strong and focused again just from the emotionally charged feeling of love for this wonderful woman.

12

ROOKIE

The shuttle was only a few minutes out from where we had started the day and I for one was ready to just get out and walk around some and maybe meet some of the other employees here at the agency, of course that's after lunch. The four of us disembarked from the shuttle and began our journey to the cafeteria, I do remember from the last time I was here the food was pretty good, especially for a government run facility. I can remember the F.B.I. food establishments were never that good during the occasions I worked with them. I could tell that I wasn't the only hungry one, Shadow's nose was perking up quite a bit the closer we got to the cafeteria. "Hey Shadow do you remember all of the chopped up steak I gave you while Cole was in his coma, I think you got pretty spoiled during that week and I guess I am to blame for your steak fetish," Sarah admittedly remarked. "Yeah I believe Shadow ate better than most of the employee's around here for that week but then again he was pretty famished when we found you two Cole," John quickly commented. As the doors to the cafeteria were now in sight my stomach was actually beginning to sound like Shadow's playful growl which led him to look up at me with one of the strangest looks I've ever seen from an animal, "What's wrong Shadow, do you think I'm growling or something, it's okay boy," I said as I knelt down on one knee and gave him a hug and let him know I was okay and not angry or another other misconceived thought's he might have had. He began to wag his tail and lick my face then he must have got a strong smell of something as the doors opened in front of us just as a couple of employees where leaving, he then started to pull away from me somewhat, "Easy boy, we'll get our food just be patient my friend, maybe we'll have Sarah get you some chopped up steak since it sounds like she's has a lot of pull around here." I soothingly said. He then regained his composure as all of us walked over to a table to stake our claim as ours.

After putting some of our stuff and attire at the table Sarah took hold of Shadow's leash and started to get up from the table, "Okay Shadow let's go get you some lunch and I know just what you want," she quickly stated. "Alright then, how about you and I get us some of the same, the food is pretty good here but probably not as good as your sister's café I bet," John confidently remarked. "Sounds great, I'm starving and I do remember the last time I ate here and the food was really good but your right sir, nothing can beat my sisters cooking, have you ever eaten at her place, it's called Miralani's," I quickly commented. "I can't say that I have Cole, I don't usually stray too far away from here and when I do I just usually pick up something on the way home, I'm pretty sure my eating habits are quite unhealthy and I know I really should change them," John said. "Well you look pretty damn healthy to me sir, you must be doing something right," I strongly replied. "Well maybe just somebody upstairs likes me and wants to keep me around for a while," he suggestively replied. The two of us headed up to the beginning of the buffet style cafeteria and began to pick out the food of our choice, I assumed it was all you could eat but I never really asked Sarah before or if we had to pay for our meals, I really hoped not because I was used to getting my meals for free. With our plates full the two of us headed back to our table only to find Shadow and Sarah already sitting down and chowing down on some beautiful chunks of what looked like New York strips, "Hey where did you get that steak, I didn't see any up there in the buffet line," I quickly inquired. Sarah just looked up at me and smiled with a mouth full of steak that is. "Wow I guess you do have some pull around here, next time I'm going with you and Shadow," I sadly remarked. John began to chuckle a little as we sat down at the table. Sarah had even brought out what looked like a little table the size of a foot stool just for Shadow to eat on. "You know he's really got your number sweetheart, he's going to be impossible to live with pretty soon if we both keep spoiling him so much," I said. "I know Cole, I'm sorry but he's just so smart and it's hard not to spoil him," she explained. "I know, I guess I'm just as guilty of doing it too," I quickly agreed.

Over the next half hour or so the four of us just sat and talked or I guess Shadow just listened about the different teams of agents that I would be meeting over the next few days and the scheduled aggressive training program that John and Sarah had in mind for me, most of which was skill based or self-defense programs that would benefit me once out in the field. John also mentioned that I would need to become familiar with older firearms and the ability to use them if needed, John explained that we don't take anything back in time with us from the future unless it's an absolute emergency or a very abnormal situation, he said it was just too risky and could lead to all kinds of horrific time related paradoxes. John also mentioned the ability of the re-atomization process also included the healing of any injuries you might sustain while back I time, in other words if I were to break my arm or some other bone on one of these missions or what Sarah calls saves the re-atomization process would fix or correct any physical abnormalities that would pop up from the original body scan that all agents have saved in the medical data reconstruct files, in other words it could utterly fix any physical injury or for that matter even a sickness like the flu. John said later down the road this type of equipment and the processes we use hopefully will be allowed to migrate into the civilian populous and that the possibilities were limitless for the medical field. It was a lot of information that was mostly still going over my head but I did understand and agree in regards to the medical first aid and treatment prospects.

As we were all nearing the end of our delicious lunch Charlie from the guard shack approached the table then pulled up a chair and sat in between Sarah and I, "Hey Coop, I got your man's window sticker here, his badge will be ready by the time you two leave today, I'll have it at the guard shack by the time you go home this afternoon," he stated. "Thanks Charlie," she replied. "Yeah thanks a lot Charlie, maybe I can drive the Bronco in tomorrow if she lets me," I eagerly remarked. "That would be great, I've heard a lot about it, especially the fancy patriotic paint job it has, I promise you Mr. Youngblood if you drive it to work here I'll get you a special parking place to protect that paintjob, I would hate see a bunch of door dings hammered into it from some of the nitwits that work here, they drive and park like idiots, I guess because most of them drive government furnished vehicles which they don't give a damn about," Charlie excitedly and somewhat angrily replied. "Wow, I really appreciate that, please call me Cole if you'd like, Sarah has told me how you like to work on older cars and restore them, maybe sometime later we could sit down and pick each other's brains on this subject, I have a feeling there may be another vehicle in Sarah's future that will need some restoring and she and I could use all the help we can get," I suggested. "Yeah Charlie, Cole's going to help find an older Bronco like his and we're going to restore it, I've driven his and I think that I really would like to own one of those great pieces of American automotive history," Sarah commented. "I'd love to offer any help you need on that project, just let me know, I love this little lady here, I know John thinks I treat her too much like if she was my own daughter but he's okay with the two of us spoiling her, I'll just say this Cole, you take care of this woman and listen and learn from her because she's the best at everything we do here, you can learn a lot from this wonderful lady," Charlie emotionally stated. "Don't I know it, she's one in a million and I know I can trust her with my life, you don't have to worry about me not taking care of her, although I think she'll be the one taking care of me for a while, at least until I get familiar with everything," I reassuringly replied.

As Charlie said his goodbye's too everyone and left the table I could tell that John had great respect for him and the two of them were as close as you could be without being family, I guess that's part of the reason why Sarah had such a fondness for him. "Cole, speaking of learning you can learn a lot from that man there, if you ever need someone to just talk to or vent out some personal feelings about what's going on around here please seek him out and ask him for advice, he is always willing to help," John said as Charlie had just left the cafeteria. "I will sir, thanks," I replied. "He has helped me through some tough times here Cole, he is family as far as I'm concerned and I will always be there for him," Sarah sincerely said. "Cole as soon as we're finished with lunch I'd like to show you a couple more areas of S.H.A.D.O.W. that will help you get a grasp of the overall structure and complexity of this place and hopefully give you a better perspective of the whole operation," John adamantly suggested. "Sounds good to me sir, I'm just finally glad to get started here at S.H.A.D.O.W. I've had so many crazy thoughts of what I might actually be doing the last few weeks that it has creeped into my dreams at night, most of which were good," I reassuringly replied. "It's almost over ranger, I mean your first day, just a few more stops, our wardrobe department and the weapons range and then we'll call it quits for the day," Sarah reassuringly commented. "The weapons range, I think I'm going to like that, finally something I'm somewhat familiar with," I quickly replied. "I'm sorry to say but you're probably not son, the weapons we have here our available for our use on our missions and mostly vintage and antique, in other words they're period correct for the applicable mission but you may be familiar with a few of them," John remarked. "Well whatever you people have here I'm pretty sure I can shoot and if I'm not familiar or an expert with the use of them I promise you, I will be," I strongly stated. Sarah smiled at me and seemed to be pleased with my firm and proud sounding statement I had just made to her father, almost as if she had been waiting for a response like that from me all day and I guess It did make me feel good and more confident about this whole new learning task that awaited me.

The three of us finally finished our lunch including Shadow and there wasn't a spec of that delicious looking steak left anywhere on his plate, or I should say bowl, it looked more like something a pasta dish would be served in. We exited the cafeteria and headed down an unfamiliar corridor that I had not seen before and it was starting to look more normal, I mean that in a way like a normal business office or building would look, there were painting's and lithographs on the corridor walls that somehow gave it a homey feeling or look about it. A couple of other employee's walked by us and I assumed they were probably heading to the cafeteria since one of them had a lunch box, pretty brilliant deduction on my part I thought, better keep that one to myself. As we walked down the corridor Shadow seemed a little uneasy and nervous, "What's wrong boy, did all that steak give you an upset belly, please don't take a dump here in the hallway, I don't have anything to clean it up with," I commented. I guess I totally forgot about where he might have to do his business, it had been over five hours and he just ate a huge meal, "Cole there is an exit to the caverns up ahead on the right, there are plenty of these doorways that are marked with a symbol that looks like a slippery when wet road sign, I think you'll be able to find a suitable area for him to do his business, I have a bag from the cafeteria that I put in my pocket just for this reason, hang on Shadow, Cole will find you a spot," Sarah quickly remarked. "Thanks sweetheart, I'm glad someone was thinking ahead, hey what do I do with it if he goes, I mean I don't want to carry a bag of crap around with me all day you know what I mean," I asked. "No worries ranger there are trash receptacles all around the path walkways every twenty or thirty feet, there are even a few benches to seat on and eat lunch for those who want to get away from the cafeteria or just want some privacy once in a while," she then replied. "Okay great, I just hope nobody is eating their lunch out there right now, I would hate to see Shadow do his business in front of someone and ruin their meal," I jokingly remarked.

After ten minutes of walking Shadow around the stone walkways and letting him slightly stray off the beaten path to find an area of his choice that he was comfortable with he finally relieved himself and was back to being his normal self, happy and calm. Shadow and I rejoined John and Sarah who were waiting in the corridor and jabbering away as we walked up to join them again, "Okay, he's his old self again, happy and relieved, poor guy, I wonder how long he might have had to go, hopefully not too long," I commented as we all started to continue our walk down the corridor. "Cole the next place I'd like to show you is our wardrobe department, after all when you travel back in time you'll have to blend in with the period correct clothing and accessories, like certain technological devices for that time period, we can't have you bringing things like smart phones back in time," John strongly suggested. "I couldn't agree more with you, I guess that could definitely affect the present and our future if someone in the past got ahold of something like that," I quickly agreed. "You see Cole, you're already thinking like a time traveler, before you know it you'll be running this place," John quickly commented. We slowly came up on another set of double doors that looked a little more traditional, what I mean was these doors looked normal with no security scanner or even locks on them, I guess that meant there was probably nothing that was highly technical or top secret that needed to be protected behind them. The four of us entered and once inside it began to look like something behind a Broadway stage or something, there were racks of clothing, shoes, hats and a section with what looked like display cases full of jewelry and watches and other small trinkets of some kind. It was quite impressive, a department store from the past filled with everything a person would need to blend in and not stick out for whatever time period they were in, I wondered if you were allowed to check this stuff out for costume parties, some of it looked pretty cool.

John began to explain the different rows and how they were organized by five-year time frames all the way up to our present time, which I thought was a little strange, I guess even if the mission only required to go back a few years in time you still had to look the part, "So Cole what do you think?" John asked. "It's very impressive sir, looks like you could have a lot of fun dressing up around this place, maybe even go to a costume party or two," I jokingly replied. Sarah then gave me a funny look as if she had already made that suggestion to her father. "We might be able to work that out on a few special occasions or something that demanded and old school presence but that can only be approved by myself or Sarah," John strongly remarked. "Okay dad, I think Cole has waited long enough, he's dying to see our gun range and the assortment of vintage firearms we have here, he's just a little timid to ask you if you could hurry up and get along with this part of the tour, right Cole," Sarah said while giving me a wink. "Well no need to rush sir, Sarah is sort of right but sometimes likes to joke around at my expense as I do with her, I'm really enjoying this part of the tour, it's kind of like being on a movie set or something like that," I remarked, quickly defending myself.

The four of us then headed back out into the corridor from which we had entered and proceeded to the gun range and weapons depository as John had called it. Shadow was still walking by my side, I guess because again he was not familiar with this part of the complex, it was nice to know that I was the one he felt most comfortable with when he was a little uneasy or in unfamiliar territory, don't get me wrong, I wasn't jealous of the relationship he had with John, I just felt a little left out in the cold because of the time I missed with him when I was in my coma. I still wondered how he could have ended up stuck in that shaft and how far away from any known indigenous locations for the breed he was, I'm just so glad that I heard his whimpers and the two of us found each other and now have this very special bond and trust that's so special, for what we experienced in those underground caverns while we were lost I truly believe that we are now blood brothers for life and beyond, our spirits will be forever be connected. Of course Sarah has bonded with him also but not quite in the same way as he and I have shared a few life threating moments together but with time I'm almost certain the three of us will have that same special bond and connection.

We kept walking for a few more minutes then came up upon

a regular looking entryway door with a scanner attached to wall next to it and on the other side of the entry door was a very large roll up door about the size of a standard garage door, it was definitely made out of some type of steel and looked very thick and very heavy. John approached the door and leaned in a little closer to the scanner and a bright green beam of light illuminated his face and began to scan it back and forth until the light quickly retracted back into the scanner. The door slowly opened and we followed John in very slowly and in a single file formation until we had gained complete entry into this facility. After ten-feet or so it opened up into several big rooms and I could make out what looked like personal lockers of some sort. "Okay Cole, here we are, the front part of our weapons storage area and shooting range, you can't quite see the range from here but it is located just around the corner up ahead, I've already taken the opportunity to assign a locker to you right next to Sarah's, that's just standard procedure for partner's Cole, So don't get any ideas of me showing you any favoritism just because of your relationship with my daughter, however I will share things such as privileged information with you that I have not shared with any other agents because you are in a relationship with my daughter, I hope you understood that Cole," John firmly stated. "No worries sir, I completely understand and I appreciate it, I mean the fact we have already have a trusting relationship will definitely speed things up regarding my training and not to mention a confidence booster when things might get a little tough or demanding," I reassuringly answered. "Great you two, now let's go check out some of our firearms we have here, I bet you'd like to shoot a few of these Cole, just wait till you see our Winchester rifle collection, you're going to love it, you'll have to get somewhat proficient with just about everything we have here Cole but with your shooting skills and the collection of guns you have at home and I don't think you're going to have any problems with this portion of the job," Sarah confidently remarked.

After a few minutes passed and totally agreeing with Sarah about my marksmanship skills and overall knowledge of vintage firearms I possessed we slowly continued towards the big opening ahead, we turned a small corner and to my amazement there standing before me was a shooting range the size of a football field, it was unbelievable anything like this could be built underground and blend in with the cavernous walls that surrounded us. I don't why but again I was reminded of my childhood experiences and memories, this time it was memories of "Knott's Berry Farm" in Los Angeles, the cavern walls and the lights reflecting off them brought back memories of the underground train ride that Miralani and I rode when we were just kids. "Cole you alright, you look like you're starting to drift away from us here, anything on your mind?" Sarah inquisitively asked. Pausing for a second and refocusing on where I was and what we were doing I replied, "No, it's just that this place keeps on reminding me of some of my childhood memories with my sister and the various amusement parks that our parents took us to." Sarah paused for a second and looked at her father, then spoke. "Yeah, it does kind of seem like that around here, doesn't it dad, I mean we do have one of the best rides in the world if you want to look at it that way." Her father then smiled and chuckled some, "Sarah's right Cole, if you liked those places as a child you're going to love this place as an adult," John remarked. "Yeah, I'm beginning to feel that way already and I haven't even experienced the main attraction," I eagerly commented. "Okay then, let's go and check out some guns, Cole I know you're going to like some of the old west style rifles and pistols we own, we don't really use them too much out in the field but they're fun to shoot and we have a great budget here at S.H.A.D.O.W. so we pretty much get whatever we think we may need someday or just get stuff anyways because we feel that we deserve a little special consideration for all of the great accomplishments we have done," Sarah said, strongly expressing her feelings on the subject.

Before we actually got to the range itself there were several small rooms with different dates or periods of time labeled above each doorway, "So by the looks of those dates above the doorways you've pretty much got it covered going back to when the first firearms were invented, I guess you really do have a great budget," I excitedly remarked. "Yeah like Sarah said Cole, quite a few of these really old firearms will never see the light of day, we just have them for our enjoyment and occasional marksmanship contests we have every couple of weeks," John quickly stated. "I can't wait to get in on that, I consider myself to be a pretty shot and have been target shooting since I was ten years old, my father was an outstanding marksman," I proudly remarked. "Well you have some pretty big shoes to fill in that respect Cole, Sarah and her previous partner had held the trophy for the last year and a half, you might want to put in some extra time here at the range over the next few weeks, I would hate to be the one who let down Sarah in the partners shooting competition," John strongly suggested. "That will never happen sir, I will always be there for her, no matter what the situation or task involved is, I promise you that," I emotionally replied. "Don't worry dad, I'll be working with Cole on his shooting techniques, I already know he's quite the marksman, now he just needs to learn a few non-standard shooting styles to compete with the other teams of agents," Sarah reassuringly stated.

The first little structure we went into had been labeled "1955 – 1990" and as we entered John spoke, "Cole these are primarily most of the weapons you'll have to become familiar with because they're the most frequently required for the time periods we travel back too. You won't have to become an expert marksman with them but you'll need to know how to use them." After John's comment I just stood in amazement at the sheer number and variety of firearms that were in just the one enclose. I began to smell the brass casing's filled with gun powder and the wonderful aroma of the blued steel barrels and the light hint of gun oil, thank god someone was taking proper care of these magnificent firearms. There were various versions of the famous and very reliable "Colt 1911" pistol that had been used in all of our branches of the military and was still being made and copied by firearm companies to this day, "Wow, I've never seen such a collection of "Colt" pistols of this size and variations, it's really impressive sir," I said standing there in astonishment. "Cole I bet you're wondering how we obtained so many vintage firearms, well you can probably guess if you put two and two together," Sarah quickly commented. "Okay, let me guess, you went back in time and stole them, then brought them back here, isn't that somewhat illegal?" I cautiously asked. "Actually we bought them back in the past, legally I might add, you see Cole everything was a lot cheaper in the fifties and sixties when it came to firearms and they were quite easy to buy, especially if you're presenting yourself as an F.B.I. agent and buyer for the government with all of the required official documents signed and authorized by that agency," John replied. "I guess I'm still not seeing the big picture in how much this place is capable of doing and orchestrating acquisitions from the past to bring to the present for use here at S.H.A.D.O.W. in order to aid in the missions or save's, I guess I just have to open my mind up to all of the possibilities that time travel can provide," I slowly remarked. "You will get there Cole, remember this is still only day one for you and I've thrown quite a bit of information your way to digest, Sarah will help in the area of technology and the overall process of how things work around here over the next couple of weeks and coming from her I'm sure you'll have no problem getting up to speed in no time," John reassuringly commented.

After touring and admiring the collection of firearms in this structure we slowly made our way out and on to the next enclose that was labeled "Pre – 1955" and once we passed through the doorway I immediately felt right at home, there were "Winchester" and "Henry rifles hanging on the walls and filling the glass-top cabinets in the middle of the room, now these I would have no problem with, I was an expert with these types of old firearms and had been shooting them all of my life. "What do you think Cole, this must look like a "Toys R Us" to you, only with guns and I know what you're thinking, the answer is no, you can't take any of these firearms out of the facility to shoot unless it's traveling back in time with them, sorry ranger that's just the way it has to be," Sarah strongly commented. "Wow, you must be a mind reader because that's exactly what I was wondering, well at least maybe we can shoot them here at the range sometime, I noticed a couple of "Henry's" over there that I would enjoy trying out, you know those are the finest lever action rifles ever made, each one is like a work of art, I wish I could afford to own a real one that survived the Civil War era but those are worth a fortune now and almost impossible to obtain," I sadly replied. "Well I don't know about owning one Cole but these are all originals from that time period and here for your use anytime you want to practice on the range or just want to admire them, Sarah can explain to you later on how we acquired most of these, it's a very interesting story that I think you'd enjoy very much," John remarked. "Thank you John, you can bet I'll take you up on that and be here in my spare time to shoot a few of these marvelous rifles," I reassuringly replied.

After admiring some more rifles and other assorted pistols we began to head back out to the main corridor and one last stop before calling it a day, I think Shadow and I were both ready to head home and just relax a bit and try to process all of this mind boggling information we were introduced to today, at least I had my own personal tutor that I could lean on at home during these next couple of weeks, not to mention she was quite pleasant to lean on. "Cole there's one more area I'd like to show you today, the main data and computer agent user facility where we keep all of our case files and perform the preliminary research for all of the missions that we encounter, then I think that'll do it for now, I think you've probably had just about enough of S.H.A.D.O.W. for one day," John remarked as we all headed down the main corridor. We quickly came upon another set of double doors with the same security set up involving an eye scanner and face recognition, "This area is a highly secure one Cole, for the obvious reason of data protection and highly classified files pertaining to every aspect of S.H.A.D.O.W. and its employees," John commented. After gaining access through John's recognition the four of us entered the huge library looking room filled with desktop computers and what looked like a checkout area for laptop computers and other electronic devices for what I assumed were there to use by the employees if needed, definitely a computer geeks paradise, I was already dreading the amount of time I might have to be spending in here to affectively do my job. I could tell Shadow was not too interested because he had already dropped to the floor by one of the desks and looked like he was ready for a nap, I almost wanted to curl up next to him on the floor because I didn't really want to get the grand tour of this place either but I stood in there and took it like a man making sure not to show any signs of disrespect or lack of interest towards John's speech.

Sarah was parading around the room checking in on some of the computers and seemed to be looking for information while John was trying to keep my attention with a brief explanation as to what all of the different computer areas and setups were used for and I was doing my best to seem interested by his comments. Shadow was out cold as John and I walked by him several times, how I envied him at this point of the tour. Finally, after a half or so and almost ready to put up the white surrender flag I heard the words come out of John's mouth that I had been praying for the last twenty-nine and a half minutes, "Well I guess that's about it Cole, have you got any questions or need me to go over anything again for you, if not I think the three of you can get the heck out of here and head home, that's if you can wake up Shadow," John suggested. "Oh I don't think that will be a problem sir, I think he was ready to go home right after lunch, He is still growing and needs his naps during the day, especially right after eating," I impatiently replied. "Hey Sarah you about ready to go?" I then asked. "Yeah almost Cole, I'm just checking up on some loose ends concerning your Escalade case, or possibly our Escalade if I'm correct about the data on the tracker program I installed a couple of weeks ago, we can go over the data result's later when we get home if you'd like, I think there's a very good chance it may shed some light on the case, I know it's not your jurisdiction any more but you may be able to help Sam out with the information we obtain," she quickly replied. "Well I guess I'll see you two tomorrow I mean three, sorry Shadow I didn't forget you my friend," John remarked as Shadow was just standing up from his power nap.

As we exited the computer room and headed in different directions once in the corridor Shadow turned around and gave a faint whimper towards John as if to say goodbye, again I had the feeling that these two developed a very close bond in the short time they were together before I came out of my coma, "What's wrong boy, don't worry I'll see you tomorrow and almost every day after that, remember Shadow you are a critical part of the team now and we will be seeing a lot each other from here on out," John remarked after turning around as if to answer Shadows cry. Shadow then turned back towards Sarah and I and seemed to be quite content with John's remark, the three of us then headed down the corridor towards the motor pool area. "Hopefully Charlie has all your permits and badge ready, maybe we can drive the Bronco in tomorrow if you'd like, I know he's been wanting to see it after hearing about it from me," Sarah suggestively commented. "That sounds good to me, I love showing that thing off to people, I'm very proud of that vehicle and what I wanted it to stand for when I had it painted the way I did," I replied. "Okay then it's settled, you're driving tomorrow if Charlie came through for you today," Sarah strongly remarked. We continued our way around the facility until I began to notice a few familiar looking doorways and corridors, I knew we were close to the motor pool and so did Shadow, he was getting a little excited and jumpy, "Yeah I know boy, I can hardly wait to get back home and just relax for the rest of the day, maybe even barbeque some chicken or ribs, I bet you'd like that, I know I would," I remarked as I leaned over to pat him on the back, he was definitely growing like a weed because I didn't have to reach down nearly as far as to when we first met.

As we entered the garage area there was Charlie standing only a few feet away talking to another employee, as we approached the two of them he turned towards us, "Hey you two perfect timing, I just got handed all of you permits and badge, Cole I'd like you to meet Gary Branson, he takes care of all the required paperwork for new employee's in regards to parking permits and I.D. Badges," Charlie stated. "It's a pleasure to meet you Mr. Branson my name is Cole Youngblood, so it will be okay for me to drive my personal vehicle in tomorrow without any problems," I curiously replied. "No problem at all Mr. Youngblood, all of your paperwork was rushed through by Sarah's father and Charlie and please call me Gary, I've heard a lot about your Bronco, I'm looking forward to seeing it," Gary replied. "Well I'm looking forward to bringing it in tomorrow, again thanks for getting all of the paperwork finished in such a short time, I really appreciate it," I kindly remarked. "Oh and by the way Cole I got you a really nice spot in one of the corners of the garage area where you have a space all by yourself and away from any possible door ding damage, Sarah told me how much that paint job was worth so I made sure it would be protected," Charlie reassuringly commented. I looked at Sarah and she just smiled and gave me a little wink, "Well I don't know what say except thank you very much Charlie, that was very considerate of you and if I can ever do anything for you please let me know, I mean outside of S.H.A.D.O.W. of course because since I'm so new I don't really know a whole lot about this place and I'll be lucky just to be able to help myself for quite some time," I somewhat jokingly remarked. "Think nothing of it Cole, I just hope you drive it in tomorrow," he replied.

I nodded my head as if to say yes to Charlie then Sarah, Shadow and I headed towards her Fj. I was quite eager just to get back outside into the sunlight and the breezy fresh air of the Sedona canyons, I was starting to get a little stir crazy being underground for so long, I think it was triggering some memories of when Shadow and I were trapped underground. The Fj was now in sight, "Hey ranger you want to drive us out of here?" Sarah softly asked. "Sure sweetheart, that just might be the perfect way to end the day here and I love driving your Cruiser," I quickly and happily replied. Shadow jumped in as I opened the driver's side door and made himself right at home on the backseat which was becoming smaller for him with each passing day, he was really starting to sprout and would soon reach his full height with those long skinny legs that wolves are known for, it would take him some time to fill out as far as his weight which should reach anywhere between one-hundred-twenty and one-hundred-sixty pounds and the way his frame and feet looked I would say he was going to be on the high end of that scale, Sarah and I both were going to have to do some modifications to the backseat areas of our vehicles and very soon. As we all got buckled in and I kicked over the motor I could see Charlie heading towards the guard shack or what looked more like a little cabin of sorts, "He's a very nice and sincere man and I believe I have made my first friend here at S.H.A.D.O.W. besides your father that is," I strongly remarked. "Yes he is, I think of him as family Cole, I believe one day you will too once you really get to know him, he and my father have been great and very close friends for a long time," Sarah emotionally commented. The three of us headed out past the guard shack as we waved and said our goodbye's to Charlie, even Shadow stuck his big head out Sarah's window and looked back as if to say goodbye to Charlie or maybe even to S.H.A.D.O.W. as well, after all he did have quite a few friends there already and hopefully I could catch up with him in regards to that area.

The camouflaged door to the base opened up and the sunlight began beaming in like a laser, once free and clear of the door we were in full view of "Secret Canyon" and the beauty of the Sedona area, God how I love this part of the country. The wind and breeze began to swirl and sing in the cabin of Sarah's Fj and it was music to all of our ears, Shadow's nose was gyrating like a spinning top as he was trying to take in as much fresh air as possible with that enormously long snout of his, "Yeah I know boy, it's nice to be back outside again and take in this wonderful fresh air and sunlight," I loudly remarked as the wind was increasingly getting stronger inside the Fj in relationship to our speed. "Yeah I know Cole, sometimes that underground air-conditioning and heating can get a little stale," as Sarah expressed her opinion on the matter. Growing up I always favored being outside versus being in the house or at a movie theater or any other indoor activity kids might prefer, I guess I have just loved nature over anything else growing up as a kid and I believe that it is a direct result from my parent's teachings to respect the land and mother nature of this great world we live on and Miralani felt just as I did. As we hit the main pavement Sarah popped in a cd into the stereo player and we listened to some wonderful relaxing native American flute music the rest of the way home. I was a bit surprised by it and had no idea she enjoyed that type of music, I guess there was still a lot to learn about each other, particularly concerning likes and dislikes. After a few minutes into the music we both reached at the same time for each other's hand to hold and met just above the gearshift knob where we locked them tightly together for a few moments then smiled at each other realizing and feeling the same emotions of love and the need for physical contact between to individuals who were so in touch with their feelings and the love they felt for one another. I began to speed up some in order to get home faster and hopefully enhance the physical contact we were sharing at the moment and I was pretty sure Sarah was feeling the same way right about now.

After a twenty-minute drive which felt more like an hour and a half from the excitement and anticipation Sarah and I were feeling, the two of us almost jumped out of the Fj while it was still moving as we pulled into the driveway. I quickly herded Shadow into the backyard and pleaded with him to do his business as quick as possible, as if to know what Sarah and I had in mind he decided to test my patients or maybe he just wanted to play around with my emotions a bit to see how long I could take it, "Come on boy, you're killing me here, hurry up okay, I know you have to take care of business but so do I," I emotionally begged him. Another couple of minutes passed then he looked at me as if to say "Okay I think you've suffered enough my friend, I'm just joking around with you" as he then took care of his bodily needs by relieving himself completely and then running up to me wagging his tail and pushing me towards the house as if to say "Hurry up and get in there and take of your business now" as the two us headed in through the patio door. Shadow loped over to his spot by the fireplace and plopped down, "I'm sorry boy but we'll have to wait a while for dinner, I'm going to be a little busy for a bit," I remarked as I patted him on his head. I could hear Sarah in the bedroom opening and closing drawers on her dresser, "Hey ranger, you coming back here or am I going to have to come and get you," she seductively yelled. I almost tripped over Shadow turning and running down the hallway so fast, "On my way sweetheart, don't start without me," I quickly yelled back while trying not to trip the rest of the way there. When I entered the room there was Sarah standing in front of me in the most scantily American Indian deerskin outfit I had ever seen in my life, it was basically a mini skirt that looked like it was made from an old cut up chamois that you would use to dry your car off after washing it. All I could do was just stand there in total awe of her beauty and the hypnotic look she was projecting my way had taken over my senses and emotions, "My god woman, I have never seen such beauty from a perspective of my own heritage, you have got to be the most beautiful woman in the world and I have got to be the luckiest man in the world," I said with a slightly nervous tone. The two of us then embraced and began our own version of a Navajo mating ritual.

After fifteen minutes of intense physical training as Sarah put it, we finally collapsed from exhaustion which led to my decision of no barbeque for this evening, instead it was looking more like a pizza delivery night. I knew Shadow would be a little disappointed there would be no steak for dinner but he did have it for lunch, I promised him I would make it up to him tomorrow. As Sarah and I moved into the living room to enjoy a relaxing evening and discuss how my first day went she pulled out a folder from her small briefcase and removed some official looking documents, "Here Cole, take a look at this information I dug up for you and our case of the missing Escalade, I think you'll find it very interesting," she stated as she handed the folder towards me. "Great, what did you find, anything that can help Sam solve the case?" I asked. "Well I'm sure it will help Sam but I think it will help us even more after you see what surfaced on these surveillance reports, just to let you know Cole this now has become our number one case at S.H.A.D.O.W. and you and I have been assigned to it, so buckle up rookie, it could be a rough ride from here on out," she strongly remarked. I paused for a second and was sort of surprised and a little nervous by her statement of me being assigned on a case already, "Wow, just like that were going out on a mission together, I mean I only have one day under my belt and what's up with the rookie comment, Coop, I hope it's okay I called you that but I really think it fit's you perfectly, If it's okay with you and Charlie I'd sort of like to use that nickname for you," perhaps slightly overstepping my bounds I asked. "Well you are a rookie and I'm sure it's okay with Charlie and I guess if I'm going to call you a rookie you can call me whatever you'd like, actually I think I would sort of like it if you called me Coop," She reassuringly expressed her feelings on the subject. We both came to an agreement on the nicknames as I began to read the documents in my hands.

Twenty minutes of intense reading passed and I was amazed at the detail of the reports and subject matter pertaining to the Escalade case that I had previously worked when I was still a ranger, "Jesus Sarah, it definitely looks like someone from S.H.A.D.O.W. is at the center of this investigation, do you have a person of interest or any ideas or leads on who or whom it might be?" I cautiously asked making sure I wasn't crossing any lines or implying anyone or particular person. "No nothing concrete but I'm pretty sure it's one of our agents and he or she has been running non-authorized missions for some time now, we just finally caught a break from the Escalade bit of evidence that fell into our lap, hopefully you and I can put this case to rest and put this person or persons in confinement, it's hard telling how much damage or changes have been made via these unauthorized trips back onto the past," Sarah emotionally replied. Seeing and hearing the emotion of Sarah's reply I could tell that she was extremely upset and very motivated towards finding out the identity of whoever was involved, "I promise you, we will get to the bottom of this, I will do whatever it takes to help you as much as I possibly can with my limited experience of being an agent," as I reassuringly made my feelings and intentions quite clear to her. "Cole, don't sell yourself short, just be yourself, the skills you have as a tracker and a hunter are one of the main reasons you're here, I have all the confidence and faith in your capabilities just the way you are," she strongly remarked. The two of us then moved over to the dining room table and began to discuss and go over the inch of the documents that Sarah had obtained, maybe together we could come up with something that only the working as partners would come into plain sight. After spending the next few hours eating our pizza and banging our heads together with all of the evidence that laid before us we just couldn't find any links to any one person or persons, "let's call it a night sweetheart, we're both getting pretty tired I think, maybe a good night's sleep will give us a new perspective on this tomorrow," I softly suggested. "Maybe your right rookie, let's go to bed, we can talk some more about your first day if you want or I can fill you in on a few more technical aspects of the time travel process and how it works in more detail if you'd like," she said with a grin. After smiling back at her we retired to the bedroom and hopefully a good night's sleep but I was pretty sure I was going to have some crazy dreams with all of the stuff I saw today.

Awakened by the alarm and then Shadow's jump on top of us Sarah and I slowly rolled out of bed, she headed for the bathroom and I headed for the patio door to let Shadow out to do his business. By four-thirty a.m. the two of us were showered, dressed and ready for a quick little breakfast, we would not have time to stop at Miralani's because we needed to get in early and get started with what was going to be a very long day according to what Sarah had laid out for the three of us. Shadow looked like he was ready for another day at S.H.A.D.O.W. from the way he was reacting to Sarah and I's comments throughout the morning. He definitely had a sense or feel of the English language when spoken. After finishing breakfast, we all loaded up into the Bronco and began our trip to the S.H.A.D.O.W. facility, "Hey sweetheart I'm so glad Charlie rushed getting my clearance sticker approved, I think I will be much more receptive to every I learn today because at the end of the day I'll know I'll be getting back into a small portion of my life that I'm quite familiar with, my Bronco," I remarked as we headed towards the main road. "Like I said before, he's someone you can always count on and always trust," Sarah reassuringly stated. I was hoping that I could spend a little time with Charlie first thing to show off the Bronco, after all I felt I owed him that much at least for all of his troubles or effort he put in regarding all of my paperwork. "Cole I wanted to let you know my father has been working on building a special area just for Shadow to hang out at or when he needs to satisfy his bowels or bladder, it will have artificial grass and running water in the aspect of a stream and some very realistic looking trees and bushes, all totally safe in case he decides to chew up or eat any of them," she excitingly commented. "That sounds great, doesn't it Shadow, I mean having your own area just to relax and maybe take a few naps during the day, I wish I could get that kind of special treatment," I cheerfully remarked.

The drive to the S.H.A.D.O.W. facility was now becoming somewhat familiar as Sarah didn't have any comments concerning the direction we were heading. Shadow was somewhat sleeping in the back occasionally popping his head up through the front seat between Sarah and me, I guess he just wanted to get his bearings to see where we might be headed. Sarah told me last night that she and her father came up with a training regime for him that might be very beneficial out in the field, I was quite curious on what it might consist of. It was now just a little before six a.m. as we pulled up to the secret entrance and parked for a moment until the front window was scanned where it hopefully would pick up the freshly applied sticker I put on last night, it only took about thirty seconds before the door began to open and grant our access. As we approached the guard shack with Charlie in it I couldn't help but wonder if he heard the glorious exhaust tone of the Bronco as we drove through the long corridor to reach this point, "Hey Charlie, good morning, hope I didn't make too much noise coming in or set off any sensors from the exhaust," I remarked after rolling down my window. 'Hell no Cole, that's music to my ears, I haven't heard anything sweet for quite some time, what's under the hood, it sounds like a big block, I didn't think you could get anything like that under the hood of these things," he remarked. Looking over at Sarah for a second and giving her a puppy dog look she knew right away what I had on my mind, "Okay rookie, you've got fifteen minutes to show off you pride and joy, I'll head up to see my father quickly and let him know we're here and then we'll meet you down here by the exit door to the main corridor, okay," she firmly stated. I could hear Charlie chuckle a bit then leaned in towards my window, "Thanks Coop, I won't keep him too long, okay Cole, just follow me and show you where your private spot is, just give me a minute to set the auto guard in full secure mode," Charlie quickly remarked while still chuckling some. "You got it," I quickly replied back.

After pulling forward and waiting a few minutes for Charlie to secure his post and start heading off to my very own personal parking spot Sarah turned and said, "I can see you two are going to become very good friends." Watching Charlie walk giddily towards my spot was so refreshing to see a man of his age so interested and excited to see an old school vintage automobile like my Bronco, Sarah was right, I think we were going to become good friends. "I couldn't agree more Coop," as I expressed my opinion. I slowly began to move forward to follow Charlie's footsteps to reach my assigned spot. "You see Cole, Shadow's not the only one getting special treatment around here," Sarah commented as we came to a complete stop in the parking spot. "Fits like a glove, doesn't she Cole," Charlie yelled out as I turned off engine. "Yeah, this is perfect," I quickly replied. The three of us piled out of the Bronco and Sarah gave me a peck on the cheek, "Hey Shadow, want to come with me boy, let's go find my father and let these two gearheads talk for a while," she said. It only took a second or two then Shadow gave me a look as if to say I'm going with her and I'll see you later, he probably thought she was taking him to the cafeteria for some steak and eggs as the two of them walked away. Charlie and I then began to go over every inch of the Bronco and I was glad to give him the grand tour with all of the restoration information and the modifications I had made. Knowing that I went over Sarah's allotted fifteen minutes she gave me I wrapped things up with Charlie quickly and told him we could check it some more at a later date and if he wanted to take the Bronco out for a spin that would be alright with me.

Just as I opened the door to the main corridor I could see Sarah, her father and Shadow coming towards me from a distance. Shadow saw me and broke out into a slight prance with quite a bit of speed, "What is it boy, did you miss me in that short amount of time?" I jokingly asked. "Good morning Cole, how did you sleep last night, I hope yesterday wasn't too much for you in one day but we really need to get you up to speed and quickly," John remarked. "Actually sir I slept quite well, I thought I might have some weird dreams but instead I think I had one of the best night's sleep in a long time," I reassuringly replied. "Sarah tells me you two went over the files regarding our internal problem we have here, what do you think Cole, any ideas or gut feelings on this case?" John asked quite directly and frankly. "Cole and I racked our brains most of the night dad and pretty much came up with nothing other than the fact the Escalade in question is ours," as Sarah then responded to her father's quarry. "Well I may have something for you two that could possibly shed some light on this case, some hidden video monitors that nobody knows the locations of except for Charlie and myself," John commented. "Wow dad, you didn't even tell me about those, any reason why or you just didn't trust me," Sarah quickly asked somewhat jokingly. I could tell she was most likely being a little sarcastic or just joking around with her father, at least I hoped she was. John turned and said, "Now you know better than that, I trust you more than anyone else in the world but these video monitors I wanted to be kept a secret just between Charlie and I." Sarah smiled and gave her father a look of understanding and forgiveness, "I know dad, hopefully they will help with this investigation, we could sure use some kind of a lead," she contentedly commented.

As we walked down the long cold corridor and passing the cafeteria I could tell Shadow wanted to turn in and perhaps get some more steak, "Oh no boy, you'll have to wait a few more hours until lunch, then we'll eat," I remarked as I reached down and gave him a big pat on his chest. Sarah and her father walked just ahead of Shadow and I and I could tell they were talking about something in great detail, I guess it didn't include me at this point in time. John slowly turned back to glance at me then turned his attention back to Sarah, "Okay Cole, Sarah has talked me into it, I'm going to accelerate your portion of the knowledge based training, she thinks you can handle it with her help if needed, are you on board with this, it will be some pretty highly technical mumbo jumbo, pardon the term, I meant no disrespect Cole," as John strongly expressed his opinion on the matter. Pausing for a second and realizing that I was the topic of their previous conversation I choose my next words carefully, "I'm on board with anything you want to throw at me, hell the sooner I can get checked out and up to speed the sooner I can start contributing to this organization and help my partner," I confidently replied. "Alright then, next stop the main medical lab where we will run a couple of body scans on you for our agent data reconstruct files," John eagerly replied. I gave Sarah a little wink and smile, then we all continued down the corridor towards what I hoped would just be the scans John was talking about and not end up being some kind of thorough physical, I didn't feel much like getting poked or having any other lab work performed on me today, It's not that I'm afraid of needles or anything like that, I just don't like people removing blood and other fluids from my body unless it's absolutely necessary. Once we were inside the main medical facility John walked over to a couple of medical tech's or at least that's what they looked like to me, "Hey Cole step over here for a minute, I'd like for you to meet Jeff and Rafael, they're the medical technicians that will be performing the scans on you, gentlemen this is agent Cole Youngblood and he is Sarah's new partner," John said as he introduced me to the tech's. "It's a pleasure to meet you, so what sort of scans are we talking about here, I mean will they pick up any health issues or other problems in my system that I don't know about?" I politely asked. The one tech named Jeff responded, "Mr. Youngblood these scans will produce a very highly detailed blueprint of your entire carbon based system, in other words we will be charting and recording every living cell in your body, then we will place them in our re-construct data files to be used during atomization and re-atomization phase of the time travel process," the man said, sounding more like a robot with every word that he spoke, I just nodded my head and softly mumbled "uh-huh" I see. Sarah let out a tiny chuckle as the two men brought me a gown to put on and escorted me to another room. I was starting to get a little nervous at this point.

After thirty minutes of scans and freezing my ass off on a cold transparent slab of something that looked like glass but wasn't, I finally headed back out to the main area to find Just Sarah waiting for me, John and Shadow were nowhere in sight, "Hey Coop, where's Shadow and your father?" I asked. "He took Shadow over to the dog park he's having built just for him and it's almost finished, at least enough for him to relieve himself if needed, we're supposed to meet them both at our next stop, you okay rookie, you're walking a little gingerly," she inquired. "Oh I'm okay sweetheart, it's just that my butt is a little numb and I have no feeling in my lower extremities, maybe you could come over here and give me a message to help start the blood flowing again," I softly pleaded with her. "I'm pretty sure you're going live Cole, you'll just have to walk it off rookie," she reassuringly commented. "Okay but when I said I was numb and lost feeling in my lower extremities I meant all of my lower extremities, so you might show just a little bit more concern for my well- being Coop," I hurtfully replied. "Well you got the little bit part right anyway, don't worry Cole I'll make sure everything still works when we get home tonight, oh by the way I forgot to let you know that Jeff and Rafael are a couple, I mean they're not legally married yet but they're working on it, so just keep in mind to respect their ways and beliefs to avoid any hurt feelings," she informatively remarked. Suddenly I was struck with the thought of an old joke one the rangers told me years ago and it was now the perfect timing to get her back in regards to the little bit comment she had just made, "Jesus Sarah, why didn't you tell me that before I went in for the scans, I mean holy crap I think I just probably offended the hell out of both of them, when I was on the scanning table laying there naked I told Jeff a joke, I asked him what do you call a male gay dinosaur and I guess that explains the dirty look he gave after he replied "I don't know, what do you call a male gay dinosaur" and now I feel horrible because I told him a male gay dinosaur is called a "Mega-sore-ass", damn I'm probably on their shit list now," I nervously replied. Sarah stood before me in total shock and disbelief as I kept a very serious and embarrassed look about me, final after a few minutes I just couldn't take it any longer and I let out a loud belly laugh that almost brought the walls down in the corridor, "Got you Coop," barely able to get those three words out amidst the continued belly laughing. "Damn you Cole, I swear I'll get you back for that one, you had me going for a second or two and ready to apologize to Jeff and Rafael," she angrily remarked, then cracking a smile before busting out into a laugh herself. "Well maybe I should have let you go in and apologize, that could have been the icing on the cake," I replied, still laughing a bit.

After gaining our composure we finally met up with John in what looked like another type of computer room which branched off into several enclosed offices, "Hey you two finally made it, I was getting a little worried something might have gone wrong with the scanning process, did everything go alright Cole, any problems?" he asked. "No problems sir, everything went great, I'm still a little amazed by what the scans are actually going to be used for and how everything works but I guess I will figure it out with Sarah's help and experiencing the process a few times," I confidently replied. "Great, that's what I like to hear, confidence in yourself and your abilities, remember if you ever feel the need to just sit down and talk to myself or any of the tech's around here feel free to do so," John remarked, putting me somewhat at ease. "That means a lot to me sir, thank you," I appreciatively replied. "Cole this is the area where we track all of the individuals we have saved and monitor their impact on modern day society, just to make sure there were no side affect's from the saved subject, we call this the "Grandfather Paradox" room," John slowly explained. I just remained silent and tried to focus on his words in order to try and fully understand this whole process and the order everything relates to as far as the overall process of this whole facility. "Don't worry rookie, we'll have plenty of time to go over all of the terminology and phrase's used here and what exactly they all mean," Sarah reassuringly commented. "Well I know what a grandfather is but what the hell is a paradox?" I jokingly inquired. "Okay smartass, I think that's enough from you, I'm not falling for another one," Sarah quickly and strongly replied.

After a few minutes of watching Sarah and I go back and forth with verbal jabs John decided to intervene by suggesting we head over to the main offices of all of the agents and he would introduce me to any of the other agents that might be around, "Sounds good to me sir, I think Sarah and I needed a little time out," I concededly remarked. "Yeah dad, I think that's a good idea also before I take the rookie here out to the hand to hand combat training area and give him a beat down," as Sarah confidently expressed her feelings. Even Shadow seemed like he was ready to move on, I just hoped he realized that Sarah and I were just teasing each other with our slightly aggressive verbal remarks, by the slow wag in his big bushy tail I would venture to say he knew exactly what was going on. I had come to know the body language of Shadow and I guess that of all wolves over the last few months and I must say that the intelligence level of these magnificent animals was off the charts, I began to have thoughts again of trying to teach him some type of sign language that could be beneficial out in the field, the prospects of this would be limitless and quite useful for Sarah and I. That's it, my mind was just made up, I would begin his training this weekend and get Sarah involved as well since she would be working with him just as much as I. The four of us then continued down the main corridor and with my second orientation day, it was sort of weird that I hadn't once thought of or even missed any aspects of the ranger job that I had left behind, maybe this was truly my destiny all along.

As we got closer to what I assumed the main office area I finally began to see other people use the corridor we currently occupied and I must say it was a slight breath of fresh air to be around and see a few more people. We made a slight turn to the right when the corridor split into two directions and I could then hear several voices coming from a pair of opened doors just ahead on the right, "Well Cole this is our main office and where you'll have an office of your own in a couple of days, we're just getting it ready for you and Shadow, it will have a few extra perks and modifications to support Shadow's needs," John proudly remarked, I could tell he was a man that was very prideful of his accomplishments and successes. I could definitely tell where Sarah gets here drive from, he is a great man and she will probably take over for him someday and probably try to match his achievements, it was obvious she did not want to disappoint him in any way. As we entered through the doorway I could now see several people standing around a central area that looked like a small hotel lobby or lounge with some of the ugliest chairs I've ever seen and some small tables that only midget's or Hobbit's could sit at and just to give it that homey touch a few magazines and fake looking plants on them, kind of cheesy looking but a lot better than just an empty room, "So Sarah was this lounge area taken right of the fifties to save money or something?" I jokingly asked. Once again I may have just crossed the line again with that smartass remark, John just smiled a bit then turned away holding back from laughing, I hoped he wasn't offended by my remark, I'm pretty sure he wasn't, he just turned away to keep Sarah from seeing his facial expressions knowing it might upset her more, "Well it doesn't look like any of the other agents are around Cole, I'll just have to introduce you to them when we come across them here at the facility," she then remarked, quickly changing the subject. Nodding my head as if to say that's fine the four of us continued on with the orientation.

As the day progressed and past lunch Sarah and I headed to a security monitoring room which was only accessible by Sarah or her father, "Hey rookie, I thought we could spend the rest of the day looking at the video footage my father gave us and go over the rest of the footage as well and try to see if we missed anything or this new video might give up some leads," Sarah suggested. "Sounds good to me as long as you think Shadow will be okay with your father for that long of a period," I quickly replied. "No worries there Cole, those two have a great relationship and trusting bond just as we do with him," she reassuringly remarked. Once Sarah was cleared through her badge and facial scan we entered the highly technical looking room, there were computer monitors like I had never seen before with bright and clear images of S.H.A.D.O.W. employee's under surveillance from multiple areas of the facility, Sarah immediately headed for a blank monitor and video feedback player underneath it. Sarah then removed several cd discs from the bag her father gave to her earlier in the day. After inserting the first one we began to view the parking garage area first which overlooked all of the company Escalades and other smaller vehicles used by S.H.A.D.O.W. employee's. The installed cd was an eight-day segment of time and would take a while to go over, even at a slightly advanced speed. Hopefully we would catch something early on. The hidden surveillance equipment that the cd's came from were of the highest quality and probably not available to the public would be my guess. Everything looked pretty normal according to Sarah at this point and it was now past three o-clock and we would soon be heading home or to Miralani's cafe for dinner, I had called her earlier and Sarah and I both agreed it would be nice to see her again since we hadn't seen her in a few days.

We continued on watching more video and then all of a sudden I saw Sarah's eyes light up which was followed by a puzzled look on her face, "Now that's odd," she blurted out. "What is, did you see something?" I quickly and anxiously asked. "Notice anything different about these two views of the same Escalade, I mean one is from the standard video and this one is from the bag my father gave us," she asked as she pointed to the image on the left side of the screen. "Wait a minute, give me a second look at this, hold on, yeah I got it, I do see it, I think, are you talking about all of the dirt on the side of the rear passenger fender behind the wheel well, is that it, is it?" I eagerly asked. "Nice job rookie, pretty impressive, the attention to details is always going to lead or perhaps uncover hidden clues in any case, you just might have a future in this type of work," she jokingly remarked. "So what exactly does this mean Sarah?" I asked. "Well what it means is, how can the vehicle be clean in one frame and within a second or two of the same time stamp but from another monitor be dirty in the same area of the vehicle without physically being moved or driven by anyone, can you provide have a theory or offer up an opinion on this rookie?" as she explained with a question of her own. I'm pretty sure she already had one so I just remained silent for a few seconds, "Well you're the expert here Coop, how about you tell me your theory then I'll tell you mine," I smartly replied. Smiling then rolling her eyes somewhat she looked back down at the video monitor, "Okay rookie, listen up because here is your first lesson on time travel uses and the endless possibilities once you open your mind and except the fact that anything is possible utilizing the technology we have at our disposal, okay my theory and I'm sure it's probably very close to yours, it is my belief that someone or possibly even more than one person has doctored the main video feed from the security cameras that are visible in the motor pool area in the hopes of covering up their unauthorized use of this particular Escalade and that also happens to be the one that was removed from the Sedona impound yard that you and Sam had it towed too," she thoroughly explained with conviction. Once again I remained silent for a few seconds, "I think I understand and I'm also beginning to understand the overall complexity that this whole time travel stuff can lead to or create and cause, I keep thinking in the back of my mind it's just for limited situations and circumstances but I guess it's really limitless to the individuals who can think up applications on how or what to use it for," I somewhat confidently replied. "Very good rookie, you're already accepting the reality of time travel and have begun to open your mind but you have a long way to go and I'm going to do my best to get you down the road as fast as possible, I think we just got our first big break and lead into this case and I believe it's going to resolve a lot of unanswered questions, let's go get Shadow and call it a day and then go to your sister's place for dinner," she said with excitement and a renewed sense of energy and resolve.

After picking up Shadow and saying our goodbye's to Sarah's father we heading off in the Bronco to Miralani's, after I called her to see if she was going to be there. When we pulled up to the café Shadow began to get excited, he had built a close relationship with her as well as Sarah's father and other's at the S.H.A.D.O.W facility. He was getting to be quite the celebrity and friend of many. We walked into the café and Miralani greeted us with big hugs and kisses, of which Shadow received the most. Miralani had reserved our table an hour prior to our arrival, what a sister. We sat and ate and talked for quite some time, Shadow ate his ground up burger cooked with chunks of carrot's and mixed in with rice and a little beef broth, "I hope this is okay for you Shadow, Cole told me on the phone no more steak for a couple of days, he said you were getting to spoiled on it and might get to the point of not eat anything else, besides too much cooked steak is probably not very good for you my friend," Miralani remarked with great concern and love for him. "Sorry buddy but I tell you what, the hamburgers here are the best in Sedona," as I quickly added my input to her remark. Sarah and Miralani talked about my first day and second day with little input from me and I was okay with that, the two of them were also beginning to build a trusting and great friendship. After a couple of hours and big full belly's mostly the result from my sister feeding us some cheese cake for dessert we said our goodbye's and then out headed to Sarah's place to pick up a few things then back to my home or I guess I should say our home because it was quickly beginning to feel as if we should call it our home. On the way back Sarah kept rattling our brains about who or whom might be behind the Escalade mystery and the reasoning behind it all, mostly it was all of her opinions and expertise relating to S.H.A.D.O.W. and its employee's, primarily the other time traveling agents because there had to be a connection of some kind.

The garage door closed behind us after pulling the Bronco in and I began to feel a sense of warmth and completeness in my life as I had finally found my spiritual partner in life and death, we were truly connected as one spirit and would be forever, we both felt the same in that respect and whatever powers of destiny or faith had brought us together we both knew it was for a good reason and meant to be.

13

GOOD TO GO

Over the next few weeks the routine was pretty much the same with the exception of a little more training and education on quantum physics and the theories of time travel. Sarah and I also were now quite prepared to take on anyone in the shooting competition as I had honed my marksmanship with the vintage firearms at S.H.A.D.O.W. and I must say I think Sarah and her father were impressed with my progress and the quick study of the brainy portions of my training, I was quite surprised myself. There was still not much progress made in the aspect of identifying who or whom was behind the Escalade mystery but we were both sure it had to be one or more of the agents or other employee's that I had met over the last several weeks, Sarah had warned me that we must proceed slowly with this case until we have something solid in the way of a lead or more than just circumstantial evidence. Whoever it was had to be a very cool and calm individual with plenty of confidence they had gotten away with whatever illegal activity they had performed or are performing. The other agents were broken up into three teams of two agents each and then of course there was our team which was now unique and the first to enlist a canine as an agent. The teams were identified by the first four letters of the alphabet, "A" team which included Sarah, Shadow and myself, then "B" team which consisted of agent Dan Sutter and his partner Bill Casper who was the senior, age wise of all the agents, then "C" team which was another male and female partnership of agent James Kelly and Erin Lovell and finally "D" team with agents Troy Garner and Cindy Collin's. After meeting all of them it's hard to believe that one or more may be involved with the Escalade case, they all seemed very nice and sincere in regards to their job and the belief of what S.H.A.D.O.W. was trying to accomplish.

Over the past few weeks I had also been working with Shadow as much as possible regarding his training in the use of sign language that we could use out in the field if needed, he was such a fast learner that he mastered the basics of sit, stay, heel and lie down in just one day so Sarah and I began with an accelerated program consisting of the basis of the human sign language for the hearing impaired, at first I thought it was a crazy idea but he once again showed his intelligence and quickly learned everything we showed him and has retained all it. Sarah and both agreed that we would work with and keep him proficient in this skill and try to keep it just between us for now. Sarah had been working with me as well in regards to all of the time travel processes at S.H.A.D.O.W. and broke them down for me in a way that even an ex-park ranger could understand the principals and applications that were in place at the facility. I can proudly say that I now know the current seven states of matter of the universe which are Solid, Liquid, Gas, Bose-Einstein condensate, Quark-gluon plasma, Degenerate matter and Fermionic condensate, just don't ask me which ones represent what. The only thing that's important to know about them is that they exist and help make up the main sections of the "Orthogonal Wormhole" used on the sending and retrieving platform of the time travel process. I also learned the basic principal of the large particle accelerator which resided underneath the S.H.A.D.O.W. facility and how it was the necessary power source to achieve particle de-atomization and re-atomization in order for us to return from the past in one piece and not scattered all over the universe. Sarah told me that she believed her father had help from the hand of God to finish his research and get the technology online and working and safe for human travel. I agreed with her that her father was a very religious man and seemed to have an aura about him that was different from anyone I had ever met before. When I questioned her more about this belief and why she was so sure about the divine intervention she said that I would soon feel the same way after the first mission or two that we went on. I just told her I hoped she was right because it would make me feel a lot more at ease with changing the future if I knew the all mighty was on our side.

It was Sunday night now and Sarah and I were just getting ready to turn in, "Hey you need to get a good night's sleep Cole, tomorrow will be a cram session of just about everything you've learned up till now and my father will probably question your knowledge on several subjects but I'm one hundred percent sure you are more than ready for whatever he can throw at you, just remember he thinks the world of you and all that you have accomplished in such a short time, he just wants to put his mind at ease and make sure you're ready to go out on your first mission and be successful," Sarah confidently remarked as she reached over to give me a kiss goodnight. "No worries Coop, Shadow and I are more than ready, I won't disappoint your father or you for that matter," I reassuringly replied. The two of us drifted off to sleep with Shadow on the floor at the end of the bed, I did feel a little uneasy about Sarah's comment but deep down inside I knew I would never be more ready than I was now, maybe just a little nervous about the fact that very soon I would be getting de-atomized and my atoms sent back in time and re-atomized somewhere in time, hopefully I would get more at ease with the process the more times I experienced it. I had asked Sarah several times to try to explain how it felt but she said it was something she couldn't describe and that I would know what she was talking about soon enough.

The morning came very quickly and the two of us hopped into action getting ready for work, yes work, I've actually become quite comfortable calling it work now and the distant memories of being a ranger have begun to subside in the back reaches of my mind, I was truly happy now and knew that I had made the right decision in pursuing this path of destiny for myself and together with Sarah and Shadow our lives would be forever etched in stone, my father once told me the path and journey of our lives is what we make of it, only you can decide what is right or wrong and that it can always change at any given moment, he always said trust in your heart and your soul, they together will always guide you. Those were powerful words and words that will stick with me forever, I really miss his wisdom and his knowledge of the Navajo ways and spiritual teachings he gave my sister and I, he was a great man and someday I know I will see him again in the spiritual world. As those thoughts weighed heavy on my heart Sarah stuck her head out of the bathroom, "Hey you okay Cole, you look sort of distant or something, hey you're not afraid of today's tough schedule and the meeting with my father are you?" she curiously asked. "No, I was just thinking about my father and how nice it would've have been if he could've met you, he would have really liked you," I emotionally replied then smiled at the beautiful woman standing before, once again realizing how lucky I was. "I wish I could have met him too Cole, I'm sure he was a great man because he raised such a great son and daughter, you and your sister are a reflection of his upbringing and all that he taught you and I'm pretty sure is very proud of what you have become and the accomplishments you have achieved," as she proudly expressed her feelings on the matter. The two of us quite hungry headed out to the kitchen for breakfast where Shadow had already resided to, probably wanting his breakfast as well.

As the three of us finished our breakfast Sarah called her father and let her know that we might be a little late because she wanted to stop and pick something up on the way. We then all loaded up into the Bronco which now had a modified and much larger rear seat area for Shadow and padding on all of the metal areas that could have cut his paws from getting in and out of the vehicle, his weight and size had now reached just over one hundred pounds and he still had at least another six months of growing, he was going to be one awesome looking wolf. Once we reached downtown Sedona I pulled over at a mini mall area and parked and waited for Sarah to pick up her package that she said was for her father and wanted to surprise him with it today. As I watched her walk away from the Bronco I was still so amazed at her beauty and how she carried it, I mean she looked like the girl next door but with a very serious business look to her at times, she was so stunning in just about every way possible, she was quite an extraordinary woman. As Shadow and I waited he pushed his head forward through the opening between the two front seats and gave me a sad look, "Don't worry boy, she'll be back in a few minutes, hey are you ready for today, I know I am, hopefully John doesn't give you a verbal test like the one I'm getting of everything we've learned up to this point," I remarked as I stroked his big broad chest. He gave me a wet kiss on the cheek and his tail began to wag as he saw Sarah returning to the Bronco, "See I told you she'd be back," I quickly added. Sarah hopped in and we were off to S.H.A.D.O.W. for what was going to be my most trying day yet, at least as far as nerves go that is.

After twenty minutes of easy driving which means nice and slow for me we finally reached the secret entrance, "Wow Cole I didn't think we were ever going to get here, you're not feeling a little apprehension are you?" she jokingly asked. "No I just wanted to make sure Shadow gets comfortable with his new seating arrangements back there without me bouncing him around all over the place," I reassuringly replied hoping she would buy it. As Charlie checked us through I slowly parked in my spot which now was called the "Corral" by the other agents here at S.H.A.D.O.W. which I guess was fitting since I drove a Bronco, kind of corny but I did like it, I just wasn't going to let anyone know that. Shadow was so big now that he had to get in and out through the back tailgate. We gradually made our way towards Sarah's father's office for what I was hoping to be my final test and acceptance to be become a fully trained and vetted agent. Sarah and Shadow seemed to be quite excited to be here, I on the other hand was just wishing for this to be over quickly and get on with my progression towards becoming a great partner for Sarah and able to contribute to the agency. "Hang in there Cole, just think after this is over with you'll be that much closer to me not being able to call you rookie anymore, that day will come after your first save mission," she confidently remarked. "Thanks, that makes me feel a whole lot better," I nervously replied. As we entered John's office he was sitting at his desk going over some paperwork or files of some kind, "Good morning, did you eat breakfast yet, this won't take very long if not, but if you want to grab a bite it's okay with me, I'm just going over all of your training records and progress report's, I must say Cole what you've done in less than three weeks usually takes most agents three to four months, you should feel proud son, that's quite an accomplishment," he commented as he flipped over a few pages of the documents in front of him. "Thank you, I am proud and I would just like to say I couldn't have done it if it were not for Sarah's commitment to helping me and providing the push and confidence I needed at times," I strongly replied sounding like a Marine who just made it through boot camp. "I really just have one question to ask you Cole and I'd like an honest answer even if you feel it might be insulting to me, are you okay with that?" he asked. "No problem sir, I will be totally honest and sincere," I quickly replied.

After a few minutes of complete silence and going over some more documents from my folder John looked at Sarah and gave a wink, I thought to myself what the hell was going on here, "Cole, my question to you is do you have a big head?" John asked with a look of seriousness. I looked at him for a second then said, "What, a big head, what's going on here?" I somewhat angrily replied. Sarah began to laugh behind me, "Got you rookie, I told you I would get you back," she said holding a black graduation cap with a couple of feathers attached to it sticking straight up, they were beautiful, they looked like they belonged to a Red Tail Hawk, that's what was in the box she picked up on the way in. "I'm sorry Cole, she put me up to it, congratulations Mr. Youngblood, you are now an active agent of S.H.A.D.O.W. and welcome aboard," John proudly said. "Wow, you two got me good, John if you ever think about trying a second career I would think you have a great shot at being an actor and a damn good one at that," I said as I graciously acknowledged the performance from both of them. "I've got to say rookie I do feel a little bad about this but I'm sure you'll find a way to get even," Sarah remarked with a look of love and a little regret. "It's okay sweetheart, I probably deserved it and I really do like the cap, I think I'll hang it up on the living room wall when we get home," I happily replied. "I also have a certificate for you and Shadow that might look pretty good on that same wall with the cap," John quickly added. "Thank you and thank you for believing in Shadow and I, we won't let you down sir," I proudly expressed my gratitude.

After a half hour or so of celebrating Shadow's and my accomplishment's John shook my hand one more time, "Cole I want you and Sarah to take the next couple of days off and just relax or go somewhere on a little short vacation and clear your head, you two have earned it and I will start prepping for your first assignment together when you return, oh yeah and you too Shadow," John recommended as Shadow let out a little whimper as if to understand exactly what he had just said. "Thanks dad, we could sure use it, I mean you don't know the uphill battle I had training this guy," she jokingly remarked. "I love you too Coop," I quickly replied. John smiled at my response to Sarah's comment then reached down to give Shadow a big hug and congratulate him on his successful training, "Well done my friend, if you ever need anything you know where to find me," he conveyed to his four-legged friend. Shadow acknowledged the hug with a lick on John's cheeks which just about knocked him over backwards. "Well this has turned into a short day, what do you want to do for the rest of it Sarah," I curiously asked. "I would really just like to go find a nice quiet spot in Oak Creek Canyon on the way home and sit on some rocks by the water and relax and enjoy each other's company and maybe clear up any concerns you might have with our upcoming mission, that's if you have any, if not we could just relax and enjoy the sound of the water cascading down the rocks and into the pools," she emotionally suggested. "That actually sounds like a fantastic idea sweetheart, I think maybe that's exactly what we both need at this point, just some quiet time together, like when we were at Havasupai Falls," quickly agreeing with Sarah. We said goodbye to her father one more time then headed out as fast we could, even Shadow was in a high speed lope for him.

Clearing the guard shack with Charlie in it we just waved and didn't even slow down enough to say anything to him, we were like two high school graduates leaving the campus and starting the first day of our adult lives hoping to make it out in the real world. "Hey rookie, have I told you how much I love lately," she said as we emptied out into Secret Canyon after passing through the hidden entrance or in this case exit. "Actually I've been wondering if you stopped loving me after all of that intense mean training you've beat into me over the past few weeks, I think there's some making up to do on your part if you ask me," I sadly replied. "Well you might have a little bit of a case in that respect, I guess over the next couple of day's I'd better make it up to you, I'll leave that up to you on how, when and where, how's that sound rookie?" she seductively suggested. The two of us just smiled at each other. Twenty minutes passed and it was now high noon and the weather was wonderfully warm and pleasant, the hills of the surrounding area were gleaming with the bright colors of red, brown and orange topped off with brilliant puffy white clouds filling the majestic blue skyline, it was like looking at a giant post card from one of the local gift shops, we were truly blessed to live here and experience this masterpiece of mother nature. Once in Sedona Sarah suggested we stop and get some cheese, crackers and a nice bottle of wine to enjoy at Oak Creek Canyon. "Hey we should pick something up for Shadow, like some jerky or rawhide chews maybe, he's going to want to be a part of this relaxation excursion," I strongly recommended. After picking up our items on our small list including Shadow's treats we were back on our way, it would only be another fifteen minutes or so to reach the main parking area by the old bridge which overlooked the creek area.

The exhaust tone exiting from the dual pipes at the rear of the Bronco was really quite pleasing to my ears as I turned the music down a bit, "What's the matter, you don't like that song," Sarah asked. "No sweetheart I love that song but I love the sound of this masterfully built American made muscle V-8 under the hood even better," I said with a calmness in my voice. After reaching the parking area we piled out and loaded up our little knapsacks of food and drink, "Let's head down the main trail and then when we get to the bottom we'll turn left and head upstream on the main trail for about a half mile, after that there are plenty of nice quiet spots to enjoy the water and tranquility of this place," I remarked as we headed off down the trail. Shadow kept his perfect pace or lope between Sarah and I, even with the leash and harness attached to him I couldn't feel him at the other end, he walked with such grace, almost as if his paws were not touching the ground, such a magnificent animal he was and becoming more and more impressive with each passing day. "Wow this is really pretty down here, all the years I've lived here I never had a reason or I guess just too busy to come and see this beautiful part of Sedona," Sarah commented. "Well now you have a reason and there's so much more around here than most people ever get to see and I plan on showing you every one of them sweetheart, you too Shadow," I reassuringly expressed my feelings on the matter. "You've already shown me so much Cole, I just wish I could do something as nice for you, I mean the only thing I'm an expert on is time travel and maybe some limited history," she said sadly and somewhat depressed. "Hey you are the most interesting, impressive and wonderful woman I've ever met in my life, I'm the one that's comes up short in the skills, qualifications and expertise areas compared to you sweetheart, believe me it would take me years to even come close to what you already know and I'm so lucky to have you as a mentor," I reassuringly expressed my personal feelings to her.

Once we found our private little spot next to a slow swirling deep crystal clear pool with small water falls flowing into and out of it we began to set up our eating area with a blanket which was the foundation for the cheese and wine, the red plastic cups were a little of a drawback and taking some of the beauty away from the place but still it was a gorgeous day and we were going to enjoy it.

Shadow had made himself comfortable lying on a big rock next to us and he was enjoying the cool breeze blowing down the canyon, sounding so surreal as it whistled through the tops of the trees and danced with the surrounding scrub bushes and shrubbery, it was truly peaceful. Sarah and I began to relax and talk about what we had just accomplished together and I was still somewhat curious about several aspects of the agency and if there was still a lot for me to find out about or learn, "So sweetheart I do have some questions that I was a little hesitant to ask your father that I was sort of saving for you," I asked after deciding this was a perfect time to do so. "Okay Cole, fire away," she quickly replied with an authoritarian tone. "Alright, my first question is mostly based on a concern I have about the symbols all over the walls, corridors and doorways at S.H.A.D.O.W. that look like a pentagram or some kind of religious sign, I know your father knew I was checking them out over the first couple of days on the job and I was hoping he would volunteer that information, because I was a little too cautious and nervous I was afraid to question him on it, I just want to know their meaning or purpose for being there," I respectively asked. "Well I was wondering when we would get around to having this talk and hopefully I can explain as much as possible without breaking my promise to my father," she then replied. "Wait a minute Sarah I don't want you going back on your word or breaking any trust you have with your father on this issue, never mind the question," I quickly remarked as I interrupted. "No Cole, I want to tell you as much as I can, you deserve to know what you're getting into and hopefully what I don't tell you now my father will eventually tell you when he feels it's right, okay here it is in a nut shell, you remember when I told you I could guarantee you that every save mission we do will always turn out right and not change the future in a worse way but positive, the thing is my father basically has a direct line to God, I mean he speaks with him and I know that sounds a little grandiose but I can tell you that it's one-hundred percent true, I just can't tell you why at this time and as far as the symbols you asked about they're pentagrams to keep out evil spirits and demons from infiltrating the S.H.A.D.O.W. agency, just one other bit of information that might get you a little upset, you remember that blood test you took, well it actually was a blood transfusion of sort I mean you're blood received a treatment of thousands of tiny nanotech cells in the shape of a pentagram to protect you from demonic possession or control, so I guess that pretty much clears that up right, any other questions rookie?" she remarked followed with an extraordinary smile I had never seen up to this point of our relationship. "Sure, no worries, that's what I thought, you want to eat now or latter," I said then paused a second, "What the hell are you talking about Sarah, demonic possession, super tech blood, I mean what's next vampire's and mummy's, what else aren't you telling me sweetheart, I love you more than life but are you really telling me that we're are going to be actually working for God himself?" I emotionally asked. The two of us just sat there totally quiet and staring deep into each other's hearts and souls.

After complete silence for what seemed like eternity Sarah reached for and then grasped my hand tightly, "Cole you know that I love you and would never lie to but please trust me on this and everything that I've told you today, it is all true and there is more to it than that and once you know everything it will be much easier to accept and understand, if you'd like I can approach my father about it and ask him to talk to you and maybe he will open up to you and fill in the blanks but if not please don't pressure him on this Cole because it's probably the single most important secret at S.H.A.D.O.W. and only he will know when it's time to fully explain to you the gravity of the subject," she reassuringly remarked with teary eyes. I could only respect her father's wishes at this point and could see that she was highly emotional about this subject so I decided the only right thing to do was respect her wishes, "Sarah, I will trust and respect the faith and honor you and your father have, I would never want to be the cause of putting that in danger, I do believe in you and in your father, you know that I'm a very spiritual person and that I do believe in God, I just hope I don't disappoint him in anyway or dilute his trust in me or the faith that I have in him," choosing my words carefully and respectfully I replied. "Thanks Cole, you know it's tearing me up inside keeping anything from you but I have a feeling you'll know everything there is to know about S.H.A.D.O.W. very soon," she thankfully replied. Over the next couple of hours Shadow, Sarah and I just enjoyed the calm and the beauty of our surroundings and relished our food and drink.

After the short hike back to the top of the hill and reaching the parking lot the three of us headed home to enjoy the rest of the day just relaxing, Sarah and I agreed to talk only about what we wanted to do over the next couple of days before returning to S.H.A.D.O.W. for our first assignment together and what would be my first overall experience with time travel, I was quite anxious yet very nervous at the same time about the upcoming ordeal. Once we parked in the garage and I had let Shadow out to take care of his urgent business in the backyard we staked our claim in the living room and began to express some ideas pertaining to the next few days, Shadow had assumed his spot by the fireplace and was ready for his late afternoon nap. We talked about from everything to flying up to Vegas for a couple of nights and seeing some shows to just pitching a tent in the backyard for just the fun of it. After an hour or so we finally agreed to just pitch a tent in the backyard and watch the stars at night, I think Shadow was on board with this idea also, at least I didn't hear any arguments from him on the decision we made. So it was decided we would pitch the tent early in the morning and load it up with some basic supplies and our sleeping bags and a dog bed for Shadow. We also agreed to go over and check in at Sarah's place and pick up some more of her stuff, I think eventually we would have to come to a decision on the living arrangements because trying to live out of two houses was becoming somewhat of an inconvenience for her. I believed that both us preferred to stay here at my house since it was so much bigger and had more open land for Shadow to enjoy. We turned in early for the evening because we were both pretty tired from all of the sun we got at Oak Creek Canyon earlier in the day, it didn't take long for us to drift off and reach a deep sleep for the entire night.

The morning came quickly after the great night's sleep we both got and even Shadow slept through the night. We quickly ate breakfast then began to set up our camp in the backyard, we packed full a couple of coolers with beer, water and enough food to last a couple of days, I know that's sounds a little crazy with the kitchen only being a minute away with a completely stocked refrigerator but we wanted to make this feel like a real camping trip. Over the next two days we would have one of the best times yet, we talked about life, religion, mother nature and Sarah asked if I could work with and teach her some advanced tracking skills as much as possible in the backyard and surrounding areas of the property, it sort of reminded me of when Miralani and I played hide and seek all over this place, I think even at that early age I wanted to become a tracker and learn the skills my father had been taught from his father. I had even taken it a step further by becoming a member of the Shadow Wolves tracking unit that the government still uses today to track and arrest drug smugglers and even out of country assignments tracking high value terrorist targets. Sarah was intrigued by my answer and the fact how many references we both now had in our lives pertaining to the word shadow, she then questioned who some of the terrorist targets were, I told her anyone and everyone you could possibly think of that were major influences or players in the middle east, she was astounded by my answer, however I did agree with her on the shadow reference, it almost seemed like some kind of a sign from above. So I did indeed teach her some advanced tracking techniques and with the little time we had it was a very concerted effort from both of us. I could tell at this point that she and I were going to make one hell of a working team at S.H.A.D.O.W. just because of how easily we could communicate with each other and almost know what the other person was thinking. We also worked together with Shadow some more on his sign language training, I swear he could almost teach it if he could move his feet like a pair of hands, he was that good. We were having so much fun just enjoying each other's company and the friendship we had developed over the past four months, we truly were a family in every aspect.

The two days off had come and gone and Sarah, Shadow and I

had just pulled out of the driveway in the Bronco and headed for the S.H.A.D.O.W. facility to begin the first day of my new career as a fully vetted time traveling agent working for the almighty himself, I wondered what lied ahead for the three of us as a time traveling team that was about to change history for the better and under the guidance and grace of God, the overwhelming scope of that thought was still a little incomprehensible even though I was very close to experiencing it firsthand. We had already talked to Miralani last night on the phone and said that the three of us were going on our first real assignment today and might be gone a few days or so and that's all we could tell her because the location was classified, we did tell her we would stop by first thing when we got back in town. I was sort of uncomfortable lying to my sister like that but it was a necessity and a requirement of the job. Sarah had told it would become a little easier to accept the more you realized the importance of keeping as many people in the dark about S.H.A.D.O.W. as possible especially those who were very close or family in order to keep them safe. The closer we got to "Secret Canyon" the more uneasy I began to feel, "You okay Cole, it's okay to be a little nervous, hell I actually got sick right before the first time I traveled, it was so embarrassing, I'll never forget it but I'm sure you'll be okay rookie," she reassuringly remarked. "Hey how long are you going to keep calling me rookie anyway," I quickly replied. "I tell you what rookie, when we all get back in one piece from this save mission, then I'll call you whatever you'd like," she jokingly said. "You got a deal Coop, I'll try to come up with something else or maybe you could," I replied. "I'll work on it," she answered. We slowly pulled in through the hidden opening that was unbelievably camouflaged into the hillside, you could almost stand within a couple of feet of it and not even detect that it was a twenty-five-foot door that opened up like it belonged on a garage, it was a work of art all hand made from carbon-fiber and a thin layer of re-enforced concrete.

Slowly making our way up to Charlie at the guard shack he greeted us and as usual he was cheerful as always, "Hey good morning Charlie, how's everything going?" I asked. "Good morning you guy's, I'm doing great and how's my favorite team of agents doing on this glorious morning, that includes you too Shadow?" happily expressing his mood and asking the same of us. "We're doing great Charlie, hey I'm sure you already know but if you don't, today is Cole's first mission, I think he's a little nervous," Sarah replied followed by a little chuckle. "No I'm not nervous I just was wondering if you wouldn't mind taking care of the Bronco if this thing ends up being a little longer than a few days or so, I mean maybe just take her out for a spin in the canyon a bit then back just to keep everything lubricated," I asked with a worried tone. "You got it Cole, just leave the keys with me after you park if you want but I don't think you got anything to worry about, especially with Coop here being your partner," he reassuringly replied. "Yeah right, I know she's the best this place has got but it's me I'm worried about so just in case I'll leave the keys with you for my own peace of mind and thanks, I owe you one Charlie," appreciatively I said. "Don't worry about it Cole, it's my pleasure to look after her," he happily replied.

After parking and dropping off the keys with Charlie, Sarah, Shadow and I headed up to her father's office to get our pre-mission briefing, I was warned by Sarah this could take a couple of hours depending on the complexity of the mission. I knew from the classroom training I had received over the past couple of weeks that the mission could be one of three types, SC-1, SC-2 and SC-3, the SC stood for "Save Classification" and SC-1 being the most dangerous and complicated. I knew from my training that the SC-1's consisted of prevention of the assigned target's death and the apprehension of the suspect or in most of these cases the convicted individual from the closed case. I was hoping we wouldn't start out with one of these for my sake but deep down inside I knew that I was quite ready to handle it if that's what we were assigned. Upon entering John's office that feeling of warmth and calmness came over me again like from the first time I met him, "Hello you guy's, how was your time off, you look great and quite relaxed and refreshed, you too Shadow," He commented after turning to face us. "It was great, Cole, Shadow and I we just decided to campout in the backyard of Cole's place, it was so much fun and I think we both learned a lot from each other," Sarah remarked. "Yeah, it was very nice and I think even Shadow had a great time," I reassuringly expressed my opinion on the matter. "Well are you three ready to get started on your fist mission together?" John quickly asked. Sarah and I both looked at each other then said yes at the same time followed by a moan from Shadow. "I'm going to take that as a yes Shadow," John said with confidence. John slowly walked back behind his desk and grabbed a folder which I assumed contained the save target and all of the pertinent information we needed to accomplish our mission, John then handed the folder to Sarah.

After a pause of several minutes and Sarah's scanning of the folder John looked at her as if to ask her approval on the selection, "Well, do you think you and Cole are up to a SC-1 mission to start out with?" he slowly inquired. As I heard John ask the question my heart began to race a bit, "Excuse me for interrupting but I'd like to put my two cents in if that's okay, we're as ready as we'll ever be sir and you can have faith in our abilities and the cohesion we have developed as a team, we're good to go," strongly expressing my feelings on the subject. "Sorry Cole, we didn't mean to leave you out but my father has always given me the final say on whether or not to accept a mission, that's including all of the missions with my previous partner too," she quickly remarked. "Okay then, the three of you can get started with your procurement of the supplies, wardrobe and firearms you will need for this mission, after that I'll see you on the pad in a couple of hours." John adamantly suggested. "Okay dad, we'll see you later," Sarah replied as the three of us then headed out of his office and began our pre-mission preparations. When we got in the corridor I quickly remarked, "I hope your father knows I didn't mean any disrespect about my comment back in there, I just sort of felt like I was being left out, I hope he understands how passionate and excited I am about this opportunity he has given me and I just wanted him to know that I was indeed ready and that I will not disappoint him," I strongly and confidently commented. "He knows that Cole, he trusts you with my life and that should tell you how much he respects and thinks of you, you've come a long way in a very short time and I just think he wants both of us to be comfortable with this decision," Sarah reassuringly replied.

After picking up all our supplies and firearms it was off to the wardrobe department to fit us with the proper attire for the mid nineteen seventies, how fun was this going to be I thought to myself, I could hardly wait to see what Sarah was going to look like dressed in bell bottomed pants that were cut around the waist below here belly button, at least that's what I was hoping for anyways, I think Shadow was the only one that was safe from this upcoming hell of looking like a couple of rejects from a seventies themed costume party. Too bad Miralani and the rest of the gang at the café weren't here to see this. When we got to the wardrobe department there were two backpacks already loaded with several changes of clothes and undergarments waiting for us and as we approached them two S.H.A.D.O.W. employees began to assist us with our current change of clothes, Sarah went one way and I went the other to our own dressing rooms and several racks of preselected and properly sized items of my choosing, including shoes, hats and even sunglasses. The next thirty minutes or so we spent selecting our clothes that would be on our backs while making the trip back in time, it was actually pretty nerve racking for me because of all of the horrible thoughts and memories of old movies that kept creeping into my mind as I was trying to decide, I just tried to focus on one of my favorite television shows as I was growing up, "Starsky & Hutch" had what was probably the most god awful compilation of seventies attire that was ever on television.

After a long and hard choice between a pair of bell bottomed blue jeans or suede pants that probably belonged to Tom Jones I decided to go with the blue jeans and a deep V-neck long sleeved shirt that was going to expose all five of my chest hairs, I'm sure Sarah was going to love it, how I envied Shadow right about now, he at least didn't have to go through this humiliation. When I was fully dressed I made my way back out to the front lobby of the department and there standing before was the most beautiful seventies looking hippie girl I had ever laid eyes on or dreamed of, her bell bottomed multi-colored jeans were outrageous, "Hey Coop, where in hell did you get those pants, they look like they belong to a color blind leprechaun from the seventies, Jesus those are definitely period correct with the bright yellow, green and black stripes in them, I must admit it does give you a certain look of hotness, I love the top too, that must have come from the "Sonny and Cher" show, we've got to take a selfie of us together and send it to Miralani before we go," I said waiting with anticipation for her retaliation concerning my attire. "You should talk rookie, what the hell are you supposed to be anyway, a white pimp who's been through some hard times and has been stealing his clothes out of a "Goodwill" container, really Cole those threads blow," she said barely holding on to her composure before letting out a gut wrenching laugh that even scared Shadow. "Wow, that bad huh, what's with the seventies lingo, are we supposed to try to even talk like we're from that era and I don't look like a pimp, maybe a disco reject or something along that line but I kind of like it," I proudly replied. The two of us began to laugh uncontrollably and embraced each other with a very sexy hug and physical pat down of each other's outfit, Shadow then nestled his way in between us and wanted in on the show of affection. Fully packed up and loaded with our firearms of choice from the seventies we headed to the shuttle and what was soon to be the most exciting and important moment of my life.

Once the shuttle stopped at the passenger platform the three of us headed down stairs and then towards the seventies, all I could think about was completing this mission and getting back in one piece. The past few weeks and all of the training that Sarah and especially her father's teachings of the process of de-atomization and re-atomization and the riding of gravitational waves that provide the actual movement in time were slowly taking over all of my thoughts. Before I knew it we were standing on the platform with John in distance peering down from his lookout station along with a few other employees, "Well this it rookie, you didn't forget your recovery watch did you?" Sarah quickly asked, referring to the method of returning back to the present which was explained to me as a watch that was equipped with a small particle de-fusion processor when activated opens up a one-time use wormhole to return us to the present, every agent was equipped with one but one was all that was needed for the return of the team. I rolled back my sleeve to reveal the watch to Sarah, "You mean this cool looking watch Coop, I just hope it works, I don't want to be stuck having to wear this horrible get-up any longer than I have to," expressing my sentiments to her. "Don't worry Cole, even if we do get stuck we can always make a good living as a couple of "groovy" P.I.'s, don't you think?" she jokingly asked. After that remark Sarah slowly lifted her hand towards her father and gave a thumbs up gesture, "Hold on rookie, here we go," she then said with a loud tone and full of excitement. I stood in silence looking at her and then at Shadow. We were just about to be on our way to save a young fifteen-year old girl from Denver Colorado named Nora Jacobs, that was our save target and my inaugural baptism into this holy sanctioned new career of mine. As the pad below us now began to glow in a very light blueish color a slight feeling of warmth consumed my body as I looked at Sarah and could see her smile and giving me the reassurance that I needed at this point, slowly a translucent bubble encased the three of us and suddenly just like that Sarah and Shadow began to fade away as well as what was outside of the bubble, this was truly happening, seventies here we come.

14

ROUNDTRIP TICKET

As if only a second or two had passed I began to see Sarah and Shadow materialize right before my eyes and we were standing in the middle of a clearing surrounded by woods, Sarah had told me we would be targeted for re-atomization ten miles outside the Denver in a heavily wooded area. I guess the first order of business was to make sure everything was connected and where it was supposed to be, I mean like arms, legs and feet, "Hey Coop is my nose upside down or something, I'm having a hard time catching my breath," half-jokingly I said. "Maybe a little sideways but definitely not upside down," being quick witted she replied. "Hey Cole don't worry about the shortness of breath it will pass in a few minutes, your lungs have to use to the immediate relocation of being at such a high altitude, in other words you haven't had enough time to adjust to the thinner air at this elevation," she quickly added. "I guess we should make our way out to the main road and see if we can hitch a ride or just start walking to the city limits of Denver, hopefully we can get a hotel and a rent a car right away," I suggested. We both had plenty of pre-nineteen-seventy-five currency and would probably need most of it to complete this save mission, Sarah had prepared me for what she called crazy expenses when on a case that involved an unsolved case in which the body or remains were never found and the individual who actually committed the crime was never found. Like so many other cases the Nora Jacobs case had no closure for her family members and we were planning on changing that outcome, we had arrived here exactly seventy-two hours prior to her disappearance and we were going to make sure she would never go missing at all and catch the suspect in order to put him away in a very far-away place that's not even of this earth, the holding facility for all of the arrested suspects was an interdimensional holding tank which held their de-atomized carbon based signature's in one of the many agencies high orbit satellites, I guess for eternity the way John had put it, he said it was Gods will and that they would be judged when the time was right. The three of us began to walk, heading north to the main road according to the map we brought, there were no GPS guidance devices available to the public of this time period so we both had a very nice compass we brought with us. According to my watch it was just passed eleven a.m. and should only take us a few hours to reach the main road if we kept up a good pace.

As we walked towards the main road and after an hour or so of talking and planning what our options might be pertaining to the case we decided to take a well-deserved break by a little stream, "Hey Cole how about some of that beef jerky you brought along, let's see if it made through without turning into a piece's of rubber," she jokingly remarked. I began to rummage through my backpack while she and Shadow got comfortable on a thick padded area tall green grass that looked as soft as a pillow, "Hey I found it, it looks okay, do you want the seasoned one with some kick or just the regular beef flavor?" I asked. "I'll try the hot one," she replied. After passing the jerky to Sarah and getting a thumbs up from her we sat and talked about this Nora Jacobs girl who according to her file was to become a very distinguished D.A. and on to becoming a prominent judge in our time, "So Coop, what's our first move after we get a hotel room and a car, do we just stakeout the area where we know she lives and wait or do we try to pick up on some of her daily routines in order to get some idea where she went missing and who is involved," I inquired, sounding and living up to my rookie nickname. "Great questions rookie, you're right on both suggestions, we'll definitely stake out her residence and see if we can pick up anything suspicious on her outings or playtime away from the house, since it's summer vacation and she's out of school right now it will be much easier to keep an eye on her and hopefully we get lucky and don't have to play this thing out and take it down to the wire," she confidently replied.

After our quick fill of jerky and getting somewhat of a recharge of energy we resumed our trek to the main road. Shadow was leading the way like he knew exactly where we needed to go, maybe he could hear the cars from this great distance with his super sensitive hearing. Our pace had quickened and Sarah and I could actually hear the sound of vehicles echoing through the thick beautiful green pine trees that surrounded us in every direction, the wind whistling through the pines with the occasional trace of a mechanical sound riding on its tail was music to my ears. Another twenty minutes passed when we had breached the edge of the forest and emerged on the roadway, which was actually quite busy, hopefully we wouldn't have to wait too long before we caught a ride into Denver. The three of us sat down on the side of the road on top of our backpacks with our thumbs out, except for Shadow of course, "Hey Cole, I don't know about you but I can hardly wait to get into a hot shower and wash all of this sweat and dirt off of me," Sarah adamantly commented. "Yeah I know, I've been downwind of you for the last two hours and I couldn't agree more," I jokingly said. Just as Sarah was about to knock the crap out of me a gorgeous early model Chevy van pulled over and stopped right next to us, "Hey you kids need a ride, I'm heading up to Grand Junction, I can take you as far as that if you'd like," the man who looked to be around sixty remarked. "Thanks, we're heading in to Denver to meet up with some people we know and we sure appreciate the offer, it's okay for my dog too?" I gratefully asked. "Hell yeah hop in, I love dogs, although I think he's probably just a little more than a dog, he's a beautiful animal, my name is Tom, what's all of your names?" the man asked. I could tell right away he was a very friendly and peaceful man and probably had a big loving family. "Well my name is Cole and this here is my girlfriend Sarah and the bigger than normal dog is Shadow, you don't have to worry about him, he's as timid as a bunny rabbit and smarter than most people I know," I quickly replied as the three of us were getting into the van. We had found our ride and it looked like it was going to be a pleasant one, "So tell me Tom did you do the airbrushing on the side of the van, it's really nice, I love the American flag theme and anything that represents this great country of ours," I curiously asked hoping to find some common ground to strike up a friendly conversation. "No I didn't paint it Cole, my son did, the two of us live in Brush and we have a little custom paint shop there, he mostly does custom work on Harley's and other bike's, he's about the best there is in this part of the country, he learned his trade over in Vietnam painting "Huey's" for the army, I guess he painted some pretty crazy stuff on those old whirly birds," he proudly replied.

As we made our way down the road I could begin to see the outline of the city, the biggest thing that stood out was all of the greyish brown haze that hung over the entire skyline, I guess I never really new how bad the smog levels were back in this time period, it was unbelievable, you could really see how switching all of the gasoline products to unleaded fuels only had really cleaned up our present day air quality. Sarah had moved up a little closer as she was in the back with Shadow, "Say Tom, you know any good hotels up ahead once we get close to the center of the city, or even better the Lakewood area, that's sort of where we planned to meet up with our friends," Sarah asked politely. "Well yeah, I know there's a bunch just off the highway but if you're looking for a nice one I'd stick to some of the bigger names, there's a really nice Hilton not too far from Lakewood or there's an old pioneer style looking place called the "The Table Mountain Inn" just outside of Lakewood in Golden and it's really cool and not too expensive either, not sure if they take pets though," Tom eagerly replied. "Great, that sounds pretty nice, I like the sound of that Table Mountain place you mentioned, I'm sure they'll let Shadow stay there, after all he's a working dog with a badge and everything," she gratefully replied.

After fifteen minutes or so Tom exited the freeway and headed southwest towards the hotel chosen by Sarah.

Once we parked in front of the lobby passenger drop off area Tom stepped out of his van and gave Sarah a hand with her backpack but even more so he wanted to give her a hug, "You better take care of this little lady Cole, she's something special, I've got a funny feeling about you guy's, I mean I hope you find what you're are looking for and complete your business at hand, if you're ever in Brush look me up, take care my friends," Tom said as he finally let go of Sarah and climbed back into the van, "Thanks again Tom and maybe we'll see you again sometime in the future," I said after leaning into the passenger side window. Tom slowly pulled away and Sarah, Shadow and I entered the lobby towards the check-in counter. This place would be our base camp for the next few days or longer if need be. Tom was right, this place was cool, it looked like it was right out of some kind of mining town and very authentic looking. Right away the clerk keyed in on Shadow and gave a look of amazement, "Wow sir, is that a real wolf, I mean is he tame and friendly?" the clerk nervously asked. "Yes he is a wolf but you don't have to worry about him, he's a professionally trained service dog under the F.B.I. and he is part of our team, this is agent Cooper and I'm agent Youngblood," I replied while showing him our readymade credentials from S.H.A.D.O.W. that were actually put into the system here one week before our arrival. The clerk now looked even more terrified from my remarks, "Don't worry young man, our case doesn't concern this establishment, we just need a home base to operate from for a few day's maybe longer, oh yeah is there a place to rent a 4WD vehicle around perhaps nearby or maybe a part of your concierge service could set it up for us, we may need to head up towards Fairplay or near those whereabouts," I quickly added before he could say anything. The young man stood there in silence for a minute or two fiddling around with his guestbook and available room list that lied in front of him, "Well of course we will do our best to satisfy your every need during your stay here sir, your wolf is an amazing looking animal, is there anything special needs he might need as far as food or bedding or anything else?" he then asked. "That's a very good question young man, I'll send down a list of the special foods he likes to eat and anything else I can think of, by the way his name is Shadow and again he's very friendly and quite smart as well," I reassuringly remarked. "Well that's good to know sir, here are your room keys and its pleasure to have you staying with us agent Youngblood and agent Cooper, I will check on that four-wheel drive rig for you and let you know right away on your room phone as soon as I have any information for you, also we have a very nice breakfast in the morning I would highly recommend it," the young man politely commented. Thanking the young man, we then headed off to our room which was number twenty-one, "Twenty-one, that's my favorite number Cole, I think that's a good sign," Sarah excitedly remarked.

Once we entered the room we were both surprised by the enormous size of it, "Wow, this is great Cole, I'm beginning to feel like we just might be in a mining town, what do you think?" she asked. I could see the glow coming off her beautiful face as if she were a little kid at an amusement park or something like that, "I think it's great sweetheart, I think Shadow really likes it too, I guess I should get busy on that menu of Shadow's and take it to that young man, he was very helpful and professional, I felt a little bad about deceiving him in regards to us being F.B.I. agents though," I said with some remorse. "Better get used to it rookie, there will be times when we have to impersonate various types of agents to do this job and besides, we actually are agents working for the government," she reassuringly remarked. "I guess you're right in that aspect, I guess I'll have to get used to playing the part depending on what is needed for each case," I replied. Sarah then moved up very close to me and put her arms around my shoulders, "Hey, the way you handled that situation at the check-in desk was very impressive and I must say very quick thinking on your part, hell you had me a little intimidated and believing you were a real F.B.I. agent," she proudly remarked. "Yeah I guess I did okay at that for my first time trying to lay down a cover story of sort, I think I may have a bright career as a con man, I mean if this time traveling thing doesn't work out," I jokingly replied. Sarah began to laugh so loud that Shadow got excited and started jumping up on her waist and legs, I guess he wanted in on the joke.

As we emptied out our backpacks onto the bed Sarah began to laugh again all of a sudden, "Jesus Cole, did you really pick out those clothes because you liked them or were you just trying to be funny?" she asked while still cracking up. Starting to laugh somewhat myself and then regaining my composure, "Hell yeah, I've always loved the styles and fashion statements from the seventies," I answered, as I held up a long-sleeved white denim shirt that almost looked holy or something that a religious hippie might have owned at one time. "Yeah with your dark skin tone I must admit I can't wait to see you in that shirt," she remarked. We spent the next couple of hours planning out our surveillance schedule of Nora Jacobs and some of her known close friends, the timing of this case was going to have be just right in order to save her and apprehend the suspect, we had a very strong lead pointing towards her assistant gym teacher, a twenty-eight-year old man by the name of Gary Barnett. He was questioned as a possible suspect after Nora went missing but there was insufficient evidence to charge him on anything, soon after her disappearance he was let go by the Green Mountain High school board where Nora attended as a junior and he was never seen again a few weeks after her disappearance. If this was the guy we had to make sure we knew of his whereabouts at all times and be ready to intervene at a moment's notice. Sarah was going to have to be the expert on the surveillance portion of this operation because I was just a little too wet behind the ears in those techniques.

We knew that late tomorrow afternoon would probably be when the abduction would go down and from previous reports from her friends saying the last known sighting of Nora was when they all went to "Elitch Gardens" amusement park which was known to be a popular hangout for teenagers. The time was now almost six pm and we were starting to get a little hungry, just then there was a knock on the door and it was the lobby clerk, "Hello Mr.

Youngblood, sorry to interrupt but I wanted to let you know that the only available 4WD vehicle I could get on such a short notice would be a very expensive fully loaded and modified Ford Bronco, I know you probably were wanting a jeep of some sort but this is all that's available for now, would you like me to reserve it?" The clerk nervously but professionally asked. I could hear Sarah let out a slight chuckle behind me, "The Bronco will be fine, go ahead and make the arrangements and just put it on the bill if that's okay, oh and if Mr. Youngblood here can't handle that type of vehicle I'll take over the driving responsibilities," Sarah sarcastically remarked. "Yeah that'll be fine, thanks again for your help and support on this case young man," I quickly added with a little embarrassment on my face. The young clerk acknowledged my praise for him and then returned to his post. After closing the room door, I just couldn't keep it in any longer, "Yeah, can you believe it Coop, a Bronco for our rent a car, it just doesn't get any better than that, it has to be a sign or something, don't you think?" I ecstatically asked. "Settle down rookie, it's not going to be like yours you know that right, I mean even if it's brand knew it's still not going to drive or have the power like yours, it's probably going to have all of that smog bullshit on it that all of the cars had to have during this time period, in terms you can relate too Cole, it probably couldn't pull a sick crack whore off the toilet," she said and deflating my moment of joy and expectations.

After ordering some food from room service we hit the files again making sure there wasn't something there we had missed, we decided to stake out Nora's home residence beginning early in the morning then follow her once she went on the move to the amusement park, from the information in the files she caught a ride with one of her friends and the older brother of one of them who had dropped them off since she nor her friends were old enough to drive yet. The three of us were going to have to keep a very close watch on her and wait to see if the prime suspect in the case would show up like everyone had presumed but could never prove, it's too bad they didn't have all of the high tech video monitoring systems we have in our present day lives, if they had this case would have been solved and maybe even would have found Nora alive somewhere. We did know that this Gary Barnett fellow had an older brother who lived in Fairplay Colorado, which was about two hours away, it was a very small and tightknit community and it would most likely be hard to get any help or information out of its citizens regarding Gary or his brother Sam, they were both experts on outdoor survival techniques and sometimes lead backpacking trips into the high country of the Rockies for extra money as a part time business. Sarah and I were hoping we could wrap this thing up quickly if it indeed happened at the amusement park, we had the authority to arrest and apprehend this individual who would later in life become a hardened criminal and serve time for several other murders over the span of the next twenty years. No matter how this case would play out, Sarah, Shadow and I had a job to do and that was to put this guy away forever in a place he could never return from, the S.H.A.D.O.W. holding facility, it was more like a science lab than prison, the prisoners being held there were in a state of stabilized and stagnant atomization to be judged at a later date by from the almighty himself.

The evening was progressing into the late hours and after thoroughly reviewing the files as much as possible we finally had enough. The two of us were quite comfortable with our strategy so we decided to watch some late night news just to give us some perspective on our situation and make sure there wasn't something happening tomorrow that could possibly affect our plans. It was so weird not seeing any of the news channels that were available in the future, another part of modern day technology that we so easily accepted and forgotten how far we have come in social media crazed world that we all live in today. Shadow had his fill of the special food that was prepared for him by the hotel kitchen, the staff here really had been bending over backwards to satisfy our every need including those of Shadows. We finally called it a night knowing that tomorrow would be a big day, especially for me. Deep down inside I could already feel a few small butterflies starting to dance around, I mean tomorrow hopefully would be my first time arresting someone for something other than drunk and disorderly at a public campsite, a far cry from what I had been training for over all of this time not mention that I now had two partners to watch my back as I would theirs. I was really impressed and happy on how far Shadow's sign language training had come, his ability to understand most of the human sign language was absolutely astonishing, there was still something quite unique and special about him that I just couldn't figure out but with time I knew it would become quite clear. Sarah had fallen asleep right away while I stared up at the ceiling wondering if maybe all of this was one very long dream I was having after climbing or perhaps falling into that shaft where I found Shadow and brought all of this in hopefully into fruition.

The morning came all too fast and I felt like I had just fallen asleep, Sarah was already up and in the shower, "Hey Coop leave it running and I'll be in a second, I have to take Shadow out first," I loudly requested. "No worries rookie, I already took care of that for him, you were out cold I didn't want to wake you," she yelled back with the faint sound of water trickling down the glass walls of the shower. I guess I must have agreed with the hotel mattress which are usually horrible and feel like a piece of plywood, I made my way out of bed and quickly headed for the shower, "I'm coming in sweetheart, you feel like getting dirty again Coop?" I eagerly asked. "Why do think I was taking so long," she seductively replied. The two us then embarked in a passionate game of love making which was enhanced by the presence of being in a very nice and romantic hotel. After getting dressed there was a knock on the door and it could only be one thing, at least I was hoping it could only be one thing, the clerk with the keys to the rented Bronco. I quickly opened up the door, "Good morning Mr. Youngblood, Miss Cooper, agent Shadow, I hope everything has been to your satisfaction so far," the clerk politely said. "Everything has been great, your hotel's customer service is outstanding, even Shadow here agrees, he loved the dinner your cook prepared for him last night, Agent Cooper and

I will be giving this place the highest recommendation possible," I gratefully remarked. The clerk smiled while looking at Shadow, "Yes sir we aim to please, I must say again that's one beautiful animal, oh and by the way your Bronco is parked right out front with a full tank of gas and I made sure they put in some very detailed maps of the surrounding mountain areas that included most of the 4WD trails and parks, the gas mileage isn't the greatest on it but it does have two extra five-gallon gas cans on the back full of gas, just in case you get out in the middle of nowhere with no fillings stations in sight, so here are the keys and let me know if you need anything else sir," the young man thoroughly explained. "Thank you so much, I will personally put in a good word with the management here and there will be a generous tip for you upon checking out," I reassuringly replied.

After loading up the Bronco we were just about ready to head out to Nora's residence, we let the lobby clerk know that we might not be back today but to keep the room available for one more day if they could, also that we would check out this morning and pay our bill and pay for the deposit and rental fee of the Bronco up front just in case we were not able to personally return back to settle the bill. The clerk agreed and said the hotel would hold the room for two more days no matter what with no extra charges. Again I was very grateful and expressed our gratitude and the governments. Sarah, Shadow and I then jumped into the gorgeous midnight blue Bronco decked out with oversized wheels, custom light bars on the roof and front bumpers, it also had the latest high tech CB radio on the market, which was light years behind the average modern day smart phone of our time but it was all we could use here in nineteen-seventy-five. As we pulled out of the parking lot I couldn't stop noticing all of the old muscle cars of the early seventies, they were everywhere, I wish there was a way to take some of them back with us, they're worth a small fortune back in our time, "No Cole, don't even think about it, I know what you're thinking, we just don't have the authority to bring back something as large as a car or truck, my father has been trying to perfect that process over the last year and a half, there's just not enough accuracy in the return coordinates of something that large, so don't get any ideas of trying to sneak one of those cars back you've been checking out ever since we arrived," Sarah strongly emphasized. "Whatever gave you that idea sweetheart, I've just been checking out the scenery and along with a few cars maybe," I strongly replied pleading my innocence from her comment. We soon were only a few minutes from Nora's parent's house and once we got close enough we would set up our surveillance spot down a few houses where we would have a clean line of site to the front of the house. Shadow had finally found a comfortable position in the back and was snoozing pretty good, thank god he traveled so well, he would be a handful if he didn't, his size and weight was well over one-hundred pounds and his height was already halfway between my knees and waist, he was becoming a magnificent looking wolf, I was now leaning more towards him being more Timberwolf than any other of the wolf species, his coloring was turning a darker brown with light shades of black and grey on top and a solid white underbelly, he was definitely special.

Soon we were set up and staked out in Nora's neighborhood and now was going to be the hard part of waiting and watching for the start of the events that Sarah, Shadow and I would put in motion in saving this young girls life and putting away an evil twisted man to prevent any future criminal atrocities on his behalf. The time was now eight-thirty and hopefully her friends would be showing up soon. The amusement park opened up at ten o-clock and was at least a thirty or forty minute drive from here, I would imagine she and her friends would want to get there right when it opened in order to get in as many of the so called good rides as possible, from the information I read last night the park was not really that big but definitely had quite a selection of rides crammed into it, not to mention all of the fair like games and food establishments, I just hoped it wouldn't be too crowded making our job somewhat easier to follow her. It was close to nine a.m. when a small Ford Pinto wagon pulled up into the driveway of Nora's residence, two girls and the young man driving all got out and made their way to the front door, after a couple of knocks I could see in plain sight the young girl who was our target for saving, Nora Jacobs, "There she is Cole, so innocent and so young," Sarah slowly and somewhat sadly commented. "Well she doesn't know it yet but this is going to be the most important and best day of the rest of her long and distinguished life, no harm will come to you today, I promise," I emotionally remarked as her friends all entered the house. "Don't worry Cole, we've got this, she's going to come through this okay and so will we," as Sarah confidently expressed her feelings. We gave each other a very serious look and knew right away that we were both committed to doing whatever it took to save this young girl, Shadow seemed to pick up on the emotionally and serious conversation Sarah and I were having buy shoving his big head forward between us as if to say don't forget about me, I'll do my part as well, "I know boy, I'm sorry, we're definitely going to need all of your skills and help to be successful on this save, we're a team and you're a special team member the likes of nobody has ever had the pleasure to work with, Sarah and I are proud to be your partners and friends," I said as I gave him a great big hug around his huge neck and head.

Finally, after another twenty minutes had passed Nora and her friends all emerged from the house and got into the Pinto. The older brother of one of the girls got behind the wheel again of the mustard colored ticking time time-bomb, a thought I couldn't get out of my mind, Ford had so many lawsuits against them for rear end collisions on this type of car that resulted in the gas tank exploding and killing quite a few people, I just hoped they wouldn't get into any type of accident on the way to the amusement park, that situation would be out of our control. I quickly pulled out from where we had parked and maintained a good distance between us and them, being teenage kids they probably were distracting the driver enough to where he probably wouldn't even notice Sarah and I if we were right on his ass, not too close though I wouldn't want to possibly rear end them and explode the gas tank, I don't think that would look too good on my record for my first assignment. Once we got on the freeway it became a little more difficult to follow them, this part of the job was totally new for me as I never had to tail a person for not having the proper permit for camping or campfires, "Hey rookie, don't drop back too far, we wouldn't want to lose them," Sarah quickly commented. I nodded my head and closed up the gap by several car lengths, as we were quickly leaving Jefferson county and only twenty minutes or so from "Elitch Gardens" amusement park. The park which was located in downtown Denver originally opened in 1890 as a green oasis and zoological garden founded by John and Mary Elitch, it also became the first zoo to open west of Chicago. Even in our present time of 2016 the park still thrives to this day with many modern day attractions and themes.

After twenty minutes of doing the posted speed limit we finally got off the freeway and I could now see the Ferris wheel and the roller coaster, "Well I guess that must be the place," I suggested. "Doesn't look like much from here," Sarah commented. "Well it's not Disneyland but it's supposed to be pretty good and has one of the best roller coasters around, for it's time that is, maybe we'll get lucky and get to ride it," as I expressed my feelings on the matter. As we got closer to the park and just around the corner from the main entrance of the parking area we were only five cars behind them, we would have to stay very close to Nora and her friends especially when checking in through the security gate instead of buying tickets, we had all of the required authorized identification for us to gain entry and that's including Shadow as a working dog for the government. We would have to park up front in the security parking area and hope that it was close enough to where Nora and her friends were going to get dropped off, this would be the most difficult part of the surveillance and the biggest chance of us getting separated and losing them in the crowds at the entry gates. I followed them as long as I could to get a fix on the nearest parking lot I.D. sign closest to them, we then headed for the security parking area as fast as I could. It must have been our lucky day because when we parked I could see the entry gates and there was only about twenty people in line at four different gates, in other words Sarah, Shadow and I just had to get over there before Nora and her friends got to the entry point.

After attaching Shadow's working dog harness which even had a little I.D. badge sewn into it and on the top part it said "Working Dog" sewn in the middle of it, not sure if that was even an authentic harness from the F.B.I. or not from our time but I know Sarah's and mine were real F.B.I. badges and our covers were actually inputted into the agencies system before we got here, all part of the pre-mission setup performed by S.H.A.D.O.W. ahead of each save mission. The three of us moved at a very quick pace to get through the security gate with our identification in hand, we wanted to get inside the park before Nora and her friends, "Well let's hope there's not a problem with Shadow being allowed in the park," Sarah quietly commented. "No worries, I've got this Coop, let me do all of the talking, I mean please let me do all of the talking," slightly begging. "Alright rookie, let's see what kind of game you got," she quickly replied as the gate was only a few feet away. "Good morning officer Price, how are you doing on this fine day, my two partners and I need to gain access to continue our surveillance and the probable arrest of a top ten most wanted suspect on the F.B.I.'s list, he has been identified as being in your park and some of his known associates have just parked and on their way to the entry gates as we speak, we need to handle this very discretely without alerting any of the park's guests, this is agent Sarah Cooper and agent Shadow and I'm agent Cole Youngblood, here is our identification and department headquarters number if you need to verify any of which I have just told you but beyond that the rest is highly classified, the need for urgency cannot be emphasized enough here officer Price," I said with conviction and a very firm tone of authority. The guard was probably in his early sixties and just absolutely froze after my comment, after a few seconds of trying to regain his composure he slightly turned to his right and then reached into a small cabinet below and to the right of the access gate, "That's okay son, you, your dog and the pretty agent lady can come through and let me give you one of our security walkie-talkie radios in case you need any help or directions inside the park, wow we never had anything like this happen in the thirty years I've been working here, can't wait to tell the misses when I get home, imagine that, me working with the F.B.I. to apprehend a top criminal on their most wanted list, hell son if you get this guy will you let me take a picture with all of you, just to show my grandkids, you know just so they believe me and all," the man enthusiastically replied. "Well maybe, we'll just have to wait and see how this thing plays out," I courteously remarked.

After thanking the security officer for the use of the hand held radio which was actually a very crude version of a cell phone Sarah, Shadow and I made our way into the park and set up our position in order to fully view all of the entry gates in order to pick up on Nora and her friends for our surveillance and protection of all of them. It only took about ten minutes before we got an up close visual on them and a chance to get a good look at their attire which would be needed to keep up with them when it came to the crowded areas around the main attractions of the park. I immediately pulled out my collapsible white cane and extended it fully, this was to make sure we posed no threat to our suspect leading up to his apprehension, at least I hoped I would be able to get the jump on him before he tried to bolt or resist in any way. This was going to be a little nerve racking for sure, I mean we were here to stop an abduction and the probable murder of a fifteen-year old girl who destined to do great things in the American justice system and it was only us that could do this. The young girls walked by us quickly on the way to what I assumed was one of the main attractions, which was more likely to be the one of the several roller coasters in the park. Sarah and I decided we would take turns if necessary when it came to sticking close to them on the rides themselves. The park was amazing considering the time period and all, the trees were gorgeous and the amount of green foliage all over gave you a feeling of being in a state park or something, this was the beginning of the summer so it hadn't quite reached the hottest part of summer but it was going to be a nice warm day probably somewhere in the low-eighties. You could easily hear the sounds of water falls or fountains cascading through the walkways and echoing through the beautiful trees. The closer we got to some of the bigger rides we could begin to hear the screams of joy from their riders, it was slowly drowning out the peaceful and calming we had experienced when we first came into the park. This was going to be a good test for Shadow in regards to the number of people he has been around up to this point, so far he was handling it quite well, I just hoped I could stay as calm when the time came for us to go into action.

Shadow was leading the way and Sarah had one arm interlocked with mine as we rapidly approached one of the roller coasters in the park, this must have been the one everyone wanted to ride the most because the line was pretty long. Nora and her friends were just thirty-feet or so ahead of us heading towards the end of the line, "Hey Cole there's some shade over there next to that bench, I'm sure Shadow would appreciate the cool grassy area too," Sarah suggestively remarked. "Yeah that sounds great to me, we can get a clear view of the exit area from the ride," I quickly agreed. Sarah and I sat down on the bench and talked some about how lucky we were to be given this opportunity to be able to change history and under the guidance, approval and strong faith in us that God himself must have in trusting us with the lives of others and their fate. Shadow had somewhat fallen asleep and was napping pretty hard, it must have been the cool breeze that was continuous and quite relaxing, I think Sarah and I both were still lingering a bit from the time travel lag, sort of like jet lag but it seems to just linger on more. "One of us had better stay awake," I loudly remarked. Sarah turned, then laughed a bit, "No worries rookie, if you want to take a nap go ahead, that line looks at thirty minutes long, I'll wake you if something happens before they get off the ride," she reassuringly said. I slowly drifted off but I'm sure Sarah couldn't tell because of the dark glasses, hopefully I wouldn't fall of the damn bench.

The rest of the day was pretty much the same, well at least after I woke up anyways, Nora and her friends were hitting every big ride at least twice and a few of them even three times. Sarah and I took turns keeping a close eye on them and Shadow had adjusted quite well to his surroundings, the heavily populated park didn't seem to bother him one bit. It was around two o'clock when we finally caught the break we were praying for, our suspect Gary Barnett had just walked by us and appeared to be stalking the girls about the same distance Sarah and were from them. He was way off to the right of us and definitely behind the girls, "Okay rookie don't get too eager to jack this ass-clown, we have to let him make the first move, then we move in as close as possible without alerting him," Sarah strongly stated. "How far back should we stay, what if all these people get in the way when we have to make our move?" I asked somewhat impatiently. "Relax Cole, we've got this, our main priority is to make sure nothing happens to Nora, then we apprehend Mr. Barnett," she quickly reminded me. Nora and her friends were now about fifty feet in front of us and our suspect was smack dab in the middle of that distance. "Okay, I guess I can always get Shadow to take him down if need be, we've been working on that command for weeks, I definitely felt he was ready for anything we asked of him," I confidently replied. "Well that it'll be our last resort or option if needed, I'm pretty confident we can do this very quickly and quietly if he doesn't try resisting arrest," she reassuringly replied.

Keeping our distance from Mr. Barnett Sarah, Shadow and I brought up the rear of our little tight conga line. Another hour and a half passed and it was just a little before four o'clock and according to the statements of Nora's friends they left the park around four-thirty to be picked up by the one brother of her friends, Nora was going to stay until six o'clock or so to wait for her father to pick her up after he got off work, of course when he showed up she was nowhere to be found and she was never seen again. We had to stop this evil deed from happening, I know I was going to make sure of it, this guy had to be put away. The distance between everyone had now started to shrink significantly, the girls had just stopped at a fast food vender for what I presumed would be their dinner or a pre-dinner snack and the time was getting ever so close to four-thirty. Sarah, Shadow and I had sat down on a bench about thirty feet from the girls and again we had a clean line of sight of Mr. Barnett. The suspect was now more than ever starting to have the look of somebody stalking and planning something very wrong or highly illegal at the least, "What do you think Coop, should we began our intervention or wait until he actually physically tries to grab her?" again I impatiently asked. "Hold on rookie, let's wait until she splits up from her friends, we don't want to cause any collateral time damage," she quickly replied. I nodded my head and I kept silent as to not lose my focus on the girls, I'm pretty sure Shadow had already picked up on our target and was waiting for some kind of command from Sarah or myself, I knew I could count on him, Sarah and I had worked feverishly over the past three weeks on all of the commands we thought might be useful out here in the field, our cohesion as a team was outstanding and in sync.

The girls had just finished eating their burgers and fries, also it looked like they had ordered several milkshakes to go, suddenly the girls all began to form a big group hug then after a few words were exchanged Nora's three friends took off towards the park exit not realizing this was to be the last time they would ever see her again, that was the old time stamp of history and we were about to change that in order to give this young girl her life back so she could fulfill her destiny. Nora sat back down at the table where they had all been sitting at and began to study the park brochure she had from her entrance to the park. I guess like any normal teenager she was probably trying to figure out how many more rides she could get in before she was to meet her father at the pick-up area by the entrance. Sarah and I had just finished powering down a greasy cheeseburger and Shadow got a couple of hamburger patties from the girl at the fast food cook on the grill, he was quite pleased with them, "Hey Cole, you know you eat pretty good for a blind man, don't forget to play the part or you might draw some unwanted attention from some park guests," Sarah commented. "I know but for some reason the food seems to taste so much better in this time period, Jesus that was a good cheeseburger, I guess they didn't use so many healthy preservatives now as compared to our time," I replied as I wiped the grease from my hands and cheeks. Nora just seemed to sit and relax at this point I guess she was tired from the day's activities. "Remember Cole when this thing goes down and Mr. Barnett makes his move we have to be extremely careful not to cause any physical harm to any bystander's that could possibly affect the future," she adamantly stated. I acknowledged her comment by nodding my head and placing my hand on her thigh, then turned all of my focus back on our suspect, I was getting a very strong sense that he was getting ready to make his move, my grip on Sarah's leg was tightening as I was slightly broadcasting my emotions to what was about to happen, "Coop, I think we should get in much closer, don't you?" again impatiently asking. "I think your sense of urgency is right on the money this time Cole, let's move in," she said quickly agreeing.

The three of us moved in closer to within fifteen feet from Mr. Barnett and Nora was now within five feet of him, it was about to go down. Within just a few seconds the suspect quickly turned and sat down at Nora's little table, I could almost hear their conversation, something like what are you doing here all by yourself Nora? Sarah and I then moved in towards a table behind them and slowly sat down as I purposely bumped our table and one of their tables empty chairs, "Excuse him sir he's still learning how to use his cane," Sarah apologetically remarked. "No problem Miss, I completely understand," our suspect sincerely replied. Sarah and I quickly sat down as if we were going to order something and with me ever so playing the blind man part, I thought to myself how quick Sarah was to lay down that line in conjunction with me bumping them, it wasn't even planned, just two minds in complete sync with each other and knowing one another so well. Shadow was sitting next to me in his full attention mode sensing the inevitable event that was only moments away. Sarah and I made idle conversation for the next five minutes while trying to listen to every word the two of them were saying to each other, I could pick on and I'm sure Sarah heard the same line coming from Mr. Barnett about him offering to give Nora a ride since he lived out that way but she firmly refused telling him her father was already on his way and would be here shortly, good girl I thought to myself. It appeared that he backed off from that plan and the two of them just talked for a few more minutes, then he got up and the two of said their goodbye's, Nora then headed off in one direction and our suspect slowly headed off in a different direction, "What the hell do we do know Coop," I asked with a certain panicked look about me. "We stick with Mr. Barnett, we know he's the guy and our acquisition target," she strongly stated.

After leaving our table at the food establishment we followed our suspect for around ten minutes before he somehow had returned his direction back towards the route Nora had taken. This had to be his final play at grabbing Nora, if not we were running out of time according to all of the extensive files and notes we read a hundred times. Within a few minutes he was back on the scent of Nora, she was now only fifty-feet from him as she took her time traversing the gift shops while making her way to the exit, it was still a half hour away from six o'clock. Sarah, Shadow and I were now positioned only seconds behind Mr. Barnett, "Cole let me make the initial contact please, I'm going to try to make this as peaceful and low key as possible," Sarah quietly asked. "Hey Coop no argument from me but remember I'm not going to let this guy hurt anyone if I can help it," I reassuringly replied. A few seconds later the suspect began to move in faster and closer to Nora, "It's really going down this time Sarah," I emotionally remarked. "I know Cole, let's do this," she confidently said. The suspect was now only a couple feet behind Nora when Sarah jumped into action, "Excuse me Mr. Barnett, Mr. Gary Barnett," she said. "Yes that's me, how do you know my name?" the man asked. Sarah paused for a second then pulled out her F.B.I badge, "Mr. Barnett I am agent Sarah Cooper and these are my partners, agent Cole Youngblood and agent Shadow, you need to come with us for some questioning sir," Sarah strongly remarked. "F.B.I., what the hell do you want with me, I didn't do anything illegal, I think you better get a warrant or whatever you people use," the man angrily replied. I couldn't hold my tongue any longer, "Mr. Barnett we can do this the easy way or the hard way, it's up to you but if you take the hard way you will be charged with resisting arrest and possibly a felony," I said as I moved in very close to him trying usher him to the side of the walkway and put some distance between him and other park guests. Sarah gave me sort of a surprised look but a look of approval, "Well since you put it that way, I guess the easy way is the only way," he slowly replied.

The four of us were now shuffling down the main walkway of the park and seemed to have everything under control until a cleanup maintenance worker began to pass us on the left, "Cole look out," Sarah screamed from behind, the suspect had pushed the worker down while grabbing his push broom, before I even had a chance to react to Sarah's warning my ass was hitting the ground hard from a quick blow to my midsection from the push-broom, Sarah tried to grab the man but he used the broom like some kind of ancient martial arts weapon, Shadow too was immobilized from the broom and hit the ground hard. When the three of us had regained our senses the man our suspect had disappeared in the crowd. Sarah, Shadow and I had just had our asses handed to us and granted there was no physical injury to any of us we had just been outwitted by this assistant high school gym coach and he made it look easy. We quickly made our way out to the front of the park by the pick-up area to make sure Nora got picked up by her father. We had totally blown this opportunity to apprehend our suspect, he now was aware of us and would probably go on the run. After watching Nora get into the car with her father we at knew we had set a different set of time stamps in motion and Nora was probably not going to ever see this man again, "Alright Cole, chalk up the first round to this dirt bag, I'm really pissed, when we find him and we will, I'm taking this peace of crap down," Sarah remarked with a tint of red on her face I had never seen before, she was hot and embarrassed as was I. "It's my fault, I should have been ready for something like that, I'm sorry I let you down," I apologetically replied. "Hey rookie, we both got our asses kicked, you too Shadow, this is our fault, we must have missed something back at S.H.A.D.O.W. during the pre-screening of this man's history, I'd say everyone involved with this case dropped the ball," Sarah quickly reassuringly said. "I know one thing for sure I'm not going to be caught off guard the next time we meet Mr. Barnett, I feel horrible and I know Shadow feels the same way," I deeply and sadly remarked. "Let it go rookie, we'll get this bastard and put him away for eternity," she reassuringly said.

Once we were one-hundred percent sure that Nora was safe and sound back at her home Sarah, Shadow and I stopped by a sporting goods store to pick up some hiking supplies in order to play out our hunch that Mr. Barnett was going to run where he was the most familiar and experienced at and that was where he and his older brother grew up in Fairplay Colorado, it was about two hours away up in the high country of the Rockies and was quite an open range with a very low population compared to the size of South Park grassland basin at an elevation of ten-thousand feet, so needless to say we would need some warmer coats and some hiking shoes that were pre-broken in to spare us the blisters. I wasn't sure how hard it or long it would take to track this guy but this was his home and I'm sure he knew it like the back of his hand. Mr. Barnett's brother Sam still lived in Fairplay according to our files we had on him and I'm sure that's probably the first stop our suspect would make, I don't think we were going to be able to beat him there but we were definitely going to grill his brother on his possible whereabouts. After getting the needed supplies for our impending pursuit we were on the road and on our way to Fairplay Colorado. Sarah had a gleam of anger still in her eyes and was still very upset that this guy got away from us so easily and I guess I couldn't blame her for that, "Hey we're going to get this guy sweetheart, I will track this guy to the ends of the earth if needed, so believe in me and trust me, I will find him," I confidently said. "I do believe in you and so does everyone back at S.H.A.D.O.W. I believe this is why our destinies crossed paths and that you're here for a reason Cole and it's all part of one grand scheme for us to be successful at what we do, this is what you're great at and Shadow and I would follow you to the ends of the earth," heartfelt she replied.

Within two hours we were in Fairplay and at the residence of Sam Barnett, thanks to my breaking the posted speed limit most of the way. As we pulled up along the side of the lot which was quite small with a very small house and carport we immediately noticed Mr. Barnett's early seventies Jeep parked out on the backside of the house. It would have been so much easier to just have given the plate number to the Highway patrol here in Denver but our goal was to capture Mr. Barnett and send him to the S.H.A.D.O.W. holding facility where there is no parole reviews every couple of years, this man needed to be removed from society permanently until judgement day. Sarah and I both had our firearms loaded and ready if needed, we weren't taking any chances from here on out. The three of us got out of the Bronco and slowly approached the front door, "That's far enough you two, what are you doing on my property, you'd better have a good reason for being here," a voice projected outward through the screen on a window adjacent to the door. "Sir just relax were from the F.B.I. and were looking for a Gary Barnett believed to be in this area, we know this is the residence of his brother Sam, is this who I'm talking to?" Sarah explained and asked. "Yeah my name is Sam and I don't want know trouble with the Fed's you two got some identification I can see?" the man asked. "Yes sir we do, I am agent Cooper and this is my partner agent Youngblood, we don't have any business with you just your brother, we want to ask him some questions about his whereabouts on some certain past dates that's all, he had willfully come with us earlier today for a very short while until he decided to run, we just want him to clear up some things for us, I'll put our I.D. badges up to the window over here if you'd like to check them out," Sarah replied quite professionally. "You do that miss, then I'll decide whether or not to let you in," the man abrasively replied.

The next few minutes were nerve racking for me, I was having a hard time just standing there on the front porch waiting for this guy to make up his mind whether or not to let us in or even talk to us, we were losing valuable time. Finally, we heard the latch on the front door being released followed by the creaking noise of old rusty hinges as door swung wide open, "Alright, you two can come in but that damn wolf of yours has to stay out, that's the deal, take or leave it," the crotchety angered man remarked. "No problem sir, Shadow sit and stay," Sarah commanded in a very stern voice. I was impressed by Sarah's demeanor and professionalism even if she was not being truthful with the man about his brother and what we really intended on doing with him but she had no choice in the matter, we both would stop at nothing to recapture our suspect and secure him forever. The place was very run down and looked to be in very bad shape as far upkeep, the man was definitely living in poverty, "Okay now what's the real reason you people want my brother, I know he's not the perfect model citizen but he's never done anything bad enough to get the F.B.I. involved, at least as far as I know," the man asked. "First of all let me say thank you for talking to us but you need to know your younger brother has done some very serious and horrible things in the Denver area over the last twelve months and must be stopped, we know he was here not too long ago because his Jeep is out back and we could still see the heat rising from the hood," Sarah then explained. Wow, again Sarah was amazing with her observations and focus, I had totally missed that, I would have had to go over and put my hand on the hood or in front of the radiator grill in order to confirm if it had been driven recently.

The man sat and pondered his thoughts for a moment, then spoke, "Okay but I need to know what exactly he's being accused of before I say anything." Sarah looked at me then turned her attention back to the older brother Sam, "I know this will be hard for you to accept but we have evidence to support the arrest warrant of your brother for the kidnapping, rape and murder of three women in the Denver area," Sarah confidently explained to the man. What the man didn't know was that the three victims and the crimes Gary Barnett committed were in the future and he was the prime suspect but was never convicted because none of the bodies were ever found, once again Sarah was flawless with her somewhat factual bending of the truth in order to get what she needed from the man. The older brother sat in total shock for a moment after Sarah's statement then looked up at the two of us and shook his head in disbelief and embarrassment, "I'm so sorry, I had no idea he was doing these things, he told me he got into some trouble with the high school he worked at involving the selling of drugs to the kids, I thought that was bad enough but now you tell me he's out murdering and raping women, I'm so sorry, whatever I can do to help I will," the man tearfully said. "Mr. Barnett we need to know how long ago he left here, where he was headed and what was he driving, it would be a great help if you could point us in the right direction," Sarah asked pleading with the man. "Okay, he left about an hour ago, I let him use my Jeep Wagoneer, it's an older model but it's been heavily modified to go just about anywhere, if gets past the Mosquito range of mountains you'll never catch him, from there he'll head to Leadville but anywhere in between he could hide out for months and never be found, he's a very resourceful outdoorsman and survivalist," the man replied almost sounding proud of his brother for a second. "Thank you so much Mr. Barnett, with your help you might have just saved a life or two," Sarah quickly replied as the two of us made our way out and back to the Bronco as fast as we could, releasing Shadow from his stay command along the way.

As we left the residence of Sam Barnett Sarah was already plotting our route to the Mosquito mountain range, our suspect definitely had a good head start on us but we had an advantage of knowing where he was headed. Before we left the house of the older brother Sam he gave us a light coat that his brother Gary had been wearing early in the day, he offered it to us to maybe aid in the tracking and capture of his brother and asked that we try not to harm him. Sarah and I both agreed not letting on to what the real outcome would be. In a matter of just a few minutes we were out of the town of Fairplay and heading out on State Hwy 9 to intercept County Road 12, from that point it would start to get a little rough and I would definitely have to slow down to keep from breaking this Bronco, it was nice but not as nice as mine and the off road equipment in the future was so much more advanced and capable to handle just about any terrain. Once on County Road 12 we would then look for Mosquito Pass Road which recommended the use of High 4WD clearance vehicles to traverse this road, we had to go over twenty miles and it would be at a very slow pace. Eventually that route would end up in Leadville via County Road 3 if that was our suspects intentions or he could just try to get lost in the vast remote areas of these passes. An hour had passed and we were now traveling on Mosquito Pass Road and the terrain was just as described by the map, the windy switchbacks with the deeply rutted washout areas were definitely a huge challenge for the Bronco, "Jesus Cole, how much farther do you think we can go without getting stuck or breaking down, I mean I keep hearing the bottom of this thing hitting rocks and the ground," Sarah asked with great concern. "We'll do whatever it takes to follow this guy, I may get off the trail and try to proceed on the grassland areas but that could be a little risky if I end up missing something beneath the tall grass, we could break an axle, it's still not bad enough to have to make that call yet," as I reassuringly expressed my feelings about our current situation.

Another half hour had passed and suddenly we both saw a Jeep Wagoneer that matched the description of Sam Barnett's vehicle, "Hey there it is Coop, that's got to be it, it looks like he broke down or something," I quickly barked out. The vehicle was abandoned and there was no sight of our suspect anywhere close by, "I don't see anyone around Cole, do you?" she asked. "No I don't, he's on foot now and this is our chance to catch up with him at first light, we only have about an hour of light left let me pull off the main trail and we'll make camp," I suggested. Sarah agreed that if we rested overnight that he would be cold, hungry and tired in the morning and just maybe easier to track. The three of us huddled in the cab of the Bronco as temperature dropped significantly once the sun went down. We heated up our freeze dried dinner's refueling our bodies for the expected strenuous challenge that awaited us in the morning then quickly fell asleep with the complete darkness and total silence of these beautiful mountains called the Rockies, the stars were unbelievably bright and seemed like you could reach out and touch them, the three of us quickly drifted off to a very deep sleep.

After waking up abruptly from the sun beaming in through the front windshield we quickly got ready to get started after surviving the overnight cold, "Hey Coop the ground is still pretty damp since we are so high up in elevation so he shouldn't be that hard to track," I confidently replied. "It should only take a few minutes for me to get our gear and Shadow ready," Sarah quickly remarked. A few minutes later I quickly locked up the bronco after we jumped out with our fully loaded day packs, hopefully we could catch this guy within four to six hours depending on how many breaks he took compared to ours, which would be none at this point of the game, the only thing I worried about was the high altitude and the thin air and how it would affect us probably more than him because he was from the area and grew up here, hopefully that part of the equation would not come into play. I knew Shadow would be fine, wolves are known to track and hunt there pray at relentless strides over great distances, if it came down to it I would release Shadow ahead of us if he picks up Mr. Barnett's scent. I had easily picked up on our suspect's track's and they looked like he was pretty heavily loaded with gear and in a hurry by length of his strides. I had put the light coat belonging to our suspect in a big Ziploc bag in order to preserve the scent of Gary Barnett our suspect and soon to be prisoner I hoped. It was still a little hard for me to understand how he was going to be able to travel in time like us without having a re-construct signature to be put back together in one piece, Sarah kept trying to explain it as simple as possible by saying he was never going to be reconstructed by anyone other than God and not until judgement day, he would just be suspended in a carbon based container with no sense of existence whatsoever.

We began heading out towards the west tracking the heavily

laden footsteps from our suspect, the fact that his shoe size was probably at least a size twelve made it that much easier to follow, the damp ground spread out with each footprint like a child playing in the mud, the vegetation was light except for the surrounding wooded areas which I'm sure he would eventually end up in to make it more difficult just in case he believed he was being tracked. According to his files he was an avid outdoorsman and had some experience with providing guided tours of this area in his younger days along with his brother so Sarah and I had to be on our toes and be ready for anything, "Hey Cole can you tell if we're getting any closer to him yet?" Sarah impatiently asked. "Well we've been at it for a little over an hour and I can tell you this, at this point his pace had slowed down considerably probably due to the loss of light and I'd say we have covered the same distance up to here at least twice as fast, so depending whether he stopped altogether or not last night the difference could be even closer than that, we should start to see some signs of whether he made camp overnight or not pretty soon," I confidently replied. "Sounds good to me rookie," she remarked. Once I felt we were within an hour or so of him I would try to put Shadow on his scent with the coat his brother gave to us, I was hoping Shadow would be able to provide the extra punch we needed to really close the gap quickly due to the fact he was going off scent and not tracks on the ground, in other words our speed of pursuit would only be restricted by the physical stamina of Sarah and I.

After almost three hours now of what I would call a very good pace of tracking the three of us finally came upon a small campfire site that was still pretty warm, that was the most telling sign yet, we were within an hour of him now and I would guess he got less than three to four hours of sleep, that makes him tired and hopefully a little off guard. Now was the time to turn Shadow loose on this guy and with a little luck end this mission quickly and the three of us could then get back home. I quickly removed the light coat from my backpack and pulled it out of the Ziploc bag and began to rub it on Shadows snout and slightly played with him to get him excited and alert from the scent, a method I observed from working with the F.B.I. and their search dogs, "Okay Shadow we need to find this guy in a hurry and take him down, you up to it boy?" I asked as he was now jumping up and down slightly and pulling on one of the coat sleeves. "You think he has the scent Cole, I mean it looks like he's excited about something," Sarah asked, again showing emotions and eagerness to put an end to this manhunt. "Yeah, I believe he's locked in on the scent now," I reassuringly replied as Shadow was rooting around the area of our suspects footprints and the smothered out campfire, he had definitely been here and not too long ago. "Okay Coop, this is where it's going to get a little more intense on my part, I mean this is what your father brought me in to do right, I swore to him I would not let him down, from here on out I'm going to use the "Cutting Sign" skill, a long and traditional way of tracking something in the most vast and baron types of geography using only the smallest of signs such as broken twigs, hair or fur and any leftovers or crumbs of evidence from a meal of some sort, Sarah this technique and knowledge has been passed down to me from my father and his father before him, it's time I earn all that money you guys are paying me," I said with extreme confidence.

Shadow was keeping his stride as Sarah and I were falling back some paying close attention to the signs if any around our suspects footprints, which by now he had slowed to somewhere between a very slow walk or almost even a crawl of sort, in other words he was starting to feel it, the lack of sleep, the physical expulsion of his adrenaline and his nervousness of knowing the authorities were probably following him were beginning to take their toll on him. We began to enter a wooded area of beautiful dark green whispering pines full of life with their movement from the high altitude breezes and Shadow had now dropped back some to join us as if the scent was getting a little harder to follow or he was sensing that we were closing in, I was hoping for the latter. We decided to take a short break and talk over our plan of apprehension and the very good possibility of our suspect putting up a fight or resisting in some other way and that we had to be prepared for anything, it had appeared from our first meeting with him he was well trained in hand to hand combat techniques and definitely some martial arts skills too, the way he kicked our asses at the amusement park with just a broom handle said this guy was extremely dangerous, we were not going to let that happen again at any cost, I had never shot anyone before but I was fully prepared to do so if warranted by the situation, the weeks of training at S.H.A.D.O.W. had hopefully prepared me enough to react quickly and properly if needed and it didn't hurt any to have such a great partner like Sarah who was sort of a modern day Anne Oakley, I had total trust and faith in her to handle any situation that came our way.

After our break we quickly picked up the trail of our suspect again and were ready and alert for anything, our senses were on high and even Shadow seemed to know that we were getting extremely close, I had the same faith in him as I did Sarah, he was trained and ready to accept any command either verbally or by hand signals that Sarah or myself would ask of him, I'm sure his focus and senses were peaked out right now. Everything that my father had taught me and all of our Navajo traditional tracking skills were in full play now as I seemed to almost fade everything out around me accept for the signs and tracks left by our suspect, I was in a zone of mental concentration that was almost spiritual as if I was being guided by the spirits of the great Navajo medicine men and their knowledge, every footprint, twig or broken blade of grass was now standing out like it was a thousand times larger than normal, this was a sense that was quite familiar too me from over the past years of tracking with the F.B.I. and all of the training and contract work I had performed for the Homeland Security department over the past ten years involving the tracking, capturing or eliminating of certain high profile terrorist targets, this was a state of mind that was essential to become an expert reader of the "Cutting Signs" method of tracking. After ten minutes of slow and careful tracking Shadow stopped and seemed as if he wanted to go a different direction from where the footprints were leading, "What's up Shadow, do you sense something that way, sit and stay,"

I quickly and softly spoke the commands, if we were real close I didn't want to make any loud noises or verbal commands, we had to be in stealth mode from here on out, "Sarah, you and Shadow loop around from those thicker pines off to the right, I'll continue on his trail, stay back from my position at least a hundred feet or so, let me draw him out if possible," I very softly and confidently requested. She nodded her head, "Cole you be careful, remember stick to our plan, she replied. The two of them then began to fade away behind the cover of the heavily wooded area, a slight chill ran down my spine as they became totally engulfed by the forest as I was hoping I would see them again in a few minutes and this whole thing would be done and over with.

As I continued on my own at least visually that is I began to regain my focus and mental concentration on my surroundings and the signs in front of me. The stride of our suspect was now very slow and almost as if he were lost or confused on what his next move or plan of direction was going to be, he had doubled back a few times already, maybe deciding to look for a place to hide or attack, hopefully not the latter, I really wanted this thing to end peacefully and let god judge his outcome, not us. I could no longer see or even hear Sarah and Shadow which was great, my crammed teachings of how to track and tread lightly to not be heard or seen so far was paying off, she was so motivated to learn everything about the Navajo culture and the various types of skills that could benefit the two of us in our working relationship and at the same time would strengthen our personal relationship. I immediately stopped in my tracks when I noticed some increased and erratic bird activity just ahead in the tops of the heavily wooded area, this was it, I was probably within seventy-five feet of our suspect and neither one of us was moving, I could sense him and his approximate location by the triangulation of the direction from which the birds were coming from, he was very close, I had to be careful, I quickly held up my hand and gave the signal for Sarah and Shadow to circle around and try to get in front of our suspect after pointing to the general direction of his position and that I was now going to move in and hopefully surprise and then contain him until they arrived from their position to keep him from bolting and then contain and finally apprehend him.

I slowly removed my shoes and socks to in order to get a true sense of the ground beneath me and careful not to disturb any loose twigs or any other object of mother nature that might alert my presence to Mr. Barnett, I then began to creep forward moving like a snail on a sheet of ice, careful to not cause any vibrations or noises with my footsteps, It was only a matter of minutes before I saw a silhouette of a man about thirty feet in front of me between the tree trunks, he was moving very slowly and looked lost. I took a chance and decided to get just a little closer in order for him to recognize me from the amusement park and hopefully just turn himself in, I quickly drew my fire arm and held it ready by my side, then stepping in his shoeprints I made my move at a rapid pace in order to surprise him, before he could even hear me coming I steadied my weapon at his torso, "F.B.I. Mr. Barnett, stop and turn around, "I aggressively voiced my command. The man slowly turned to face me, "Put your hands on top of your head now," I quickly demanded. The man slowly complied, "I was wondering when you'd catch up, you're a very good tracker, I couldn't shake you or your partner, speaking of that where is she?" the man asked. "Right behind you, so don't get any ideas of running, you won't get two steps before I drop you," Sarah confidently remarked as she and Shadow came into play just as we had planned, "Good job Coop, what took you so long?" I asked. "Oh I just wanted to see how you were going to handle this, well done agent Youngblood," she proudly remarked. "You want to cuff him while I cover you, I'm getting tired of holding this gun up at him and I'm sure he would tend to agree with me," I impatiently remarked. Sarah quickly moved in and cuffed our suspect, it was over, we could go home now and relax, maybe even go back to Havasupai for a few days.

After putting my socks and shoes on about fifteen feet away from Sarah and Shadow who were now herding Mr. Barnett towards me I began to realize how lucky we were that he gave up so easily, I guess the lack of sleep, the cold and knowing you were being hunted like a rabid dog just wore him out, just as I was about to stand up I heard two gunshots that whizzed by the left side of my shoulder and as I looked over towards Sarah, Shadow and Mr. Barnett I almost collapsed in agony, "Sarah!," I screamed. All I could see was her lying on the ground next to our suspect and both of them bleeding out from their midsection. Shadow had taken off and disappeared during this brief horrific moment, "We'll agent Youngblood, looks like you've totally failed on your first and last mission, you should have stayed at being a ranger handing out citations for illegal campfires, now toss that weapon over here towards me," the stern voice from behind me said. I tossed my gun backwards over my shoulder then ran towards Sarah, I could tell she was breathing and barely conscious but was losing a lot of blood, the same could not be said about Mr. Barnett, he was lifeless and not breathing, as I leaned over to hold Sarah's hand I could hear some soft rustling in the bushes, it was Shadow and he was giving me a look of aggression like I had never seen before, I could tell it was totally directed at the man coming up from behind me, I quickly gave him the hand signal to lie down and stay. As the man came around to face me I could slowly began to recognize him, it was agent Dan Sutter and I immediately noticed the sunflower seed shells flying out of his mouth after his comment, I remained calm and on my knees putting as much pressure as I could on Sarah's bloody wound. I was going to have to come up with some kind of plan of action and soon, "So it was you all this time, you were the one that stole the Escalade from the impound yard and whatever else you were doing illegally behind the shield of S.H.A.D.O.W. but why the hell shoot one of your own, I mean are you in that deep?" I nervously asked while keeping an eye on Shadow and Agent Sutter's position, if I could just get him to turn his back towards Shadow we might have a chance to come out of this alive.

The blood from Sarah's wound had somewhat slowed from the compression I was applying to it, as I began to slowly shift my body around over to Sarah's other side agent Sutter followed in tandem with my every motion, just what I needed, "So where's that super smart wolf of yours Cole, I guess he had a little yellow streak in him, well you know what they say, your pets usually take after their owners, don't bother trying to save her, you'll be joining her in a second, I just wish she could have heard me tell you that I was the one who went back and killed her last partner, just like I'm about to take care of both of you," agent Sutter said with absolutely no remorse or emotion. "Why do this now and here, wouldn't it have been easier just to take care of this back in our own time," I asked trying to buy a few more seconds of repositioning him. "You still don't get it do you ranger, it's a lot harder to get away with murder in our present day time then it is back in the past, you see nobody can make a case against you if there's no evidence or bodies to be found and believe me you two will never be found," the rogue agent remarked with a hint of pride in the statement. Agent Sutter was now in perfect position to absolutely blindsided from Shadow if he could get to him quick enough, I slowly and discretely got ready to give him the command to attack, I could tell he was watching my every move and ready to pounce like a mad and vengeful wild animal, it was time, "So agent Sutter just tell me one thing, why, changing history wasn't good enough for you, you had something better in mind," I slowly remarked. As he was about to answer I gave the hand signal for attack and harm, one of the commands we had worked on so diligently back at S.H.A.D.O.W. and before I could even react to the action I had just initiated Shadow was out of the foliage and flying through the air after taking only a few steps, in just a matter of seconds I heard a scream that could only be described as tortuous and horrific, Shadow had attached himself to agent Sutter's arm and hand and causing his gun to drop to the ground immediately, I quickly leaped for it as Shadow continued to rip and shred the agents arm to pieces, I could actually hear his the breaking and crushing of his two major bones in his arm, finally after agent Sutter's arm detached completely from the elbow down and exposing his broken and severed ulna and radius bones he punched Shadow with his one remaining fist in the midsection and ran off as fast as he could into the woods holding his severed limb, Shadow started to get up and go after him but I quickly yelled, "Shadow, no boy, stay, come here and sit." We needed too fallback and regroup. I quickly turned to Sarah again who was just coming to and conscious once again, "Cole you have to go after him, don't worry about me I'll be alright, I love you," she weakly and softly spoke as Shadow was now laying by her side, "I am going after him, he's not going to get far, he's bleeding out from his severed arm which by the looks of it has his broken and chewed up S.H.A.D.O.W. watch on it or at least what's left of it but first I'm sending you and Shadow back home, you need a doctor and fast, Shadow you go with Sarah and keep her safe on the journey home, I will see you again soon my friend, thank you for saving our lives," I emotionally said to him while hugging him around his shoulders which were slightly shrugged and covered in blood either from the blow inflicted by agent Sutter and he might of thought he had done something wrong by his aggression towards the rogue agent, I patted him on the head and acknowledged the fact that he had done exactly what I asked of him and assured him that he had done no wrong. "Sarah I love you, hang in there sweetheart, I'll be holding you in my arms soon, remember you promised me this was a roundtrip ticket for all us," I said as she drifted off again.

I quickly set Sarah's recovery watch for a thirty-second time delay alloying me time enough get back and out of range from the return time bubble that was about to appear and engulf them both, at least that's how Sarah had described the return process. As I walked away from her and Shadow I could only hope to god that she would survive the return trip home and get the medical care she badly needed, she had lost a lot of blood as it was now all over Shadow's white fur on his underside. As her watch began to glow a bright neon blue I noticed Shadow looking at me as if he wanted to say something or come to me, "Stay boy, you stay with Sarah, I'll see you soon, you protect Sarah," as I voiced what might be my last command to him, if I didn't make it back. As the time bubble slowly started to appear I could see Sarah slowly lift her head and smile, she then laid her head back down next to Shadow's head who was now lying next to her, they both now seemed to be content and comfortable for the return trip. The two of them slowly began to fade away as did the blueish time bubble, then they were gone and so was our suspect Gary Barnett, he was dead but still on his way to serving time in a state of timeless confinement to be judged by God, Sarah and Shadow were now far away into the future to where I hoped to join them soon, now it was my turn to hunt this rogue agent as he had hunted us all day, I knew he would be very easy to catch up with because of his condition and the amount of blood he was losing. I kept a fast and furious pace not holding back on any emotions, more like feeding off the anger and feelings that had taken over my body, I was in control of them but just barely, I was thinking what I was going to do to this guy once I caught up to him, my mind was on maximum overload filled with crazy thoughts, emotions and feelings of loss and heartache, I was enraged yet somehow under control, I had never felt like this in my life before and it was scaring the hell out me, not to mention the fact I was fully armed with two guns now, his and mine. Poetic justice I thought for a moment, maybe I'll shoot him with his own gun, then my senses took over once again and I settled down to the situation in front of me, tracking and the relentless pursuit of this murderer.

After fifteen minutes I began to hear heavy footsteps and moaning and groaning, it only took a second to lock on his expressions of pain and suffering before I got a visual on his location, he was hunched over and leaning up against a pine tree, I was only twenty feet away and he was not aware of my presence, most likely because of the pain he was feeling from Shadow's wrath, "Hey agent Sutter, you taking a break or are you done running, I can keep this up forever, how's the arm or what's left of it, you know you were right, dogs do take after their owners and I guess you were a little off base with that yellow streak comment," I yelled with a touch of sarcasm and revenge for the insult he had said about Shadow. Suddenly the rogue agent began to dive down the side of a nearby embankment, I quickly matched his move with an intercepting run and leaped over the edge of the embankment, the two of us became one tangled ball of bloody flesh as we tumbled over rocks and pinecones the size of footballs, the pain was sharp and sudden, I quickly reached down to grab my survival knife attached to my lower left leg, after securing a good grip on the knife I plunged it repeatedly into the ground trying to slow our tumble, it worked right up to the point where we both went over an edge of a cliff hanging on only by my knife in the ground and my other arm clinching onto a small rock the size of a pillow, after a minute or so of trying to pull myself up and agent Sutter trying to pull both of us over the edge and down to the bottom of the canyon where a watery death waited us I finally made the decision take this man's life and save my own, "Have it your way you son of a bitch, this is where you get off," I said as I quickly rolled over onto my back and with one powerful swift move I raised my free leg up as high as possible and came down as fast and as hard as I could on agents Sutter remaining arm that was holding on to my foot and ankle, it was at this point that I had felt cheated or robbed of the opportunity to take this dirt bag down and bring him to justice for Sarah, her father and God to judge, instead the laws of gravity had taken him down and over the edge of a very large cliff down to a fast moving river that lied below, it had to have been at a least a hundred and fifty foot drop, nobody could have survived that, especially a one armed man, then after a few seconds I saw the body of agent Sutter cascading over the rocks off the fast flowing rapids, I then collapsed to my knees and activated my recovery watch, it was over and all I could think about was Sarah and if she had made it back alive. As the time bubble slowly started to encase me I thought to myself how badly this mission had gone wrong and how I had failed in my promise to keep John's daughter safe, maybe I wasn't cut out to be an agent of S.H.A.D.O.W after all and at this point I really didn't care, all I wanted was to get back and hold Sarah in my arms once again. The scenery of the Rockies outside the time bubble was now almost totally gone, finally I was on my way home.

After re-atomizing back on the platform and the blurriness of the time bubble began to clear I could see what must have been a hallucination perhaps resulting from a side effect of the return process, as the bubble began to dissipate I could now clearly see Sarah, Shadow and her father standing just off the edge of the platform, "Cole," I heard her scream as loud as she could, I was still not able to move yet as the process was not quite finished. Once the time bubble had completely dissipated I could see Sarah and Shadow moving towards me, "What the hell, you're okay, my god what happened, how are you completely healed from your wound, I mean you had a hole in your stomach the size of a plum, how's this possible?" Emotionally and shocked I asked as she and Shadow met me on the platform as we all began to share a group hug. "I'll explain everything Cole in our post debrief meeting, I'm glad to see you made it back son, Sarah told me what happened, you must have a million questions and it is time for me to answer them all," he remarked with a certain tone of pride in voice. "I'm sorry sir, I let you down in the fact that I didn't keep Sarah safe, I was caught off guard, while tracking our suspect I became so focused on what lied in front of us I never realized we were also being hunted by agent Sutter, I totally screwed up and maybe I'm not what you thought I was in offering me this job," embarrassed and ashamed I replied. "Cole be quiet and listen to me, you saved everyone, you changed history and you and you alone I presume took down a rogue agent that killed my previous partner and tried to kill us, I'd say you did as well as a seasoned agent could have ever done, not mention the fact how you tracked Mr. Barnett down in his own backyard of the Rockies, if we were in the military I'd put you in for a "Medal of Valor" because you earned it quite frankly," she passionately and emotionally remarked. "Thanks sweetheart but your father is right, I do have a million questions and I'd like some answers, I think I've earned at least that much sir," as I directed my statement towards the two of them.

As we began to move off the platform I could still not let go of Sarah, "I'm never letting go of you again Coop, I'm so glad to see you alive, I would have never been able to forgive myself self if this turned out differently, I love you so much," I said as we began to follow her father to what I hoped was going to be the finishing touch to closing out this case and then Sarah, Shadow and I could head home. I was exhausted mentally and physically. As the four of us headed down the long and cold corridor beneath the hills outside of Sedona I began to wonder if John was just as proud of me as Sarah was or was he going to critique everything that went wrong and how we should have handled it. Shadow's tail was wagging and he was right in between Sarah and I as we walked. We entered the debriefing room which was a very secure room with the latest digital hardware and internet capabilities on the planet and probably the most advanced by far, "Please sit down you two, you too Shadow, there's some refreshments and snacks over in the fridge on the counter if you're hungry or thirsty, this shouldn't take too long depending on your satisfaction or acceptance of what you're about to learn Cole, Sarah has already been through many of these debriefings and the other facts that I'm going to reveal to you because you are ready and have proven yourself to me, Sarah and the powers above," John confidently remarked. "Sir let me just say that your daughter will always be the most precious part of my life and I hope you can trust me to always be there for her, I won't get caught off guard again, I have accepted the truth that in our world of this fantastic facility of technology we have here at S.H.A.D.O.W. that anything is possible," I quickly and reassuringly stated.

John sat down at the end of the conference table like a father would have sat down at a dinner table with his family, "I know that Cole and believe me when I say you came very highly recommended for this job, everything I expected from you has come to fruition and I couldn't be any more pleased with your performance, I will tell you that all of this mission was planned by myself and requested from God himself in order to prevent a very evil man from committing horrific murders and spreading the evil of Lucifer himself. You see Cole what Sarah has been keeping from you at my request until I was convinced about you is the fact that what we do here at

S.H.A.D.O.W. is just more than stop and prevent bad things from happening in the past in order to change the future, that is a big part of the picture but it all driven from the hand of God himself, the balance of good versus evil has been around since the beginning of time and always will be, although it has shifted way over towards the evil side of things over the past thirty years or so, I know you're are probably thinking if all of this is really true and you believe that I'm not a madman why doesn't God just fix everything himself," John explained sounding like a Sunday morning sermon you might hear at church. Keeping my composure and being respectful I just looked at John with an open mind and open heart. "Why doesn't God just fix everything himself sir," I cautiously asked. "Okay Cole this is how it works in the spiritual world, you see there are some things God cannot do as hard as that sounds to believe, particularly when it involves the past or the future, God can only help mankind in present time, things that were missed or considered failures by his standards cannot be fixed once they happen, so this is why the two of us have developed a very unique relationship to go back in time and save some of the souls that were never meant to be taken by the evil hands of Lucifer and his army of demons," John explained, then paused a moment while looking at me to see if I was still listening or rolling my eyes in the back of my head, funny thing is I believed every word he said, somehow I knew he was speaking the truth and that he did have a personal relationship with God.

Sarah sat quietly and Shadow was lying on the floor while John continued to talk, "Cole I know this is a lot to take in and grasp but I am pretty sure you are quite ready for the whole truth behind S.H.A.D.O.W. and what our main objective is here, your save mission has changed the world drastically and has involved more than just the life of Nora Jacobs and her family, you see Cole after preventing her abduction and murder miss Jacobs went on to become the prominent District Attorney she was destined to be, her main case of interest concerning S.H.A.D.O.W.'s need involved the prosecution of two young teenagers that she eventually sent off to a correctional facility in 1998 which changed their lives forever and saved the lives of many pertaining to a certain High school shooting in Colorado during 1999," John emotionally stated. "All of that changed just from saving one life, I guess I'm still not seeing the big picture when it comes to the whole time travel theories and the affects we actually can create on purpose," I remarked. "Yes Cole, we have an opportunity to reshape the world we live in today and restore the balance of good versus evil," John proudly replied. "I think I understand now the feelings that I've been experiencing over the past month and the overwhelming sense of a spiritual connection of some kind, John if you don't mind can you please tell me how is it that you can communicate with God and was he the one who healed Sarah?" I cautiously asked. "I'll answer the second part of your question first because I believe Sarah has already explained to you how and you just didn't see the gravity of her explanation before, Sarah wasn't healed at all, she was simply put back together using her existing carbon blueprint of her atoms and during the cellular reconstruction phase of the return process, in other words Cole, no matter how badly any of our agents get injured they will always return in perfect health or at least in the way their carbon blueprint reads which brings up something else I should tell you while we're on this subject, we basically will never age from the day your body scan was formatted into a blueprint unless you want to and that will be something you need to sleep on for a while," John answered with his explanation that was really starting to get a little above my paygrade I thought.

I really almost was at the point now where I wouldn't have minded at all if John decided not to answer the first part of my question, "Okay Cole here's the rest of your answer and this is the part that Sarah has been keeping from you by honoring my wishes, Sarah and I are the only ones that know what I'm about to tell you, the best way to do this is to start at the beginning I guess, you see when I developed the Synchronized Hadron Atomizing Directional Orthogonal Wormhole system and process I was the first one to try it because I didn't want to put anyone else at risk if something went wrong, well something did go wrong, I had made a fatal error in my calculations concerning gravitational waves and the affect's on the human DNA, to make a long story short when I returned from the first attempt at time travel I did not come back in the correct format of the human body, my internal organs had been scattered around like a tornado had gone through me. This is the part where the divine intervention took place from none other than God himself, he put me back together and gave me something extra and the part that is probably going to be a little hard for you to swallow Cole, I'm not totally human anymore after my reconstruction from God, I had become sort of a hybrid human slash angel, God even created a new name for my type of existence, he appropriately called me a Shadow Angel," John emotionally and slowly remarked. "I believe you sir, I've sort of always had a strange sense or feeling from the first day we met, and I almost have that same feeling when I communicate with Shadow, is he connected in some way, I mean he's so smart and has been so easy to train there has to be something special about him," I once again cautiously asked being careful to hopefully not over step my bounds. John stood and looked at Shadow after my statement, "Shadow has been touched and blessed from the hands of God Cole, I hope you don't get mad in what I'm about to tell you, Shadow was put into that shaft once we knew you were close by, he was the last of his siblings who had been killed by hunters in Alaska, his parents also had been slaughtered by the vengeful ranchers whom are at war with wolves, Cole your father was the one who recommended you to us and believed that you would be exactly what this organization needed in order for us to take these save missions to the next step, it was hard to keep this from you but it was for your own safety and Sarah's and Shadow's too. Remember you asked about the pentagram symbols all over our facilities, well there for the primary reason of keeping demons and evil spirits out, which is the same reason why all of our agents are injected with the pentagram cell infusion process during their physicals, demonic possession is impossible with these artificial cells protecting the human body," John replied, sounding like a sermon and with holiness of God himself. I sat in total silence, maybe all of this had finally gotten to me, I was in a to say the least, a mild state of shock.

After sitting for a few minutes and regaining my composure and actually processing everything that John had just said especially the part about Shadow and my father I took a deep breath, "Mad, no I'm not mad John just a little disappointed I couldn't have been told about this a little earlier, so you can talk with my father, how does that work if I'm allowed to ask, I mean can't he just talk to me?" I impatiently asked. "Cole I wish I could tell you how it works but the truth is he may someday be able to talk to you either in your dreams or in person but for now you'll just have to believe and trust me when I say he's probable the proudest out of all of us about how you have become such a good man and the great things you have done here and what lies ahead for you, Sarah and Shadow. He's also very happy that you have found your true love in Sarah, that by the way was purely accidental and was not planned in any such way or form, he says you two found something in each other that was missing from your lives and now you are complete, one spirit and one soul forever, those were his words exactly," John emotionally explained. Hearing the words that John had just spoke I knew that they came from my father, it was how he spoke, he was in a way speaking to me now and it was a wonderful feeling knowing he's still looking out for me, "Thank you John, if there is any way you can tell him how much I miss him and how much I love him I would be forever grateful," I asked emotionally and shaking somewhat. "I will Cole but I really don't need to, I believe you just told him yourself," John replied.

After hearing John's answer Sarah came over and put her arms around me, "I'm so sorry I couldn't tell you everything before but I had to honor my father's wishes and it was to keep you safe and to keep from perhaps influencing your actions on this first case, oh and by the way thanks for taking care of agent Sutter, I hope he got what he deserved and in a way that was justified, I can finally put my last partner's death behind me now and move forwards in that regards, I wonder if we'll ever know how much damage or carnage he has done, I love you Cole," she said while tears slowly ran down her cheeks. I held on to her as tight as I could, not saying a word, just looking into those big beautiful eyes of hers and projecting my thoughts of love and care for her. "Okay you two I think that's enough for today, the three of you have a couple weeks off again and I need to find out how our late rogue agent was able to travel back in time and who was his accomplice is and how it was possible nobody here at S.H.A.D.O.W. knew about it, so go and get some rest or take another trip somewhere, that's another one of the things we didn't tell you about Cole, after every save mission you'll get a couple weeks off to mostly just relax and try to put everything into perspective of how you changed history and how important everything is we do here, oh and remember you two, I'm still half human and I do like to eat once in a while, it wouldn't hurt if you had me over for a dinner or lunch, I'm just saying," John remarked trying to sound like a concerned parent or something. Sarah and I looked at each other and together we said, "You got a deal." Then Sarah reassuringly remarked, "We'll call you dad, Cole will barbeque some of his famous southwestern steaks, you'll love them." John then grabbed a very long and somewhat thin box wrapped in brown paper and handed it to me, "Cole this is a little something I'd like you to have in appreciation for everything you have accomplished here in such a short time and becoming an agent of S.H.A.D.O.W., it's just a little something that every agent receives after completion of their first assignment and maybe I went a little overboard on yours but believe me you've earned it son," John emotionally remarked. "Why thank you sir, I don't think I deserve any gift but I will except this with the promise that I will get better with every mission and always protect your daughter," I emotionally and graciously replied. I quickly shredded the brown wrapping off and knew right away it was some kind of rifle just from the weight and shape of the box, I then slowly opened the side fold of the box to reveal an unbelievable site, an 1860 Henry rifle that looked brand new, I just stood there in shock. I could then see

Sarah's eyes begin to well up with tears, "Cole, you don't need to say anything or thank me son, I want you to have this piece of American history because I know how much of a patriot you are," John said while looking at Sarah and I, quickly I reached for John's hand and thanked him properly and that was the end of it, Sarah smiled and gave me a big hug then smiled at her father for his act of kindness. Sarah, Shadow and I then headed out of the conference room and to what we hoped was going to be a very relaxing couple of weeks off, God knows we deserved it.

As Sarah, Shadow and I began to pull out of the S.H.A.D.O.W. underground parking facility and as we were waving goodbye to Charlie my "Bad Company" cd started to play one of my favorite songs from the nineties, the timing and significance was almost as if some divine intervention was selecting which track to play, of course it was perfect for the feelings I was now having from my first experience with time travel, saving Sarah and Shadow and the life from the past which has now changed the world in a positive way and last but not least the unbelievable feelings I have for the woman I love so much, the name of the song, "Holy Water" and it completely describes the events of my life over the recent months perfectly, "Hey Coop, I think this song will be our song from now on, I mean it's us, what we do as S.H.A.D.O.W. agents and it says how much I love you," I passionately remarked as I turned up the volume to its maximum setting, "Yeah, this is a great song, I think your right agent Youngblood, this will be our song," she replied with her raised voice, as she then leaned over and put her arm around my shoulder then kissed me on the cheek. "Agent Youngblood huh, that sounds a lot better than rookie, let's go home sweetheart and I think I'll take the long way, after all we have all the time in the world," I remarked with an unbelievable feeling of calmness and inner peace. The sun was now reflecting off the hood of the Bronco and lighting up the American Bald eagle's wings with the red, white and blue colors gleaming and looking like a neon sign, just maybe a sign from God or perhaps even my father that I had made the right choice in taking this path for my life and this was their way of saying thanks, the three of us headed home and now more than ready for whatever tomorrow could throw at us, even if it meant going back to yesterday to make it right....

Cole, Sarah and Shadow will return in "S.H.A.D.O.W. Kill"

Lightning Source UK Ltd.
Milton Keynes UK
UKOW05n0646020117
290957UK00009B/19/P